I0708992

STARBOUND

A Starstruck Novel

BRENDA HIATT

dolphin star
PRESS

STARBOUND

A Starstruck Novel
Book 3

Copyright © 2014 Brenda Hiatt
Cover art by Ravven Kitsune

All rights reserved
This is a work of fiction. Any resemblance between the events or the characters in this story and actual events or persons, living or dead, are purely coincidental.

License Notes
This ebook is licensed for your personal enjoyment only. This ebook may not be re-sold or given away to other people. If you would like to share this book with another person, please purchase an additional copy for each recipient. Thank you for respecting the hard work of this author.

Dolphin Star Press
ISBN-13: 978-1-940618-06-7

+
. +
. +

DEDICATION

For the hero hidden in each heart.

+
. +
. +

THE STARSTRUCK SERIES BY BRENDA HIATT
Starstruck
Starcrossed
Starbound
Starfall
Fractured Jewel: A Starstruck Novella
The Girl From Mars

Contents

———————————————————

1

Emileia

———————————————————

EMILEIA (EM-I-LAY-AH): *current Banfriansa (Princess), daughter to Mikal son of Leontine; sole heir to the Nuathan monarchy*

A year ago, if someone had told me I was born on Mars, heir to the last legitimate Sovereign of a three-thousand-year-old underground colony there, I'd have thought they were crazy. Of course, I also would have thought they were crazy if they'd told me nearly every cool kid from Jewel High would be at my sixteenth birthday party. My last birthday party had been a three-person sleepover with Bri and Deb, my whole circle of friends at the time.

A year ago, I was plain, acne-ridden Marsha Truitt, twice-orphaned nerd, being unwillingly raised by an "aunt" and "uncle" who had no more idea who my real parents were than I did. It had been a pretty big shock to learn last fall that I was really Princess Emileia, born Sovereign of Nuath, the secret colony on Mars, and of all the *Echtrans* (expatriate Martians) on Earth.

Not that any regular Earthlings, including my aunt and uncle, knew any of this. That wasn't why I was so much more popular now than last year. No, that had to do with my (real) relationship with Rigel Stuart since the start of the school year, and my (pretend) relationship with Sean O'Gara since Christmas.

"Gee, M, maybe you should've asked Rigel to have your party at his house, it's so much bigger than yours." My best friend Bri shoved her way through the crowd, her dark curls swinging behind her. "Though maybe that would be awkward these days?"

I shrugged, not sure how to answer. I mean, she had a point, since Rigel's house was about four times the size of my aunt and uncle's "historic" little cracker box. But it *would* have been awkward.

"C'mon, everybody, let's do cake!" Sean—tall, handsome, and the reason for the awkward—called from the small dining room across the hall.

The crowd moved in that direction but I hung back a little, hoping to at least brush Rigel's hand first. Suddenly, there he was beside me, dark-haired, broad-shouldered and gorgeous, just like he'd sensed my thought—which, of course, he had.

"Did you actually invite this many people?" he whispered, brushing my hand to give me the boost I craved. He had to be craving it, too, since we got so few chances for physical contact these days. Now that most people thought I was dating Sean instead of Rigel.

Craving is right. It sucks to go so long without touching you, he sent silently in response to my thought. *Their stupid antidote hasn't changed that.*

I smiled up at him, trying to hide my frustration from him the same way he was trying to hide his from me. "I originally invited about half of these people," I whispered back, "But Bri mentioned it at lunch on Wednesday, so…" I waved a helpless hand at all the people who'd have been hurt to be left out.

Rigel and Sean, and Sean's sister Molly, were the only other *Echtrans* attending Jewel High, and all of them were here because of me. Shortly after Rigel moved here in August, he and I discovered we had a special bond, the *graell,* that was so rare most Martians didn't even believe in it, outside of fairy tales. Because of our bond, even though I was a nobody and Rigel was the new star quarterback of Jewel High's formerly lame football team, we started dating.

Thus my meteoric rise in popularity.

Sean was no slouch, either, of course. He'd come to Jewel late in the fall semester and almost immediately became the star of our also formerly lame basketball team. Unfortunately, Sean also happened to be the guy that Nuathan tradition said I was supposed to pair up with. And Nuathans, I'd learned by now, were *all* about tradition. Way too *much* about tradition, in my opinion.

To keep the peace, especially on Mars, which was teetering on the edge of civil war, I was now having to pretend I was with Sean, even though Rigel was, and would always be, my soul mate and the love of my life. I knew this. Rigel knew this. The whole *Echtran* Council knew this. And Sean knew this, though he clearly kept hoping I'd buy into the make-believe and become his girlfriend for real.

Thus, the awkward.

"C'mon, M." Sean brushed a coppery strand from his forehead and motioned to me. "The candles are going to burn out before you can blow them out."

Go ahead, Rigel thought. *I'll still be here.*

Thanks, I thought back, grateful—again—that Rigel and I had never told anyone else about our ability to communicate this way, since it was practically the only thing keeping us sane these days. Besides which, if the Council knew, they'd no doubt try to find an antidote to *that*, too, instead of just to the awful physical symptoms we both suffered whenever we were apart too long. Not that we'd been apart long enough since receiving their serum to know how well it *really* worked.

And I hope we never will be, we both thought at the same time.

With secret smiles, Rigel and I linked pinkies for a second. Finally, I moved forward, the crowd of jocks, cheerleaders and actual friends of mine parting with difficulty to let me through. I saw Sean's bright blue gaze flick to Rigel behind me for a fraction of a second and noticed a very slight tightening around his mouth, but then he was grinning again.

"Make a wish." Sean threw an arm around my shoulders. "A good one," he added, giving me a little squeeze.

I didn't stiffen like I used to, but I also didn't look at him, not wanting to see what I knew I'd see in his expression. Instead, I faced the cake and took a deep breath.

I wish for a permanent, perfect solution to our problem, I thought to Rigel, then blew out all the candles in one try.

✦

Even though it was a Saturday night, people started leaving my party around ten o'clock. I figured part of the reason was my Aunt Theresa,

3

who was becoming less and less gracious the later it got (she and Uncle Louie were usually in bed by ten).

But I knew the main reason was that Trina Squires was throwing a party tonight, too—a last-minute thing, announced *after* word got out about my birthday party. Which was Trina all over. I tried not to let it bother me, though I did wonder how she'd managed to bully her parents out of the house for the evening. Of course, they pretty much gave her everything she wanted, from a new car to the latest fashions, so it probably hadn't been hard.

Even Bri and Deb left around ten-thirty, though probably not to go to Trina's. They'd always hated her as much as I did, and it was definitely mutual, though Trina reserved her worst nastiness for me.

By quarter to eleven, only Rigel, Sean and Molly were left. Aunt Theresa pointedly started picking up plates and napkins and yawning widely. Uncle Louie had gone upstairs a while ago and was already snoring so loudly we could hear him through the ceiling.

"Let us do that, Mrs. Truitt." Molly smiled, her gray eyes wide and innocent as she stacked a bunch of paper cups to throw away. "You can go on to bed and we'll head out as soon as we've cleaned up."

My aunt hesitated for a second, then smiled back—something she rarely did at me. "That's very thoughtful, Molly. Thank you. Marsha, don't let your friends do all the work. Anything not done by eleven o'clock you finish up by yourself, since their parents will be expecting them."

I nodded and she headed up the stairs. Before she even reached the landing, I was reaching for Rigel, dying to take advantage of this brief opportunity when we wouldn't have to pretend. His hand met mine halfway and our fingers intertwined, a blessed relief. I was tugging him unresistingly toward the kitchen when Molly spoke.

"Wow, quite a crowd, huh?" she said a little too casually, watching my aunt's retreat. "I think everyone had a good time, though." Then, more quietly, "We have news, and thought this would be our best chance to tell you."

"News?" I reluctantly delayed the Rigel-kiss I so desperately needed. "You mean from—" I hesitated, then heard my aunt's bedroom door close. "From Mars?" I exchanged glances with Rigel, along with a spike of shared anxiety, since in our experience most news from Mars hadn't been good—at least for us.

Sean picked up the trash bag my aunt had brought out and started tossing paper plates and plastic forks into it. "Yeah. Our folks suggested we let you, um, both of you, know right away." Though he frowned at our still-clasped hands, he continued without trying to provoke Rigel, like he did way too often. "There's more and more call for elections, not just for legislators, but for a President or Prime Minister or something."

My heart beat a little faster. "You mean, somebody more permanent than the Interim Governor they have now? Somebody who could lead long term?" Maybe this would let me off the hook! It's not like I *wanted* to be a leader, even after months of studying Nuathan history, government, society, and protocol. If I didn't have to be Sovereign, I could live a normal life, be Rigel's girlfriend openly again… It sounded too good to be true.

"It won't really happen, of course." Sean sounded certain. "But the Interim Governor is already campaigning, building support, and a bunch of Royal *Echtrans* are heading back to Mars as soon as possible to do the same thing."

"Gee, that wouldn't include your Uncle Allister, would it?" Rigel crumpled up the paper tablecloth and shoved it into a trash bag with unnecessary violence.

Molly shook her head so vigorously her dark hair flew around her head. "There's no way they'll let him go back after what he tried to do to you, Rigel. Mum says he and his pal Lennox are still under guard in Montana, and a good thing, too."

I heartily agreed. Allister Adair, ex-member of the *Echtran* Council, and Lennox, former governor of the Martian compound in Montana, had conspired to take Rigel out of the picture permanently. I'd been incredibly lucky to make my deal with the Council—the deal involving Sean—in time to save Rigel's life.

"So, um, what am I supposed to do about all this?" I asked before I could think too much about that close call and upset Rigel with my feelings. "I already made that video they wanted right after Faxon was ousted and I've recorded two more statements since then."

"My dad says those last two statements didn't get nearly as wide an airing on Mars as they expected." Rigel's voice was factual but I could feel his excitement at the idea of me not having to be Sovereign after all.

Sean frowned again, though not at Rigel this time. "My folks said the same thing. Of course, communications are still screwed up there, so some villages used that as an excuse not to air them, especially villages that are either still anti-Royal because of Faxon's propaganda or that have Royal leaders with their own agendas. Disloyal, short-sighted *dabhal* —"

"Sean," Molly cautioned him, though *dabhal* really wasn't much worse than "damn" in English. Then, to me, "Anyway, Mum's worried you haven't had a chance to start building support of your own."

"I thought that's what our trip this summer is supposed to be about. Isn't that why your mom fixed it with Aunt Theresa so I can to go 'Ireland'—" I made air quotes— "with you guys?"

"Yeah, but now she says summer will be too late." Sean threw the last few paper cups into the trash. "That some Royal or other might have enough support by then that it'll be almost impossible to get you Acclaimed Sovereign. Especially since people have got used to not having one the last fifteen years. I mean, most of them hated Faxon, but now he's out . . ." He trailed off with a shrug.

I didn't say anything for a few minutes, carrying the trash and recyclables into the kitchen, throwing away potato chip crumbs and rinsing out the empty onion dip bowl, trying to get my confusing emotions under control.

A part of me was almost giddy at the thought that I might not have to do the Sovereign thing after all. At the same time I couldn't help feeling a little betrayed, after everything I'd been told about the Nuathan people *needing* me and *wanting* me so badly. Also disappointed, mainly because I'd been looking forward to seeing not only Mars, but the all-Martian village in Ireland where Molly and Sean had lived for a year and a half before coming to Jewel.

Once or twice Rigel brushed my arm or touched my hand as we handed off bags of trash. I appreciated it, though the hints of elation coming through told me he was *totally* fine with the idea of me maybe not becoming Sovereign after all. And so was I. Of *course* I was.

Just as the last traces of the party were dealt with, right on the stroke of eleven, there was a light tap on the front door. Swallowing, wondering what other "news" I'd have to hear tonight, I opened it. The O'Garas stood on the porch.

"Happy birthday, Emileia," Mrs. O'Gara greeted me with a smile. "Again."

My real birthday, I'd discovered last fall, was actually a week earlier than the one I'd always celebrated—the one on my faked birth certificate. The O'Garas had thrown me a private party last weekend at their house with just them, Rigel's family, and the two members of the Council who'd recently moved to Indiana. For three wonderful hours Rigel and I hadn't had to pretend, which was the best present they could have given me, though I doubted they thought of it that way.

"Thanks. Do you want to come in?"

Lanky, sandy-haired Mr. O'Gara glanced past his wife toward the stairs. "Have your aunt and uncle gone to bed?"

Uncle Louie's snoring was louder than ever, so I nodded.

"Even so, outside might be safer."

"Safer, maybe, but it's like ten degrees out there." In fact, I was already shivering. We'd had a late cold snap yesterday, not terribly uncommon in early March in north-central Indiana. It had dropped temps by almost thirty degrees, along with a foot of snow, and the O'Garas, who'd lived in a climate-controlled underground colony their whole lives, weren't exactly used to that.

"I've got my omni." Sean pulled the amazing little Martian device out of his pocket.

Rigel scowled—I knew how he felt about Sean owning one while he didn't. Rigel's grandfather, Shim, a senior Council member, had helped draw up some guidelines for *Echtrans* new to Earth, and carrying things like omnis around was definitely discouraged.

I just said, "Will it work for this many people?" Because it *would* be safer to talk on the porch, if it was going to be about Martian stuff.

"If we're all touching." Mr. O'Gara didn't seem to register Rigel's disapproval. "All right, then, everyone outside."

We all trooped out to the front porch and as soon as I closed the front door behind us, Sean flicked on the omni's holographic screen, punched in the settings, then stuck it back in his pocket. He put one hand on my shoulder and the other on his mother's, who touched Molly, etc. Rigel was on my other side. As soon as Sean touched me, the cold disappeared, of course. Personally, I thought the omni was beyond awesome, like an iPhone on steroids.

"So, did Sean and Molly have time to tell you about the change of plans?" Mrs. O'Gara loosened her scarf, revealing hair as coppery as her son's.

"Um… That we might not go to Mars after all?"

"That's not what we said," Sean protested. "We're still going, right, Mum?"

"You lot are, along with your dad. I need to stay here to deal with things at this end. The Council feels that could be important." Mrs. O'Gara had replaced her brother Allister on the *Echtran* Council when he was booted off.

I glanced at Sean, confused. "But you said that by summer the other guys will already have all their, um, political machinery in place. It sounded like there wouldn't be much point in me going."

"By summer, possibly," Mr. O'Gara agreed. "That's why the Council believes the timetable should be moved up. They want you to leave on the very first transport rather than a later one."

"The summer dates were chosen to interfere with your school year as little as possible." Mrs. O'Gara spoke briskly now. "But these new developments outweigh that in importance."

Sure, all of this was way more important than school—I'd realized that a while ago. But it would still cause a lot of questions, both at school and at home, to leave before the semester was over.

"Can two or three weeks really make that much difference?" I knew from my longtime astronomy hobby (with an extra focus on Mars these past few months) that launch windows between Earth and Mars only happened every twenty-six months, and only lasted a month or so.

"You're thinking of Earth ships." Mr. O's smile was almost—but not quite—patronizing. "Ours travel much faster, giving us a longer window of opportunity for launching."

Oh. I hadn't studied much about the Martian space program yet, but I should have guessed that, as advanced as they were. "Then when *would* we leave?"

"The first transport is scheduled to leave around the start of your spring break, three weeks from now."

"Three *weeks?*" I practically squeaked. I'd been excited about leaving in three *months*, but— "That's…that's crazy. Isn't it? I mean, the politics on Mars can't change *that* fast, can they?"

Mrs. O'Gara leaned forward and caught my eye, then turned to the others. "I need to discuss a bit of private Council business with Emileia. Would you all mind waiting in the car? It will only take a moment, and then we'll take you home, Rigel."

Though Sean and Molly looked surprised and Rigel looked

worried, no one argued. Mrs. O waited until they were inside the van with the door closed to put a hand on my shoulder—which I appreciated, since she now had Sean's omni.

"It's important for you to know that there's much more at stake here than mere politics." Her blue eyes held mine, her voice deadly serious. "None of the others, not even my husband, are aware of the larger issue, but you should be."

Breathing suddenly became harder. "You mean…the Grentl?" I'd gotten in the habit of *never* thinking about that race of potentially hostile, super-advanced aliens, since it was such a huge secret I'd promised not to tell even Rigel.

Mrs. O nodded. "A message has come from them—the first since Faxon's overthrow—and no one on Mars can decipher or respond to it. Our hope—our *fervent* hope—is that you will be able to do both, as soon as possible. The fates of both Mars and Earth may depend upon it."

$$2$$

Sean O'Gara

SEAN O'GARA (SHAWN OH-GAYR-UH): *Son of Quinn and Lily O'Gara; destined Cheile Rioga (Royal Consort) to Princess Emileia*

Sean

"So, what was that last bit about?" I ask when Mum joins us in the minivan.

She raises an eyebrow at me, the way she does. "Council business, as I said, and none of your concern."

I glance over at Rigel, on Molly's other side. "You mean something *he's* not allowed to know about?" I can't resist the dig. I saw how he acted the second M's aunt went up to bed, like he wanted to drag M off to some corner and make out with her. Plus M seemed just a little too happy at the idea of not becoming Sovereign after all, and I know Rigel's the reason why.

"No, something that concerns *only* the Council and the Princess." Mum gives me one of her looks and I know better than to push it.

I remember when she first replaced Uncle Allister on the *Echtran* Council back in December, there were a couple of meetings so secret she couldn't even tell Dad what they were about, even though she was clearly upset after that second one.

"So, Rigel, are you excited that we're leaving for Mars so soon?"

Molly obviously wants to change the subject before I can take my bad mood out on Rigel again. "I can't wait to get back and show you and M around and all."

He shrugs. "I guess." Then, to my parents, "These Royals who don't want M to become Sovereign, they won't do anything worse than campaign, will they? I mean, could she be in any actual danger?"

"I wouldn't think so," my dad says, with a quick glance at Mum.

She shakes her head. "We certainly don't expect that, though of course, as her Bodyguard, you'll be told if we hear anything along those lines."

Bodyguard. Right. It's all I can do not to laugh. Rigel's a year younger than I am, just a sophomore, nowhere near old enough to be a proper Bodyguard to our next Sovereign. But that's one of the conditions M insisted on when she made her deal with the Council back in December.

Molly starts talking about Mars again, and Bailerealta, where we lived for almost two years before moving to Jewel, but I'm really not paying attention. It's taking all my self-control not to say any of the stuff I want to say to Rigel while M's not here to stop me.

Because while I've done my best to ignore the truth for the past two months, it's always there, niggling at me: M is no closer to being my girlfriend now than she ever was. It's still purely an act, a part she only plays because the Council says she has to. Not that she's been doing a great a job of it. Hell, she usually avoids touching me at all, because of that tingle we both get. The one she refuses to acknowledge. It must be as obvious to everybody else as it is to me that we're not really a couple, that her heart isn't in it.

And that's what hurts. Because my heart definitely is.

During all those years everybody believed Princess Emileia was dead, I clung to a hope—a wish, really—that they were wrong. Even though I couldn't remember her, could barely remember a time before she was presumed dead, I grew up thinking about her, thinking about what my life would be like if she was still around. I thought about her so much I practically conjured her. For a few years, when I was little, I actually believed she—or maybe her ghost—was always with me. That we were friends. *Best* friends, even though nobody could sense her but me.

I outgrew that particular fantasy by the time I was nine or ten, but I still thought about her a lot. When word came last fall that Princess

Emileia really was alive, I was beyond happy. It was like every wish I'd ever made had come true. When Uncle Allister suggested we move to Jewel so she and I could get to know each other, I wanted to leave on the very next plane.

But dear Uncle Allister didn't bother to mention that Emileia was already dating another *Echtran*. Sure, the whole Stuart family was mentioned in reports of the big battle with Faxon's people that came so close to killing our Princess for real, but only in passing. So I knew Rigel Stuart existed, but it wasn't until my first day at Jewel High that I had *any* inkling something was going on between them. It's possible I overreacted a little when I found out. But who could blame me?

Anyway, ever since that first two or three weeks, when I was still struggling to reconcile the real Emileia—M—with my fantasy version, I've behaved pretty decently to Stuart, all things considered. I mean, not only is he dating the girl *I'm* supposed to be with, but he manages to form some stupid genetic anomaly *bond* with her, which is totally not okay. Then he puts her in danger all over again, not to mention risking every Martian on Mars and Earth, by running off with her! The worst is, she acts like he didn't do anything wrong at all.

Meanwhile, no matter how well I play basketball, no matter how much every *other* dumb girl in Jewel flirts with me, I can't even get M to notice me. At all.

So yeah, I have lots of reasons to hate Rigel Stuart. But because M wants me to, I try to act like we're friends. In spite of how much he's screwed things up for me, for Mars, for the future of the whole damned human race. About the *only* good thing I can say about him is that he seems to love M almost as much as I do. And, much as it kills me to admit it, M loves him back.

Which will make it a lot harder to convince her that *I'm* the one who's her ultimate destiny. Still, I'm not giving up. Ever. There's way too much at stake, and not only for me.

I just have to get smarter about it.

3

Grentl

GRENTL (GREN-TUHL): *advanced non-human alien race from an unknown part of the galaxy; likely founders of underground human colony on Mars*

Sitting in church the next day I still felt dazed. How could I possibly be leaving the *planet* in just three weeks? Maybe to save the *world*?

By now I was almost used to these disorienting, living-in-a-sci-fi-novel moments. But the idea that the fate of two worlds might rest on *my* totally unprepared, inexperienced, inadequate shoulders went beyond disorienting to downright terrifying.

Rigel picked up on my fear the moment he and his parents arrived, even from the opposite side of the sanctuary. *What's wrong?* he thought, clearly alarmed.

One *more* thing to worry about: keeping Rigel from picking up on how freaked I was, and why. I took a deep breath, tamping down my fear before answering him.

My aunt, like always. I couldn't remember ever outright lying to him before. I didn't like it. *Plus the whole going to Mars in three weeks, thing,* I added truthfully. I worked harder to squash down my anxiety, along with any errant thoughts about scary, non-human aliens.

Yeah, that's pretty freaky, he agreed, *especially for you. All I have to do is play Bodyguard, which I'd do whether they wanted me to or not. But you—*

Sean leaned over just then and Rigel broke off his thought.

"Hey, you okay?" Sean asked in that sub-whisper only Martians could hear. "Guess we shouldn't have sprung the change of plans on you so suddenly last night, huh?"

Oops. I obviously needed to control my face as well as my thoughts. "I'm fine, just not used to the idea yet." Lying to Sean didn't make me feel nearly as guilty as lying to Rigel.

Even though the Stuarts no longer shared our pew, Rigel and I had gotten so good at communicating over distance recently that he was still able to sense more of my thoughts and feelings than was safe.

You're still way on edge, M, he sent halfway through the sermon. *Anything I can do to help? They can't expect you to do the impossible, you know. Just your best.*

And if my best wasn't good enough? I hastily stifled that thought and tried to focus on the sermon instead, but it might as well have been random words in Greek.

What would the Council do if Rigel found out about the Grentl and they found out he found out? I remembered them using the word "treason" at least once when swearing me to secrecy. If nothing else, it would give them the excuse they needed to separate us again.

What was that? Something about the Council? They're not threatening you—us—again, are they?

Crap. Just a bad dream I had last night. Sorry, didn't mean to worry you.

To my relief, he seemed to believe me—and it wasn't *so* far from the truth. I'd lain awake half the night, too scared to sleep.

For the next few minutes I deliberately counted the bricks on the wall behind the altar, forcing myself to take deep, even breaths like during meditation in taekwondo class. It helped. Some. Then the sermon ended and everyone started singing, which helped even more, since we couldn't sing and "talk" at the same time.

That left me free to worry—*very* privately—how long I could keep such a big secret from Rigel and exactly how big a disaster it might be if I didn't.

⁙

That evening, I found out. Sean invited me over after dinner, which he did a lot these days and, like always, Aunt Theresa was totally okay with me going—which she never used to be when it was Rigel.

But it was Mrs. O'Gara, not Sean, who opened the door when I knocked.

"I hope you won't be disappointed, dear, but Sean and Molly have gone out with their father so we can discuss Council business more thoroughly—and privately." I could hear voices in the living room behind her, which meant other Council members were already there.

"No, that's fine. I, uh, need to know exactly what they expect of me." I *definitely* wasn't disappointed Sean wouldn't have yet another chance to convince me to play my "girlfriend" role more believably.

I followed Mrs. O into the living room and was startled to see the entire *Echtran* Council standing there, all seven of them, though only Breann, Malcolm and Mrs. O lived in Jewel. Those must have been some quick travel arrangements! They all saluted me by bowing, right fists over hearts. I used to flinch or blush when they did that, but now I just inclined my head like I was supposed to.

Rigel's grandfather, Shim, by far the oldest member of the Council, spoke first. "Thank you for joining us this evening, Excellency. We all felt that the more quickly we could acquaint you with the situation, the better."

I stepped toward him with a smile, trying to decide if it would be undignified to hug him. Shim was my favorite member of the Council, even though he could be intimidating, what with being so tall and so old. He *looked* maybe mid-seventies, his white hair still thick, but I happened to know he was closer to three hundred.

Just as I was about to touch him, I noticed a tiny flicker, then realized at nearly the same instant that I wasn't feeling any *brath,* or Martian vibe, off of him. I stopped, confused.

"Wait, are you really here, or are you a, um, hologram?"

Little Nara, another Council member I liked, answered. "I'm sorry, Princess, didn't Lili tell you? In the interest of expediency, those of us not in Jewel conferenced in."

"Though I do expect to be in Jewel in the flesh in a few days," Shim added.

I blinked. They all looked so *real*. So...solid.

"Oh. That's...that's great. I didn't realize... Must save a lot on airfare, huh?"

Several of them chuckled, but Shim quickly brought us back to the business at hand. "Excellency, how much has Lili already told you?"

"Um, just that a message has come from the Grentl so we're

moving up my visit, hoping maybe I can somehow reply to it. We didn't have much time to talk last night."

Mrs. O sat on the couch next to Breann, who I assumed was really here. I sat in the only empty chair left. Well, technically the ones with holograms in them were empty, too, but I couldn't exactly sit on top of someone.

"That is indeed the gist of things." Shim's expression was kindly but serious. "However, there is more that you should know, that you would have been told sooner, had not certain objections been raised." He glanced at Kyna, who pursed her lips and frowned. Or, rather, her hologram did.

"Get on with it," she snapped.

Shim merely smiled at her before turning back to me. "As you might expect, Nuath suffered a fair degree of chaos during the days and weeks following Faxon's ouster, including the disruption of normal communications. Not until six weeks ago, more than a month after Faxon was imprisoned, did we learn the full story of his overthrow. Interestingly, it appears the Grentl may have been the deciding element."

"Huh?" I definitely hadn't expected *that*. "How?"

"According to an Informatics Engineer who has worked at the Royal Palace since your grandfather's time, the Grentl activated their communication device late in Faxon's tenure. Using rather brutal methods, Faxon forced the truth about the device from a fellow Palace Engineer—now, alas, deceased."

I assumed Shim meant murdered. I shuddered.

"The Grentl apparently allowed Faxon to communicate with them for a time, perhaps to gain information. Whatever their motives, after a few exchanges, the Grentl used the device to, ah, disable Faxon, at which point a few loyal Palace staff members were able to imprison him, allowing for a quick and nearly bloodless overthrow of his regime."

For a few seconds I just stared at Shim, trying to wrap my brain around what this meant. "So…the Grentl are good guys after all? They found out how bad Faxon was and took him out?"

"We can't know that." Kyna's image leaned forward earnestly. "The Grentl still have the potential to be extremely dangerous. No one knows the content of Faxon's communications with them, only that information *was* exchanged, and that Faxon was subsequently rendered unconscious. He has not been forthcoming with details since regaining consciousness. In fact, our Healers believe it likely he does not even remember those details."

"So…where do I come in? Mrs. O'Gara said they've sent another message?"

Shim nodded. "Six days ago the device activated again. Our best guess is that the Grentl wish to learn the outcome of their last interaction, but when our remaining Palace Engineer attempted to respond, he was denied access. It appears they are again willing to communicate *only* with our Sovereign."

"Or, perhaps, they wish to verify that we still have one," Malcolm theorized. "You are the only one who can find out what they want—and reassure them."

"Reassure them? About what? That I exist?"

"And that Nuath is back on a peaceful path," Shim said. "If indeed the reason they took action against Faxon had to do with his departure from that path, they may wish to know it has been restored. Whatever they want, history suggests the Grentl are apt to take offense should you not respond in a timely manner."

I swallowed nervously. "Offense? What will they do?"

Shim lifted a shoulder in a half shrug. (He looked *so* real!) "We prefer not to find out."

Obviously it would be a bad idea to antagonize aliens way more advanced than even the Martians. But— "Why don't we *know*? Haven't we been communicating with them for like three hundred years?"

Kyna answered me. "It took years—decades—to establish a true two-way communication. That only occurred after Sovereign Aerleas, your great-grandmother, imprinted on the device, for want of a better term. Since then, all attempts at communication were necessarily conducted by the Sovereign, as the Grentl were emphatically unwilling to talk with anyone else. Until Faxon, and then only briefly."

"But…all those years. Surely we learned *something* about who the Grentl are and what they can do to us? What they want from us?"

Shim took up the explanation. "Over the years, some essentials were shared with certain trusted Scientists. We know that the Grentl are non-humanoid, seemingly composed of both matter and energy, and reproduce by fission. But only the Sovereigns have ever known the full content of all communications."

"Remember, Excellency, that until the, ah, events in December, Shim and I were the only people on Earth who even knew of the Grentl's existence," Kyna added. "Due to the extreme sensitivity of that information, only a few specifics, thoroughly encrypted, have ever been sent to us here. However, we believe there is at least one Scientist in Nuath who can show you how to access the complete historical record. Only then will we have a clear idea of what we are facing."

Which was why they needed me on Mars ASAP.

"Then is it still important to keep it such a huge secret?" I held my breath, hoping the answer would be no.

"Absolutely." Kyna's sharpness made me wince. "We even took the precaution of having former Council member Allister's memory modified, to remove everything he learned about the Grentl. If anything, maintaining secrecy is more important now than it has ever been, given the current instability in Nuath. *You* haven't happened to mention this to anyone outside the Council, have you, Excellency?"

"Kyna!" Little Nara, who'd always been my champion, sounded horrified. "How can you even ask? She promised us."

Kyna bowed her head slightly, though she still frowned. "I apologize, Excellency. I did not intend to imply you might not honor your word. But you are still…young, and the young sometimes speak without thinking, only to regret later."

"That's okay." Now I was extra grateful they didn't know Rigel and I could communicate telepathically. My insides quivered, remembering how close I'd come to telling him about the Grentl a few times. "And no, I haven't told anyone."

Mrs. O watched me closely as I answered, no doubt using her "lie-detector" ability. Sure enough, she gave Kyna a small nod to indicate I'd told the truth.

Kyna looked relieved, as did the rest of the Council. Apparently they'd all been worried I'd slip up, no matter what Nara said. Crap.

"Lili, may I assume neither of your children are aware?" Kyna asked then, making me feel a *little* better.

Mrs. O'Gara shook her head. "You've been very clear they're much too young to be told."

"And your husband—"

"He is extremely honored by this mission and wants me to convey his thanks. You can trust him to guard the secret—and the Princess—with his life."

This was news to me. "Wait, Mr. O'Gara knows?"

"Given his extraordinary contributions to the resistance during Faxon's reign and his willingness to sacrifice all for the good of Nuath and its people, his loyalty and discretion are above reproach." Connor's expression was downright reverent. "That is why he has been deputized by the Council to be our representative on Mars in the days to come."

"I must say, he took the news about the Grentl rather better than I did." Mrs. O gave a slight shudder.

"But I can't tell Rigel? Even though we're bonded? Even though he's my Bodyguard?"

"No." Kyna was emphatic. "Forgive me, Excellency, but because of your youth, I argued strenuously against *you* being told about the Grentl. Sending other young people to Mars with that knowledge would be foolhardy, as an indiscreet word could easily lead to widespread panic. Part of Quinn O'Gara's mission is to make certain that does not happen."

It still didn't seem fair. At all. "What's the rest of his mission?"

"To do whatever is necessary to get you Acclaimed Sovereign," Breann answered firmly. "Something he was already strongly motivated to do. He will endeavor to accomplish this before any opposition can become organized. To that end, he will act as your political advisor as well as your *in situ* guardian."

Shim spoke more gently. "Once Acclaimed, you will have access to the Palace and the device. At that point, an Informatics Engineer familiar with the device and with prior Grentl communications will assist you. In fact, Eric Eagan will likely contact you shortly after your arrival with more specifics. You can trust him completely."

"Which brings us to logistics," Malcolm said. "The first ship launches three weeks from tomorrow from the Irish port. You and the O'Gara family will leave for Ireland the Wednesday before."

"And Rigel," I put in quickly. "He's coming as my Bodyguard, remember?"

At least half of the Council started shaking their heads, nearly all of them frowning. My stomach clenched.

"But that was our deal! Rigel and I get to be together as long as I play along in public. And I have." Way more than I liked, in fact.

"Here on Earth, while you were simply attending high school, that seemed harmless enough." Connor received nods of support from everyone but Shim and Nara. "But with this new development, you will need a real *Costanta*…that is, a properly trained Bodyguard. An adult. Which would make explaining young Stuart's constant presence a bit awkward."

I turned accusingly to Mrs. O. "Did you know about this? You told me they were okay with Rigel being my Bodyguard! And last night you didn't say a word about him not coming."

She shrugged apologetically. "I did try to plead your case, dear, but those more experienced in such matters feel strongly—"

"I don't care," I snapped, anger finally crowding out panic. "We had a deal! You all voted on it."

"We did promise," Nara said to the others. "Suppose Rigel goes along in a different capacity? He could pretend to be young Molly O'Gara's boyfriend…"

Ew. It would be better than him not going at all, but— "That wouldn't give him any excuse to be near me unless I'm with Molly all the time. And I won't be, once we get to Mars, will I?"

"If Molly is named your *Chomseireach*? Then he might have reason —" Nara began tentatively.

"Handmaids aren't allowed such visitors, you know that," Kyna broke in. "Nor can I see him going as the Sovereign's Bodyguard. That requires very specific training, which—"

"He can train before we leave," I insisted. "He's a *really* fast learner, and he's way more motivated to protect me than anybody else ever could be. Besides, my Bodyguard should be someone I trust completely and I trust Rigel more than *anyone* on Earth—or Mars."

When they still hesitated, I used the only real bargaining chip I had. "I won't go to Mars without Rigel. Period. If you guys won't honor your side of our deal, I won't honor mine. Go find yourselves another Sovereign."

I glared around at them all, waiting, just like I'd done back in December when I'd first thrown out that ultimatum. And, just like then, they caved. To my massive relief, each of them eventually nodded. Some were clearly reluctant, but all that mattered was that they agreed.

"Very well." Connor's tone made it obvious he didn't like it. "Though once she reaches Mars, at least one more Bodyguard must be assigned, perhaps more. Until then, I suppose young Stuart will do." Then, to Shim, "Can he be trained in time, do you think?"

"I'll see to it that he is. In fact, I will leave for Jewel tomorrow and remain there until they leave for Ireland to oversee his training myself. The Sovereign is correct that he will be highly motivated, both to learn and to protect her. Their bond—"

"Yes, yes, we know." Kyna was the only one with the nerve to interrupt Shim. "But that very bond makes Rigel Stuart our biggest security risk. If there's anyone she will be tempted to confide in, it is he."

Shim inclined his head. "A fair point, and one you've made often. Excellency, I must again stress the importance of keeping all information pertaining to the Grentl absolutely to yourself. Should Rigel learn anything about that aspect of your mission, he will not accompany you to Mars in *any* capacity. I assure you that between Lili O'Gara and myself, we will know if that stricture is violated. Will that content you?" This last was to Kyna, who reluctantly nodded.

I remembered suddenly what Rigel had told me about his grandfather practically reading his mind sometimes. In fact, I'd experienced that with Shim myself more than once. Between him and Mrs. O, they'd *definitely* know if I told Rigel.

My heart in my throat, battling between relief and dread that I'd screw this up, I nodded. "I understand. Thank you."

4

Jewel

JEWEL (POP. 5,013): *town in north-central Indiana noted for corn, artisan jewelry and annual Jewel Jewelry Festival*

The next day at school I worked harder than ever before to shield my thoughts from Rigel. What I *couldn't* hide was the fact that I was shielding my thoughts.

You're really worrying me, M, he told me halfway through first period. *If you're scared or have some problem, I want to help. Don't shut me out.*

The pleading edge to his thought twisted my heart—I knew how I'd feel if he were doing this to me. *I don't want to, Rigel, I promise. But there's stuff I can't…that would be bad if you found out, okay?*

Bad? You mean it would piss me off? It's something about Sean, isn't it? I know you were at his house last night.

I sighed, exasperation starting to crowd out sympathy. *No. It's not. Please don't push me, Rigel. It only makes it harder.*

Fine. Sorry.

But I could tell he wasn't going to give up and I couldn't really blame him. I'd be every bit as obsessed with finding out the truth if he were hiding things from me.

As we were leaving class, he came close enough to "accidentally" brush my hand. "Don't put up walls, M," he murmured so no one else could hear him. "I just want to help. You know that."

"I know." I started to link pinkies with him, like at my party, but noticed Trina watching us, her eyes narrowed. I took a reluctant step back from Rigel and turned away. *We'll talk later*, I promised him silently. Not that there was much I could safely tell him.

Rigel wasn't in my next class, which I spent trying to convince myself there was nothing to worry about. I'd just go to Mars and do whatever the Scientists there told me to do. Until then, I didn't need to think about it at all. Which meant there wouldn't be anything for Rigel to accidentally "overhear."

That pep talk helped me relax a bit next period. While I could sense Rigel's amused irritation at Trina's blatant flirting, I deliberately didn't probe his actual thoughts, since I wasn't willing to share most of mine. Trina clung to his arm all the way to Earth and Space Science, something she did way too often now I was supposedly dating Sean. Even though it distracted Rigel from trying too hard to get into my head just now, I still didn't like it.

Once in class, I tried my best to focus on what the teacher was writing on the board about the space program. But when I heard Trina whispering softly to Rigel right behind me—they were lab partners— of course I had to pay attention to *that*. She probably didn't think I could hear but, like all Martians, I had super-sensitive hearing. It wasn't always an advantage.

"—deserve so much better, Rigel," she murmured, probably right in his ear. "No girl in her right mind would throw you over for someone else, even if he *is* a junior and can invite her to prom. After all you did for her last fall, too, plucking her from obscurity and making her more popular than she's ever been in her life. Believe me, before you did that, somebody like Sean *never* would have asked her out!"

I knew I should be happy Trina was distracting Rigel so effectively, but happy wasn't how I felt when Rigel responded.

"M's free to date whoever she wants. She and I are…over. We're just friends now."

Ouch. I mean, that *was* the front we were putting on these days, but it stung to hear him say it to Trina, of all people.

"Then you need to move on, Rigel. It's pretty obvious *she* has, the way she's practically glued to Sean O'Gara these days."

It was hard not to turn around and contradict her, but Rigel did it for me. Sort of.

"They're close, yeah, but mostly just friends. We're all friends."

"Friends? Don't make me laugh! Maybe they act that way when *you're* around." Trina snickered softly. "Behind your back, they're all *over* each other, believe me."

Not true! Not true! I thought quickly to Rigel, breaking my mental silence.

Oh, so you are *there?* The resentment that came through with his reply proved I hadn't been as subtle about blocking him as I'd hoped.

"Everybody knows she's over at Sean's house practically every night," Trina continued with smug mock-sympathy. "You need to forget her, Rigel, give other girls a chance. If you'd come to my party Saturday night I would have—"

Luckily the teacher turned around right then, forcing Trina to shut up, but I could feel Rigel's frustration and jealousy from what she'd already said, along with his worry about what I *wasn't* saying. My compromise with the Council had been tougher on Rigel than anyone, no matter what Sean claimed. I'd gotten pretty good at defusing Rigel's occasional spurts of jealousy, but keeping big secrets from him was bound to make that harder.

Ever since that one almost-fight last fall (which I'd broken up), Sean and Rigel hadn't exchanged anything worse than occasional snide comments, instead making an effort to at least *pretend* to be friends, for my sake. I was proud of them both and hated to think that truce might be threatened now.

"I heard everything Trina said," I told Rigel as we left for the cafeteria, wishing more than ever I could hold his hand. Stupid deal. No, a deal that saved Rigel's life, I reminded myself sternly—and quietly.

"Yeah, I wish she'd lay off." Waves of irritation poured off him, distracting him. "If she's not trying to set me up with one of the other cheerleaders, she's trying to get me to ask *her* out or go to some party."

"I guess she's made a project out of you." But my attempt at a joke backfired.

I hate everyone feeling sorry for me! he thought fiercely. *I mean, I know you still…that we're still…*

I surreptitiously brushed his hand. *I still love you more than anything, Rigel! That hasn't changed at all! But if it would make you feel less…feel more… I don't know…feel* better, *you can go to parties and stuff. I won't get mad. I'll know it's just part of the act.*

"Hey, guys." Sean came up from behind and wedged himself between us. "No need for a Bodyguard now that I'm here." He grinned at Rigel and threw an arm around my shoulders.

When the O'Garas first got to Jewel, I'd learned there was some kind of Martian taboo about people touching the Sovereign. They'd been so careful about it at first, it made me feel weird. Now I wished I hadn't given Sean blanket permission to do this sort of thing whenever he thought it would "look good." He was definitely taking way too much advantage of it.

That's for sure. Rigel's thought reminded me yet again how careful I needed to be. *He's the one you need your body guarded from.* His irritation surged back, along with a seriously rude comment about Sean he luckily didn't say out loud.

"You coming to the game tomorrow night?" Sean asked, oblivious. "First game of Sectionals, can you believe it?"

Rigel answered for both of us, managing to sound like he wasn't gritting his teeth, though I could tell he was. "We'll both be there, unless M's aunt keeps her home."

"She's been loads better lately." I wondered how either of them could even think about basketball when we were leaving for freaking *Mars* in three weeks.

"Loads better than when *we*—" Rigel began, then broke off.

Between us, Sean grinned widely. "Hey, it's not my fault she trusts me more, or likes me better, or whatever."

"Stop it, Sean," I snapped. "It's your mom she likes so much, and you know it. And you know why."

In addition to her lie-detector power, Mrs. O'Gara had the Royal ability to gently persuade other people to her way of thinking. Sort of a psychic "push." It creeped me out at first, but now I was figuring out how to use it myself, it was kind of cool. Especially when it worked on super-strict Aunt Theresa.

Sean shrugged, still grinning. "If you say so."

From beyond him I felt Rigel's jealousy surging up again.

I sighed audibly so they'd both know I was tired of playing peacemaker. To my relief, Sean stopped his needling and Rigel's emotions eased back down to reasonably normal levels. When we got to the lunch table Bri, Deb and Molly had already staked out, I made a point of sitting next to Rigel, something I couldn't often do these days. The seat on my other side was empty, but only because Sean had been waylaid by a bunch of other basketball players and a few cheerleaders.

I tried not to be annoyed how everyone took it for granted now that Sean and I would sit together. Instead, I took my opportunity to talk silently to Rigel before we got sucked into any of the conversations already going on around us.

Don't let Sean get to you, I thought as I opened my milk carton. *You know he just likes getting a rise out of you.*

I know. Sorry. It's not fair to you, especially when you feel everything I feel. I'll try to do better.

It won't last forever, I promised. *Maybe once we get to Mars, everything will change and we'll be able to—*

Don't! His sudden anguish startled me. *Don't get my hopes up, when for all we know we might have to do this for months or even years. I'm just… taking it a day at a time, okay?*

It helped *me* to believe things would get better soon, to look ahead to a day when we wouldn't have to pretend anymore, but I couldn't force Rigel to share my view. Instead of arguing, I offered him one of my cookies, which he took with an answering smile and a noticeable lessening of tension in his face and emotions. *Better?* I thought, losing myself in his eyes for a moment, something I used to do all the time before—

"Don't you two look cozy." Sean scraped back his chair and thunked into it. Of course, every head within earshot turned to see what he was talking about, but by then Rigel and I had broken eye contact and were focusing on our lunches.

"I just gave him a cookie, Sean. What's the big deal?"

"Yeah, I saw. Very nice of you." Then, so softly only I—and maybe Rigel and possibly Molly, across the table—could hear, "Everyone else saw, too. You guys aren't doing as good a job of cooling it as you think you are."

I turned to glare at him and noticed Trina standing a few feet away, smirking in our direction. She must have said something to get Sean riled up about Rigel, just like she'd done to Rigel last period.

"Look, we're doing our best, okay?" I whispered back. Then, to Bri, who was starting to look a little too curious, "Did you hear Matt broke up with Alicia over the weekend?"

Since Bri had gone out with Matt several times last fall, that snagged her attention immediately. "Really? Did you hear why? I'll bet she cheated on him, the little—"

"I heard it was the other way around," Molly said, giving me a half wink.

Then Deb weighed in with her own bit of gossip and I was free to communicate with Rigel some more, though I was careful not to look at him.

You guys need to stop listening to Trina. She's just trying to make both of you mad at me.

Out of the corner of my eye I saw him give a hint of a shrug. *Problem is, some of what she says is true.*

Not when she says I'm over you, it's not! You know she's always—

"Are you going to finish that?" Sean asked, pointing at my untouched roll.

"No, you can have it. And my other cookie, too, if you want." Maybe he'd realize how ridiculous he'd been a minute ago.

Instead, he frowned across me at Rigel. "No, *I* know how much you like the double chocolate ones."

"Only the ones from Dream Cream," Rigel shot back. "The school ones, not so much. Maybe you don't know her as well as you think?"

And so it went for the next few minutes, both guys making little digs till I pulled out the big guns. "Let's talk about our history projects now, okay?"

It always surprised me when my "push" worked, but I was grateful when they obediently started discussing how far they'd gotten on their respective projects.

⁙

U.S. History, after lunch, was usually my favorite class, since Rigel, Sean, Molly, Bri and Deb were all in it, but Trina wasn't. But today, less than five minutes in, Mrs. George called Rigel and me and both O'Garas up front.

"You've all been asked to go to the office. No, I don't know why," she said when Sean started to ask, "but try to come back as quickly as possible, since you all still have a lot of work to do on your projects."

After the tension at lunch, my first thought was that Rigel and Sean had been caught fighting, but that didn't explain Molly and me being summoned, too. Maybe it had something to do with our upcoming trip?

My second guess was right.

"Congratulations, all of you!" Principal Johannsen greeted us when we were shown into her office. "I've just received word that the four of you have each finaled in an essay contest, which means full scholarships to a study-abroad program in Ireland that I take it you've all applied for? I hadn't heard about it before, but the paperwork seems clear enough. Was this something your guidance counselors told you about?"

"Our mum, actually," Molly replied while I was still groping for a good answer. "She heard about it from friends in Ireland and suggested we all apply."

The principal nodded. "I see. Very resourceful of you all to have followed through. Now, we'll have to work out transfer of credits and other details, but assuming you decide to go...?" We all nodded. "It shouldn't set back your graduations. Would you like to tell your parents, or shall I call them?"

This time I spoke up. "Uh, I think my aunt would really like to hear it from you, Ma'am. Just so she knows it's official and everything."

"Of course." From the principal's knowing smile, she was well enough acquainted with Aunt Theresa (who taught third grade at Jewel Elementary and knew everybody in the school system) to understand why I requested that. "The rest of you?"

"We can tell our folks, since they already know about the program," Sean said.

Rigel nodded. "Me, too. But thanks for offering."

Principal Johannsen beamed around at us. "Wonderful. That's settled, then. You'll want to make appointments with your guidance counselors this week to be sure you're on track with everything, since it's a very short time frame. Congratulations again!"

"That was pretty slick," Rigel murmured as we headed back through the mostly deserted hallways. "I didn't think they could manage it that fast."

Sean glanced at me. "Mum said the Council started setting things up a few days ago. I think they just wanted to run it past you first, M."

Though I was still feeling a little stunned, I had to laugh. "Run it past me? You make it sound like I was given a choice."

I didn't usually pay attention to the morning announcements, since Trina was one of the announcers, but I glanced up at the video monitor the next day when I heard, "And special congratulations to four Jewel students for winning full scholarships to the Irish-American Cultural Enrichment program, which will allow them to spend the spring studying in Bally . . . Bail . . . in Ireland. The winners are—" Suddenly Trina looked like she'd swallowed something disgusting. "—are Sean and Molly O'Gara, Rigel Stuart...and Marsha Truitt. Now, here's Carly Morehouse with an update on tonight's game."

The camera switched to Carly. Next to me, Deb started laughing.

"Did you see her face? That was awesome! I mean, I already thought it was way cool that you guys won this thing, but that makes it even better."

I had to agree. Especially when Trina came into the room a few minutes later, her expression still sour as she glared across at me. I just smiled sweetly.

She didn't look at me again for the rest of class. But as we were all leaving for second period, she sidled up to me. "There's no *way* you won that thing on your own, Marsha," she hissed furiously. "I'm going to find out who pulled what strings to get you in, and then I'm going to make sure *everybody* knows about it. So don't you start packing for Ireland just yet!"

$$
\begin{array}{c}
\rule{6cm}{0.4pt}\\[4pt]
5
\end{array}
$$

Pleanal

<hr>

PLEANAL (PLENN-UHL): *advance planning; scheming*

Now it was Rigel's turn to tell *me* not to listen to Trina, that she was just jealous, but I was uneasy. I'd had way too much experience with Trina's vindictiveness from second grade on and knew what lengths she'd go to pay off a grudge. She'd already been pissed at me about Rigel and Sean, both of whom she'd decided she had first dibs on. Now this. At least I only had to keep my guard up for a couple more weeks.

At lunch, Rigel got mobbed by cheerleaders while Trina waylaid Sean again. This time I focused, so I could hear what she said.

"Hey, Sean, congratulations on that scholarship. I guess you guys found out about it because of being from Ireland, huh? I *so* would have applied if you'd told me, I've *always* wanted to go there!"

From several yards away, I snorted to myself. Trina had already spent a summer in Paris and at least two winter breaks in the Bahamas, as she told anyone who'd listen. Must be nice to have rich, doting parents.

"So how come just you four knew about this thing?" Her voice was still syrupy sweet.

"Um, well, our folks are friends with the Stuarts, so I guess my mum mentioned it to them. And M is my girlfriend, so of course I told her."

I stiffened, even though I'd heard him use the word before. (I'd definitely never used the word *boyfriend* to refer to Sean!) Trina obviously didn't like it, either.

"So you two really are *official* now, huh?" The honey had disappeared. "When did that happen?"

"It's been kind of gradual, I guess, ever since the winter formal."

Trina made a rude little "tch" noise. "When are you going to wise up, Sean? Everyone *else* knows her whole innocent girl-next-door thing is just an act."

"What do you—? No, never mind."

Sean walked away from her then, but still looked upset when he sat down beside me a second later. He dumped ketchup on his fries, then frowned at me. "There's nothing everybody else knows about you that I don't, right?" His bright blue eyes bored searchingly into mine and I met his gaze steadily.

"Of course not. You need to ignore Trina, Sean. She's just trying to make trouble for me, like always."

Rigel reached the table before he could respond, sitting down with a thump. I jumped a little, thinking he'd seen that look between Sean and me. "Sheesh! I didn't think I was going to get away from them in time to eat lunch."

I forced myself to laugh. "You can't really blame them for trying, Rigel. I mean, you *are* the quarterback and super popular, and, um, single these days." *Not to mention the best looking guy in the school, by a couple orders of magnitude,* I added.

He grinned, though I knew it was at my silent comment and not the word "single." I hoped.

"So I'm the best catch in school, is that what you're saying?" *And no, I was* not *smiling about being single. I'd change that in a heartbeat if I was allowed to, you know that!*

I only replied to what he'd said aloud. "You think I'll puff up your ego any more by admitting that?" Though of course it was true. He had to know it as well as I did.

Bri was distracted from her latest gossip session about Matt by the scent of something potentially juicier. "So, Rigel, who *do* you have your eye on these days? I know Hailey Wallace was really hoping you'd ask her to the Valentine's dance, but then you didn't go at all. And Amber says you've been talking to her kind of a lot these days…"

Rigel shot me a quick glance. "Nobody special right now, but who knows?"

Of course, that got Bri pumping him even harder for hints, which she did often now she'd regretfully decided Rigel and I weren't getting back together.

I tried not to listen as Rigel gave a mostly flattering assessment of the various girls Bri suggested. Even though I knew he was just toying with Bri and the gossip mill, I didn't like hearing it. I really hoped this trip to Mars could somehow change things so we wouldn't have to pretend anymore. But I didn't dare let Rigel pick up that thought, either.

.⁺.

That evening, the O'Garas and I rode to Sean's basketball game in the Stuarts' SUV, which meant Rigel and I got to hold hands in the back until we reached school, a too-rare treat. I focused on how wonderful his touch felt to keep more dangerous thoughts from intruding. It mostly worked.

Once we got there, though, I had to sit with the O'Garas at mid-court, where Bri had saved seats, while Rigel went to sit with some fellow football players. Molly waved to us from the court, where she was practicing with the cheerleading squad. That prompted Trina to send a nasty glance my way, after which she immediately started talking to Molly. I couldn't make out everything over the noise in the gym, but I caught a few words.

"…ask if they're taking late applications…know what Marsha's essay was about?…helped her?" Molly just shrugged and shook her head, so after a last comment that sounded like, "Promise to let me know?" Then Trina took her place again so she could wiggle seductively for the benefit of the basketball team, which had just come out of the locker room.

To nobody's surprise, Sean played ridiculously well again, scoring twice as many points as anyone else on either team. We won easily, advancing Jewel High to Regionals for the first time in living memory. The spectators erupted in cheers at the final buzzer, then rushed the court to congratulate the team.

Like he always did these days, Sean greeted me with a hug. Conscious of interested *Echtran* eyes in the crowd, I hugged him back —just for show. I must have played my part a little too well, though, because Sean pulled me closer, then suddenly swooped his mouth down to mine.

Since I thought I'd made it crystal clear during our first "date" at the winter formal that kissing was *not* in my bargain, I was caught totally off guard. Sean managed to graze the side of my mouth with his lips before I jerked away to glare at him.

"Oops, sorry." But his eyes made it clear he was only sorry he hadn't made it a *real* kiss. "Got a little carried away for a second."

"Don't." I stepped away so his parents and Molly—and about a hundred other people—could congratulate him.

I sensed Rigel watching from somewhere behind me. Worse, I sensed his shock and pain, which hurt me almost as much as it did him. Remembering how destroyed I'd been when he let Trina kiss him after a football game last fall, trying to misdirect the bad guys who were after me, I felt like a hypocrite—even though *I'd* pulled away in time.

If he tries that again, I'll kick him right in the stomach, I thought to Rigel, desperate to make it clear I had nothing to do with that almost-kiss. *You know I can do it, too. I have my blue belt now!*

Hoping no one was watching too closely, I turned around to look at Rigel, separated from me by a couple of yards of surging crowd. He met my eyes and attempted a smile that only squeezed my heart harder. No matter how I tried not to, I somehow kept making things worse for him and I hated it.

It's…not your fault. But you just reminded me—want to meet me in the arboretum after your taekwondo class tomorrow?

It was all I could do not to nod furiously. *Absolutely! We're way overdue for some alone time. I'll be there even if it's blizzarding.*

The Stuarts crammed all of us into the SUV using the drop-down middle seat and took me home first, since my aunt was still strict about my school night curfew. Sean followed me out of the car to walk me to the door, even though no *Echtrans* were around to notice.

Tomorrow, I caught from Rigel as I started up the walk, pointedly not touching or even looking at Sean. I was still pissed at him.

Tomorrow, I thought back. I couldn't wait.

"Hey, I really am sorry." Sean's breath fogged in the cold as we reached my front porch. "I was out of line to…you know."

"Yeah, you were." No way was I letting him off the hook on this. "Don't let it happen again or I *will* make you sorry. Got it?"

He actually hesitated for a second, but when I narrowed my eyes at him, he nodded.

"Got it. G'night, M."

I went into the house without another word, not wanting it to look to Rigel like I was unbending even a little.

Because I wasn't.

⁘

During taekwondo the next day, I was so psyched about my upcoming date with Rigel I kept having to pull myself back so I wouldn't hurt anyone. Because of the way our bond had changed me—not just perfect eyesight, super hearing and speed-reading, but also faster reflexes and greater strength—I had to be more and more careful when sparring. Especially today.

Rigel and I hadn't had any real alone time for over three weeks— an eternity. Every time we'd tried to meet lately, Mrs. O'Gara came up with something I had to do instead, even though I never mentioned our plans to anyone. She must have figured out Wednesdays were my best chance to slip away without my aunt noticing. All day I'd worried some "important" thing would pop up again, but for once it hadn't.

I was so eager to spend time with Rigel—to touch him, to kiss him—I didn't even worry about how I'd keep my secret for the next hour. As soon as class ended, I changed out of my do-bok at lightning speed and ran all the way to the arboretum, trying to make it look like I was just out for a jog despite my gear bag swinging at my side.

I entered the snowy walled garden only slightly out of breath and felt a jolt of pleasure at the sight of Rigel—and no one else—inside. By the time we got back from Mars, the roses would be in bloom and people would be here all the time, but for now this was a perfect place to be private.

The moment we were completely screened from anyone on the street, we hurled ourselves at each other, kissing like there was no tomorrow. It was the best feeling in the universe. This, *this* was what we really needed, the physical contact both our bodies craved.

And it was something we could *only* do when no one could possibly see us. Maybe by summer the cornfield around our secret clearing would be tall enough…

Rigel ran his hands up and down my back, pulling me more tightly against him as I threaded my fingers through his dark hair, deepening our kiss. If I could have melted right into him, I would have. His energy recharged me while mine did the same for him. That had always been true but lately, because our chances were so rare, it had become even more intense. More necessary.

"Mmm. I will *never* get tired of this," he murmured against my mouth when we finally pulled back a fraction of an inch so we could breathe. "I've missed you *so* much, M."

I knew exactly what he meant. Sure, the three or four hand-brushes we managed most days at school kept us from feeling physically ill (or maybe it was that stupid "antidote" the Council's scientists had given us?) but there was nothing like a good makeout session to make me feel *right*. Whole. In balance. Sometimes I wondered if that was our bond, or just what being in love felt like. Not that it really mattered.

No, it doesn't really matter, Rigel thought, since his mouth was now occupied, kissing me again. *Even if they've cured our headaches and stuff, I think I'd still die without you.*

I pressed myself even closer to him, agreeing with all my might.

Because we both knew this could be our last chance to make out for a long, long time, when Rigel's hands roamed a little more than usual I didn't discourage him. In fact, probably the only thing that kept us from doing something we both might regret was complete impracticality in the freezing, semi-public arboretum.

Not until I was home, nearly an hour later, did it occur to me that I hadn't needed to block my thoughts once during my whole time with Rigel this afternoon.

✦

I was extra grateful for my stolen hour with Rigel after our meeting at the O'Garas' that evening. Judging by the schedules Mrs. O gave us both, we wouldn't have ten spare minutes between now and our departure for Ireland in two weeks. Rigel had Bodyguard training every day after school, while Sean, Molly and I would be drilled on protocol almost daily. I was also given another huge batch of reading on my electronic book-scroll (I had my own now, though of course I had to keep it hidden from non-Martians).

I hadn't learned much Martian yet, since I'd thought I had more time, so I'd have those lessons, too. Even though English was spoken more than Martian in Nuath these days (except in schools, where it was required at all times), I'd be expected to use it for formal occasions.

Molly was officially appointed my *Chomseireach* or Handmaid—sort of a combination companion, chaperone and lady's maid. I hated the idea of her being some kind of a servant, but Mrs. O insisted the position was considered a huge honor, especially for someone not born Royal.

"If not Molly, it would be someone else, and I'm sure you'd rather have her than a stranger, dear." I couldn't argue with that.

At school we'd already been given a ton of extra homework to make up for missing the rest of the semester. Plus, Aunt Theresa seemed to think I'd create some kind of diplomatic incident in Ireland if she didn't drill me on my manners every chance she got. While that was kind of hilarious under the circumstances, it meant I had to deal with her etiquette lessons on top of everything else.

"Oh, and this from the Council," Mrs. O added after going over our schedules. "It is imperative you and Rigel remember that the relationship between a Sovereign and his or her Bodyguard is *strictly* a professional one. However close the two may have been beforehand, once that position is accepted, *no* sign of intimacy will be tolerated in public. It has always been thus."

Sean looked as pleased by this reminder as I was irked. Until his mother's next words.

"There are also protocols governing a Sovereign and his or her future Consort, prior to the official pairing. Any time you and Sean are together you'll be strictly chaperoned, either by the Princess's advisor —" She nodded toward Mr. O— "her *Chomseireach,* or by her personal Bodyguard, who will never be far from her side."

Now it was Rigel's turn to be pleased. *Excellent,* he thought to me, though he carefully kept his expression grave.

"Wait." Sean's smile was gone. "You mean once we get to Mars, M and I can't *ever* be alone together?"

"That is indeed the custom before your joining. Proper impressions are extremely important, as they will help the Princess to gather the support she needs to be Acclaimed."

All things considered, I decided I could live with that—especially since it meant Rigel would *have* to stay close enough to me that we'd always be able to talk. Silently, anyway.

Yeah. It also means I get to watch Sean trying to "court" you, or whatever.

Maybe it'll be funny.

Maybe. But now his emotions held a sour edge. Again.

6

Chomhaerle

CHOMHAERLE (KOM-AHR-LEE): *advice; counsel*

Time seemed to speed up over the next week, between my ramped-up schedule in and out of school and yet another holo-meeting with the full Council for an update from Mars.

"The Grentl appear to be growing impatient for a response to whatever message they've sent," Shim informed me. "They've activated the device again."

A knot of tension formed in my midsection. "Do you think they've issued some kind of…ultimatum?"

"We won't know that until you can decipher the messages, Excellency," said Kyna gravely, her eyes reflecting some of the same fear I felt. "But their repeated attempts at contact make your mission all the more urgent."

After that, it became even harder to keep my secret from Rigel. No matter how I tried, I couldn't completely prevent stray Grentl thoughts from popping into my mind at odd moments. Friday at lunch, Rigel caught at least part of one.

What was that? Something about a code?

I clamped down my mind immediately and just shook my head.

Sean, on my other side, noticed. "Something wrong, M?"

"No. Just, um, thinking about stuff."

He put his hand on my arm and I did my best to ignore the tingle his touch always gave me, maybe half what I got from Rigel. "You know you can always talk to me, M. Any time, day or night."

"I'm fine," I snapped. But the violent surge of jealousy I felt from Rigel proved he still believed my secret had to do with Sean.

I was *dying* to just tell Rigel the truth and swear him to secrecy, but Shim was staying at his house now and would surely be able to tell if Rigel learned something that big. Plus there was always the chance Mrs. O might ask me about it directly again. I *had* to hold out, at least until we were both safely on our way to Mars.

For the rest of lunch I concentrated—hard—on my food and on the gossip Bri and a couple of the JV cheerleaders were sharing, but I was starting to doubt I could keep this up for another two weeks.

Though I missed Rigel, Saturday was almost a relief since I could finally obsess to my heart's content. At least during my few free moments between Aunt Theresa's etiquette lessons, taekwondo class and another protocol training session at the O'Garas.' But Sunday at church was worse than ever. Shim, sitting right there in the pew with the Stuarts, was a constant reminder of the consequences if I screwed up. I couldn't even properly appreciate the little boost I got from Rigel's *brath* after our day apart.

During the sermon, I found myself wondering—very, very privately—if there was some trick I could use to quiet my thoughts when I really needed to. Maybe some Martian meditation or discipline...or would anyone else even need such a thing? The *only* other people I'd ever heard about who could do what we did were Rigel's parents.

Which suddenly gave me an idea.

So, what are your plans for the day? I thought to Rigel as everyone stood after the benediction.

Dad and I are going to a firing range up in Kokomo. I suggested adding practice with Earth weapons to my other Bodyguard training, just in case. Grandfather agreed. He's coming, too.

Good plan. I hoped he'd assume my eagerness was about him being my Bodyguard instead of the perfect opportunity he'd just given me. *Hey, maybe I can teach you some taekwondo, too.*

Yeah, if they'll let us spend ten minutes together before we leave. I shared his frustration, but halfway hoped they wouldn't. At least until I found out if my idea was possible.

I waited until after lunch, when Uncle Louie had gone upstairs for his Sunday afternoon nap and Aunt Theresa had taken a crossword puzzle into the bathroom, also upstairs. With just one phone in the house—and not a cordless, either—private calls were always a challenge.

I called Rigel's home line and, as I'd hoped, Dr. Stuart answered. "Oh, hello, M. I'm afraid Rigel's not home right now. He and his father—"

"That's okay. It's really you I wanted to talk to, Dr. Stuart. I, um, need some advice. Can we maybe meet someplace? I don't know how long I'll have the kitchen to myself and it's kind of, um, personal."

She only hesitated for half a second. "Of course. Would you like to come here, where we can be private? I can pick you up."

I exhaled with relief. "That would be perfect! Is it okay if you pick me up at the corner? I'd, ah, rather not tell my aunt where I'm going, since she'd want a reason, but she'll be fine if I say I'm going over to the O'Garas' house."

There was a longer pause this time. "I can't say I approve of you deceiving your aunt, but under the circumstances, I suppose it's often unavoidable. I'll be there in ten minutes."

I thanked her profusely and hung up just as the toilet upstairs flushed.

As I'd predicted, Aunt Theresa had no objection to me going over to the O'Garas' for an hour or two. It usually bothered me how much she liked the O'Garas, since I knew it was at least partly because Mrs. O used her Martian Royal ability to influence her, but at times like this it worked to my advantage.

Dr. Stuart pulled up about five seconds after I reached the corner of Garnet and Opal, halfway between my house and the O'Garas.'

"Thanks." I climbed into the car. "This probably seems kind of weird…"

"Not really," she assured me. "I'm always willing to talk with you, M, or just listen. I know it must be hard for you, not having a mother, and your aunt and uncle not knowing the truth. I'm sure Lili O'Gara would say the same."

I warmed at her tone as much as her words. "She has. But she can't help me with this particular problem. Plus, she's on the Council—"

"I understand. A promise of confidentiality could conceivably conflict with her oath."

Though I'd suspected as much, her words underscored just how careful I needed to be around Mrs. O. "Exactly. I'm glad you, uh, understand."

I wasn't sure she'd be as understanding once I explained my problem, though, since Rigel and I had never told anyone what we could do. I spent the rest of the car ride rehearsing just how I was going to reveal it, hoping I could convince Dr. Stuart to keep our secret.

When I stepped inside the Stuarts' house a few minutes later, I was hit by a wave of nostalgia. For several glorious weeks, when Rigel and I had been openly dating and the O'Garas hadn't yet shown up to complicate things, I had spent some of my happiest hours here. This was my first visit since their New Year's Eve party, shortly after that awful compromise went into effect.

Dr. Stuart led the way to the kitchen—the place I'd learned that I was a Martian—and motioned me to a chair at the table. She poured us each a glass of milk and set a plate of oatmeal cookies on the table between us.

"Now, what did you want to talk about?"

I swallowed, my prepared speech evaporating in the face of her concerned, motherly expression. "I, er, well…you know how, um, you and Mr. Stuart can sometimes, uh, talk without talking?"

Her eyebrows rose, but she nodded. "I assume Rigel told you about that? Or did you deduce it on your own?"

"I, uh, both, I guess. The thing is," I said in a sudden rush, "Rigel and I can do it, too. Talk telepathically, I mean." I braced myself for her reaction, but all she did was smile.

"I've rather suspected that for a while." Her hazel eyes, so like Rigel's, didn't betray shock or even surprise. "In fact, I considered cautioning you both to be more discreet if you don't want others to guess, but I didn't want to force your confidence before you were ready."

I closed my mouth, which had dropped open. "You knew? Are we…that obvious?"

"Only to those who know the, ah, symptoms."

Relieved, I made a mental note to be a *lot* more careful. I definitely didn't want the Council, or even Sean, to find out what we could do.

"Is that what you wanted advice about?" she prompted, when I didn't immediately say anything.

"Um, yes. I mean, most of the time it's great, being able to talk whenever we want, without anyone else listening in. Not that we're always 'talking' in class and stuff! But since we're not allowed to act like we're together, it…helps a lot."

Her smile was understanding. "Yes, I can imagine it does. You've been put into a very difficult situation, one that's not easy for either of you."

I stared down at the table, willing myself not to cry at the sympathy in her voice. It felt so *good* to know someone else understood. That alone made me glad I'd come here. But I still needed a solution to my problem. Taking a deep breath, I looked up.

"The thing is, even though I love being able to think back and forth with Rigel, there are times when it's, well, awkward. I thought if anyone might have tips on how to keep *some* thoughts to myself it would be you."

She chuckled. "Yes, there certainly are some thoughts a girl needs to keep to herself. Van and I developed our telepathic link gradually, over a period of many years, which no doubt made it easier to learn control as our ability matured. I take it your link with Rigel developed rather abruptly, when your *graell* bond formed?"

"Not *instantly*. It was just feelings at first, and only if we were touching. It wasn't until the battle with Faxon's people in the cornfield that we exchanged actual words. Then later, after Thanksgiving, when we were apart for ten days and got so sick and all? Well, when we got back together it was like our bond…doubled or something. After that, the mind-reading got way easier until, well— *Do* you have tips on how I can sometimes…shield what I'm thinking?"

Her cheeks inexplicably pinkened as she hesitated. "The best way I've found to block the mental give and take is to focus on the, ah, physical."

"You mean like being hungry or hurt or something?" That made sense, since it *was* hard to carry on a mental conversation with distractions like that. It wasn't something I could easily control, though.

"That too. But what I… That is…" Her color deepened further. "I assume you and Rigel have never, ah, escalated your relationship to a…physical level?"

Now it was my turn to blush. "Oh, um, no! I mean…we kiss and hold hands and stuff. Not that we get much chance these days. But we've never—"

She bit her lip and nodded. "No, I thought not. But that makes this a bit more awkward."

I nearly fell off my chair. "What? Do you mean we *should*—"

"No! No, no, no, that's not what I meant at all! In fact, that would be a *very* bad idea given current circumstances. When I said 'focus,' I only meant your thoughts. Especially Rigel's thoughts."

"Rigel's thoughts?" Now I was confused again.

"Given how you and Rigel feel about each other and the fact that you are both sixteen years old, I'm sure *thoughts* about the, ah, physical pop up quite often?"

Though I felt my face getting hot again, I nodded. "I...I can't help it. I mean, he's so—"

She held up a hand, though she was smiling now. "No details, please. He *is* my son."

I fell silent for a moment, thinking hard. "So...you mean if we're, uh, thinking about each other *that* way, we can't read each other's thoughts?" I suddenly remembered our last makeout session in the arboretum...and how I hadn't needed to shield.

"I can't know for certain in your case, but from my experience it's likely that if Rigel is preoccupied with such thoughts it will tend to block his ability to pick up on anything less...primal. For a while, at least."

"How long is a while?" To keep him from learning about the Grentl, I'd to need to do a lot of blocking—preferably without making Rigel too suspicious.

Clearly still embarrassed, she didn't quite meet my eye. "As I said, it may not work exactly the same for you. But I've found that the more, ah, intensely my husband thinks about such things, the longer before he can pick up on anything else I'm thinking."

I was sure my face went redder than hers as her meaning sank in: to block Rigel from picking up my thoughts, I would have to make him think about sex. A lot.

✦

Monday morning, I did my best to dress "sexy" for school, choosing my tightest jeans and a clingy green sweater Rigel had once said looked hot on me. I also put on extra makeup—eyeshadow, mascara and super-shiny lip gloss—but after I got to school, so Aunt Theresa couldn't make me wash it off. I didn't look anywhere near as sexy as Trina did every single day, but it was the best I could do.

Leaving the girls' room for first period, doubts assailed me again. I didn't have a *clue* how to act sexy and even if I could, it seemed mean to get Rigel all hot and bothered when we couldn't *do* anything about it. But…what choice did I have?

When I walked into class, my first thought on seeing Rigel wasn't about distracting him but about how hot *he* looked in a long-sleeved t-shirt that outlined his chest and shoulders. His thick, dark, perfect hair fell across his forehead as he turned his head, then his amazing hazel eyes widened and he smiled his incredible smile.

Wow, looking good today, M, he thought.

Ditto, I thought back, giving him a half-wink that I hoped looked seductive instead of like I had something in my eye. When Trina glanced my way, I headed to my desk. But slowly, so Rigel could watch me from behind.

"Are you okay?" Deb asked as I sat down next to her. "You look flushed."

"What? Oh, I…spent too long in the girls' room and had to rush, that's all."

I peeked over my shoulder to see Rigel still looking my way. I was reminded of his very first day at Jewel High and how I'd kept sneaking looks at him—and how intensely he'd affected me before he even noticed I existed. A sudden, overwhelming wave of longing hit me—a longing for those wonderful days when we could spend hours together, holding hands, whispering together, touching…

Rigel echoed my longing with a nonverbal surge of agreement. Quickly steeling my resolve, I tried a little test. *I wonder if there's going to be a pop quiz today?* I thought, though without specifically directing it to Rigel. *I really should have studied instead of playing with my pet unicorn last night.*

No response. Not even a flicker of amusement. Focusing, I still felt that longing from him, though it was starting to fade a bit.

Maybe I'll go for a walk today instead of eating lunch, I thought then.

When he still didn't respond, I repeated the same thought but "pointed" it more his way.

Huh? You want to do what instead of lunch? he thought back, clearly startled.

Oh, sorry. Nothing. I was thinking some exercise would be better for my figure than eating, that's all.

Another burst of desire came from Rigel. *There's not a thing in the world wrong with your figure, M, believe me!*

Dr. Stuart had definitely known what she was talking about! *Thanks,* I replied, opening my math book with a secret smile.

When class ended, Jimmy Franklin, my old "crush," made a point of stopping to talk to me about our assignment. He'd shown some brief interest in me when Rigel and I had our first fake breakup last fall, but mostly ignored me now I was supposedly with Sean. So this was new.

I answered his question, which he'd clearly made up just to talk to me.

"Thanks, M. I guess I'll see you around. Have a great day."

"You, too," My smile slipped a little at the flare of jealousy I caught from Rigel, leaving the room with Trina.

Really? When Trina's on your arm half the time these days?

Even though my thought had been directed right at him, he didn't seem to have heard me, so I repeated it.

What about Trina? he asked belatedly.

Never mind. I just shook my head, letting him feel my exasperation, then headed off to second period.

7

Triail

TRIAIL (TREE-AYL): *test or audition; ordeal by trial*

Dr. Stuart's strategy worked so well I kept it up for the rest of the week even though it soon became obvious Rigel and Jimmy Franklin weren't the only boys who "appreciated" my new, marginally sexier look. Guys I barely knew went out of their way to talk to me, which was funny considering all I was doing differently was wearing clothes I'd started to outgrow, plus a little more makeup. What was less funny was Sean, who kept trying to sit way too close at lunch or any other time we were together.

As a result, it didn't take me long to figure out that jealousy worked nearly as well as desire to distract Rigel, since of course he noticed how Sean and other boys were responding.

So, unfortunately, did Trina.

"Wow, Marsha, love the new trailer trash look," she sniped at me in the lunch line Friday. "Guess you can't afford clothes that fit anymore?"

I glanced back, then down at her super low-cut, clingy blue top. "What, you don't like the competition, Trina?"

"Comp—? Don't make me laugh! As if!"

I turned away from her ice-blue glare with a little smile and continued through the line, though I knew she was adding this to the list of things she intended to make me pay for. Like I didn't have enough to worry about.

All week I'd had to exert both diplomacy and Royal "push" to keep Rigel and Sean from fighting anytime we were all together. Ironic that now I could finally shield my thoughts from Rigel, I never had a chance to think about the Grentl anyway, I was so busy defusing the *other* results of my new strategy.

Meanwhile, our training took up nearly every moment we weren't in school. Rigel was getting most of his instruction at home while I studied at the O'Garas' every afternoon and most evenings. Sean and Molly at least got to go to basketball and cheerleading practice, since neither of them were the stupid Princess. Besides which, having grown up on Mars, they already knew the language.

Saturday I had my last taekwondo class, then went to watch Sean in the State 2-A basketball championship game in Indianapolis. We lost, since Sean was our only really good player while the other team had three or four, but everyone was still super pumped about it, except maybe Rigel. I was careful not to give Sean another opportunity to kiss me.

Sunday, just three days before we were to leave for Ireland, the Council summoned us all to the Stuarts' house so they could evaluate our progress.

"We'll start with the Bodyguard certification," Kyna informed us briskly when the O'Garas and I arrived. "We thought you should observe that, Excellency, so that you will know what our decision is based upon."

"Decision?" I exchanged a worried glance with Rigel. "I thought the Council agreed—"

"We agreed that *if* he could be trained in time, he could accompany you as Bodyguard, yes. This test will determine whether he was able to acquire the necessary knowledge and skills over the past two weeks. If you'll follow me to the back yard?"

You have, right? I thought to Rigel, trying to hide my sudden panic.

Hope so. The main emotion I caught from him was grim determination, costing me another pang for what I'd put him through this week.

Not caring whether anyone noticed or not, I moved to his side as we walked and gave his hand a quick squeeze. "Good luck."

He shot me a smile, the first genuine one I'd seen on him in days, and squeezed back. *With you here I'll do fine.*

And he did. *More* than fine.

First, he scored perfectly on the target practice with both Martian energy weapons and Earth firearms. It was obvious now why the testing had to be here instead of at the O'Garas'—the Stuarts' restored farmhouse was out of sight and sound of any neighbors.

Next, he fought two trained security men, the biggest *Echtrans* I'd ever seen, in hand-to-hand combat. One was on the ground in under two seconds. The other grunted his surrender before the first could even get to his knees, when Rigel pinned the man's arm behind his back. It was all I could do not to laugh at the Council members' reactions.

"Oh, well done!" Nara clapped her hands. The others wore expressions ranging from grudging respect to outright shock. Molly was clearly awestruck, her eyes huge, while Sean looked both impressed and irritated, though he was obviously trying to hide both.

"Looks like you've been holding out on us, my boy." Shim clapped Rigel on the shoulder as we all trooped back indoors.

"Guess I do better under pressure." But Rigel's sidelong glance let me know our bond, my touch and nearness, had really made the difference.

"Now dinner." Kyna reverted to her usual calm professionalism. "This will be a practicum of sorts for all of you." Her gaze encompassed me, Rigel, Sean and Molly. "Excellency, you and your affianced Consort will precede the rest of us into the dining room."

At the words "affianced Consort," Rigel's emotions abruptly shifted from triumphant to outraged. I stifled a sigh at the wave of jealousy that emanated from him—again—after too brief a respite.

Under the watchful eyes of the entire Council, I placed my left hand on Sean's right sleeve and approached the table, set for a formal state dinner. I quickly scanned the finger bowls at each place setting and identified mine by the pale green orchid adorning it. I moved to that chair, which Sean obediently pulled out for me, waiting until I was seated before taking his own seat on my left. Rigel then took up his proper position, standing at attention directly behind me. His jealousy faded somewhat as he went through the protocols that had been drilled into him—into all of us.

Shim, as the oldest Council member, took the chair to my right and Mrs. O'Gara, as ranking Royal, sat to Sean's left. Molly stood in her Handmaid spot to Rigel's right, where she could serve me.

The rest of the Council, along with Rigel's parents and Mr. O'Gara, proceeded to take the seats their status decreed. Once everyone was seated, Sean ceremoniously lifted my finger bowl and presented it to me with a small bow of his head. I dipped my fingers the prescribed three times, then dried them on the tiny linen cloth provided for that purpose. Sean then offered my bowl to Rigel, who dipped his fingers, and used my same cloth. Rigel held bowl and cloth for Molly, then handed them back to Sean, who set them back at my place. Finally, Sean dipped his fingers in his own bowl, which was the signal for everyone else to do the same.

The two security guys who'd fought Rigel during his test came in with platters of food and started serving. For me, that meant Molly dished a bite of everything onto a small plate, in full view of everyone, then handed it to Rigel for tasting. Only after none of the dishes made him gag or drop dead was she allowed to spoon proper helpings onto my plate.

This is stupid, I couldn't help thinking to Rigel. *If someone was really going to poison me, they'd probably be smart enough to use something that wouldn't work instantly. And it totally sucks that you don't even get to sit down!*

Yeah, well, it beats the alternative of me not going at all, right? I can deal. But I could tell he'd way prefer to be sitting where Sean was, next to me.

The touchiest bit came at the end of the meal, when we all rose (me first) and Sean turned to Rigel, who still stood at attention.

"You can run off to the kitchen and get some dinner now." He wore a definite smirk. "I'll take care of the Princess for the rest of the evening."

Rigel's jealousy and anger roared back. He kept his expression carefully blank since most of the Council was watching, but I could tell he was itching to punch Sean in the face.

It's part of the test! I thought to him quickly. *Don't let him provoke you, Rigel. Please!*

He must have registered my worry, if not my words, because he gave a terse little nod, then bowed, first to me, then to the rest of the group, turned on his heel and marched into the kitchen, Molly one step behind him.

I let out the breath I hadn't realized I was holding. He'd passed. We'd all passed. In a week, we'd be on a ship to Mars!

On Monday, Trina's revenge campaign kicked into high gear. She needled me constantly, whispering insults under her breath every chance she got. Whenever she wasn't calling me a slut, a two-timing tease or a pathetic orphan with daddy issues, she watched me like a hawk. Sometimes she even snapped random pictures of me with her phone. She clearly hoped to either provoke me or catch me doing something, anything, she could use to get me in trouble.

I ignored her completely, knowing that would bother her way more than anything I could say, but it was unnerving the way she was always *there*, wearing that nasty little smirk like she knew something I didn't. Every now and then I allowed myself a superior little smile, since whatever secret Trina might have, *my* secret easily trumped it.

But Tuesday, the day before our departure, Trina took things to a whole new level. Rigel showed up for English, Trina on his arm, more upset than I'd felt him yet—and wouldn't look me in the eye. Worse, when I tried to ask him silently what was wrong, he shut me out completely. I couldn't pick up a single thought from him, though jealousy, rage, anguish and even fear were coming through loud and clear.

What? Rigel, please *tell me what's going on!* I kept sending frantically, but even when I looked directly at him, he shrugged, still refusing to meet my gaze. As upset as he was, I doubted he could hear my thoughts at all.

Trina walked with him to Science, patting him sympathetically on the arm while I followed a few steps behind. So *she* knew what was upsetting him but he couldn't tell *me?*

During class, I focused all of my attention on the two of them, right behind me, and none at all on the teacher. Neither of them said anything for most of the period, though I was still getting waves of awful emotion from Rigel. When I did catch occasional snippets of thoughts, they didn't make sense: *Can't be true. But is that why she—? Would explain a lot...*

Finally, just before the bell, I heard Trina's whisper. "Rigel, I really am *so* sorry I had to be the one to tell you. If there's *anything* I can do..."

"You've done enough, Trina. Thanks." Then, straight to my mind from his, *How could you, M? I trusted you!*

I sat frozen for several painful heartbeats, before glancing over my shoulder. I had to stifle a gasp at the agony I saw on his face.

Rigel! What do you think I've done? What did Trina tell you? Why would you ever believe anything she tells you? Whatever she said, it's a lie, I promise!

For a moment uncertainty mixed with the pain, anger and jealousy I felt from him, but all he thought back to me was, *Later.* That one word was so harsh, it struck me like a physical blow, making me reel again.

Steadying myself, I followed them to the cafeteria, determined to clear things up even if I had to sit on top of Rigel to make him answer me. By now I felt pretty betrayed myself, that he'd ever judge me based on anything *Trina* said. Didn't he know her better than that? Didn't he know *me* better than that??

Halfway to the cafeteria, Trina gave Rigel one last soothing pat on the arm and peeled off down another hallway. Glancing after her, I saw Sean coming our way, so I hurried to Rigel's side to snatch a brief moment of relative privacy.

"Rigel," I hissed, "you *have* to tell me what's going on! What the hell has Trina been saying about me?"

He shot me a quick, pained glance then looked away. "It's not what she *said.* I don't— But I guess it explains why lately you've been so—"

"Hey, you two." It was Molly, though I'd expected Sean. "What's up?"

I shrugged, not wanting to admit there was a problem until I knew what the problem was. Looking back, I saw Trina talking to Sean a little way behind us. Great. Whatever she was saying to him, it was guaranteed to make things worse, not better.

"We leave *tomorrow,* can you believe it? Are you all packed?" Molly whispered, apparently not noticing the tension between us in her excitement.

"Um, mostly." I tried to hide my frustration at the interruption. "How about you?"

"I thought I was, but mum says I can only have two bags, so now I have to decide what I can do without for…however long we'll be there."

Normally I'd have commented on that, since everyone had been vague about when we were coming back no matter how much I tried to pin them down. But right now I was way more worried about Rigel and whatever awful thing he seemed to believe. I just nodded and let Molly ramble on about layers and two sets of weather conditions and whatever else was on her mind while I tried again to make Rigel answer me.

Look, no matter how Trina has managed to convince you, I promise I haven't done anything at all to make you feel like this. Can you please, please tell me what I'm being accused of, so I can at least defend myself?

After the way you've been shutting me out? Anyway, I can't, not now. Not with— He jerked his chin toward his shoulder, in the direction of Sean and Trina half a hallway behind us. *Or...I might do something we'd all regret.*

I nearly stopped walking to stare at him, remembering just in time that I didn't want to alert Molly to any of this. So it was something to do with Sean? Something Trina told him I'd *done* with Sean? I knew he was jealous, and that *was* partly my fault, but there was still no way he should believe anything like that.

"I'll be there in a minute," I told Molly when we reached the doors to the lunchroom. I needed to pull Rigel and Sean aside and make Sean tell him that whatever it was wasn't true. How could Trina think a ridiculous lie like that would hold up once I found out? It seemed stupid, even for her. Not that it made me any less furious with her for upsetting Rigel like this.

"Oh, um, okay." Molly looked curious now but, to my relief, didn't ask questions before heading off.

I immediately grabbed Rigel's arm with both hands. "Stop. You have to—"

Sean's snarl cut me off. "So, now you've passed their stupid test you're not even bothering to pretend anymore?" He stared at my hand on Rigel's sleeve. "Are you *trying* to ruin everything? To make *me* look stupid?"

Rigel turned and he and Sean glared viciously at each other for a long, tense moment. Then Rigel made a convulsive motion with one clenched fist and wrenched away from me to follow Molly into the cafeteria. Trina was nowhere to be seen.

"Are you crazy?" I practically yelled at Sean. "Are *both* of you crazy? What has Trina done to you two today?"

"She's shown me what's really going on." He glowered down at me from on high. "If Stuart's that upset, I guess *he's* not so proud of what you two have been doing behind my back. How does that make you feel?"

"Doing—? What are you—?" But he spun away from me before I could form a coherent question.

More confused than ever, I entered the lunchroom, bypassing the line to go straight to our table, though neither Rigel nor Sean were there yet. Off to one side I saw Trina again, this time talking to Molly and a couple of other cheerleaders. It looked like Trina was showing them something on her cell phone, while her pals Nicole and Amber squealed, giggled, then turned to stare at me.

Molly stared too, her expression shocked and upset. After looking again at Trina's phone for several long seconds, she shook her head violently, then hurried away—toward me. I assumed she was going to tell me what was going on, but as she neared the table, she veered away, not making eye contact.

Sick of all the secrecy, I leaped up and moved directly into her path. "Molly, stop!" Like I had with Rigel, I grabbed her arm, forcing her to look at me.

For a second I thought she was going to pull away, too, but then she jerked to a halt, so upset she seemed on the verge of tears.

"You have *got* to tell me what's going on." I used all the Royal persuasiveness I could summon. "What is Trina showing people?"

Molly blinked rapidly a few times, her lower lip trembling, then seemed to get a grip on herself. "It's... She's... M, she's got *pictures*, on her phone, of you and some guy half naked, like you're right in the middle of...of..." She stared helplessly at me. "How—? Who—?"

"Yeah, I want to know both of those answers, too." I kept looking Molly in the eye. "She obviously faked the picture somehow, but who is the guy?"

"Faked? But... Oh! Of *course!*" Her relief was so great, so obvious, that for a second I could almost feel it, like I did Rigel's emotions. "The picture doesn't show the guy's face, or even his hair, so there's no knowing who it is. But she's definitely got *your* face on there!"

"That obnoxious little—!" Rigel's and Sean's behavior suddenly made sense, though I was furiously insulted either of them could have *possibly* thought the picture was real.

Molly flapped her hands apologetically. "I'm sorry, M. I...I should have known the second I saw it that she'd stuck your face on some- body else—maybe some porn picture she found online, I don't know.

But…it looked so real. Whether she faked it herself or had someone do it for her, they did an awfully good job."

I glared in Trina's direction, where she and a few others were still giggling over her phone. "I'm pretty sure Trina has shown it to Sean and Rigel and they both assumed it's the other one in that nasty picture with me. She probably even told them that."

Molly gasped. "What a—"

"Exactly. And I'm going to tell her so to her face. Can you find the guys and explain to them what's *really* going on? And if you want to tell them they're both jerks for believing that about me, I'm okay with that, too."

She hurried off and I headed toward Trina, determined that this would be the *last* time she ever messed with me.

$$8$$

Camastall

CAMASTALL (KAM-UH-STAHL): *deception; deceit; falsification*

Sean

Instead of trying to eat lunch, which is impossible now anyway, I head to the nearly-deserted gym to shoot some baskets and blow off steam. Of course, I'd rather do it by pummeling Rigel into jelly. I came close just now. I was still reeling from that disgusting picture of M and Rigel on Trina's phone when I looked up to see M hanging onto his arm, right in front of me...

It's been bad enough, the way M's been acting this past week, all sexy with her tight sweaters and extra wiggle in her walk. Guess now I know why.

With a groan, I shoot another three-pointer, trying to shove that awful image out of my head, afraid the rage will take over again. Afraid I really will kill Rigel, which would probably put a crimp in our plans to leave tomorrow. I only have till the fifth period bell rings to—

"There you are!"

I miss my next shot as I whip my head around to see Molly coming toward me. "Go away."

"Not a chance. You know you're an idiot, right? And a jerk?" She walks right up to me, where we'll be out of earshot of the guys horsing around at the other end of the court. She looks pissed but also a little smug.

"I mean it, Molly. Leave me alone."

"I already told you, no way. I know why you're upset, Sean, and it means you're an idiot. I saw the picture, too—and I'll admit I believed it for a few seconds. It looked pretty real. But come on, Sean! It's Trina!"

Hope and relief I'm afraid to feel start to bloom in my chest. "*Looked* real? What do you mean?" But even as I ask, it's obvious. Even a stupid *Duchas* like Trina probably knows how to doctor a photo.

Molly confirms my belated revelation. "She faked it, of course. All she needed was a good picture of M and Photoshop."

"And a picture of Stuart. Naked. Don't forget that."

She shakes her head. "Nope. Wasn't Rigel. Wasn't you. She just wanted both of you to think that. Probably some random guy off the internet—though she probably had to hunt to find one that anonymous. Just a naked back, no head. C'mon, connect the dots! Aren't you supposed to be smarter than the average *Duchas*?"

She's right, of course, and I feel like a moron—and like the scum of the Earth for believing, even for a few minutes, that M would do something like that. Because when I let myself remember that picture, I realize Molly's right. The guy's head *wasn't* in it. No wonder Rigel was pissed, too. Trina played us all. Just like M's been warning us she would.

"Obviously not even as smart as Trina." I feel dumber than ever. "How pathetic is that? Do you think M will ever forgive me?"

"That's between the two of you, but I'd say some groveling is in order." She shakes her head at me in exasperation—or maybe pity— then heads out of the gym, leaving me alone.

Leaving me to writhe in mortification. And guilt.

Now that Molly's pointed out the obvious, I can't figure how I ever believed that stupid picture in the first place. Why was I so ready to jump to such a terrible conclusion about the girl I love, who I've loved all my life, since way before I even met her? Is it because I'm still so jealous of Rigel Stuart that I saw exactly what I expected to see in that picture?

The bell rings. I toss the basketball into the bin and head to History class, eager now to throw myself at M's feet and beg her forgiveness. Maybe, with luck, M will be even more pissed at Rigel than she is at me. It's about all I can hope to salvage out of this.

9

Hiarmarti

HIARMARTI (HEE-EHR-MAHR-TEE): *consequences; results; price to be paid*

Trina saw me coming from across the cafeteria. She whispered something to her friends, then just stood there, smirking, as I closed the distance between us. My right fist positively itched to punch that smug face but I told myself—firmly—that I could *not* get expelled for fighting the day before leaving on our trip. Something in my expression must have scared her, though. Her smile slipped for a second and she glanced at her friends again, like she was making sure they were still there.

"Is there a problem, Marsha?" The smirk was back, her voice full of fake, syrupy sweetness.

"*You're* the problem, Trina," I snapped. "You've done a lot of nasty things to me over the years, but this is a new low. You think even your so-called friends will trust you again after seeing what a weasel you are? Go ahead. Tell them exactly what you did. Or I'm going to turn you in for this."

Her smile turned ugly. "Yeah? You really want the principal and your aunt and everybody to see this picture?" She held up her phone.

Before I could stop myself, I looked—and nearly gagged. It was me, all right, apparently in the naked throes of passion with some faceless guy. Now I knew why she was snapping pictures of me yesterday. This one was actually me laughing, but in its new, nasty context it totally looked like I was doing something else. No wonder Rigel and Sean were so upset! I didn't even want to think what my aunt or anybody else would think if they saw it.

"Aren't you the Photoshop wizard?" I snarked, trying to decide what to do.

Her sneer broadened as she sensed my hesitation. "Aren't I? In fact, I'm so proud of this, I think I'll post it online so everyone can admire it. All I have to do is push this button—" Her finger hovered over the screen of her phone.

I didn't dare assume she was bluffing. More quickly than she could react, I snatched the phone out of her hand. I'd shorted out electronics by accident all my life, but this was the first time I'd ever tried to do it on purpose. It was surprisingly easy, since being upset always made my static problem worse. The moment I touched the phone it crackled and the screen went black.

When Trina grabbed the phone back I didn't try to stop her. "What did you do, you freak?" Vainly, she tried to turn it back on. "This is a brand new phone!"

Now it was my turn to smirk. "Guess you should have been more careful with it. And if you post that picture from your computer, it'll be super easy to trace it to you."

"You—!" Her hand flashed out to slap my face, but I was much too quick for her and instinctively whacked her hand aside with a taekwondo block.

"We're not on the playground now, Trina. Your days of beating me up are over. Or do you plan to have your posse hold me down, like you used to do in elementary school?" But the other girls had backed away, joining the loose circle that had formed around us, watching avidly.

Trina's eyes narrowed nastily. "I could always take you, Marsha, posse or not, and I still can." Her pretty face distorting into something almost bestial, she aimed a punch at my nose. Though I dodged, she caught me in the shin with one of her pointy boots, then immediately lunged at me again.

I easily danced aside, her swinging fist missing me by several inches. "Give it up, Trina. You played a really rotten trick and paid for it with your phone. Let's call it even."

"Even? Not a chance! I'm sick of you getting everything I want!"

She shoved her phone into her pocket and rushed me, both hands ready to claw my face. Fast as she was coming, it still seemed like she was moving in slow motion. I waited until the last possible instant to sidestep her. With no time to stop or change direction, Trina slammed so violently into the table behind me that she doubled over and smacked her face hard onto its top, scattering abandoned lunch trays.

She screamed and whirled around, green Jell-o and blood streaming down her face. "How did you—? Where—? You broke my nose!" She flung out an accusing hand, pointing at me.

"Me? Everybody here saw what—"

"Girls, is there a problem?" It was vice-principal Pedersen, the "Warden." Over his shoulder, I saw Ms. Harrigan, an *Echtran* who'd been posing as a student teacher to keep an eye on me since before Christmas, watching with shocked disapproval. Great.

"Yes!" Trina cried, still pointing. "Marsha attacked me without provocation, Mr. Pedersen, and broke my nose!"

A babble of voices broke out, some supporting Trina's story and others denying it, but when Mr. Pedersen held up a hand it stopped.

"To the office, girls. Both of you."

Trina looked like she wanted to argue, but I followed docilely. The sight of Trina's blood had brought me abruptly—and belatedly—to my senses.

What was wrong with me? I was a blue belt in Taekwondo *and* a Martian with extra-human reflexes and strength. I could have kept Trina from hitting me without making her hurt herself, or using abilities in public that would prove to everyone I really was a freak. When word got back to the Council—and I was sure Ms. Harrigan would see to that—I'd be in *way* bigger trouble than anything the school might do to me.

When we reached the front office, Mr. Pederson made us sit down and called the school nurse over to deal with Trina's nose.

"Is it going to heal crooked?" she whined as the nurse mopped her up and tried to stanch the bleeding. "Will I need plastic surgery? Omigod, the cheerleading banquet is Friday night! I can't accept my award with my nose all bandaged up!"

Principal Johannsen came out then to see what was going on, so Mr. Pedersen left our questioning to her and headed back to the cafeteria to talk to the students who'd witnessed the "fight." Trina tried hard to convince the principal I'd attacked her for no reason but by now I'd recovered enough composure to give my side of the story.

"That's enough." Principal Johannsen's voice cut through our escalating accusations about who'd started it (Trina's totally false). "You know the policy about fighting in school. Until Mr. Pedersen sorts things out, you're both suspended from classes. Marsha, it will be up to your aunt and uncle to decide whether you may still go to Ireland. Now, go sit on opposite sides of the office until I can contact your parents or guardians to pick you up."

Trina actually opened her mouth to argue—probably about some stupid cheerleading thing she'd miss—but shut it quickly at the look the principal gave her. Instead, she moved sulkily to the chair indicated. (I was already sitting in mine.)

It was only a couple of minutes later that I heard Rigel's voice in my head.

I'm so, so incredibly sorry, M! So totally stupid… Don't know what I was thinking.

So Molly made you finally see sense, huh? I assumed he must be on the other side of the wall, in the hallway.

No, I figured it out on my own, as soon as I cooled down a little. Of course it was fake. I can't believe I was that stupid, even for an hour or two.

Yeah, well, you are a guy. Guess you heard what happened?

Word is you broke Trina's nose. She definitely deserved it!

She actually broke it herself. All I did was dodge. But we both might get expelled anyway.

Even through the wall I could feel his guilt. *I can't tell you how sorry I am, M! If I'd blown her off from the first, maybe you wouldn't have… Will you ever forgive me?*

It was a little harder to communicate through walls, and I used that as my excuse to not respond right away—because I felt like he deserved to grovel a little, after jumping to such an awful conclusion.

Finally, after he'd been sending increasingly frantic pleas for forgiveness for at least two minutes, I relented—a little. *I won't pretend it didn't hurt—a lot—that you could believe that about me, Rigel. But Trina showed me that nasty picture and… it did look awfully real. So I get why you were upset. But if you ever assume anything bad about me again without at least asking me first—*

I won't! Never, never, I promise! So you forgive me?

Yeah. It's not like I can live without you, you know.

I could feel his relief through a foot of cinderblock. *Thank you! I don't deserve it, but I'll try to make it up to you. I love you, M!*

The bell rang for fifth period then and he had to leave. A few minutes later, Trina's mom came to take her home. As she was leaving, she turned to me with as much of a smirk as she could manage with a bandage on her nose.

"Told you I'd keep you from going to Ireland, you freak," she hissed as she passed me. "Even a broken nose is worth that."

When my aunt took me home at the end of the day—more than an hour after school ended—I thought Trina would get her wish. Aunt Theresa ranted and raved about the calls she'd received, from the principal and then from Trina's parents threatening lawsuits and I don't know what all else. Of course I told her Trina started it, but that didn't make a dent in her anger.

"The Squires are one of the most prominent families in Jewel, you know that, Marsha. No matter what that girl did, you had no business fighting with her. If her parents decide to sue, it could ruin us. You can kiss that trip to Ireland goodbye—and after I paid all that money to get you a passport, too."

Luckily the principal called before dinner to say I wasn't suspended after all since witnesses, and even a cell phone video, verified that Trina had attacked me and I'd only defended myself. But even *then*, Aunt Theresa wouldn't say if I could still go to Ireland tomorrow. She only let me go to the O'Garas' after dinner when Mrs. O came over to invite me personally.

When I got there, there was no sign of Molly or Sean, but Mr. O and half of the Council were assembled in the living room—the ones who lived in Jewel, plus Shim. I knew at once from their grim expressions that I was in big trouble.

Sure enough, the moment I sat down, Shim said, "It goes without saying that we're very disappointed, Excellency. We'd thought by now you had a better grasp of how important it is not to jeopardize the impression we've all been working to create as to your suitability to lead."

"I do," I earnestly assured him—assured all of them. "Honestly, I do. But Trina totally started it. And she hurt *herself*. I didn't hit her or anything, no matter how much she deserved it."

Breann cut off my babble stream. "That's not the point. Using abilities beyond those of most humans, especially in front of so many witnesses, showed *very* poor judgment. I'm afraid if word gets around it will prove a serious setback to our campaign to present you as your grandfather Leontine's logical successor."

I swallowed. Much as I didn't *want* to be Sovereign, I hated that I might have screwed it up for all of these people who had worked so hard on my behalf. And the deal I'd made before Christmas *had* included a promise to do my best to assume that role.

Shim almost seemed to read my mind. "I would hate to think that you would do anything to deliberately sabotage our efforts on that front, Emileia."

Somehow, his use of my real first name made me feel even worse. Way worse than all my aunt's shouting had.

"No, it wasn't deliberate, I swear! I...I didn't think at all. Though I guess that isn't much better. When Trina kicked me, then tried to punch me again, I—" I broke off at Breann's, Malcolm's and both O'Garas' concerted gasps.

"Molly told me that Trina used to bully you, Excellency." Mrs. O'Gara looked shocked. "But I thought she meant teasing, not physical abuse!"

I shrugged. "It was mostly teasing. And playing mean tricks on me. But she sometimes beat me up, or talked somebody else into doing it. Trina herself usually just shoved me or pulled my hair—stuff that never got her in trouble. Especially since nobody would ever take my side when teachers asked what happened."

She nodded. "Molly also told me what Trina did that compelled you to confront her, and I admit I can't blame you for *that*. It's the failure to control your, ah, reflexes that has us concerned." Then to the others, almost pleadingly, "This Trina really is a nasty-tempered girl. My Molly has said so more than once in the past. And we mustn't forget that our Princess only just turned sixteen. Surely some leeway—"

"Yes, yes, but that's not the point, is it?" Malcolm broke in. "And where was young Stuart, when this girl tried to strike the Princess? No matter how well trained he may be as a Bodyguard, this confirms my belief that he is far too young for such an important role."

"I've already spoken to him," Shim said. "He was apparently unaware of the two girls' confrontation until afterward, but I have now impressed upon him that it is his duty to be aware of *any* potential threat to the Princess."

Malcolm didn't seem reassured at all. "I still feel this demonstrates that he does not possess the maturity or experience for such a vital position. I can't help remembering Allister's concerns about the boy. I suggest we take another vote—"

My heart jumped into my throat. "It wasn't his fault at all!" Okay, maybe it was, a tiny bit, but *they* didn't need to know that. "There's no possible way he could have known. Besides, it's not like he can stay glued to my side at school without us violating my agreement with you. Much as we both might like that."

Malcolm frowned at me for a long moment, then shrugged. "Very well. Though his actions will be watched even more closely after this, as will yours, Excellency." He looked pointedly at Mr. O, who nodded, though his expression was *slightly* more sympathetic.

"Indeed," Breann agreed. "Right now, however, our task is to undo the damage by countering this negative impression and, most importantly, to make certain you are on that ship next week."

"I'm on excellent terms with her aunt," Mrs. O'Gara told the others. "I'm certain I can convince her the Princess should still go, given the extenuating circumstances."

"Please do," Shim said. "And keep us—the entire Council—apprised." Then, turning to me, "For your part, Excellency, please do nothing whatsoever that could further antagonize your guardians before you leave in the morning."

I shook my head eagerly. "I won't. I'll be an absolute angel. I promise."

"Very well." Shim favored me with a slight smile. "Though Malcolm is right. This will mean even closer scrutiny of your every move, and Rigel's as well, going forward. You *must* do everything possible to insure you are acclaimed Sovereign. That is the only way you will gain access to the communication device in the Palace, which is absolutely essential, for all of the reasons explained to you."

More frightened than ever by that reminder of the potential stakes, all I could do was nod.

10

Orinacht

ORINACHT (OR-IN-OTT): *propriety; seemliness*

Mrs. O'Gara walked me home, then talked with my aunt while I washed the dinner dishes and wiped down the counters. I put my nervous energy to work, scrubbing until every single surface gleamed. When Mrs. O left, my aunt came into the kitchen and glanced around with grudging approval.

"Lili O'Gara has been pleading your case, Marsha. She told me how you were provoked, which I will certainly share with Miss Squires's parents, should they issue any more threats. Of course, you still shouldn't have let her goad you into a confrontation, but I've decided that this scholarship is too important to your future to allow you to throw it away."

A huge weight lifted from my chest and the eager anticipation I'd suppressed all evening came bubbling back. "Thank you, Aunt Theresa! I promise you won't regret this. I've totally learned my lesson."

"Lili suggested you stay the night at their house, so you can get off for Chicago more quickly in the morning. Quinn will be coming by to pick you up in an hour, so you'd best finish packing."

"Oh. Oh! Great! I'll get right on that. Thank you, Aunt Theresa, thank you!" Overcome with relief, I surprised both of us by throwing my arms around her and giving her a hug—the first time I'd done that since I was little.

Even more surprising, after a startled moment her arms came around me and hugged me back. "You're welcome," she mumbled. "Off with you, then."

I let her go with a nod. Then, before I could say anything that might break the mood, I ran upstairs to pack my toiletries, the only things left.

I was going to Mars! And Ireland! I really, truly was! I could hardly believe it, even when Mr. O'Gara knocked on the door an hour later.

"Thank you, Quinn," Aunt Theresa said as he took my bigger suitcase. "And do thank Lili for me again, won't you?"

"Of course. Shall we go, then, M?" The little bob of his head showed he still had a hard time restraining his urge to bow to me.

I said a strangely unemotional goodbye to my aunt and uncle, then followed Mr. O'Gara outside. It occurred to me to wonder what my aunt would do if I never came back. Get angry? Celebrate? Either seemed more likely than tears.

"M! Yay!" Molly greeted me a few minutes later as her dad brought in my suitcase. "Mum had us so worried earlier, when your aunt was saying you couldn't go, but I knew she'd bring her round. Come in, do, we're all going to have a spot of tea before bed."

Glancing up, I saw Sean hovering behind her. "Give us a sec, Mol?" he murmured to his sister.

"Oh. Um, sure." She headed to the kitchen, where I could hear the clatter of cups and spoons.

For a long moment, Sean just looked at me, anguish in his blue eyes. "M, I wish I knew how to say how sorry I am that I was so horrible about that thing Trina did. How I could have ever believed—"

"Yeah, how *could* you believe that picture, Sean? Especially knowing Trina? I mean, how would she have taken that picture even if it *was* real? Apparently neither you *or* Rigel thought about that." I'd had way too much time to dwell on details like that during my long afternoon in the school office.

He hung his head. "I know. It was stupid. Of both of us. And if we both hadn't been so *twillya* to you, you probably never would have got mad enough to—"

Molly rejoined us and he broke off. "Tea's ready. And M, I've gotta say, even though it caused all this trouble, I'm glad you made Trina break her own nose. So are a lot of other people. She *so* deserved it!"

I had to laugh at the relish in her voice. "Yeah, she really did. Though I still shouldn't have done it."

Molly headed back to the kitchen, but Sean hesitated, still with the puppy-dog eyes. "So...do you forgive me? At least a little?"

I nodded. His assumption hadn't been nearly the betrayal Rigel's was, and I'd forgiven him. "Just don't go assuming things again, okay?"

"Deal!" A grin broke like sunshine across his face, making him almost as handsome as Rigel for a second.

But only almost, because of course that was impossible.

.⁺⁺

We went up to bed an hour later, since we had to be up early. Looking around Molly's room, I asked what she'd done with her plants. The last time I'd been in here, there had been at least a dozen, all, unfortunately, in varying stages of decline.

"I gave them all—well, the ones that were still mostly alive—to Heather. She's better with plants than I am, even though she's pure *Duchas*, go figure."

Molly had mentioned more than once how frustrated she was with her "brown thumb." As someone born into an Agricultural *fine* (the O'Garas had adopted her as a toddler) she was supposed to have a special gift with plants and kept hoping it might miraculously kick in. That it still hadn't was obviously a sore point.

"So, you never said, did you have a boyfriend in Bailerealta?"

My change of subject worked, and we ended up talking until well past midnight. Even so, when Mrs. O'Gara woke us at six the next morning we both bounced out of bed. As we scrambled into our clothes, Molly chattered nonstop.

"You are *so* going to love Bailerealta and Nuath, especially Glenamuir. I can't wait to show you around! Dad says we might even be able to visit Elana in the hospital."

Elana was Sean and Molly's much older sister, who'd been snatched by Faxon's forces just before the O'Garas escaped to Earth. Not till last week had they learned she was among the hundreds of political prisoners released after Faxon's ouster. Like a lot of Royals, she was undergoing treatment for memory tampering, which explained why she hadn't tried to contact them. I hoped she'd be okay.

After yesterday, I completely abandoned my "sexy" look. The side-effects just weren't worth it. Besides, I was now resolved to tell Rigel the whole truth as soon as we were safely on our way to Mars. As my Bodyguard, he needed to know, no matter what the Council said. Or so I told myself.

We'd just finished a quick breakfast when the Stuarts arrived in the full-sized van they'd rented to drive us all to Chicago so they could see Rigel off at the airport. After a last-minute panic when Molly couldn't find her book scroll, we piled into the van, everyone chattering with excitement. I managed to snag a seat next to Rigel and when Sean and his parents frowned at our clasped hands, I reminded them that this was probably our last chance for at least a month.

"Besides, it's not like any other *Echtrans* can see us."

"Yes, you're right, of course, Excellency." Mrs. O'Gara turned away with no more argument.

Sean, on my other side, still frowned suspiciously. "So when did *he* have a chance to apologize?" he muttered. "Or doesn't he have to?"

"Called her yesterday, even though I wasn't supposed to," Rigel whispered back. "Don't say anything, okay?" *That's all we need, to get in trouble for something we didn't even do,* he thought to me.

Yeah, we need to keep better track of what we say out loud and what we don't, since we'll all be together for the next month or two.

He squeezed my hand. *Together. I like that part. Even if we have to pretend we're not.*

During the drive I tried to pay attention to the political discussion between the Stuarts and O'Garas, though a couple of times it veered into territory that *almost* made me think about the Grentl. I scooted an inch closer to Rigel, so we were touching from hip to knee. That helped keep him from picking up any forbidden thoughts, even if it made Sean glower again.

The Stuarts had allowed extra time, so even with the awful Chicago traffic we got to O'Hare Airport nearly three hours before our flight. Mr. and Dr. Stuart came inside with us to spend the extra time with Rigel before we had to go through security. When Dr. Stuart finally hugged Rigel goodbye, with tears in her eyes, I felt a pang.

What would it be like to have parents who loved me like that? She hugged me, too, but it wasn't quite the same.

At security, I worried we might set off the scanners because of our Martian static thing, but none of us did. When Mrs. O handed out our boarding passes, I saw Rigel and I were in different rows.

"Um, shouldn't Rigel and I sit together on the plane?" I whispered to her. "He's my Bodyguard after all, plus it might be the last time—"

"I'm sorry, dear," she whispered back, "but there are other *Echtrans* on this flight. You didn't feel their *brath* while we were in line?"

"Oh. I, uh, no." I didn't mention that when I was with Rigel, I rarely noticed anyone else's Martian vibe unless I was really paying attention.

When we reached the gate, though, I had no trouble identifying the *Echtrans*, even apart from their *brath*—two men, talking quietly together, both a little too handsome. In fact, when the taller one turned his head I had to stifle a gasp, he was so over-the-top gorgeous. Dark-haired and strong-jawed, he looked a bit like an older version of Rigel.

He glanced over and caught me looking, then whispered something to his companion. They immediately headed our way. Before they reached us, Mr. and Mrs. O'Gara both stepped casually in front of me while Rigel and Sean just as casually flanked them. Though I appreciated it, their protectiveness seemed kind of silly in such a public place, especially since the men didn't seem at all hostile.

"I see we're all on the same flight." The super-gorgeous one's voice was as amazing as his smile, low, smooth and assured. "Devyn Kane. The O'Gara family, right? I believe we met once, back in the, ah, old country."

"Yes, of course." Mr. O'Gara shook his extended hand. "How have you been?"

"I've been well. Even better these past months, of course, as I assume we all are." His eyes flicked to me, where I still stood behind them, then back to Mr. O. The other man wasn't as restrained, blatantly staring at me. Devyn glanced his way. "Have you met Gordon Nolan?"

"Pleasure." The shorter, fairer man stuck out his own hand. "Pleasure. Would these be your children?" His gaze roved over Rigel, Sean and Molly before coming to rest on me again. I stiffened slightly. In addition to the usual *Echtran brath*, Gordon Nolan also had a faint whiff of what I termed "bad guy vibe," something I'd picked up from some of Faxon's followers last fall. This one would bear watching.

Got it, Rigel thought, edging a little closer, creating more of a barrier between me and the newcomers.

Mrs. O'Gara smiled back, not appearing to sense anything sinister. "Sean and Molly, here, are ours. These are Rigel Stuart—" She nodded his way— "and Marsha Truitt."

Neither man showed any surprise.

"Hello." I managed a smile. "It's nice to meet you."

"Honored, of course." Devyn gave a very slight bow of his head, which his companion, still staring, echoed. "I regret we can't greet you properly in such a venue. Please know we mean no offense by it."

"No, that's fine," I said quickly. "I appreciate your, um, discretion."

"I imagine we'll see you all in Bailerealta." Gordon's smile now seemed forced, his eyes darting from me to Rigel, then back.

The O'Garas assured them they would. When they headed back to the other side of the gate, I let out a relieved breath. "Are those some of the Royals you mentioned before?" I whispered.

Mrs. O nodded, frowning at their retreating backs. "Planning to take the same ship we are from Bailerealta, no doubt to build support of their own." Her mouth primmed with disapproval. Maybe I *wasn't* the only one who'd picked up that questionable vibe.

"Devyn Kane was becoming quite prominent in political circles before Faxon's uprising." Mr. O'Gara kept his voice low. "The youngest minister in a century or more, on track to become High Chancellor one day. Possibly your most serious competition for leadership of Nuath. I notice they were careful not to pledge their allegiance to you, for all they showed outward respect. I'd hoped such shifts in attitude were exaggerated."

I wasn't particularly surprised when the two Royals boarded with the first class passengers. I wondered if they were surprised I didn't. Boarding several minutes later, the six of us made our way to our assigned seats: three rows of two, one behind the other, along the windows. Sean and I were in the middle two, with Mr. and Mrs. O'Gara in front of us, Rigel and Molly behind.

Sitting next to Sean for the whole flight, ignoring that faint tingle I always got from him—and making sure Rigel didn't pick up on that *at all*—was going to be a challenge. At least I had a window. I stared out of it during taxi and takeoff, watching everything below us grow smaller and smaller until Chicago looked like a model of a city and the Great Lakes like ponds. Then we climbed into clouds and there was nothing to see but a floor of dazzling white foam with brilliant blue skies above. I released a small sigh.

Glad you enjoyed that. Rigel's mental tone was indulgent, making me smile.

"I forgot this was your first time flying," Sean said at almost the same time, probably in response to my sigh. "Glad you're not scared."

"Scared? I'd better not be, considering—" *Considering I'll be getting on a spaceship in a week,* I thought to Rigel. Then, aloud, "I think it's awesome." I turned back to the window, wondering how it would feel to watch the whole planet getting smaller the way Chicago had.

11

Aitlean

AITLEAN (AYT-LEE-AN): *airplane; primitive aircraft used extensively by Duchas; Earth's primary means of intercontinental travel*

Sean

M finally falls asleep somewhere over the Atlantic, not long after they take our dinner trays away. She's been so keyed up all day, I figured she'd crash eventually. Can't blame her, I'm excited too. It's going to be way cool to show her around Bailerealta and I can't *wait* to get her back to Mars. I wonder how much has changed in two years?

Some attitudes, for sure, like Dad said after those two *Echtrans* talked to us at the gate. How anybody who calls themselves Royal can possibly *not* want M to take her place as Sovereign of Nuath is beyond me. Almost makes me wish they could get demoted to another *fine* or something, even though I know it's genetics and not a choice. Still.

My eyes are beginning to get heavy when M starts to lean… toward me. I hold my breath as her head droops further and further my way until, finally, her head is resting on my shoulder. I slowly lean my own head back, careful not to jar her awake. It's beyond awesome that she trusts me enough to relax so completely against me, especially after yesterday. For a long moment I savor her closeness, her wonderful scent, the soft sound of her breathing…until something painful twists my gut. Because I know, deep down, she'd never let me be her pillow if she were awake.

I try to push that thought away, pretend she's leaning against me on purpose. Pretend she's sitting next to me on this plane by choice and not because Mum assigned her this seat. But my gut knows perfectly well that if it were up to her, she'd be one row back.

With *him.*

But that doesn't mean I can't enjoy having her head on my shoulder for as long as it lasts.

I wake up a couple of hours later and pleasure lances through me when I discover M is still snuggled against me. I smile down at her for a long moment, then look past her out the window, where the sun is just rising…over Ireland!

Much as I don't want to wake her, I don't want M to miss her first sight of Ireland even more. Gently, I touch her arm, the one that's not pressed against me, then shake her just a little. She stirs, then opens those amazing green eyes, looking adorably confused. But then she wakes up for real—and immediately pulls away from me, obviously embarrassed.

"Oh, I'm sorry!" She struggles to sit upright. "I didn't—"

I grin down at her. "No, it's fine. I hated to wake you, you looked so peaceful, but…look out the window."

She does, and gasps. Because Ireland is spread below us in every conceivable shade of green, dotted with lakes and crisscrossed by roads that are getting bigger and bigger as we start to descend.

"Wow, no wonder they call it the Emerald Isle. It's beautiful!"

I'm grinning again, drinking in her pleasure and sharing it. "Isn't it? I knew you'd like it. And I promise, you'll like our, uh, final destination even more."

I keep an eye on those two disloyal Royals as we go through Immigration. They're near the front of the long non-E.U. passport line, which means they must have come to Earth via Montana instead of Ireland. Unfortunately, M and Rigel have to wait in that line, too, while the rest of us breeze through the E.U. line.

"Guess we'd better go find our bags," Dad says. "Anyone want to wait here for the others?"

I volunteer, since I'm watching M like a hawk anyway. She and Rigel are standing way too close to each other, in my opinion, even if those Royal *Echtrans* are already through and gone. They're not all lovey-dovey like when I first got to Jewel last fall, but they still act more like a couple than a Bodyguard and the person he's protecting.

The way they look at each other, smile at each other, sometimes it's like they can communicate without words, they're so tuned in to each other. Even in the middle of conversations with other people. Impossible, of course, bond or no bond. Just me being paranoid again. I still don't like it.

Finally they're through and we all head to where Mum, Dad and Molly are waiting with our luggage. Customs is quick, then we go pick up our rental, an SUV big enough for all six of us. I don't see those Royals again. Probably had a limo waiting.

I get to sit next to M in the car, since there's no knowing what *Echtrans* might be on the roads. It's obvious she and Stuart don't like being split up, but that's tough, since the point is to get her Acclaimed Sovereign ASAP. Unfortunately this car has separate seats in the middle, so she doesn't even have to try to keep from touching me. Still, if I concentrate, I can feel a hint of that tingle from her—which means she must feel it, too.

"Don't let me miss any castles, okay?" M's staring out her window.

"You know I won't," I promise. "Hey, Mum, how come we didn't fly into Shannon? Isn't Dublin a lot farther?"

"It is, but between no nonstop flights to Shannon and this new highway, this was the faster option."

"So we're driving all the way across Ireland?" M sounds surprised. "Bailerealta's on the west coast, isn't it?"

"Yes, but it should only take four or five hours," Dad says.

"Oh, I don't mind." She sounds upbeat, even sitting next to me instead of Rigel. "It means I get to see more of the country."

"It is pretty, isn't it?" Molly's upbeat, too.

M nods, still staring out the window. "Even greener than I expected, and you told me it was really green."

"Wait till we get to the Burren." I grin. "Nothing green about that. Though the bit right around Bailerealta is."

Finally M turns to me. "Tell me more about the village. I studied everything I could about the colony on Mars but hardly anything about Bailerealta, since we'll only be there a few days."

With her looking at me like that, I want to tell her that her eyes are as green as Ireland, and more beautiful. I stop myself in time. "It's tiny, only about four hundred permanent residents. Purposely hard to find, if you don't know where to look. But once you're there, it looks about like any other little Irish village—at least from the outside."

"But not from the inside?"

"Depends. There are the *teachneaglis*—technophobes, I guess you'd say, maybe a hundred of them, who are practically Amish, the way they refuse to use any Martian technology, or even most Earth technology."

Molly pipes up from the back. "Yeah, until we got to Indiana, I didn't know there were *Duchas* like that, too. Though these aren't anti-tech for religious reasons, I don't think. Anyway, they mostly keep to themselves, and the rest of the villagers are pretty normal."

"You mean, using omnis and stuff?" M glances at me again with those incredible eyes.

I nod. "You'll see. I can't wait to show you around."

For a second I wonder if Brenna will be happy to see me. We'd had kind of a thing going before the news came about M. Funny, I've hardly thought about her at all since then. Or maybe not so funny.

Because M is my life now...or she will be.

12

Bailerealta

BAILEREALTA (BAY-LUH-REE-AL-TUH) (POP. 412): *village on the western coast of Ireland, est. circa 1575, populated entirely by* Echtrans

Despite my nap on the plane, we'd only been driving for an hour when I found myself getting sleepy again. Which I guess wasn't surprising, since it was about four o'clock in the morning back in Indiana. I was just starting to nod when Rigel's voice startled me back to alertness.

M! Look! A castle!

"Where?" Jerking upright, I looked around. Only when I noticed Sean's confused expression did I realize Rigel's comment had been silent. Oops. "Dozed off," I explained with an embarrassed shrug. But then I saw the castle, only a stone's throw from the highway, and pressed my face against the window. "Oh, wow! I've never seen a real castle before, not up close! How old is it?"

"That one? No idea," Sean said. "Probably hundreds of years— most of them are. Ireland is lousy with castles."

Even Rigel laughed at his phrasing. "Well, for us New Worlders, it's pretty cool to see something older than the United States. Hey, are there castles on Mars?"

"Not like the ones here," Molly told him, "but there are some fortress-y things left over from the early days of the colony, before we had Sovereigns. Maybe half the villages have one, or at least the remains of old stone walls."

"Huh. So are there Martian archaeologists?" Rigel asked.

I knew there were, because of all my studying, but I let Molly answer again. "Oh, sure. They're still finding out stuff about those early days, since almost nothing was written down. I'm not sure people back then could even read and write."

That and similar topics kept my mind away from more dangerous stuff for the next couple of hours, as the countryside got wilder and more rolling and even greener than before. I did more listening than talking, quietly enjoying how well Rigel and Sean seemed to be getting along, away from Trina's poisonous influence. I hoped it would last.

We stopped for lunch halfway, at a cute little village called Horseleap that Sean said was about the same size as Bailerealta. Mrs. O'Gara took over the driving after that, and after another hour or so we turned off the highway onto a smaller road. Then, half an hour later, an even smaller road, then another. Abruptly, the landscape changed from green to gray.

"Wow! It's...like another planet." I gazed wide-eyed at the wide expanses of stone stretching as far as I could see, obscured in places by patches of mist.

"The Burren." Sean said. "We told you about it, remember? Nothing can grow here, obviously, so no one ever built here. Kind of cool, though, huh?"

I nodded wordlessly.

"Bailerealta isn't far now," Mrs. O'Gara said over her shoulder. "It's at the edge of the Burren, so *Duchas* rarely wander in by accident. Which was the idea, when it was first founded back in the fifteen hundreds."

Ten minutes later she turned onto a dirt track that looked more like a cow path than a road—just a pair of parallel ruts with a strip of weedy rock in between. We slowly wound our way up and over a barren crag and on the far side the green returned, first in patches, then suddenly all around us. At the same time, the mist thickened into real fog, making it hard to see very far ahead.

"There." Sean pointed.

I squinted and saw rooftops in the near distance, poking up above the fog. As we got closer, they resolved into a collection of one- and two-story, mostly stone houses, some thatched, some tiled. *Thatch? Really?* Although this village supposedly housed nearly four hundred technologically-advanced *Echtrans*, so far it looked a lot like Horse-leap. In other words, impossibly quaint.

Suddenly, a man sauntered out of the mist onto the road in front of us. Mrs. O'Gara stopped and rolled down the window.

"Lost, are ye?" the man called out in a thick Irish brogue.

"Nay, we're here for the star gazing," she called back, like it was some kind of password. "How are you, Cory?"

Now the man broke into a big smile and hurried forward. Like most *Echtrans*, he was way more handsome than average, with wavy red-brown hair and a strong jaw. "Ah, it's you, then, Lili! I dinna recognize ye from afar. So, do you be bringin'—" He broke off, peering into the back of the car, his eyes wide.

"Yes, she's here. You may as well go spread the word."

He took a hasty step back, bowed in my direction, fist over heart, then, with another grin and a touch of his finger to his forehead, he turned and loped into the village.

"I feared there'd be no bringing you in quietly, Excellency." Mrs. O sighed, slowly driving forward again. "You'd best brace yourself."

"Um, brace myself? For what?"

"You'll see." Sean and Molly spoke at the same time, sounding amused rather than apprehensive.

Rigel's anxiety nearly matched my own, but he tried to reassure me. *Don't worry. Probably just some ceremony or something.*

We reached a fork and turned right. Abruptly, the fog thinned to reveal the whole village, spread out around us. People began pouring into the street from all sides—men, women and children, many of them waving red and green banners.

I shrank back against my seat. "What...what do they want?"

"You, dear." Mrs. O'Gara stopped the car and turned around with a smile. "I'd have warned you, but thought it might make you nervous. This first-ever visit of their Sovereign is nearly as much cause for celebration as when we got the news you were alive last fall."

More and more people crowded into the street, laughing and cheering, until I was sure every single one of Bailerealta's four hundred inhabitants must be out there. When they started chanting, I was even more freaked out.

"*Faoda byo Thiarna Emileia! Faoda byo Thiarna Emileia!*"

"This is crazy!"

"They're happy, that's all," Mrs. O'Gara assured me. "Just smile and wave and try to enjoy yourself. Come now, don't be shy. It means so much to everyone."

I swallowed. "All right, but everybody stay close, okay? My Martian isn't very good yet."

Molly laughed. "Don't worry, M, everybody speaks English. Even the Irish accents are mostly out of habit, for show. They're just shouting—"

"Long live Sovereign Emileia. Yeah, I got that much." I steeled myself for the role I had to play, knowing Mars would likely be even worse. "Okay, let's do this."

Sean climbed out, then held out a hand to me. Taking a deep breath, I put my hand into his, resolutely ignoring that little tingle. *Stay close, okay?* I repeated to Rigel, as much to reassure him that the hand-holding didn't mean anything as because his nearness gave me courage.

Like glue. And I know—it's all just for show. But I still sensed that tiny twinge of jealousy that never completely disappeared these days.

The second I stepped out, the crowd exploded in cheers. Fighting the urge to dive back into the car, I pasted a smile on my face—probably not a convincing one—and waved. They cheered even louder. I tried not to shiver visibly in the cold, damp breeze off the North Sea.

"What now?" I asked out of the corner of my mouth, trying not to let my smile escape. I was starting to feel stupid, just standing there waving like a mechanical doll.

As if in answer, a tall, dark-haired woman stepped forward and the crowd quieted to an excited murmur.

"Welcome, Excellency! I am Liana MacMurrough, *Meara*, ah, Mayor of Bailerealta. Please let me express how very honored we are to have you here. I'm sure you—all of you—are tired after your long journey. May I show you to your lodgings?"

It took me a second to realize it was on me to respond. "Thank you. Yes, that…that would be wonderful. I'm, um, very glad to be here." Then, raising my voice a little, "Thank you all! I feel very welcome."

More cheers. My smile became more genuine, their enthusiasm warming me. All these people, total strangers, really *were* overjoyed I was here, as bizarre and overwhelming as that seemed.

Just as I thought that, I saw, near the back of the crowd, the two Royals from our flight, deep in conversation with a tall, blonde woman and another man. None of them were cheering. Okay, maybe *everybody* wasn't overjoyed.

I see them, Rigel thought before I could frame my vague concern into mental words. *More ambitious Royals who aren't thrilled with the idea of another Sovereign, I'm guessing. I'll keep an eye on them.*

Thanks. I turned back to the mayor, who was gesturing toward the first two-story house on the right, which boasted a slate roof and gorgeous lead-mullioned windows. I assumed it was what passed for a hotel here, or maybe a bed and breakfast. We had a few of those in Jewel.

The crowd now lined both sides of the street, occasional cheers still breaking out as we walked the short distance while Cory, the man who'd first greeted us, drove the car around back to unload our bags. We were nearly to the front door when a little girl, maybe four years old, ran up to me.

"Princess, this is for you," she said with an adorable lisping Irish lilt. "I made it." She held up a piece of paper with a crayon drawing that looked vaguely like a girl wearing a crown.

Ridiculously touched, I took the drawing. "Thank you so much. This is beautiful! Is that me?"

She nodded, grinning, and a woman, her face as red as her hair, rushed up.

"Oh, Excellency, my apologies! I was fussing with my two others and Ginny clear got away from me before I kenned it. I do hope she hasn't—"

"No, no, it's fine," I broke in quickly. "Ginny just wanted to give me a present." I displayed the drawing. "It was really sweet of her."

The mother's eyes went wide. She opened and closed her mouth a few times before bowing to me with the Martian fist-over-heart salute and backing away, dragging little Ginny by the hand.

"That was very gracious, Excellency," Mayor Liana murmured, unlocking the front door.

Gracious? Had they expected me to be offended? "I thought it was sweet," I repeated, confused.

Liana just smiled, then opened the door and stepped back so we could enter. I was clearly expected to go first, so after a second's hesitation I did.

"I hope this will be suitable?"

The house was as charming inside as out, the short entryway opening into a cozy parlor with overstuffed chairs and a sofa. I caught a glimpse of a huge kitchen beyond that.

"It's beautiful! Are our rooms upstairs?" A wave of fatigue suddenly hit me.

Liana stepped inside and closed the door, muting the boisterous crowd outside. "Four bedrooms are upstairs, yes, with another two on this level. The largest has been made up specially for you, Excellency, but of course you may choose whichever room appeals most."

"Are we the only ones staying here?"

"Of course." She seemed startled. "This house has been set aside for you and your companions. I know it's not much, but it's the biggest we have. Normally Mrs. Cleary runs it as a bed and breakfast, but she would never ask you to share a roof with strangers. She'll come in to cook for you, but she and her family will sleep elsewhere while you are here."

I glanced at the O'Garas, but none of them looked surprised at all. "But…they shouldn't have to leave their own house. Should they?"

"So very gracious," Liana whispered to Mrs. O'Gara, looking almost awed.

Mrs. O just nodded, smiling at me in a motherly sort of way.

"Believe me, Excellency, the Clearys are extremely honored to have you in their home," Liana assured me. "It will give them a story to tell for generations. But no one would think it proper for them to remain while you're here."

Just one more example of the weirdness of being the Princess. I still felt guilty about displacing the Clearys, but I didn't want to say anything else that might delay a nap.

⁘

A tapping on the door woke me a couple of hours later. "Yes?"

Mrs. O'Gara cracked the door open. "I'm sorry to wake you, dear, but if you nap too long you'll never sleep tonight. And we've all been invited to a dinner in your honor."

"A dinner?"

"More of a festival, I imagine. The whole town will likely be there. You'll be wanting to change, I'm thinking?"

I looked down at the rumpled t-shirt I hadn't even bothered to take off before passing out. "Um, definitely. Do I have time for a shower?"

"Of course. We'll all be in the parlor."

She left and I glanced around at a room so nice I suspected it was Mr. and Mrs. Cleary's own bedroom. I'd been too tired to notice more than the soft mattress earlier.

After a quick shower, I put on a purple paisley dress Bri had given me last year and grabbed my nice jacket, hoping I wouldn't freeze. If the whole town was coming, the festival must be outside, but my parka seemed too informal for the guest of honor. When I joined the others downstairs, I saw Sean and Molly had spiffed up, too, Sean in a well-cut suit and Molly in a shimmery, long-sleeved blue dress. Smoothing the creases in my skirt, I suddenly felt underdressed after all.

"Don't worry." Mr. O'Gara correctly interpreted my renewed nervousness. "This won't be as…intense as your greeting when we arrived. People have had time to calm down a bit."

Rigel came in and I turned to him for more reassurance. And immediately did a double-take, my eyes widening. Instead of the shirt and slacks I'd expected, he was encased in a form-fitting navy blue body suit with a brown leather strap crossing his chest from left shoulder to right hip, where a small holster protruded from his wide leather belt. Sleek black pants went from waist to mid-thigh, with the navy body suit continuing underneath, outlining his perfect calves.

It was all I could do not to fan myself in appreciation. He'd always looked impossibly fine in his tight-fitting football uniform, but this was over-the-top *hot!*

Wow! I like! Then, out loud, "So…what's with the new outfit?"

Rigel gave an embarrassed shrug. "Now we're in Bailerealta, I'm supposed to wear the official Bodyguard uniform. Do I look as ridiculous as I feel?"

"Ridiculous?" Ridiculously *sexy*, maybe. "Um, no. Definitely not."

Molly shook her head in agreement while Sean scowled. I couldn't seem to stop staring.

Did you get a good a nap? Rigel's question snapped me out of my ogling.

Yeah. Am I the only one who crashed like that? How embarrassing. "I, uh, guess we should get going, huh?"

The sea breeze made me shiver as we walked, despite the hotness that was Rigel just behind my right shoulder. Sean was on my left, as protocol demanded. The village was roughly circular, the main road one big loop with a town square in the middle, footpaths radiating out from the center like spokes. As we approached I heard a clamor of voices, verifying that we'd be outside. *Brr.* If it wouldn't upset Rigel, I'd ask Sean to use his omni to warm us all up.

The moment we reached the edge of the big square, at least fifty yards on a side, cheers broke out. And I was suddenly as comfortable as if *Sean* had read my mind. Startled, I glanced up at him. "Did you do that?"

He grinned down at me, his teeth flashing white in the dusk as he shook his head. "The square is climate-controlled. And see how the fog is above and around us but not at ground level inside the village? Makes Bailerealta almost impossible to spot from the air or sea."

I glanced up, and sure enough, the sky was obscured by low clouds. Cool! I shrugged out of my jacket, only then noticing that no one but Rigel and I had bothered wearing one.

They might have told us, he thought sourly, taking my jacket to carry along with his own.

I glanced at Sean, half expecting him to object, but he and Molly were already being greeted by about a dozen teenagers, obviously friends from when they'd lived here. They both seemed totally at ease —unlike me.

Is this what it feels like to be the new kid?

There was a chuckle in Rigel's reply. *You're hardly the average new kid, so more for me than you.*

Yeah, but you've had practice!

Mayor Liana came forward with a bow. "Perhaps you'd like to meet some of the younger people, Excellency? This will be an informal gathering, as the O'Garas said you would prefer that."

"I would, yes, thanks." I smiled gratefully.

"Come meet Princess Emileia." She beckoned and the group of teens approached me, some more eagerly than others.

"Um, just M is fine." I noticed one girl clinging to Sean's arm possessively, though he looked uncomfortable about it, and three or four others eyeing Rigel with frank appreciation. Not that I could blame them.

Molly stepped up to cut through the awkwardness. "Remember, she didn't know anything about being a Princess, or even about Mars, until last fall, so she still feels a little weird when people make a big deal about it. Especially since she's always lived in a town where *nobody* knows the truth. Right, M?"

"Right." Mindful of nearby adults, not all of whom were necessarily delighted to see me, I added, "I've been learning everything I need to know as quickly as I can, but I'm still getting used to the whole idea."

"That must be hard," one girl said, her blue eyes sympathetic. "I'm Tamra, by the way."

I smiled at her, relaxing a tiny bit. "Hi, Tamra. And yeah, nobody warned me how much work it would be when they first told me…everything."

That broke the ice and a moment later I was being peppered with questions and names as people introduced themselves—first the teens, then more and more adults. Everyone seemed friendly and eager to know more about me. I did my best to attach names to faces and to answer all the questions I could.

By the time a bell rang signaling the opening of the buffet line, I felt a warm glow at so much kindness—helped by Rigel staying right behind me the whole time. A few days in Bailerealta would be fun after all.

$$\rule{6cm}{0.4pt}$$

13

Agoid

$$\rule{6cm}{0.4pt}$$

AGOID (AH-GYOYD): *organized protest; opposition*

I felt horribly conspicuous going first through the buffet line, but knew arguing would make it worse. Prompted by his mother, Sean came next, followed by Mr. and Mrs. O'Gara, then all the visiting Royals and the mayor (who I assumed was also Royal), then everyone else, more or less from oldest to youngest.

Rigel and Molly paced along behind me the whole way, two or three feet away from the table, not taking any food yet. At least no one insisted Molly serve me, which would have been extra weird at a buffet.

Stupid Martian tradition, I thought, since Rigel was even hungrier than I was. Everything looked delicious—probably everyone had made their own specialty. Lots of seafood and fresh greens, which was fine with me since I loved both. I put a big helping of broccoli salad on my plate and was startled by a mental groan from Rigel.

I glanced back at him. *What?* I queried, turning back around before Sean could frown.

Nothing. Just…I hate broccoli.

Oh, I forgot! You don't really have to—

Yeah, I do. It's my first day on the job. Gotta make it look good.

Gripping my own plate tighter, I frowned. *What if the food runs out?*

You want me to take some extra, to make sure you don't starve? What do you want most of?

That's against the rules, too. It's fine. Broccoli's good for me. Don't take any banana pudding though, okay?

Like I would. He knew I didn't like bananas any more than he did. Once through the line, I waited for the mayor to tell me where I had to sit.

"As it's not a formal occasion, Excellency, you and your friends are free to sit with the young people. Though if you could say a few words later on, we'd all appreciate it."

"Um, okay. Thanks." I was glad I didn't have to sit at a special table, but nobody had warned me about a speech!

You'll be fine. Rigel sent a burst of confidence my way. *Just say how much you appreciate the welcome and the food and how pretty the town is. Stuff like that.*

Easy for you to say. You're not the one who has to—

"C'mon, let's go eat." Sean glanced suspiciously from me to Rigel, reminding me how observant he was—about me, anyway. We definitely needed to be more careful.

I immediately nodded. "Yeah, I'm starving."

We all went to one of the long wooden tables that had been set up around the buffet. Since there were no finger bowls, I just sat near the middle. Sean took the seat to my left while Molly stepped up and put a dab of everything I'd taken onto Rigel's still-empty plate.

Sorry about the broccoli, I sent as he dutifully tasted everything. He suppressed a smile.

"Now, go get your own food," I said the moment Rigel and Molly finished the silly ritual. "Consider it an order," I added when Rigel opened his mouth to protest.

By the time Molly and Rigel returned, the very last ones through the line, the rest of the teens had joined us. The pretty, dark-haired girl who'd been clinging to Sean's arm earlier was quick to grab the seat on his other side, strengthening my suspicion that she'd been his girlfriend before. Not that I was bothered by that.

I'd saved the two seats on my right for Rigel and Molly, since it was an informal occasion, and insisted they both sit.

"Wow, Molly, you really have been appointed *Chomseireach.*" Evelyn, the redheaded girl across from us, looked frankly impressed. "Very cool." Apparently Mrs. O had been right about the position being an honor. She shifted her gaze to Rigel. "And the *Costanta* here —your new beau?"

Molly looked startled. "My...? Rigel is, um, *mainly* here as M's Bodyguard." She'd obviously remembered, just a hair too late, that she and Rigel were supposed to play along if anyone assumed they were a couple.

"Mmm, so that's the Royal Bodyguard uniform? I approve." A blonde who reminded me uncomfortably of Trina, but even more ridiculously pretty, flashed a flirtatious glance his way. "I'd seen pictures, but it looks way better in person. I'm Rowena, by the way. Nice to meet you, Rigel."

"We all heard how you saved the Princess from Faxon last fall," Tamra, the blue-eyed, black-haired girl who'd seemed so nice earlier chimed in. "No wonder the Council appointed you Bodyguard. My dad says there's never been one so young. Congratulations!"

I could feel Rigel's embarrassment. "Um, thanks? I mean, I do feel honored, of course."

"You must have so many great stories to tell." Rowena fluttered her lashes again. "I'm going to be on the ship, too, and can't *wait* to hear them all. Will this be your first trip to Mars?"

"Yeah, it will." His embarrassment started to fade. "Anything special we should see?"

Immediately, every girl at the table started offering Rigel advice on what to expect and what he had to see while he was there. I told myself their flirting was inevitable, considering how incredibly good-looking Rigel was, even by *Echtran* standards—especially in that uniform. It wasn't like he was actually *encouraging* them.

"Make sure you take a trip to the central pillar." Evelyn included me in her smile. "I hear it's the one place you can get a real feel for how high the, uh, ceiling is."

"I'll make sure they see it," Molly said. "You've never been, though, have you, Ev?"

The girl shook her head. "Born and raised here in Bailerealta, like my mum and dad. Rowena's from Nuath, though."

"We came here when I was eleven." The forward blonde leaned toward him across the table, reminding me even more forcibly of Trina. "Mum can't wait to get back, now Faxon's out. My father and brother are still there, keeping the family farm going. They sent us here when things started getting dangerous."

The conversation shifted to how Nuath had changed since the last launch window. The girl on Sean's other side, Brenna, mentioned messages from friends talking about shortages and transportation problems.

"But it's getting better now, they say. Now that there's no tyrant stepping on everyone's rights." She shot a glance my way. "We'll be on this transport, too, but *we* got bumped down to steerage."

I wondered if my emergency trip to Mars was the reason, and if that explained her slight hostility—though Sean was the more likely reason. Not my business, I reminded myself.

"So, have any of you been to Thiaraway?" Some looked startled at my first words since sitting down. I hoped they didn't think I was stuck up, they'd all been so friendly. "I've seen a video, er, hologram," I continued. "It looked pretty amazing."

No one had, but Rowena offered that her father used to go there a lot. "He said it really went downhill under Faxon, but I'm sure they're cleaning it up now." She sent a totally unnecessary smile at Rigel. "I hear there's tons to do there—or used to be."

I found myself fighting that increasingly familiar sense of unreality, listening to them all talk about life on Mars, relatives on Mars, like it was some little country in Europe. Not like it was another freaking *planet*. Not that they'd be so casual if they knew about the possible threat from— I shut down that thought before Rigel caught it.

Glancing around for a distraction, I saw three of the Royals I'd noticed earlier heading purposefully my way—more distraction than I'd bargained for. I felt my stomach clench, despite the big smiles they all wore. Rigel immediately stood up and moved into position behind me.

"Good evening, Excellency." The woman greeted me with the traditional right-fist-over-heart bow. "I hope you will forgive me not welcoming you sooner, but I wished to let you eat and relax after your travels and the undoubted stress you've been under. I am Annwyn Walsh, and I believe you have already met Gordon and Devyn?"

"Nice to meet you." Annwyn didn't have the unpleasant vibe I got from Gordon, but I could almost feel her tension—or maybe it was just the stiff way she was standing.

Devyn bowed then, positively oozing charisma. "Excellency, allow me to place myself and my colleagues at your service, something we could not discreetly do before arriving here. If there is any way in which we can assist or advise you—here, on the ship, or on Mars—I hope you will not hesitate to ask."

So they'd decided to suck up after all. Just to be safe?

"Thank you." I raised my chin, refusing to let my misgivings show. "I've done a lot to prepare already but appreciate your offer."

Now Gordon spoke. "I take it you have been receiving instruction from the O'Garas now that Allister Adair is, ah, no longer available? The amount of information you've been expected to absorb in such a short time must be overwhelming, even without a change in advisors to complicate things."

"Believe me, the change in advisors has been very much for the better. I've learned much more from the O'Garas, and from books, than I ever learned from Allister," I said firmly.

A spasm that was almost a frown flashed across Gordon's face, making me wonder if he and Allister were friends. That would explain a lot. "I, ah, was not trying to imply otherwise, simply expressing the sympathy we all have for the suddenness with which you have been thrust into a position of such responsibility."

"Yes, a great burden for one so young," Devyn agreed. "That is why we wished to assure you of our support. Believe me, Princess, one can never have too many allies."

A friendly warning or a veiled threat? I hoped the former, but would keep my guard up.

So will I, Rigel thought.

All conversation at our table had stopped the moment the three Royals reached me. Now everyone hung on my next words. Great.

"Yes, I've come to realize that. Your allegiance is greatly appreciated." I'd learned that the word *allegiance* held special overtones involving loyalty to the point of sacrifice. That they knew it too was clear from the slight widening of all three sets of eyes, though none of them disputed the word. If anything, I detected a trace of increased respect.

"And our honor," Devyn replied after only the barest hesitation. "We will leave you to your new friends, with the hope you will enjoy your brief stay in Ireland." All three again bowed in unison and moved away.

Silence gripped the table for another five seconds, then everyone started whispering at once. Rigel silently congratulated me on how well I'd managed the exchange and Sean did the same, out loud.

Conversation gradually resumed, but a few minutes later Mayor Liana cleared her throat at my shoulder.

"Excellency, now you've finished eating, might you honor us with a few words? Not to worry," she added in response to my undoubtedly panicked look. "No one expects a prepared speech."

Rigel immediately sent a bracing wave of strength and confidence my way. *You'll be great. Just keep it short and sweet and smile a lot. They'll love you. How can they not?*

I turned a smile at his thought into a smile at Liana. "Sure. I mean, I'll do my best."

Liana led me to the edge of the town square, where a large rectangular platform slowly rose about six feet out of the ground. Though startled, I followed the mayor up the short flight of stairs cut into one side. The thing even had a podium.

"Here." Liana pulled something almost too small to see from her pocket and attached the tiny button to the neckline of my dress. She then turned to the crowd, which had fallen expectantly silent. "I give you…Princess Emileia."

They cheered enthusiastically but I swallowed. Then swallowed again. There seemed to be twice as many people out there as there'd been a minute ago.

Go ahead. You'll be fine. Rigel stood at attention at the edge of the platform, scanning the crowd.

"Hello, everyone." Magnified by that tiny button, my voice boomed across the square, startling me again. I took a deep breath, drawing on the courage Rigel was sending me.

"Thank you all *so* much for the wonderful welcome you've given me today. I already feel like one of you." A burst of applause gave me time to come up with my next sentence. "Everything I've seen of Ireland and of Bailerealta so far has been beautiful. I wish I could stay longer, to see more of it, and I promise that if I get a chance to come back, I'll do just that."

More applause. Really? I wasn't being clever or original, just sincere. I decided to try something a little more substantial.

"I'm sure many of you are wondering whether a teenage girl who found out less than a year ago who she really is will be able to do all the things expected of a Sovereign. To be honest, I don't know, but I promise to do my best. I have some great advisors and I know I'll have more in the days…years to come. Believe me, I have as much reason as any of you to hate what Faxon did to our people and I intend to do everything possible to put things right and undo the damage he caused."

The crowd clapped and cheered again. Then, suddenly, there was a shout from the back of the square. "How about free elections?"

"Aye, let the people decide!" came another.

"No Royals needed! No Royals needed! No Royals needed!"

I blinked, only locating the source of the disturbance when several people converged on two men waving their fists in the air. Before I could react, the men were hustled out of the square into the surrounding darkness.

"Go on," Liana whispered. "Please. Pay them no mind, Excellency."

Like I could just ignore something like that? I hesitated, badly rattled, until Liana gave me another urgent nod, her eyes begging me.

Just give them a good finish, Rigel sent, along with another wave of love and strength. *Short and sweet, remember?*

He was right, of course. It wasn't like I could address what had just happened without knowing who those men were or what they wanted. Squaring my shoulders, I cleared my throat and continued.

"Over the next few days, I hope to get to know as many of you as I can, and to understand your hopes and concerns. And during my time on Mars, I intend to learn more about our people and about Nuath itself, so I can craft a course to lead us all into the best possible future. Again, thank you—all of you."

I looked to Liana and she nodded, now smiling ear to ear. She seemed to think I'd done fine and, judging by the reaction of *most* of the crowd, they did, too. I nearly slumped in relief but caught myself before anyone—especially my detractors—could notice.

Told you you'd be great. Rigel's thought was smug, and it drew a smile from me that provoked even more cheers.

I couldn't have done it without you. Thanks for being my strength.

Always, he thought back, all humor gone. *And don't worry about those two rabble rousers. Everyone else loved you.*

I wasn't as certain, but his confidence calmed my lingering uneasiness. Abruptly exhausted, I cupped my hand over my microphone button to whisper, "Would it offend people if I went to bed? Like, now?"

Liana shook her head, still smiling. "That will be fine. You've had a long day. And thank you—you were wonderful. Just what the people needed to hear from their Sovereign." She took the button from my dress and faced the crowd, magnifying her own voice now. "Please don't detain the Princess tonight, much as I know all of you want to talk to her. Tomorrow, after she's rested from her travels, will be soon enough for any private audiences. Thank you all for coming."

After one last cheer, people slowly (so slowly!) drifted away from the center square in twos, threes and family groups. It was all I could do to remain upright until I was sure I was no longer the center of attention. Keeping a smile pinned to my face, I headed toward the O'Garas, waiting a short distance from the platform.

A few people hovered nearby, clearly trying to catch my eye despite Liana's words. I was relieved when Mrs. O shook her head at them, though I pretended not to notice. That Sean did was obvious from the way he threw a possessive arm around my shoulders.

Though I would have preferred Rigel's touch, I couldn't deny Sean's was comforting. I had to resist an urge to lean against him for more physical support as we walked back to our guesthouse. The distance seemed a lot longer than it had two hours earlier.

It's okay, M. Lean on him if you want. You're exhausted. Plus, people are watching. The faint tinge of jealousy that accompanied Rigel's thoughts was nothing to the sleepiness I sensed from him. I remembered he hadn't had a nap like I had.

I almost asked Mr. and Mrs. O who those shouting men were but was afraid it might lead to a discussion I was too tired to face tonight. Tomorrow would be soon enough.

As we walked, I listed toward Sean until I really was letting him partly support me. If he seemed too pleased I never knew, since I never looked up at him, too busy focusing on putting one foot in front of the other. After what seemed like forever, though it was probably only five minutes, we were back at the house and both Sean and Rigel helped me up the stairs to my room.

Zombie-like, I managed to put on pajamas and brush my teeth before falling into a dreamless sleep, too worn out to worry about whatever challenges I might face tomorrow. Or the next day, or the next.

14

Teachneaglis

TEACHNEAGLIS (TAK-NEE-GLISH): *the minority of Nuathans and* Echtrans *who prefer to do without most modern advancements, primarily found in the villages of Bailerealta on Earth, and Keary and Eriu on Mars*

"And what might be your pleasure for breakfast this morning, Excellency?" Mrs. Cleary, our brown-haired, motherly hostess greeted me when I entered the dining room after ten solid hours of sleep. "Just you name it, and I'll whip it up in no time at all while you have a bit of toast and jam with your tea."

The four O'Garas and Rigel (who looked way too heart-stopping in his uniform for so early in the day) were already seated around the big table demolishing enormous breakfasts of their own. Apparently I hadn't been the only one to sleep late.

Mindful of protocol, I took the chair on Sean's right. "Whatever you've already made is fine. I'm not picky. Scrambled eggs, oatmeal, whatever."

"Well, aren't you a dear? I'll have both out in a jiffy. There's fresh tea in the pot and toast under the warmer." With a little bob of her head, she bustled off into the kitchen while Mrs. O poured me a cup of tea.

"Did you sleep well, dear?" she asked.

"I slept great, thanks. I feel ready to take on the world. Figuratively, anyway." I suppressed an errant Grentl thought by voicing a different concern. "I was too tired to ask last night, but what was the deal with those guys who started shouting during my speech?"

Mr. O slanted a wary glance at me. "Were you able to understand what they were chanting?"

"Sure. It was English, after all. No more Royals."

"Actually, that was in Martian." He gave me a faint smile when I blinked.

Martian? Really? Thinking back, I realized their actual words had been *Na ga Rioga.* My tired brain must have translated without my even knowing it. Which was cool…except for what it meant.

"So, who are they? Are they Faxon supporters?" I'd hoped after the big battle in October and the destruction of those nasty Ossian spheres, there weren't any more of those on Earth.

"No, rather the opposite," Mr. O assured me. "Some—though not a large or organized group—feel the reconstruction of Nuath is going perfectly well without a Sovereign in place and are opposed to another hereditary ruler."

That actually made perfect sense to me. I'd always thought the Nuathan system was antiquated. "So they want free elections and stuff? That's what I thought they said."

Mrs. O gave a dismissive snort. "We already *have* free elections for most of the legislature, and even the Sovereign only takes power after being popularly Acclaimed. These rabble rousers willfully ignore this, which is no doubt why there are so few of them. Most of our people are smarter than that."

"What Mum said." Sean patted my hand. "You heard the crowd last night. They loved you. But there are a few crazies in every crowd."

"In any event, they've been dealt with." Mr. O smiled reassuringly. "Don't worry, they won't be bothering you again."

Alarmed, I set down my cup. "Dealt with? What do you mean? What did they do to them? All they did was speak out. That's not a crime, is it?"

He seemed startled by my reaction. "Not a crime, merely a social breach. They've simply been asked to leave Bailerealta until the launch, after which they'll be free to return. Though they're likely to be ostracized unless they come to a more reasonable way of thinking."

I still didn't like it, raised as I'd been to revere free speech. Mrs.

Cleary came in with my breakfast so I allowed the subject to drop—for now. I made short work of the eggs, sausage and oatmeal, wondering how I could be so hungry when all I'd done since dinner was sleep. But both boys put me to shame, eating twice what I did on top of whatever they'd consumed earlier.

Sean swallowed a mouthful of fried potatoes. "If you want, Molly and I can show you around Bailerealta this morning, then some local sights after. There's part of a castle not far from here, and a tower at the Cliffs of Moher with great views."

I broke off my silent conversation with Rigel about how cool it was to have breakfast together. "Sounds great. I'm ready when you are."

When we headed outside a few minutes later, Sean immediately grabbed my hand. "Let's walk the circle—it's the quickest way to see everything."

"Sounds good." Resisting the urge to pull away since there were a few people around, I spoke lightly, smiling up at Sean. *For show!*

Like always. Rigel felt more resigned than upset.

The four of us strolled around the loop, Sean and Molly pointing out the tiny school, the ice cream shop next to the pub, the dry goods store. Everyone we passed greeted us cheerily. The O'Garas' previous home was now occupied by another family, but they seemed honored at Sean's request to let us peek inside.

"About like most other houses here," he commented as we glanced around the main living area. "Ionic sanitizers in kitchen and bath and a food recombinator, which we don't have in Jewel. Have you seen one?"

I shook my head. "But if there's one at the Clearys', you can show me there. We shouldn't go messing in the Kilcannons' kitchen."

"We don't mind, Excellency." But I could tell Mrs. Kilcannon was a little uncomfortable, despite her smile.

"Thank you so much, but we're already trying to squeeze in a lot of sightseeing today. I really appreciate you letting us look around."

The whole family bowed to me as we left. I didn't think I'd ever get used to that.

Gonna have to work on it, Rigel remarked.

I know. Doesn't mean I have to like it. If I ever act like I do, smack me, okay?

Oh, yeah, that'll go over well. Not that I'd ever need to. You're the least stuck-up beautiful girl I know.

Hiding my smile at the glow his words gave me, I longed to at least brush Rigel's hand. We were halfway around the loop now and hadn't managed a single touch. To hide my frustration, I asked, "Didn't you say the far side of the village is where the, um, technophobes live?"

"The *teachneaglis,* yeah, just up ahead." Molly pointed. "Some are more extreme than others, but most use electricity and modern plumbing, at least."

"You mean some don't?" Rigel was clearly startled. "Seriously?"

Sean nodded, squeezing my hand slightly—which I ignored. "Mostly just the Kellens and the Gleesons and their extended families. Their grandparents, or maybe great-grandparents, came here right after the Great Unplugging, when they didn't think it went far enough."

"The *what?*"

I glanced at Rigel, surprised he didn't know, then remembered he hadn't been cramming Martian history like I had.

And you never mentioned it, he commented silently as Sean started explaining.

"Yeah, nearly three hundred years ago on Mars, things were a lot like they're getting now on Earth—instant communication, social media, more and more personal entertainment options, stuff like that. At one point, nearly every person over the age of ten had a headset that kept them constantly connected to the *grechain*—our internet. Some even got sensory implants. Like having an omni—or at least an iPhone—attached to your face 24/7."

"I thought it sounded kind of cool when I read about it," I admitted. "But then, I'm the girl who's never even had a cell phone."

Molly grinned. "I thought that, too, until we studied it in school. It got to where everyone who could, worked from home. But instead of spending the extra time with their families, people got more and more isolated, spending so much time online they practically stopped talking face to face at all. Finally some Social Scientists convinced Sovereign Aerleas—your great-grandmother—that our whole society was being damaged, and she agreed."

Mention of her name immediately brought to mind what else I knew about her—things I immediately pushed from my mind. Instead, I thought back to what I'd read about the Great Unplugging. "Not her most popular decision, right?"

"That's for sure." Sean laughed, squeezing my hand again. "The way our grandmother told it, it triggered the closest thing to an uprising in centuries."

"But not with actual violence," Molly was quick to assure me. "Not like the uprisings Faxon engineered. Before people even got protests organized, families started talking to each other, and to their neighbors, and realized how much they'd missed it. So it turned out to be a good thing. We might have ended up, I dunno, cyborgs, otherwise."

"Resistance is futile," I muttered under my breath. Only Rigel seemed to hear, his silent chuckle just for me.

"I wonder if we'll be smart enough to keep that from happening here on Earth, or if we'll all be assimilated?" he said aloud.

Panic lanced through me at an unbidden image of the Grentl coming back to do more experiments. I suppressed it, but not before Rigel caught enough to glance at me in alarm. *What?*

Nothing. Not now.

Molly, meanwhile, was grinning at him. "Bluetooth headsets do kind of look like cybernetic implants." She'd caught the Star Trek reference after all. I kept forgetting people on Mars had access to our old TV shows.

"Do you want to wander through and meet some of the *teachneaglis*?" Sean nodded toward the two side streets and their twenty or so houses. "It's almost a village within a village. They even have a blacksmith."

"They're not anti-Sovereign, are they?" I was remembering last night.

"They mostly keep to themselves but as far as I know, they're not political at all—in any direction."

We spent the next half hour exploring what felt like a two-hundred-year-old Irish village, though the *teachneaglis* didn't dress or speak any differently than the other Bailerealtans. They seemed pleased to see me, eagerly explaining their reasons for shunning most technology.

"Not that the Sovereign has that luxury, of course," Kevin, our self-appointed guide, added at the end of a litany on the virtues of manual labor.

"Unfortunately, no." *Luxury?* Rigel's mental laughter had me struggling mightily to keep my lips from twitching. "You've been very kind, Kevin. Thank you."

I waited until we were at least a quarter mile away to say, "They seem happy enough but, sorry, you couldn't pay me to live like that."

"Luckily, they usually aren't into proselytizing." Sean shrugged. "You were great, by the way. If any of them had doubts about you before, they won't now."

I glanced up at him, startled, to find him regarding me with that warm expression that made me quickly look away. "I, uh, hope you're right. I didn't do anything special."

"Except make *them* feel special, every one of them. That's a lot."

He's right, Rigel thought before I could argue. *I've noticed it before and it's a real gift you have.*

Gift? What, paying attention when people talk to me?

It's more than that. But if I try to explain you'll over-think it, so I won't. All you need to know is that you're doing fine, just being yourself.

"Something wrong, M?" Sean suddenly asked. "It's like you…go away sometimes. You're not worrying about Mars again, are you?"

"Oh, um, maybe a little. But I'm trying not to…yet." Which was definitely true.

He looked sympathetic. "I know it's hard, but what's that saying? No point in borrowing trouble?"

Which was also true. "You're right. What's left to see in Bailerealta?"

"Not much." Then Sean grinned. "But Mum said we can take the car to see other stuff. The Cliffs of Moher and O'Brien's Tower are closest, but Dunguaire Castle is a lot older. Which are you most interested in?"

"Can't we see them all?"

"Sure, but they're in opposite directions. Tell you what, let's hit the Cliffs and the tower, grab lunch, then go north to the castle after."

"Sounds good to me. Molly? Rigel?"

I needed to talk to Rigel out loud occasionally or it would look odd to everyone who knew we were really still a couple. Which here meant just the O'Garas—who seemed to be pretending we weren't. Maybe they hoped we'd forget we were bonded if they ignored it hard enough. *Not a chance.*

"That plan's okay with me, too," Rigel said. *The cliffs and castle thing, not the other,* he quickly clarified. *That'll never happen.*

⁘

98

"Wow! Guess a lot of people come here in summer, huh?" I looked around at the enormous, mostly-empty lot across the street from the Cliffs of Moher as we climbed out of the car half an hour later.

"Yeah, it's a big tourist draw. Has been forever, I guess. O'Brien's Tower was built for tourists, not defense, way back in the early eighteen hundreds. You'll see why in a minute." Sean locked up and came around to my side. "Come on."

He reached for my hand again, but I stuck it in my jacket pocket. "There's no one around we need to convince now."

Sean's jaw jutted out stubbornly, though there was something vulnerable in his expression. "I didn't think you minded that much."

"I don't—as long as it's only for show. Let's go see the Cliffs." I turned away before the hurt in his eyes could make me feel guilty.

I was tempted to take Rigel's hand as we walked, but didn't quite dare. I couldn't absolutely *know* there were no *Echtrans* around and I didn't want to risk getting Rigel into trouble—though he'd changed into civvies before we left Bailerealta.

Hey, I'm supposed to worry about you, not the other way around. He brushed my hand with his, making it look accidental. An electric thrill went through me at the contact, our very first of the day. I'd missed this—needed this!—so much. It was all I could do not to shudder with relief and pleasure.

A moment later I was marveling at the way the green velvet top of the Cliffs abruptly gave way to sheer gray rock plunging hundreds of yards straight down. Looking along the long, curving edge of the cliffs, I watched the sea crashing magnificently against the rugged vertical rock faces and a free-standing spire thrusting up from the waves that showed where the cliff face must have been, once upon a time.

"Wow," I breathed. Land-bound as I'd been all my life, I felt overwhelmed by the raw power of the ocean. I could feel Rigel echoing my awe from a few inches away.

"It's something, isn't it?" Sean murmured from my other side. "I was hoping to be the one to show it to you. Your first real view of the sea."

I glanced up at him, startled he'd picked up on my feelings so accurately. But of course I'd mentioned more than once to him and Molly that this would be my first time seeing the ocean, so it really wasn't so strange after all.

Molly broke the awkward moment. "Let's go see it from the tower."

We climbed the path, then the tower's steep, winding stairs and admired the view from the top for a few minutes. Then both boys simultaneously declared they were starving.

"Sheesh, when aren't you?" Molly rolled her eyes. "But we've pretty much seen it. Ready to go, M?"

"We can't have these guys fainting on us. Let's go have lunch, then visit that castle." I was loving Ireland more than ever.

By the time we reached the parking lot, there was a hungry-irritable edge to Rigel's feelings and I could actually hear Sean's stomach growling. Boys really were bottomless pits.

"Maybe we should have brought a picnic, like those people." I slowed down to point while the others continued toward the car. "Then we could—"

I broke off with a gasp as somebody grabbed my jacket collar, yanking me backwards. "Hey! What the—?" I twisted around to see two strange men behind me, one still gripping my jacket.

"Yeah, that's her." The other man reached out to seize my arm. "And this must be—" He glanced toward Rigel just as Rigel's fist slammed into his jaw.

The first guy let go of me and reached inside his coat, but Rigel was a lot faster. Before the man knew what hit him, he'd joined his cohort on the ground, both of them rubbing their jaws and looking confused.

Now Sean waded in, looming over the men. "What the hell were you—?"

But Rigel cut him off, hissing, "Don't. Not here." Then, to the men, "Who are you? Who sent you?"

The men must have decided they didn't like the odds. They scooted away backwards without answering, then scrambled to their feet and ran. Sean immediately leaped in pursuit, but again Rigel stopped him, snagging him by the arm.

"We can't. Let them go."

"What? Are you crazy?" Sean tried to pull out of Rigel's grip and was clearly startled when he couldn't.

Rigel wasn't even paying attention to him. He was staring intently after the two men as they flung themselves into a black van and roared out of the parking lot. "At least they didn't think to remove the plates."

He must have loosened his grip, because Sean finally wrenched his arm away. "*Now* can you tell me why the hell you let them go? We could have taken them. They had no right—"

"No, they didn't." Rigel looked—and felt—just as furious, even though he acted calmer. "But we didn't dare take them out or cause a scene. Not here. Besides, didn't you notice? They weren't *Echtrans*."

15

Costanta

CostanTA (KO-STAHN-TUH): *Bodyguard assigned to protect the Sovereign or other members of the Royal family*

All three of us gaped at Rigel. Then, slowly, we all nodded. Because he was right. I hadn't felt the faintest bit of *brath* from either of those men, not even when one grabbed me. Clearly the others hadn't, either.

"Do you think they had that masking thing, like Mr. Smith used last fall at school?" I asked.

Rigel lifted a shoulder. "I don't think so. They didn't exactly…look *Echtran*, either."

Again, he was right. Prejudiced as it might sound, those men hadn't been at all attractive. In fact, the shorter one had been positively homely, his face pock-marked. I'd never yet met an *Echtran* who wasn't good looking. Most were ridiculously so, to the point of being conspicuous.

"So what does that mean?" Sean was still scowling. "Why did we have to let them go? They grabbed M, were probably trying to kidnap her. That's illegal no matter who they are."

Rigel's frown was thoughtful. "I'm guessing they were hired by somebody and don't know anything about…well, anything. If we'd held them, then what? Call the police? Do you really think the Council wants that kind of publicity? It's not like we could take them back to

Bailerealta with us. My orders—as Bodyguard, I mean—are clear. My number one priority is to protect M. But the second is to keep a low profile, especially around *Duchas*."

Grudgingly, Sean nodded. "I guess. Wish we'd hit 'em harder, at least."

"We? *You* didn't—"

I quickly interrupted. "So how do we find out who hired them?"

"Yeah, how?" Sean demanded of Rigel. "Think maybe we should've got that out of them before letting them go?"

Rigel was getting pissed again, so I stepped between them. "How about let's go back to Bailerealta and get some lunch into you two and report what happened and see what they say? Maybe they can run the license plate or something." I used a little "push" and was relieved when they both agreed, though that might have been because they were hungry.

Sean drove us back, grumbling all the way, darting occasional concerned glances at me and irritated ones over his shoulder at Rigel, though he did—belatedly—say he was glad I was okay. The moment we got back, he slammed into the B&B and started yelling for his parents.

His father came running, Mrs. O just behind. "What? What happened?" Mr. O looked me over quickly as though to reassure himself I was unhurt.

"You weren't in an accident, were you?" Mrs. O asked anxiously.

"Not exactly," Sean said. "But two men, two *Duchas*, tried to kidnap M, right by the Cliffs. *Rigel* decided to let them go, but at least we got the license number off their van."

"Earthers? Are you sure?" Mr. O'Gara exchanged an alarmed look with his wife.

All four of us nodded.

"He still didn't have to let them get away," Sean grumped. "I told him we should have—"

"No, Sean." Mrs. O cut him off. "That was the only thing he could do. We can't risk *any* kind of attention from the local populace with the launch only days away. Rigel's been instructed to never engage with *Duchas* unless there is no other possible way to keep the Princess safe."

Sean's sense of betrayal was so strong, I could almost feel it. He started to protest again but I spoke first.

"I was totally safe, I swear. Rigel had both guys on the ground before I even realized what they were trying to do. The second they got a good look at Sean and Rigel, they cut and ran."

"On the ground?" Mr. O looked alarmed again. "You didn't use your weapon did you?"

Rigel shook his head. "Just my fists. Like M said, that's all it took to make them back off. Maybe they weren't paid enough to risk their skins."

"I need to take this matter to the Council," Mrs. O said. "I'll call an emergency conference—most of them should be awake by now. What was that license number?"

Rigel rattled it off and she nodded, not bothering to write it down before turning away.

"Can we get something to eat?" I could feel Rigel positively starving by now, and I knew Sean was, too. I was getting pretty hungry myself, come to think of it.

She glanced back distractedly. "Oh. Of course. Mrs. Cleary left sandwich and salad things in the kitchen, and there's a recombinator. Go help yourselves." She hurried off.

.⁺.
⁺

By the time we finished lunch, the Council had met via hologram and decreed that I was done sightseeing outside of Bailerealta. They were also moving the launch up to get me off-planet before whoever had instigated the attack could try again.

"But I haven't toured a single castle yet! Can't we go see that close one Sean mentioned, the one from the fifteen hundreds, before we leave?"

"I'm sorry, dear." Mrs. O was firm. "Perhaps when you return from Mars. I've no doubt by then we'll have traced whoever hired your would-be abductors and…dealt with the problem."

"Who do they suspect?" Rigel asked. "Those guys who created a disturbance last night, during her speech?"

She hesitated for a moment. "I'm afraid that's not the only faction that isn't keen on the Sovereign traveling to Mars just now, as her arrival is likely to interfere with the support they're all trying to build there."

"How many factions are there, and what do they want?" Rigel

sounded so...official and protective and, well, *adult*. And sexier than ever.

"The anti-Royals, of course, but we know of at least two others with support here on Earth, each favoring a different candidate as Nuath's next leader. There could be others we're unaware of, as well. The van was a rental and the address given was false, so it may take a while to track the men back to whoever hired them."

I could feel Rigel's frustration at not being able to do more himself. I nearly mentioned the vibe I got off Gordon Nolan, then remembered Mrs. O's lie-detector ability—and that she hadn't liked him either. Besides, it was a big accusation to make with no more to go on than a vibe.

Sean spoke for the first time since his mother had come into the dining room. "Don't worry, Mum. I—we—won't let anything happen to M. We won't leave her side, before or after we get on the ship."

Mrs. O'Gara gave her son a sympathetic smile. "Rigel won't, I'm sure, but you can only be with her in the company of others from here on out. The Council was clear on that point, as well. Now word has gone out that you're to be her Consort, you both must follow protocol to the letter, which means constant chaperonage."

"What?" Sean surged to his feet, flipping his chair over. "You mean *he—*" He stabbed a finger at Rigel— "can be alone with her but I can't?"

"I'm sorry, Sean, but that's exactly what I mean. As Royal Bodyguard, Rigel is expected to be a constant presence, though of course he must keep any interaction *strictly* professional." She shot a look at Rigel, then at me. "You, however, must be a paragon of propriety with respect to the Princess, and she toward you. It's old-fashioned, yes, but it's important to appease the traditionalists as well as the more forward-thinking of our people."

Sean shook his head fiercely. "You can't—"

"Don't argue with me, Sean," she snapped, putting what I now recognized as "push" into her tone. He subsided with a scowl and she nodded briskly. "Now I must get back. As I'm the only Council member currently in Ireland, I am overseeing the investigation from this end."

As soon as she left, Sean turned to me. "Did you know about this? Or you?" He pinned Rigel with an accusing glare.

Rigel shook his head, carefully keeping his expression neutral despite the triumphant laughter welling up in him.

I quickly looked away so I wouldn't laugh myself. "Your mom did mention that custom before, remember? Just not how they planned to enforce it."

"It's total crap. You know I'm not going to...to try anything you don't want me to."

Now my lips did twitch a little. "Actually, the custom is more about keeping *you* pure than me. It started back in the days when only men were allowed to be Sovereigns and it was a big deal that their Consorts be, um, untouched, even by them, at the time of joining. So it's to make sure *I* don't use my authority or persuasiveness or whatever to take advantage of *you*."

Molly, then Rigel, broke into gales of laughter so infectious I couldn't help joining in. Not surprisingly, Sean didn't, though his scowl did lessen a bit.

"Yeah, okay, fine. Laugh. But I'll be the one keeping an eye on *you*," he said to Rigel. "If I have to act 'pure'"—he made air quotes— "so do you. Both of you. You heard what Mum said: *professional*. It better never look like more than that to *anyone* from now on."

Suddenly, I didn't feel like laughing anymore.

✦

At half past midnight Saturday night, I joined the others in the parlor, my heart pounding like crazy. Because this *was* crazy! How could I possibly be flying into *space*? Tonight?

Rigel, in his Bodyguard uniform, greeted me with a grin. "Ready to go to Mars?" Excited anticipation was coming off him in waves.

"As ready as I'll ever be." I knew he could also feel my excitement and hoped he'd attribute any nervousness only to the trip. Soon, soon, I could tell him—but not yet. Not until we were safely off the planet, with no chance of turning back.

Sean and Molly looked excited, too, while Mr. O was practically bouncing with eagerness. "Let's hurry. Remember what Captain Liam said about how precise the schedule is. And you'll want to see them raise the ship."

"Raise the—?"

"You'll see," Sean said. "C'mon."

We headed to the town square along with what looked like most of the town. Only a few dozen people would be on this flight, including a few more Royals who'd only just arrived in Bailerealta. I guessed the rest wanted to see us off.

The square was empty. People crowded around the edges, leaving the center clear, but there was no sign of a ship. I glanced around, confused. "So…do we go underground to board?"

"Nope." Sean was grinning. "It's pretty cool. We saw a couple of launches the month after we got here. There are access tunnels directly to the hangar for crew and maintenance, but for boarding, well, just watch."

The ground began to rumble and vibrate, like a mild earthquake or maybe a big truck going past. Then a brightly lit X appeared in the middle of the square, rapidly getting bigger and bigger until the whole thing opened up, four triangular panels retreating to the edges. Almost immediately, something enormous and black started rising up through the new opening, higher and higher until it loomed over the landscape, more than fifty feet high.

I gaped up at it. "That's the ship? It looks like a giant rock."

"By design," Mr. O'Gara said. "If it's spotted on radar, or even visually, it will be mistaken for a meteorite."

Which made perfect sense. After five hundred plus years of traveling back and forth, Martians had obviously figured out ways to keep their secrets from us easily-panicked Earthers.

Us? Rigel echoed my thought with amusement.

Oops. *Sorry. Guess you can take the girl off the Earth but you can't take the Earth out of the girl. Not completely, anyway.*

A lighted doorway appeared near the bottom of the gigantic rock, then a short ramp extended out and down. A chime sounded and Mayor Liana hurried over to me. "That's the call for boarding. You're first, of course, Excellency."

I swallowed hard and nodded, squaring my shoulders and lifting my chin as I stepped toward the ship. A murmur broke out around the square and I paused, realizing I probably should have given a farewell speech or something. I turned and waved to the crowd and, since I didn't have a mic, shouted, "Thank you all! I hope to see you again soon."

Cheering broke out. Liana nodded approvingly, then gestured for me to go on. With Sean on my left, Rigel right behind me, and the other O'Garas right behind him, I continued forward.

At the foot of the ramp, Mrs. O hugged each of her children, kissed her husband, then turned to me. "You'll remember all you've learned, dear?"

"I'll try." Right now I was too excited to remember much of anything. "Thank you. For…for everything."

Just like Dr. Stuart had done three days ago in Chicago, Mrs. O'Gara enveloped me in a motherly hug that warmed me right down to my toes. I hugged her back. I was going to miss her, even if I didn't always completely trust her motives. And then I was stepping through that brightly lit doorway onto the ship.

Captain Liam himself waited just inside to greet me. "Welcome aboard the *Quintessence*, Excellency. I hope you will enjoy your trip."

"How can I not?" I wondered if he could hear my heart thudding.

Smiling, he bowed, then motioned me to follow him down a short passageway while a crewman took over his spot by the door, murmuring greetings to each passenger as they boarded.

"This is the common area." The Captain led us to the front of a room about the size of Jewel High's cafeteria, filled with rows of theater-style chairs. "Everyone will be seated here for liftoff, after which it will be used for dining and recreation. After liftoff, I will personally escort you to your quarters. Meanwhile, please make yourself comfortable."

He turned to Molly. "You are the Sovereign's Handmaid?" She nodded. "Feel free to bring her any refreshment she desires while we prepare for liftoff." With another bow, he left us.

Trying to shake my sense of unreality, I sank into a seat in the middle of the front row and looked around, vaguely disappointed. "No windows?"

"Um…" Rigel pointed at the wall we were facing and I realized it was a huge screen.

"Oh." I guessed I'd be able to watch us take off after all. "Um, have a seat, guys."

Sean immediately sat on my left, but Molly hesitated. "Would you like something to eat or drink…Excellency?"

I grimaced, but realized she had to play her part since people were filing in, Royals first. "I'm fine. It's the middle of the night, after all."

"Pretty cool, huh?" Sean said as his dad sat next to him and Rigel took the seat on my other side. "This is the same ship we took two years ago. I'll give you a tour later on."

That'll be special, Rigel thought sourly.

Be nice, I thought back. Then, to Sean, "Definitely cool. How long after launch do we stay strapped in?"

"Not long. There's no real G-force inside the ship, since they accelerate at exactly one G—one Earth gravity. They mostly want us seated in case anything weird happens the first few minutes, and to do a head count while they run a sensor sweep to make sure no one but crew is anywhere else on the ship before liftoff."

Considering what had happened at the Cliffs of Moher, I was glad they had technology to check for stowaways.

So am I. Means if there's anyone to worry about on board, they're registered. Easier to run checks that way.

I slanted a glance Rigel's way. *Do you think there is? Anyone to worry about, I mean.*

Nobody you need to worry about. Leave that to me. It's my job. He gave me a ghost of a wink.

"Are you excited, M?" Molly asked from Rigel's other side.

I laughed. "Duh. Weren't you, your first flight?"

She nodded, looking as eager as I felt. "Any minute, they'll— Ah, there." The enormous screen lit up, then resolved into a perfect view of Bailerealta and its people ringing the square, waving. Definitely better than a window.

"Too bad we can't wave back," I said.

"We can." Mr. O'Gara pointed. "There's a camera up there, broadcasting to a screen on the square."

I glanced up at the tiny silver half-sphere above our screen, then behind me at the nearly full room. Everyone was seated now and yes, lots of them were waving. Turning back to the camera, I raised my own hand to say goodbye and saw the people outside cheer, though I couldn't hear them. Instead, as though my waving had been a signal, the faint rumbling of the ship intensified.

"This is it!" Sean pulled his shoulder strap across and clicked it into place just as an announcement directed us all to do exactly that.

The ship began to vibrate and a moment later the scene outside fell away as we rose into the air. If it hadn't been for the screen, I wouldn't have known we were moving at all, since the vibration stopped almost as soon as it started. It felt more like sitting in a movie theater than a spaceship.

But what a movie! As I watched, Bailerealta disappeared then reappeared, only now we were looking down at it from above. Our bird's-eye view quickly grew smaller, then everything was abruptly obscured by fog. I kept watching, and in moments I could see all of Ireland, the fog over Bailerealta a tiny cloud. Almost before I could blink, Ireland itself became a tiny dark mass on a much larger dark mass, and then…then I could actually see the curve of the Earth. The curve took up more and more of the screen, until it became a complete circle.

The circle—the *planet*—shrank and shrank, one thin edge brightly lit, like a crescent moon.

I was really, truly in space, on my way to Mars!

16

Probleid

PROBLEID (PRUH-BLAYD): *privilege; status*

Sean

I can't help grinning at the awe on M's face during her first launch. Watching her experience her first plane flight was great, but I'm loving this even more. I plan to be there for *all* her firsts from now on. "Way cooler than an airplane, huh?"

"Definitely." She looks away from the screen for a second to grin back and I get that belly flip her smiles always give me. "How long till we see Mars up there?"

"I haven't done the flight this direction, but maybe a couple of days? We were only a day or so out of Mars when they put Earth up there, but it's bigger."

She's looking back at the screen now, so I watch her profile for a while—until I notice Rigel staring at her, too. Jerk. No matter what Mum and everyone said, I still think he screwed up letting those possibly murderous *Duchas* get away. Maybe once we get to Mars they'll put someone else in as Bodyguard and he'll have to—

A notice flashes on the screen that we're free to get up, so I break off that thought. "You want that tour of the ship now?"

Before she can answer, Captain Liam comes up. "May I escort you to your suite, Excellency? Your effects are already there."

"Um, sure. Tour later, Sean, okay? After we've all had some sleep and I can pay better attention?"

"Yeah, probably a good idea." I stifle a yawn—and my disappointment that I can't spend more time with her tonight.

The Captain steps back while M unsnaps her harness. "If you'll come with me, Excellency? And your Handmaid and Bodyguard, of course."

I nearly gag. "What?" I swing around to look at Rigel, who I swear looks smug, though I can tell he's surprised, too. "*He's* going to be staying in her suite?"

Dad and Captain Liam both frown at me and I back off—a little. "I mean...nobody has a problem with that?"

"It's protocol, sir, as well as practical. He can't well protect her from a different level of the ship."

Dad gives me a warning look so I refrain from pointing out the obvious flaw in this setup. "Mind if I come up, too, just to check out the, uh, sleeping arrangements?" Rigel won't meet my eye now, which only proves he knows I'm right.

"Very well. You may accompany us now, sir, but you must leave the Executive Level when I do, and you're never to visit it without the Sovereign's express permission and the presence of her Handmaid. I run a tight ship and won't have it said I've played fast and loose with protocol at such a sensitive time."

Having the Captain call me "sir" helps a little. But only a little. Because this whole protocol thing sucks. "Okay, fine." I sound like a sulky kid, totally *not* how I want M to see me, so I force a smile. "Let's go, so the Princess can get her sleep."

My dad makes arrangements to meet with M over breakfast tomorrow, tells me which cabin we're in, then heads toward the main lifts, where everyone's lining up to go to their quarters. The Captain leads us to the opposite corner of the Commons, to a set of fancy bronze doors with the words "restricted access" etched across the top in Martian.

"This is the executive lift, Excellency, which only you and senior crew can access. If you'll please place your palm here, to be recognized?"

She does. The Captain punches in a code, the doors open and we all step inside. "One," he says, and a moment later we step out into the plushly carpeted VIP level, which I never got to see last time. Nice.

"This will be your suite, Excellency." The Captain points to another fancy bronze door, this one etched "private." "My quarters are across the hall, as are the senior officer quarters, should you need anything. Now, if you'll place your palm here?"

The door slides sideways into the wall and I see a room nearly half the size of the Commons downstairs. There's a huge sectional sofa, a vid screen taking up one entire wall, a big conference table with a dozen comfy-looking chairs, and crystal and gold everywhere. The kind of place M deserves.

"Wow," she breathes, stepping inside and looking around. "All this, just for me?"

"And us," Molly reminds her, grinning.

Rigel stifles a grin of his own, making me want to punch him, but then he manages to act serious again. "I'll do a recon, Excellency, shall I?" M nods and Rigel goes to look through the open doorway across from us. "This must be your private sitting room, with your bedroom beyond it." I see another open door on the far side of her parlor or whatever.

Captain Liam nods. "Those doors are also keyed to your touch, Excellency. Once you close them, they will only open for you."

M goes past Rigel into the rooms, calling back, "This looks like it belongs in a palace, not a spaceship."

"It's gorgeous!" Molly revolves in a circle in the main living room. "Are those our rooms?"

There are two open doors to our left. The first is a tiny bedroom, way smaller than the quarters Dad and I will share one floor down. It's pretty Spartan, too—a barely-twin bed, a chest and a chair. That helps make up for Rigel's duffel sitting on the chest. A little. Molly's room looks just like Rigel's except for the green roller bag next to the narrow bed. There's a little bathroom in between that they apparently have to share.

M rejoins us and suddenly Molly's back on the job. "Excellency, would you like me to unpack your things and show you how the ionic shower works?"

"Ionic shower?"

"Water is far too precious in space—and on Mars, for that matter—to waste in bathing," the Captain explains.

Molly gives a little sigh. "That's one thing I'll definitely miss. Real, hot-water showers."

Because M looks skeptical, I feel compelled to reassure her. "Ionics get you way cleaner than water can. And they're a lot faster. Once you get used to it, you'll love it. Go show her, Molly."

But M stifles a yawn and shakes her head. "I'd rather sleep first. Aren't the rest of you tired?"

I am, since none of us have slept since last night. But I shake my head. "I'm good. Sure you don't want that tour of the ship now?" It's dumb, since we have to sleep sometime and Rigel's room will still be here, but I want to put off leaving as long as possible.

"She needs to rest." Rigel shoots me this grownup, know-it-all look, even though I'm a year older than he is. "We all do."

"Quite right," Captain Liam agrees. "Mr. O'Gara, if you'll come with me?"

I start slightly at the name, then nod—reluctantly. With a last smile at M that I hope isn't too sappy and a warning frown at Rigel, I leave with the Captain. The door to M's suite shuts behind us with a click that sounds way too final.

"Shall I escort you to your quarters as well?" The Captain looks a little impatient now. I guess he's got stuff he should be doing, since we've only just launched.

"No, thanks. I can find it."

He palms open the lift for me, then disappears into his quarters across the hall, which I know has access to the Bridge, at the very top of the ship. With one last, longing glance at M's door, I step into the lift and say, "Two."

The doors open to the polished faux-wood floors and paneling I remember from my trip to Earth. This is the passenger level with the biggest rooms, reserved for Royals and anyone else important or rich enough to stay here. As I head toward the quarters I'm sharing with Dad, I see someone loitering in the doorway of the posh, deserted Level Two lounge across from the main lift. It's Brenna.

"What are you doing here?" I know her family is staying down in steerage.

"Can we talk?" She slants a look up at me through her dark lashes.

Shaking off my lingering irritation at the sleeping arrangements upstairs, I focus on her. She's just as pretty as when I first met her, maybe prettier, but I can't say I still have any real feelings for her, not since M. But I don't want to hurt her feelings, so I follow her into the lounge. "Sure. What's up?"

Brenna puts a hand on my arm. "Ever since you came back to Bailerealta, I've been able to tell you're not happy and now I get why."

"Huh? What do you mean?"

She bites her lip and looks up at me again, with that look that used to really get to me. Even now, I feel a tiny echo of those old feelings. "My mum told me about the rumors. About that Bodyguard, Rigel, and the Princess."

My gut clenches. "What rumors? What did she hear? From who?" I *knew* they weren't putting on a good enough act!

"Well, everyone knows how he helped rescue her last October. A friend of my mum's whose cousin visited Jewel a few weeks later says she saw them together right after, that it was more or less common knowledge they were together."

"Yeah, well, that was then. Before she met me. Before she knew anything about—"

She shakes her head, making her dark hair sway around her shoulders. "Like I said, I've been watching you these past few days—and watching them, too. Sure, they *act* all official around each other, but I see how he looks at her and how she sometimes looks at him. She, um, doesn't look at you that way, Sean."

"That doesn't mean—"

"Did I hear right, he's actually sleeping in her quarters?" she interrupts.

I flinch but try to hide it. "Yeah, the Captain says that's standard. Completely separate bedrooms. Molly's there, too, as her Handmaid. And chaperone."

"Think Molly's up to it? I mean, if they really want to…" She trails off, moving her hand up and down my arm. "I've…really missed you, Sean. I know you don't have any choice about this whole Consort thing and I want you to know I'm still here for you if you need to talk or…anything."

"I'll, uh, keep that in mind." But I remember how Brenna likes to gossip. Telling her the truth is *not* a good idea.

"Do. I'd like to stay…friends, Sean. Make you happy, any way I can."

Her meaning penetrates and I lean away from her. Frustrating as my not-quite-relationship with M is, there's no way I'd cheat on her.

Not unless I had *real* proof she and Rigel were—I cut off that thought. Nope, not even then. No way.

"Um, thanks, Brenna. I, uh, do consider you a friend but…not that kind of friend. Not anymore. I can't. Sorry."

She snatches her hand off my arm. "Yeah, okay. I get it. You want to play by the rules. And it's not like I'm Royal, which I guess *matters* more now than it used to. I just thought maybe, considering it's *so* obvious…" She takes a step back, shaking her head and looking away. "Never mind. Better get myself down to steerage where I belong." Without another glance my way, she heads across to the lift.

I stare after her, wondering what she almost said there at the end. What's so obvious? M and Rigel? Does she really have more to go on than that rumor from last fall and a couple of looks she probably imagined? Will that rumor have reached Mars by now? Do enough people believe it to screw up M getting Acclaimed as Sovereign?

Finally, I shrug. I'll get more details out of Brenna tomorrow and tell her not to say anything to anyone else. And let M and Rigel know what a crappy job they're doing. That they *have* to do better.

With a yawn that almost cracks my jaw, I go to our quarters, where Dad is already asleep. Tired as I am, it's a long time before I finally drop off.

17

Chomseireach

CHOMSEIREACH (KOM-SAY-RIK): *Handmaid; lady's maid, chaperone and companion to Princess or (female) Sovereign*

As soon as the door closed behind Sean and the Captain, Molly yawned. "Guess we should all head to bed, huh? Do you need anything, M—er, Excellency?"

I grimaced. "Just M, okay? You may have to do the Handmaid thing in public, but not here."

"Okay," she agreed with a grin. "But I should at least give you first turn in the bathroom."

"I have my own in there." I nodded toward my enormous bedroom suite. "You and Rigel can duke it out for this one."

Rigel shrugged. "Ladies first. Go ahead, Molly."

"Thanks!" She grabbed her toiletry bag out of her room and disappeared into the little bathroom off the main area.

I waited about two heartbeats after hearing the door lock, then launched myself into Rigel's arms. *I've been starving for this!*

Caught off-guard, he stiffened for a second. *Me, too, but—*

How many more chances like this do you think we'll get? I demanded.

Good point. His arms came around me and he fastened his mouth on mine. I immediately felt strength and health flowing into me through his touch and knew he felt the same.

Always, he thought to me, deepening the kiss. For several blissful minutes it was like we'd never been apart, like none of the political crap or awkwardness had ever interfered with our love. I wished I had the nerve to just drag Rigel into my bedroom and lock the door. Instead, I concentrated on soaking up all the Rigel-ness I could, feeling better than I had in days. Weeks.

"Um, guys?" Rigel and I broke apart to see Molly standing there, toiletry case in hand, looking acutely uncomfortable. "I had to take an oath for this job, you know."

I shrugged apologetically and he said, "Sorry, Molly," though I could tell he wasn't any sorrier than I was for that heavenly interlude.

"Yeah, me, too," Molly mumbled. I could practically feel her embarrassment—or maybe it was just mine, now that my euphoria from Rigel's kisses was starting to fade.

I cleared my throat. "Um, Molly, just how strict a chaperone do you have to be? You won't, like, *tell* anyone if Rigel and I act more...informally here in our quarters, right? Can't I order you to keep it secret or something?"

She looked away from my intentionally pleading expression, struggling between duties. I felt bad for her, but not bad enough to make any promises Rigel and I would both regret. Once we got to Mars, we might not get *any* privacy.

Suddenly Molly gasped, startling both of us.

"What?"

Instead of answering, she pointed, first to one upper corner of the big living area, then to another. In every corner, a tiny glass globe glinted. Cameras. Definitely cameras. Rigel took a step backward, away from me, as we exchanged a worried look.

Damn it! I should have noticed those before. That's exactly the kind of detail I've been trained to observe.

You were as tired and stressed as I was. Besides, I'm the one who attacked you, not the other way around!

"Do...do you think they're actually *on?*" Worry tightened my throat. What if we'd already screwed everything up?

"I don't know. Probably?" Molly sounded as worried as I was—or maybe not quite, since she didn't know the full extent of what was at stake. "We'd better assume they are, don't you think?"

Rigel nodded but I could feel his frustration. My own matched it, nearly crowding out my fear. I'd been counting on taking advantage of these few days of relative privacy.

"Fine." I glared up at the nearest camera. "Guess we'd better all go to bed, huh? See you guys in the morning."

Grumpy at being cheated out of one last good-night kiss, I hurried into my sumptuous bedroom and shut the door, wishing it was the kind I could slam. Carefully checking all the corners of my parlor and bedroom, I was relieved not to see any cameras—at least, no obvious ones. Maybe they did have a *little* respect for the Sovereign's privacy? Not that I could bring Rigel in here without the cameras in the living room recording it.

"Crap," I said aloud, fuming again at the unfairness of the whole Sovereign/Consort idiocy as I finally got ready for bed.

Not until I was under the covers did it occur to me to reach out mentally to Rigel, I'd gotten so into the habit lately of having to block him. Now that we were finally on the ship, though…*Rigel?* I thought as hard as I could in his direction. *Can you hear me?*

No response. Either he was already asleep, or the three or four walls between us were enough to keep him from hearing me…or he was afraid to answer, after the scare we'd just had.

.*.

With no windows in my room, I had no clue what time it was when I woke. Not that windows would have helped, I realized, smiling at myself—until I remembered what had happened right before bed. Surely someone would have woken me if Rigel had been hauled off or arrested?

My sense of well-being from a good night's sleep shattered by sudden worry, I got up to face the day—or whatever they called it in space.

Delicious smells greeted me when I stepped into the living room a few minutes later, along with the welcome sight of Rigel, still here and un-arrested, and Molly, sitting awkwardly at opposite ends of the long couch. Relieved, I smiled at them both.

"Mmm! Breakfast. You guys didn't have to wait for me."

"Of course we did." Molly darted an almost-glance up at one of the cameras. "If I'd known you were awake, I'd have helped you dress, too. It's supposed to be one of my jobs."

I wrinkled my nose at her. "Let's wait for Mars for that, okay?"

"Okay, though I'd like *some* practice before we get there. Shall I buzz Dad and Sean to come up? I think there's enough food."

"No kidding." The table was half covered with dishes of scrambled eggs, ham, toast, and all kinds of other mouth-watering stuff. "Yeah, tell them to come on up." Then, to Rigel, *Guess we might as well find out if we're already in trouble.*

Yeah, might as well. He was nervous, too.

Less than five minutes later the door chime rang and Molly opened it for Sean and his father.

"Sorry I slept so late," I greeted them. "I hope you haven't been waiting too long?"

"It's fine." I was relieved to see Mr. O smiling. "Sean slept late too. It gave me time to pull up information on all of the Royals on the ship."

We arranged ourselves around the table—Rigel and Molly were allowed to sit, since it wasn't a formal meal—and Mr. O launched right into business.

"As I mentioned in Chicago, Devyn Kane is your most serious opposition, as he has a strong following among both *Echtrans* and Nuathans. Gordon Nolan may have designs on the leadership as well, though he's been paying lip service to Devyn's bid. They've both spent the last year or two cultivating the *Echtran* community in Montana. Annwyn Walsh also appears to be primarily a supporter of Devyn's. In fact, she worked under Devyn in the Ministry of Culture pre-Faxon."

He paused to take a couple of bites of egg and ham and a large swig of tea before continuing. "There are four others aboard that you'll meet tonight, if not sooner."

I swallowed my toast and marmalade. "Tonight? What's happening tonight?"

"The Captain is hosting a welcome dinner in his quarters for all of the Royals aboard. I imagine that's what the message light on your vidscreen is about." Sure enough, a little blue light was flashing at the bottom of the huge vidscreen.

"A formal dinner?"

"Of course. It will be a chance for all of you to practice the protocol you've learned. We can discuss the other Royals' agendas after you've met them, but at least two appear to be angling for Regent, and can therefore be expected to support you for Sovereign. Those would be Phelan Monroe, who was Mayor of Arregaith before she fled to Earth, and Irving Kennedy, a former member of the *Riogain*."

The *Riogain*, I knew, was the Royal House, Nuath's equivalent to the British House of Lords, though more like our Senate in terms of power.

"Would you recommend either of them?" I hadn't thought as far ahead as appointing a Regent.

He lifted a shoulder. "I don't know either of them personally, though I met Phelan once, years ago. They both seem to have unblemished records. Eamon Kennedy is Irving's brother, so can be assumed to support Irving's bid for Regent. You can expect all of them to ingratiate themselves, hoping to influence your decision."

I did a quick mental count while swallowing a little more breakfast. "That's three I haven't met. Who's the fourth?"

"Rory Glenn. Slightly older, known for his traditional views. He will likely be your staunchest supporter of the lot, though he has a history of mistrusting others and occasionally making unfounded accusations. He was also a member of the *Riogain*." Though he'd barely eaten, Mr. O stood. "Sean is eager to give you a tour, I know, so I'll leave you to it, unless you have questions."

"No questions now, though I'll probably have lots after tonight. Thanks, Mr. O'Gara." As he left, I ran back over the names he'd listed, trying to commit each one and his or her agenda to memory.

I'll make some notes later, too, Rigel promised and I silently thanked him.

Sean, who had already demolished one overflowing plate, cleared his throat as he refilled it. "Um, while we're all private here, I should probably tell you about a rumor I heard last night."

"Um, we're not sure *how* private." I pointed at the cameras. "We noticed them last night, after you left." No reason he needed to know more than that.

Sean glanced up, then at me and Rigel, the corners of his mouth twitching. "I guess the security on this ship is pretty good, huh?"

It wasn't hard to guess why Sean was happy about the cameras. The exact same reason Rigel and I *weren't*.

Jerk, Rigel thought.

Be nice, I thought back, though I was nearly as irked as he was. "What kind of rumor?"

"What do you think?" Sean looked from me to Rigel and back. "Haven't I told you guys you're not...I mean..." He glanced up at the cameras and frowned.

I let out a frustrated hiss. "Let's talk in my room. As far as I can tell, there aren't any cameras in there." I had to resist a childish urge to stick my tongue out at the nearest camera.

Without a word, we all trooped into my little parlor.

I slid the door closed and turned to Sean. "Okay, spill. What exactly did you hear?"

He was examining the corners of the room. "Are you sure?"

"Pretty sure. Anyway, we need to know. Who told you what?"

Sean took a swig of the orange juice he'd brought with him before answering. "I think it was *mainly* about last fall. Before, well, you know." I nodded and motioned for him to continue. "But even in Bailerealta, some people suspect something's still going on between you two."

"Some people?" Molly echoed. "Like who?"

"Well...Brenna, for one. But—"

"Brenna? Seriously? Isn't that a little—" She stopped abruptly when Sean shot her a *shut up* glare.

He looked almost furtively at me. "It's possible she's a little...I mean..."

It was all I could do not to laugh. "Jealous?" I finished for him. "Don't look so surprised. It was kind of obvious something was going on between *you* two."

"Not any more," he said quickly. "Not even a little. I told her to cool it, that we couldn't—"

"Hey, it's not like it bothers me. And it wasn't just *her* behavior that tipped me off," I couldn't resist adding. "Maybe it's not as easy to hide that sort of thing as you think, huh?"

Rigel chuckled and Sean frowned at him. "Okay. Maybe I deserved that. Especially since Brenna and I were never as... Well, not like you two are. Were!" he corrected himself forcefully. "Right?"

"We're trying, Sean, you know that. But it doesn't mean we aren't still bonded, or that we don't still—"

"Yeah, yeah, I get it," he growled. "It's not like you ever let me forget. Anyway, I thought you should know Brenna and her mum suspect, and maybe other people on the ship, too. You know how important it is to get you Acclaimed, right?"

It was way more important than Sean knew, but I just nodded—though I could feel a silent question from Rigel. *Later.* I quickly shut off that line of thought. For now.

"We'll be careful," Rigel promised. *And try to find out who's monitoring those cameras,* he added silently.

I nodded my agreement to both of Rigel's statements and stood. "Let's take that tour of the ship."

⁺⋅

Sean led the way out of my quarters. "Dad got permission from the Captain for me to show you the Bridge and Engine Room, so I figured we'd start at the top and work our way down."

"Isn't this the top?" I glanced around the carpeted hallway.

Sean shook his head. "Bridge is above us, but we have to go through the officers' quarters to get there." He pressed the chime on the door across from mine and a moment later a uniformed crewman opened it.

As soon as the man saw me, his eyes widened slightly and he did the fist-over-heart bow. "Good morning, Excellency. I am Lieutenant Michael. I understand you wish to tour the Bridge?"

"Yes, please. We, um, won't get in the way or stay long."

"Of course. If you'll come with me?" He motioned us into the main area of the officers' quarters, about half the size of my suite's living room, with several doors leading off it—individual cabins, I assumed. A female crew member just getting up from a table immediately bowed to me before respectfully backing through one of the doors, which opened, then closed automatically.

Moving to what looked like another set of lift doors, Lt. Michael touched a panel. "Sir, permission to bring the Princess up?"

"Granted," came Captain Liam's voice.

Our guide palmed open the lift door and a few seconds later we all stepped out onto the Bridge, a round room roughly the size of my living room, with screens and panels covering more than half of the wall surfaces. Captain Liam stepped forward to greet me with a bow.

"Welcome, Excellency. I trust you slept well?"

"I did, thank you." I tried to focus on him instead of my incredibly cool surroundings.

"Glad to hear it. If you don't mind, I would prefer that none of you touch anything on the Bridge."

I quickly shook my head. "Of course not. But I'd love to know what some of these things do."

"Certainly. The main viewscreen shows the space ahead of the ship in the direction of travel. Those smaller ones show the views starboard, port, aft, above and below us." He pointed at each screen in turn. "Should any object be detected, an analysis will immediately overlay the appropriate screen. This central chair is the command console, while those other stations allow detailed monitoring and control of navigation, propulsion and various scans, both external and internal." As he pointed, the crew member at each console stood and bowed smartly to me—two women and a man. "I'll be happy to answer any questions, of course."

Momentarily speechless, I felt for all the world like I'd been plunked in the middle of a Star Trek set. I was dying to move closer to inspect some of the monitors and controls but was afraid I'd geek out and say something totally non-regal.

Then Rigel surprised me by asking, "What about security, Captain? I assume there are procedures in place to ensure the Sovereign's safety aboard?"

"Absolutely. You, of course, are her first line of defense, but every crew member aboard the *Quintessence* is pledged to protect the Princess with our lives. Her door is genetically coded so that no one can access her suite without her, and security cameras are located throughout the ship, to include the main area of her quarters."

"But not in my own private bedroom or sitting room?" Catching on, I realized this was way quicker than searching.

"Of course not." The Captain looked startled. "Even security should not supercede proper respect, Excellency."

Rigel nodded, looking impressively official, though his cautious relief echoed mine. "And where are those cameras monitored? I assume access to the recordings is restricted so that potentially sensitive matters of state are protected?"

"The recordings are never viewed at all unless there is cause. Barring an inquest, they are routinely destroyed one month after each voyage."

Even better! As long as nobody found a reason to look at those recordings, we were home free.

Though I felt like grinning with relief, I kept my smile polite. "Thank you so much, Captain. We'll let you get back to your duties."

He bowed to us again, as did all the other crew members. As we took the lift back down, Rigel and I silently cheered our narrow escape from what could have been a disaster for both of us.

18

Quintessence

QUINTESSENCE (KWIN-TESS-ENS): one of four passenger vessels used to transport Nuathans between Earth and Mars

After the Bridge, Sean showed us the suite he was sharing with his dad on Level Two, about half the size of my bedroom. The rooms on Three and Four were about half *that* size, he informed us, though we bypassed those levels and the Commons, on Five, to visit the Engine Room next, at the very base of the ship.

I was nearly as boggled by the Engine Room as the Bridge. The enormous, circular, anti-gravity drive took up nearly the whole room, totally different from any engine I'd ever imagined. Spaced around the loudly humming drive were three manned monitoring stations, each with a different holographic display. None of us had the nerve to step completely out of the lift so, after a minute or two of staring, we headed back up a level.

Steerage, on Level Six, was divided into two rooms, one bigger than the other. The smaller room, Sean told us, was general crew quarters and housed about a dozen people. The big one that the lift opened into held a lot more, with moveable partitions between groups of bunks. A common bathroom served the whole area, though at least it was divided into his and hers sections.

"No wonder Brenna's pissed," I murmured. "I wouldn't want to get bumped down here, either."

"It's not so bad," Molly assured me. "I spent a lot of time in Steerage on our trip to Earth, since one of my best friends was here with her family. They eat in the Commons like everybody else and they pipe in white noise at night to mask the sound of the drive downstairs so everybody can sleep. It's not nearly as crowded now as it was on that trip, when so many people were trying to escape from Faxon."

It still looked depressingly barracks-like but I didn't say so, because by then a few people were coming forward to greet me, seemingly delighted by my visit. Several others hung back, though, looking wary—including Brenna and a woman I assumed was her mother. Did they think I was doing some kind of inspection? Or maybe slumming it, for appearance's sake?

I'd always had a problem with the Nuathan class system, but I tried to shake off my unease at this vivid reminder of it so I could play my part convincingly.

You're doing great, Rigel assured me as I responded to all the bows, but I could tell he was unsettled as well.

For the first time, I wondered how many people on Mars thought they were better off under Faxon than under the Sovereigns. And, more importantly, how many might be reluctant to have a Sovereign again now Faxon was gone, like those men who'd protested during my speech in Bailerealta. After all, Faxon had swept to power by railing against Royals and the whole class system, so there must have been a bunch who agreed, people who'd always felt inferior under the old regime...and might feel that way again under a new one. Why hadn't this been covered in any of those texts I'd had to read?

I'd learned reams of protocol, read everything to do with the Sovereigns and their role in government, plus everything *else* about how the Nuathan government was organized. But almost nothing about how Faxon came to overthrow that government or why enough people had supported him to make that possible—which suddenly struck me as a pretty glaring oversight.

As we were leaving Steerage, I felt an uncomfortable sensation and glanced over my shoulder to see Brenna glaring at me from just a few feet away. She immediately smoothed her expression to neutrality, but the negative vibe I got off her didn't change. It wasn't like the "bad guy" vibe I got off some *Echtrans*, more a sense of her actual emotion

—like what I got from Rigel, though less clear. She must be *really* jealous, or pissed, or both, for me to be able to pick that up.

Sean followed my gaze and frowned, but Brenna turned her shoulder and walked away.

"Sorry," he muttered. "She's still kind of—"

"No, it's okay. I get it." I just hoped Brenna wasn't the vindictive sort, like Trina. "Where to next?"

"As you can see, the Commons is pretty different now than it was last night," Sean said when we reached the big room where we'd sat for liftoff. Only two rows of chairs remained in front of the viewscreen, while the rest of the big room had been transformed into a dining hall on one side and what looked like a general recreation area behind the theater-style seats.

Sean led us that way first. "They have lots of activities here, since space travel gets boring. Games, a full gym, exercise classes, all kinds of stuff. And they show movies on the viewscreen most nights after dinner." We all glanced up at the image of Earth, still receding.

"Or you can order movies from the vidscreen in your quarters if you want to watch something else," Molly volunteered. "Except in Steerage. They have to agree on a flick for the screen down there."

Yet another reason for everyone down there to resent the rest of us.

We looked around for a couple of minutes, then Sean took us across to the dining area. "We don't have to eat here, but check this out." He went to one of several little alcoves along one wall. "You like tea, right?" He punched something into the touchpad next to the alcove, and a moment later a steaming cup rose up from the bottom. "Earl Grey, but they have a couple dozen different kinds stocked."

I'd learned in Bailerealta that food recombinators weren't really like the food replicators on Star Trek, since these had to use actual ingredients on hand, but they still seemed impossibly sci-fi to me. I took a sip of the tea, which already had honey and milk added exactly the way I liked—as Sean had clearly known.

"The food's probably better in your suite, if you'd rather eat there," he said.

"No, here is fine. I don't want people to think I'm all elitist or anything." I also hoped to get an idea of the general mood on board, after that unsettling visit to Steerage. Could I pick up negative emotions from others if I got close enough? Useful as such an ability might be, I almost hoped not.

If you can, you should. I'm in favor of anything that will keep you safer, even if you find out things you'd rather not, Rigel responded, startling me. I instinctively started to shield before remembering with relief that I didn't have to. Not now.

Me too, I guess, I thought back. *But actually* knowing *every time someone resents me or dislikes me seems creepy. And depressing.*

I suppose. I wouldn't want to get into Trina's head, for example.

I was glad he understood. But then, he almost always did, I thought with a smile. If we could just arrange a half hour or so of uninterrupted silent conversation, maybe I could finally—

"Here okay?" Sean had stopped at a table. "I can get your food if you want."

"Nope, that's my job. Which I've hardly done so far." Molly sent a mock-accusing look at me.

Sean glowered for a moment, which seemed like an overreaction, then shrugged and went with Molly to the food alcoves to get his own meal. Rigel, ever conscious of protocol, stood behind me while they were gone. Did I have time to at least *start* explaining?

Explain what? he prompted.

It's kind of a lot. I don't want to confuse or worry you by starting when I can't finish.

Sure enough, Molly was back in barely more than a minute, then Rigel had to taste my food before going to get his own—which he only did when I made him, since he was supposed to wait until after I'd eaten. Sean was already sitting on my left.

"Anything else you want to see or know about the ship?"

"Not right now." I took a bite of the excellent grilled fish and steamed veggies. I couldn't imagine anything sent to my suite would be better. As I ate, my gaze strayed to Rigel, who seemed to be having some trouble with the food recombinator.

Brenna and Rowena and their families entered from the other side of the big room just then, Rowena slanting a glance at Rigel as they headed to the food alcoves. Neither looked my way, and I was just as glad. With any luck, I wouldn't see either of them again once we reached Nuath.

Rigel came back a moment later looking embarrassed, his tray heaped with food. "Took a little trial and error. Good thing I'm hungry."

"Oh, sorry, we should have helped," Molly said. "Some of the menus *are* a little confusing."

He just shrugged and started to eat, so Molly asked me what I wanted to do after lunch.

What I *wanted* to do was find some place away from any cameras, so I could tell Rigel everything I needed to. And maybe for other reasons. "Um, I've never taken a yoga class, even though they sometimes had them at my Taekwondo school. I doubt the guys would want to, though."

"You got that right. I'd rather lift weights." Sean turned to Rigel with a slightly smug smile. "As Bodyguard, are you allowed to do *anything* she doesn't?"

Rigel smiled back. "Nope, and that's exactly how I like it. Good thing I have this job instead of you, huh?"

Sean's smile disappeared. Looking around for something to distract them, I spotted that Royal I didn't trust, Gordon, wandering around the Commons. He seemed to be stopping at nearly every table to chat with people.

"Wonder what Gordon's up to?" I mused aloud. As I'd hoped, that diverted the boys' attention before they started arguing.

"Schmoozing, looks like," Rigel said after a moment. "Trying to drum up support?"

There weren't many other teens on the ship—maybe half a dozen —but Gordon seemed to be making a special effort to talk to them. He spent a long time at Brenna and Rowena's table, clearly interested in whatever Brenna and her mother were telling him.

I nudged Sean. "Brenna wouldn't *really* try to cause trouble for me, would she?"

Sean glanced her way and I saw a flash of alarm in his eyes—and even felt a bit of it coming off him, which added weight to my suspicion that I might be developing a new ability. "I'm sure she wouldn't say anything bad about you to a Royal." Despite his light tone, I could tell he was concerned. "But I'll warn her, first chance I get, just to make sure."

"Good idea." Rigel frowned over at the animated discussion that was too far away for any of us to hear. A few of them glanced our way just then and I could feel Rigel's worry along with my own. *Probably too late*, he thought to me sourly.

Guess we'll find out. There was nothing I could do about it either way.

Finally Gordon left Brenna's table and went to join Mr. O'Gara and the rest of the Royals, on the far side of the dining area. Suddenly, I was tempted to try out my new "power" on the ones I was most curious about. Or should I wait for that dinner tonight?

Go for it, if you want, Rigel urged. *I've got your back.*

You're right. Why wait? I stood up. "Back in a few," I said in response to Sean's and Molly's startled looks and headed deliberately toward the Royal table.

Gordon was the first to see me coming. He nudged Devyn, next to him, and both of them stood, quickly followed by the others. Everyone bowed, but Mr. O'Gara spoke first.

"Ah, Excellency. I didn't want to interrupt your meal, or I'd have suggested you join us. Allow me to introduce a few people you haven't had a chance to meet yet." He turned first to the oldest of the group. "Rory Glenn, Princess Emileia."

Rory bowed again, deeply, and when I focused hard, I sensed strong, positive emotion, perhaps with a defensive edge. "It is my great, great honor to pledge myself to your service and assure you of my wholehearted allegiance, Excellency."

"Thank you, Rory. I'm very happy to meet you."

Mr. O now nodded toward a tall, handsome brunette who had clearly been gorgeous when younger—not that she looked much past forty now. "Phelan Monroe," he said.

"I can't tell you how delighted I am to make your acquaintance, Excellency." Phelan's voice was rich, mellow and reassuring, but I sensed a steely determination that belied her motherly expression. "Please feel free to come to me for *any* advice or assistance you might need when we reach Mars, as this will be your first visit."

Irving Kennedy bowed nearly as deeply as Rory had. He also felt positive, but a bit overeager, while his brother Eamon radiated more nervousness and awe than anything else. When I thanked them both for their sworn allegiance, Eamon turned even redder than his hair.

I didn't particularly want to linger once the introductions had been made, so I excused myself and headed back to where Sean and Molly waited, Rigel still close behind.

Could you tell what I was sensing off them? I asked as we walked.

Some. This could turn out to be a super useful skill, M, especially if you really have to do the Sovereign thing.

We reached the others before I could comment on that "if." It made me even more desperate for a chance to talk privately with Rigel.

Both Sean and Molly seemed determined to prevent that, though, insisting we both learn a Martian version of poker, which we played with Rowena and Desmond. They invited Brenna to join but she gave a lame excuse about having to catch up on some reading. When I focused, I not only got that jealous vibe off her, but a strong sense that she was lying—though that was fairly obvious without any special powers. Still, it would be cool to develop Mrs. O'Gara's "lie-detector" ability, along with this new emotion-sensing thing.

When the game ended, I stole Brenna's excuse and pretended to read, hoping Sean and Molly would do something else so Rigel and I could finally "talk" for a while. It only half worked. The two of them did stay at the card table, but other people kept coming up to me, some just to pay their respects and others to hint about what they thought I should do once we reached Mars.

All the interruptions prevented even a silent conversation with Rigel, though they gave me plenty of chances to gauge people's emotions and motives. I found that getting easier with practice, but it was also draining. Finally, I announced I was going up to my room.

Sean and Molly immediately stood up from their game to join me, but I shook my head. "I need to decompress for a while before that dinner tonight. You guys can stay down here." Though I knew Rigel wouldn't.

Unfortunately, Molly wouldn't hear of it, either. "I'm your Hand-maid, remember? Where you go, I go, just like Rigel."

I couldn't reasonably argue, so the three of us headed for the executive lift, Sean glowering a bit because he didn't have a similar excuse to tag along.

"Mum and Dad were invited to a dinner like this on the way to Earth, our first evening aboard," Molly commented as we were whisked to Level One. "That trip was the first time I ever saw them get treated like Royals, which was kind of cool."

"So even when Faxon was in power, the ship captains didn't go along with his policies?" Interesting.

She shrugged. "Guess not. I didn't really think about the politics of it at the time, but I could tell Mum and Dad were pretty relieved they could stop pretending to be Ags."

"You don't seem very keen on that dinner." Rigel glanced at me in concern as we entered the suite, no doubt picking up on my emotions even more than my expression. "You don't *have* to go, you know."

I shrugged. "It probably won't be much fun, but it'll be good practice for Mars. There'll probably be lots of formal dinners once we get there."

"Yeah." He sighed. "Good practice for me, too."

"And me," Molly chimed in. "Come on, let's go pick out the perfect outfit for you." She was clearly looking forward to tonight a lot more than I was.

19

Fasneis

FASNEIS (FAHSH-ness): *information; intelligence*

"You might as well take a nap or something, Rigel. This may take a while," Molly said, dragging me into my bedroom and practically skipping into my huge closet. "This will be so awesome," she gushed from its depths. "How cool is it that everything in here is your size? I can't wait to dress you properly!"

Actually, it creeped me out a little that somebody, maybe a whole lot of somebodies, already knew my exact size. Mostly, though, I was just frustrated by yet another delay when I'd finally made up my mind to tell Rigel the whole truth.

"What, I've been dressing like a slob all this time?" I was irked enough to ask.

"Of course not! It's just—" Molly glanced over her shoulder and clearly decided I was teasing. "Okay, fine. You got me. Here, try these together."

By the time Molly had absolutely everything picked out for both of us, Rigel had disappeared into his room. I reached out for his mind, hoping he was still awake, but either he wasn't or a single door on this ship was enough to block our telepathy. I could have shaken Molly for taking so long.

I passed the time until Rigel woke studying recent Martian history, now that my little epiphany in Steerage had pointed up that gap in my education. Unfortunately, while my book-scroll contained a couple of accounts by Royals who'd escaped to Earth, there was nothing at all from the perspective of Faxon's supporters. Mr. O'Gara might be able to tell me more, since he'd actually been there, but he probably held the same views as the Royals who'd written these memoirs.

The *Quintessence* archives weren't much better. Though the search function put Google to shame, I found almost nothing about Faxon's rise to power. Even when I dug through old news articles from Mars, I couldn't find any—at all—from the years immediately before or after Faxon's coup. Weird. Did he have them all destroyed? Or did someone else, later?

When Rigel finally emerged from his room, I broke off my mostly-fruitless search. "Good nap?"

"I guess," he grumped. *Why haven't you been answering? I figured if I stayed in my room a while, we could talk without Molly noticing.*

I tried to talk to you, too. Something in these walls must be blocking us.

Great. Perfect. Then, aloud, "What did I miss?"

"M playing on the data console." Molly, on the couch, looked up from her book. "And grumbling."

I shrugged. "Trying to find out exactly what led up to Faxon's coup, but there's nothing to find."

"Huh." Rigel didn't seem nearly as bothered by that as I was. *So what is it you need to tell me?*

Before I could even start to answer such a complicated question, Molly jumped up. "Oh, wow, look how late it is! Time to get you dressed, M, and me, too. C'mon!"

It may be too complicated to explain this way at all, even if there was time. I wish we could talk privately for real! Especially since I didn't dare tell him about the Grentl, even silently, where Molly or the cameras might notice his reaction.

Reaction to what? he asked as I reluctantly followed Molly into my bedroom.

All the stuff I need to tell you. If I ever get a chance!

Can't you just— My bedroom door slid shut, cutting him off mid-thought and making me want to scream.

Twenty minutes later, though, I briefly forgot my frustration as I twirled in front of the mirror. For the first time since learning my status last fall, I felt like a real princess, decked out in a floaty lavender and silver dress. I also wore a necklace that looked like real diamonds —I hoped not—and a matching, tiny tiara Molly claimed my rank demanded. I'd have argued if I hadn't seen historical pictures that backed her up.

"If they didn't fit perfectly, I'd never believe all these clothes are for me." I looked over my shoulder at the swirl of the skirt behind me. "Do you think I'll get to keep them? On Mars, I mean. I can't very well take them home to Jewel."

"Yeah, your aunt would definitely freak. She'd think we bought them for you and want to pay us or something."

"You look great, too." I nodded at her blue dress trimmed in white.

Grinning, she twirled. "One of the perks of being the Sovereign's Handmaid. My wardrobe isn't as grand as yours, of course, but it's nicer than anything I've ever had."

Opening the door to the main area, Molly called out, "Rigel, come see how gorgeous she looks!"

He appeared, one eyebrow raised. "Coming into your room won't seem too…familiar?"

"I'm in here, too," Molly pointed out.

"Anyway, it's a little late to worry about that," I added. "If anybody actually looks at the recordings, I mean." Which suddenly gave me an idea.

Molly gestured toward me. "So what do you think?"

"That she's even more beautiful than usual." Rigel's words were accompanied by a wash of appreciation, love and desire—and a wariness that surprised me.

What's wrong?

He answered out loud. "You're a little intimidating. So, well, regal. But I guess that's a good thing. Got to impress the other Royals, convince them you're up to the task and all."

"I don't want to intimidate *you*, though." *Ever*, I added silently, sending all the love I could back at him. "Anyway, it's just for tonight." Except we both knew that wasn't really true.

✦

At seven o'clock we went across the hall, where Captain Liam himself answered the door chime, greeting me with a deep bow before ushering us inside. His quarters were nearly as posh as mine, though his smaller living room was currently dominated by a long dining table.

"I am honored that you were able to accept my invitation, Excellency. The others will be here shortly, so please make yourself comfortable."

In fact it was only seconds before the other Royals arrived, escorted by Commander Donia, the woman I recalled was the ship's First Officer. Each politely bowed to me on entering and I responded with the proper nod. During the small talk that followed, Rigel silently reminded me to use my new emotion-sensing thing this evening.

I'll do my best, I thought back, pinning what I hoped was a graciously regal smile on my face as I returned Annwyn's polite query about my day. I was relieved to feel nothing from her but cautious respect.

Gordon was another matter. Though he wore an ingratiating smile, I distinctly perceived hostility and resentment along with that faint bad-guy vibe. Not surprising, if he wanted to become leader of Nuath or hoped Devyn would, but it rattled me to sense it so strongly.

"It is good to see you again, Princess. I must say I commend your willingness to attempt such a burdensome role, given your youth and inexperience." His glance darted to Rigel and Molly, hovering behind me. "No doubt once you reach Nuath, you will be able to find attendants more, ah, befitting your rank, who can be of more use to you."

I carefully raised one eyebrow, which isn't as easy as it sounds. "Thank you for your concern, Gordon, but I'm perfectly happy with the ones I have," I told him—told all of them—in no uncertain terms.

"Well said, Princess," Devyn said with another smooth bow. "Your loyalty to those who have rendered you service is admirable."

His were the emotions I most wanted to probe, but what I sensed surprised me. I didn't feel anything negative from him at all—no resentment or jealousy, no hint of deceit or even irritation. In fact, something about his voice, expression and vibe made me instinctively want to trust him. Huh.

I smiled, inclining my head in response to his bow. "Thank you. I appreciate your support."

Even that didn't trigger any emotional reaction that I could perceive. Interesting.

"Shall we eat?" Captain Liam suggested then and we all moved to the table, formally set for eleven.

My special orchid-adorned finger bowl was at one end and the Captain headed to the chair at the other. As I moved to my place, I did a quick count of those present and came up with fourteen. My momentary confusion was cleared up when Commander Donia excused herself to go up to the Bridge and I belatedly remembered that Rigel and Molly weren't allowed to sit down. Which sucked. I should have made them both eat something before coming here.

It's okay, really, Rigel assured me but I still felt guilty for not thinking ahead. They'd have done it for me.

"You look amazing tonight," Sean murmured as he stepped up to pull out my chair.

I smiled my thanks, trying to ignore the spurt of jealousy I felt from Rigel along with the little tingle I got when Sean's fingers brushed my arm. Once I was seated the others followed suit, then we went through the silly finger bowl ritual.

Finally, at the Captain's signal, the food was brought in. Whether because my own hunger was augmented by Rigel's, or because I was still irritated by what Gordon had said earlier, once Rigel had tasted my food and Molly had served it to me, I cleared my throat. Every eye turned my way.

"I realize it's traditional for my Bodyguard and Handmaid to stand behind me for the whole meal and not eat till we're finished, but that custom seems very awkward and elitist to me. I may have been born on Mars, but I was raised an American. Besides, Molly is a good friend and I owe Rigel my life several times over. Would anyone object to them sitting down and eating dinner with the rest of us?"

Most of the Royals looked scandalized and Sean, of course, glowered. But the Captain, I thought, looked both surprised and rather approving.

"If it is your wish, Excellency, then of course two more places will be set at once." He nodded to one of the people who'd brought the food and a moment later an extra plate and chair was added on either side of the Captain—the only other non-Royal at the table.

Phelan, the first Royal to recover, sent me a wide smile. "I heard in Bailerealta that you were extremely gracious, Excellency. I see it's true."

I smiled back gratefully, but saw Gordon's eyes narrow speculatively and suddenly remembered him talking with Brenna at lunch today. I wondered, too late, if my impulsive request might have added fodder to any rumors about Rigel and me.

Hope not, Rigel thought to me. *I appreciate it, anyway. I was starving.*

That made me feel better. Though I was careful not to look at him, I sent him a silent *Thanks.*

Not to be outdone by Phelan, Irving spoke up. "I noticed you were reading earlier, Excellency. It's quite commendable that you are not letting the distraction of your first space flight interfere with your studies."

"Thank you." I was grateful for the change of subject. "What with all of our preparations for this trip, I had less time than usual for reading before we left." Even as I spoke, I realized this was a perfect opportunity to fill in those frustrating blanks in today's research.

"I'm currently trying to catch up on recent Martian history, but I can't find much on the beginning of Faxon's dictatorship. Does anyone know why? Most of you were on Mars back then, weren't you?"

"I believe all of us were," Phelan said as the others nodded. "Except perhaps Captain Liam?"

"I was off-planet for the actual coup, but I well remember the situation before and after." The Captain gave me a rueful smile. "I apologize for the spotty nature of the *Quintessence* archives, Excellency. The truth is, very little documentation exists about that time, either on Earth or Mars."

Mr. O'Gara confirmed that. "Once Faxon took power, he ordered anything critical of him wiped from all databases. He even had software designed to enforce it—data worms that proliferated throughout the colony-wide network, eating virtually every reference to him. A few articles and accounts were preserved on hard copy and squirreled away, but they won't have made it into any texts yet."

"But what about the pro-Faxon stuff?" I glanced around at them all. "If he was controlling the media, didn't he have them publish biased reports? Fake polls and studies?"

A few sets of eyebrows went up with what seemed to be grudging respect. "Very true, Excellency," Phelan said. "For most of his reign, news stories came out almost daily reporting how much better off the citizenry was under his rule, with fabricated statistics to back them up. At first most people accepted the stories at face value, but over time it became apparent that the news was distinctly at odds with reality."

"Right." Captain Liam looked troubled at the memory. "I heard story after story from those I, ah, smuggled to Earth during the years after Faxon took over. Disappearances and even executions covered up, falsified supply manifests showing two or three times the goods and food actually in the storehouses, even articles claiming a growing threat from Earth, when it was clear to anyone who'd been there that the *Duchas* are still completely unaware of us."

A few more such examples were thrown out by the others, their remembered indignation clear.

"But after he was ousted, those false stories were wiped from the data banks as well," Devyn concluded. "So it's not surprising you found little about that time in the *Quintessence* archives, or anywhere else."

As the salad plates were cleared away, I took advantage of the brief lull to ask my most burning question. "So, what drew people to Faxon in the first place? He must have had a lot of support to topple a government that had been operating successfully for centuries. Who were his followers and why did they go along with his plans?"

It was like the temperature of the room suddenly dropped twenty degrees. After a long, awkward pause, Phelan attempted to explain. "Faxon basely took advantage of our most vulnerable citizens, making false promises and exploiting their ignorance to create a sense of ill-usage in them that they had never had reason to feel before."

"In short, clever lies." Irving shook his head in disgust. "Unfortunately, those in a position to correct his rumors and propaganda did not realize in time how pervasive his campaign was. No one had ever attempted such a thing before, so we were less alert than we should have been. By the time the rumors reached Thiaraway, Faxon's movement was already in full sway in the more remote villages and was gaining momentum even in the larger ones."

"True," Mr. O'Gara agreed quietly, "but there was still time to mount our own campaign against him, had enough of us acted together. Truth and numbers were still on our side. It is regrettable that so many chose to abandon Nuath rather than stay and fight for it."

Every other Royal at the table reacted like Mr. O had just slapped them all in the face.

"Just because you chose to stay and play the hero," Gordon began, his face reddening, but Devyn waved him to silence.

"Surely there is nothing to be gained at this late date by debating what *should* have been done." He spoke so evenly, so persuasively that it took me a second to realize he was using Royal "push." "Our current task, surely, is to come together to rebuild what Faxon destroyed. To unite our people and to regain their trust in government—any government."

"*Any* government?" Mr. O'Gara sounded almost dangerous now. "Surely you mean their rightful Sovereign and her duly appointed and elected representatives?"

Gordon scowled, though I wasn't sure if his animosity was directed at me or Mr. O. Probably both of us. Devyn, however, smiled a genuine-seeming smile.

"Of course that would be the ideal outcome."

"I'm very happy to hear that." Despite his words, Mr. O'Gara was still watching him narrowly. "As, I'm sure, is the Sovereign."

I nodded and some of the tension seeped out of the room. Sean, Molly and Rigel relaxed noticeably. But though I was tempted to smooth over the awkward moment, if only for their sakes, there was more I needed to know.

"I'm curious." The Royals all looked wary again. "You mentioned Nuath's most vulnerable citizens. Which are those, and why were they vulnerable? And what, exactly, did Faxon promise them that they didn't already have?"

When no one else spoke, Captain Liam answered. "While Nuath has never had the economic inequalities common on Earth—no homelessness or hunger, for example—there has long been a stratification of sorts among the *fines.* Some have tended to be more respected, for lack of a better term, than others. And some *fines* have traditionally had greater access to certain, ah, amenities."

I thought I understood. "You mean the upper *fines,* the Royal and Science *fines,* live in nicer houses, have nicer clothes, eat nicer meals, that sort of thing? As well as having most of the say in government?" In recent centuries, I knew, the legislature had been composed almost entirely of Royals and Scientists.

"No one ever went without on Mars," Gordon protested. "Not until Faxon's depredations created shortages. But it stands to reason that those with greater ability, intelligence and education, those who make the greatest contributions to our society, are rewarded commensurately. It is also logical that they be the ones to take on most leadership responsibilities. You *do* understand how our government has always been structured, do you not?" He looked skeptical.

"Down to the smallest sub-ministry," I assured him. "What no one ever bothered to tell me, or even put into texts, apparently, was what life was like for those in the so-called lower *fines*. Which would you say are the very lowest?" I asked Mr. O'Gara.

He shifted uncomfortably in his seat. "I, ah, can't say I've ever thought of them that way…"

"Mining and Maintenance come to mind." Captain Liam spoke so decisively, everyone jumped. "At least, those were the people Faxon approached first, as I recall."

Sean spoke for the first time since we'd sat down. "Also Food Processing and Waste Management. I remember when we lived in Glenamuir, we had to be careful not to say anything against Faxon around them."

I glanced at him in surprise. "You never told me that."

"You never asked." His face and feelings revealed anger and hurt, surprising me even more.

But now was not the time to argue whether I should have asked or he should have offered. I'd probably done enough to spoil everyone's dinner. Still, I couldn't resist one more question while we were on the subject.

"So what *did* Faxon promise those people? More status? Money? Power?"

"All of those, at least indirectly," Devyn replied. "However, his main goal was to build resentment against the Royal *fine*. To convince people that they were being denied their fair share of what Nuath had to offer, and that they owed it to themselves and their families to demand it, even to the point of violence."

Though the violence part was clearly wrong, I suspected Faxon's supporters might have had legitimate grievances, at least early on. I knew better than to say so out loud, though. As I'd been told repeatedly, I needed every ally I could get and I'd probably just lost a few.

"Thank you." I tried to encompass all of them with an apologetic smile. "And I'm very sorry if I brought up bad memories. Is anyone else ready for dessert?"

20

Rundacht

RUNDACHT (ROON-DAHCT): *extreme secrecy; classified information*

Farewells after dinner were a little strained. Not surprising, since I'd inadvertently offended nearly everyone there. Even Sean and Mr. O radiated discomfort and irritation. Captain Liam was the only one who still seemed pleased with me—maybe even more than when I'd arrived.

"Thank you again for honoring us tonight, Excellency," he said once all the others had gone down in the lift and just he, Rigel, Molly and I stood in the hallway. "And especially for such a, ah, stimulating discussion. I must say, this was the first formal dinner I've enjoyed in years. Perhaps ever."

His gray eyes twinkling, he gave me a parting bow and shut himself into his quarters. I smiled to myself and let out a long breath, relieved that I hadn't managed to alienate *everyone*.

You'll never alienate me, Rigel promised as I palmed open the door to our suite.

That helps more than you can imagine. Please remember that when I tell you everything I've had to keep secret.

He slanted a look sideways at me. *And when will that be, M? You keep—*

"Are you two as exhausted as I am?" Molly asked as the outer

143

door shut behind us. "Rigel, why don't you take your turn in the bathroom while I turn down M's bed." She punctuated her words with a big yawn.

Rigel nodded to Molly but thought to me, *C'mon, M, it can't be that complicated.*

It is, but it's also something you should know, which is why I'm going to tell you tonight. *Since we can't think through these walls, you'll just have to come to my room after Molly is in bed.*

What? That's crazy! The cameras—

"Rigel?" Molly prompted, and he broke off that thought and headed into the bathroom.

Molly must really have been tired—the tension at dinner probably got to her, too—because she didn't dawdle in my room this time. As soon as Rigel was out of their bathroom, she headed into it, yawning again. Though I didn't leave my room, I left the door open so we could "talk" some more.

I meant what I said, Rigel. Wait half an hour, then come to my room and I'll let you in. Then I can finally tell you everything.

He hesitated in the open doorway of his own room, looking longingly at me from across the big living room. *You know how much I want to be alone with you, M! And to hear whatever your secret is, too. But what about these stupid cameras?* A glance up at the nearest one punctuated his thought.

You heard what the Captain said. They won't check the feed unless there's a reason to. And if they do look, we're screwed already after last night, so what difference does it make? In for a penny, in for a pound. Seriously, Rigel, as my Bodyguard, this is stuff you need to know!

It was that last bit that got him. Even from across the room, I could feel his concern—and longing—overcome his caution. *I guess you're right. They'll either look at the feed or they won't. Once I'm sure Molly's asleep—*

I'll be waiting. My heart already beating faster with anticipation, I retreated into my room and started getting ready for bed.

After brushing my teeth and washing my face, I was incredibly tempted to put on the most alluring nightgown in my closet. But if I did, I might not get a chance to actually *talk* to Rigel and this might be the only chance I'd get to tell him about the Grentl. I compromised with a frilly robe over a pretty but not especially sexy pair of pajamas. Then I paced my parlor for the next ten minutes.

It was funny, but what bothered me most about finally telling Rigel the truth was breaking my promise to his grandfather. Shim was bound to find out at some point and he'd be disappointed in me. Why that should matter so much when I'd been disappointing Aunt Theresa on an almost daily basis for most of my life I wasn't sure, but it did. Not that it would stop me.

Finally, I heard a faint tap on the door. I immediately opened it, pulled Rigel into my sitting room and closed it again. Unfortunately, the second I touched him, every thought left my head except needing to be closer to him. He didn't even resist this time when I threw myself at him and a half-second later we were kissing like it had been weeks instead of just one day. It was wonderful. Beyond wonderful.

Rigel's hands roamed up and down my back and I wished I'd gone with the sexy nightgown after all. Now that he was here—

"Whoa," he murmured, pulling his lips a few inches away from mine. "It's definitely not that I don't *want* to…you know."

"I know." I forced myself to go sit on the little sofa so I wouldn't be tempted to drag him into my bedroom. Into my bed.

Rigel gave a visible shudder as he picked up that thought.

"Sorry. I'll try to behave. Because I really do need to tell you the *real* reason it's so important for me to go to Mars right now, and to become Sovereign."

He started to sit in the chair closest to the sofa, but I grabbed his hand and pulled him down to sit next to me. We could have that much, at least.

"So it's not just politics?" He was working as hard as I was to keep his mind off what we both really wanted to be doing.

"Politics is part of it, since I'll need to build support to get Acclaimed and into the Palace. But honestly, Devyn Kane would probably be a better leader than I could ever be, he's so experienced and charismatic and all."

Rigel shrugged. "You sell yourself short in the charisma department, but yeah, I've kind of wondered if it would be so terrible if he, or somebody like him, got elected president or whatever and let you off the hook. Let *us* off the hook."

"You don't know how much I wish that could happen, Rigel! It's been awful having to pretend to *you* that I really want to be Sovereign, because I totally don't, not if it means we can't be together." I twined my fingers through his. "But…I have to."

He just looked at me, waiting, so I took a deep breath and launched into the explanation I'd been rehearsing, repeating everything Shim had told me back in December, when I'd first learned about the Grentl.

"Until we ran away and they had to tell the rest of the Council, Shim and Kyna were the only people on Earth who knew, it was that secret. Even on Mars, only the Sovereigns and a few Scientists have ever known."

Then I repeated what the Council had told me more recently about Faxon's communication with them and what they'd done to him.

Rigel stayed quiet the whole time I talked, a variety of emotions playing across his face and radiating from him—horror, doubt, excitement and, finally, understanding. "So *that's* what you've been keeping from me all this time. These aliens."

I nodded, beyond relieved that he finally knew, that he could finally understand everything. "I wasn't allowed to tell *anyone* for fear of starting a panic. And the Council said if I told *you*, they wouldn't let you come to Mars at all. So…I didn't. But I really, really wanted to. You can't imagine how much I wanted to."

He gathered me into his arms, but gently this time. "I'm so sorry you've had to deal with all this alone, M. I get why you had to, but I wish I could have helped. Been, I don't know, supportive, at least, instead of acting like a jealous jerk. You know I wouldn't have told anyone."

"I know *you* wouldn't, but Mrs. O can always tell if somebody's lying, and you've said that Shim usually can, too. Do you really think we could have kept either of them from knowing, if I'd told you? I didn't dare risk you getting left behind."

"No, I get it. You're right." I could tell he was still struggling with disbelief, as well as guilt for the way he'd acted when he'd thought my secret had to do with Sean. "So, what can I do to help, now that I know?"

·⁺·
·⁺

I tried to get Rigel to stay a while after we'd talked through the whole Grentl thing, figuring this was our best chance to be truly alone for weeks, but after half an hour of cuddling and kissing, he insisted on leaving.

"If I stay, you know as well as I do we'll do something we shouldn't. I need to go while I still can. I love you, M."

It helped, a little, to know he hungered to stay as much as I hungered for him to do so. I still sighed to let him go. "Yeah, I guess you're right. I love you, too, Rigel. Always."

I woke up feeling fabulous the next morning, after the best makeout session in months. I hummed all through my two-minute ionic shower and while getting dressed in the outfit Molly had laid out.

Mmm. Good morning! I thought to Rigel when I joined him and Molly in the parlor. *Did you sleep as well as I did?*

Eventually. I had a lot to process first. You look fabulous, by the way.

"There's a message." Molly pointed at the flashing light on the vidscreen.

It was from Mr. O, suggesting I eat breakfast in the Commons today. "You may have set things back a bit with some of the Royals last night but it's the common people who will vote for your Acclamation, so they're the ones you need to convince. Meanwhile, I'll do my best to bring the Royals around and make them understand they have more to gain by supporting you than by working against you."

His somber tone dampened my euphoria somewhat and Sean's foul mood did the rest, when we stopped for him on the way down. I sensed it even before I noticed his ferocious frown.

"What?"

"Last night, of course. First you insist *he*—" he stabbed a finger at Rigel— "sit at the table with us. Way to put those rumors to rest."

"And Molly." I refused to let him make me feel guilty. "It's a stupid tradition, making them stand there for the whole meal when they're as hungry as the rest of us."

"Yeah? How's a Bodyguard supposed to protect you from the other end of the table?"

Rigel immediately jumped to my defense. "You're the one always saying she doesn't need a Bodyguard when you're right next to her."

Sean shifted his scowl from me to Rigel. "That's not the point and you know it. You both know it."

The lift doors opened onto the Commons and we all shut up for as long as it took all of us to get food and sit down. Molly and I sat between the two boys, who both still felt like they wanted to pummel each other. Hoping to defuse things a bit, I turned to Sean.

"Okay, maybe having them sit at the table was a dumb move, since it was my very first formal dinner. I won't do it again, okay?"

"If you even get the chance." Sean's frown took on a slightly worried edge. "What if they decide to replace him as your Bodyguard because of those rumors? Did you even think of that?"

"They can't. The Council agreed—"

"The Council's not here, in case you hadn't noticed. And they won't be on Mars, either. Nobody there will be bound by promises the *Echtran* Council made. They don't have any power in Nuath."

The very last trace of my good mood vanished as I realized he was right. And nobody with authority on Mars knew about the Grentl, so I wouldn't have that leverage there, either. In fact, I might not have any leverage at all until I got properly Acclaimed Sovereign.

"And what was all that stuff last night about how Faxon might have been right?" Sean continued while I was still absorbing that.

"What?" My worry abruptly shifted to anger, which felt a lot better. "I never said that! Not even close. He murdered my parents, in case you've forgotten, and my grandparents."

But Sean didn't back down. "Then what was all that about inequality between the *fines*? It sounded just like the propaganda Faxon spouted when he was in power."

I blinked. "All I did was ask questions. What you're repeating are the answers they gave me. Answers nobody bothered to give me before."

"Because you never asked before!" Sean spoke so heatedly I could tell we'd finally arrived at the real issue. "I could have told you this stuff any time, or my parents could have. But no, you wait till your first formal dinner with Royals who might or might not be in a position to help you get Acclaimed, then go out of your way to antagonize them. Why?"

I glared up at him, ready with another retort, but then the justice of Sean's words penetrated and my anger disappeared as quickly as it had come.

"I didn't *plan* to antagonize them. And it wasn't until yesterday, when I started digging through the archives and not finding answers, that I even realized I needed to ask those questions." I didn't add that

I'd found the reactions of the various Royals, and the Captain, as instructive as their words.

"Yeah, well, you should have asked me, or my dad." Sean's vibe grew less hostile, along with his tone. "You could probably tell it's still a pretty touchy subject, especially among Royals. Maybe our society wasn't perfect, but what society is? Like my dad said, nobody was going hungry or homeless or anything, at least not until Faxon started taking everything for himself and his favorites."

"Okay, fine, maybe I should have asked you guys first. But I had to find out where his supporters were coming from, in case…in case there are people on Mars who still feel that way. I need to know what I'm up against because Royals might not be the only ones I have to worry about. Remember those protesters in Bailerealta? You've learned enough Earth history by now to understand that once an idea takes hold, it can take on a life of its own, even if the person who started it goes bad or even dies."

"She's right, Sean," Molly said softly, like she was afraid he might turn his anger on her. "Remember what we read about the Russian revolution? How it started and what it became? There were others, too."

I could almost see the wheels turning in Sean's head as he thought about it. Finally, he nodded. "I guess. I still wish you'd asked *me* first."

"Next time, I promise." I put all the reassurance I could into my voice, my smile. And though I could tell Rigel didn't like it, it seemed to work.

Sean heaved a big sigh and smiled back, though it seemed to cost him an effort. "My dad's talking with them now, trying to convince them you were just trying to understand, that you're not planning to go all…all Communist or anything."

"Good. Because I'm not. And I'll try not to do anything else to piss them off, okay?" I picked up a forkful of my stone cold scrambled eggs. The others finally started eating, too, and the tension at the table gradually dissipated.

At least, until Molly said offhandedly, "Yeah, you don't want to do anything that'll make them check that video feed."

I glared at her and she made a little motion like she was trying to snatch her words back.

"What?" Sean stopped with his fork halfway to his mouth,

frowning again. "What video feed? The one in your suite? Why? What's on it?"

"Nothing," I said quickly—and probably not very convincingly. "Just private conversations—"

Molly quickly helped me out. "Yeah, after dinner we were all saying stuff about how obnoxious some of those Royals were. It wouldn't be good if that got back to them."

Rigel hadn't said anything at all, but I'd sensed the same stab of fear from him that I felt myself at Molly's reminder. I shot a sideways glance his way, but he was keeping his eyes totally on his plate. Just past him, though, I saw Brenna watching us, looking way too interested. She met my eye for a fraction of a second then turned away—but not before I saw a secret little smile.

How much had she heard, and who would she tell?

Rigel's worry had started to fade, but when he caught my thought, it spiked again. *You don't think anyone will actually listen to her, do you?*

I doubt it. It's not like we actually said anything incriminating just now. Molly covered really well.

I hoped I was doing a better job convincing him than myself.

21

Coslacht

COSLACHT (KO-SLACT): *appearance; impression; influence*

After breakfast, we hung around the Commons for a while, since Mr. O wanted me to make a good impression on as many people as I could. Sean and Molly taught Rigel and me how to play skittles, a game a little like bowling, then we joined the other teens for cards again. But just like yesterday, people kept interrupting our game to talk to me.

After losing the first round rather spectacularly, I stood up. "I'll go read for a while so you guys can actually play."

Not that I managed any reading, either. If anything, sitting alone encouraged even more people to approach. In fact, the way they were lining up, I felt like I was holding court even before getting Acclaimed. Fortunately, my emotion-sensing radar was working better than ever after my makeout session with Rigel last night and it seemed most people felt even more positively toward me today than yesterday.

There were exceptions, of course, like Brenna's mom, who was clearly irritated when I couldn't tell her how soon proper elections would be held once I reached Nuath. And Gordon, who didn't speak to me but passed close enough that I was able to get a "read" on him when he glanced my way and nodded. His vibe felt ickier than ever—

angry, frustrated and resentful. Worse, I had a feeling he was the kind of guy who'd do anything to get his way—or get me *out* of the way.

Don't let him mess with your head, Rigel thought from his position behind me. *Everybody else loves you and that's what matters.*

His encouragement helped, even if it wasn't quite true. I was heartened further by the older couple who gushed (sincerely) about how happy they were I was alive and coming to Mars, and the young mother with two kids who thanked me for lifting everyone's spirits after all the damage Faxon had done.

"It was so depressing, even hearing about it from Earth, you can't imagine. You're just the tonic we all needed, Princess."

After a while, a few Royals made a point of coming over to apologize for their attitudes last night and seemed to mean it. Phelan and Annwyn, in particular, appeared to have completely put aside their reservations about me. When the two approached and bowed, I probed them both for all I was worth but didn't sense anything more negative than a bit of wariness from Annwyn. Both of them radiated an eagerness to please, along with a gratifying tinge of admiration.

"I'm terribly sorry, Excellency, if our responses to your questions last night seemed rather, ah, fraught," Phelan said. "We were caught a bit off guard, but it's both natural and prudent that you should wish to understand how the political climate in Nuath shifted over the years leading up to and following Faxon's takeover. Please don't hesitate to ask me any other questions you might have about that time."

"Or me," Annwyn chimed in. "Though I imagine Quinn O'Gara has told you all you wished to know by now?"

He hadn't had a chance yet, but it was a good reminder that I had an excellent resource who was definitely in favor of my Acclamation. "Thank you both. I can't tell you how much I appreciate your understanding and support." As I'd tried to do with everyone, I matched my words and tone to their emotions and was rewarded by pleased relief from both women.

They chatted for a few more minutes, then invited me to join the other Royals at a big table in the corner. The table where Gordon and Devyn were already sitting.

Smiling, I shook my head. "I've promised to have lunch with some of my new friends—ones around my age, I mean—but thanks so much for inviting me."

When the card game broke up, Sean and Molly headed our way

along with a couple of the others. We all found a table together, making my half-fib to Phelan and Annwyn true after all. Lunchtime conversation centered on the games they'd just finished playing, which let me relax and take a break from gauging people's attitudes.

From across the room, I saw Mr. O'Gara join the Royals for lunch. A moment after he sat down, Gordon got up and left. Jerk. Brenna and her mom left the Commons just a few seconds later and I found myself hoping none of them would come back. Negative vibes were a lot more draining than positive ones, I'd discovered.

You want to spend the afternoon upstairs again? Rigel suggested sympathetically. *I could tell you were getting kind of wrung out.*

I'm fine for now, but I'll take another break if it gets to be too much, I promise. His concern gave me another little boost of strength. A good thing, since the minute I left the lunch table I was besieged again by people wanting either reassurance or favors. Even Devyn stopped by. Like last night, I felt nothing but goodwill and honesty from him, making me wonder if projecting positivity was *his* special power. It would definitely be a useful one for a politician.

When Rigel, Molly and I finally went up to our suite late that afternoon, I found another message waiting from Mr. O, this one super upbeat.

"You'll be pleased to know that I've spoken with the other Royals as well as a fair cross-section of the passengers and they all seem extremely well-disposed toward you, Excellency. Still, I recommend you continue to engage as many people as possible for the remainder of the voyage. You can never have too much support, though at this point I predict your Acclamation will be a mere formality when we reach Nuath. Well done!"

All three of us cheered and Rigel and I exchanged what amounted to a mental hug of relief and congratulations. It looked like we were in the clear after all!

✦

Molly insisted I dress a little nicer for dinner, even in the Commons. "It shows respect for everyone else. Trust me on this."

"You know, sometimes I think you'd be a lot better at this Sovereign thing than me." I was only half teasing. "Are you sure you don't have a little Royal blood in you somewhere?"

The sudden hurt I sensed from her took me by surprise. "Just because I kill every plant I try to grow—"

"No, Molly, I didn't mean that at all!" I felt mortified by my stupid slip. "I'm sure you'll be the best Agriculturalist ever, one of these days. I just meant you're so good at all the protocol stuff. Way better than I am, even though I've studied it till it's coming out of my ears."

She smiled reluctantly, the hurt fading. "Then thanks, I guess. And really, being the Sovereign's Handmaid is way further up the social ladder than even the top-ranking Ag, so it's not like I can complain. Here, why don't you wear this?"

Though it seemed like she pulled the outfit out of my closet almost at random to change the subject, it was perfect, nice but not too fancy: a swishy green skirt and a cream top with matching green trim. The green was the exact shade of my eyes so I knew it would be flattering.

"Thanks, Molly. You have a great eye, even better than Bri. Which is lucky for me, since I've always been hopeless in the fashion department."

I swirled for Rigel when we came out of the bedroom and was rewarded by a wash of appreciation and love that nearly made me throw myself at him again, since I'd decided not to worry about the stupid cameras. But it would embarrass Molly and she'd feel obligated to remind us again about her chaperone duties, so I restrained myself. Still, I was in a great mood when we headed down to dinner, already wondering if I could talk Rigel into another late-night rendezvous.

Mars was finally on the Commons viewscreen tonight. The sight of that reddish sphere brought my excitement surging back—an excitement I'd almost forgotten, with everything else going on. I was *born* there! It was still impossible to believe. I had to pull my gaze away when Sean called us over to the table he and all the other teens— except Brenna—had staked out. During dinner, everyone talked about what they wanted to do first once we reached Nuath, all of them as upbeat as I was.

Mr. O stopped by our table as we finished eating, looking the most relaxed I'd seen him since leaving Indiana. "You got my message?"

I nodded. "Everything's been going great at my end, too. Thanks!"

"This will make things go much more smoothly in Nuath. I've already written a message to the Council I can send once we land. Are you ready for your first gravity reversal?"

Sean had told me about that earlier today. We'd all be strapped in while the ship switched over from acceleration to deceleration, since that would make the gravity go wonky for about half an hour. Sean claimed it was fun, but I was a little worried I'd get queasy.

"I guess so. Do you, um, want to sit with us?"

He waved a hand dismissively. "No, no, I'm sure you'll enjoy yourselves more if I don't. And there'll probably be a movie afterward, there usually is. We can talk tomorrow. Perhaps over breakfast?"

I agreed to that and he left us. Not long after, a ship-wide announcement reminded everyone that they had fifteen minutes to report to the Commons and secure themselves for deceleration. Of course, most people were here already because of dinner. The latecomers started eating more quickly while a few others who'd been elsewhere filtered in.

The changeover of the Commons from dining/recreation area back to theater-style seating was pretty cool all by itself. We all stood to one side and watched as tables, chairs and all the games and workout equipment sank into the floor. A moment later panels slid over everything and, after some rumbling, the airplane-type seats rose up again to fill most of the floor space.

"Everyone please be seated," the Captain's voice boomed over the speakers. "Deceleration will commence in five minutes."

"C'mon." Sean grabbed my hand and pulled me toward the front, nearest the viewscreen. "You're going to love this! I've got ping-pong balls and stuff."

"Huh?" I was totally confused and could tell Rigel was, too.

"You'll see." Molly was grinning. "I've got a hair clip and a pen."

Still baffled, we accompanied Sean, Molly and several other teens to the third row of seats, which Sean insisted was the best place to sit. Just like for takeoff, Sean sat on my left, Rigel on my right and Molly on Rigel's other side. I wished Rigel and I could hold hands. Not that I was exactly nervous, but—

Yeah, I know, me too. But it'll be fine, he assured me.

I didn't have time to wonder if he was right because just seconds after we'd latched our harnesses, the ship shuddered slightly and then I felt…weird. Sort of like going down fast in an elevator, making my stomach feel higher than it should be. Was this weightlessness?

Sean nudged me. "Check this out." He pulled a ping-pong ball out of his pocket, held it out in front of me, then let it go. It drifted slightly upwards, then to the left, where it stayed motionless, spinning. On my other side, Molly set a hair clip in midair and when it didn't do anything, she tapped it my way. It spun lazily past Rigel's nose, then mine, toward Sean. In front of us, I saw kids, teens, and a few adults releasing other lightweight, relatively harmless objects into the air in front of them, just to watch them be weightless. Awesome!

"Can I try?" I asked Molly. Grinning again, she handed me a ball-point pen.

I held it at arm's length then let it go, half expecting it to fall, like everyone else knew some trick I didn't. But no, it just hovered there for a good minute before gradually starting to sink toward my knees.

"Ship must be almost turned already." Sean sounded disappointed. He quickly pulled another ping-pong ball out of his pocket and lobbed it up toward the ceiling. Like the pen, it hung suspended for several seconds, ten feet above us, then slowly, slowly drifted back down, gathering speed toward the end. "Ah, well, still fun. Don't you think?"

"Absolutely." I dropped the pen again. This time it fell a little quicker. What an amazing life I was leading! A year ago I could never have imagined any of this.

Definitely cool, Rigel agreed. *I only wish—*

Yeah, me too. I sent the longing I felt from him back his way with a little sigh. Still, if I could get Acclaimed as quickly as Mr. O predicted, then deal with the Grentl issue, our path would *have* to get easier.

On that exact thought, the image of Mars on the big screen in front of us pixelated.

"They must be about to start the movie," Molly remarked. "Probably a Disney flick or something else family-friendly."

That made sense, since every passenger was trapped here at the moment, including a few younger children. Like everyone else, I watched the screen, figuring we'd decide whether to stay once we knew what the movie was.

But no movie started.

Instead, the screen went completely blank for about five seconds, then another image appeared—the living room of my suite, with Molly, Rigel and me standing in the middle, talking without sound. What the—?

Up on the screen, Molly was smiling as she said something to me. I gestured toward my bedroom as I responded, then Rigel shrugged and said something to Molly. Molly went into her bedroom and came out with her toiletry kit, then headed to the bathroom. My heart thudded up into my throat as I realized what we were seeing—what everyone was about to see. I could feel Rigel's panic, as intense as my own, but there was nothing—*nothing*—we could do but sit and watch, just like every single other passenger on the *Quintessence.*

22

Beidan

BEIDAN (BID-DEN): *gossip; scandal*

Sean

I'm wondering if I'd be dumb to try holding M's hand during tonight's movie when suddenly I'm seeing her—and Molly and Rigel —up on the big screen instead of "Transformers" or whatever. Huh? It looks like a video feed from her quarters but it can't be live, since they're all sitting right next to me. I keep watching, trying to figure out how the heck we can be seeing this, when suddenly M—on the screen, I mean—starts making out with Rigel.

My breath huffs out like somebody just punched me.

I can't look away, even though it kills me to watch them kissing… and kissing. Finally I turn to look at M, though to say what, I don't know. She's staring straight ahead, her face tense and paper white, like she's as shocked as anyone. And she probably is—shocked that everybody's *seeing* this.

The kissing goes on and on and what began as startled murmurs rises into a babble of confusion and outrage. I know exactly how everybody feels—only more so. Finally the picture freezes, M still in Rigel's arms, their faces all mashed together. Then, mercifully, it disappears.

But only for a second. Another video pops up, this time of Rigel tiptoeing across the now-darkened living room to M's bedroom door. He taps on it soundlessly, the door opens and there's M, in a frilly nightgown, obviously expecting him. He goes into her room and the door shuts behind them. Then suddenly Mars is back up on the vidscreen, like it never went away. If it wasn't for the shocked faces and voices all around me, I'd almost think I hallucinated the whole thing, like some horrific waking nightmare.

I barely hear the announcement that we're free to undo our harnesses, I'm still so gut-punched. I turn to M again, praying she has some explanation, but she still won't even look at me. People in front of us, behind us, on either side, are all yelling questions and accusations at her and at Rigel but it's like she can't even hear them.

Molly's the first to speak. "We…we should probably go." M doesn't respond. It's like she's retreated into another dimension or something. Probably from shame and embarrassment.

Pissed but also a little worried now, I reach over and grab her arm. "Come on. We can't stay here."

She flinches and finally turns wide eyes to me. "Sean, I—"

"Not now." My voice is harsh, but harsh is how I'm feeling.

The four of us stand up. I don't look at Rigel. I can't. We move to the end of our row. The Captain and my dad are standing there, waiting for us. For M.

"Excellency, I must ask you and your attendants to come with me," the Captain says.

She nods, her face expressionless. I'm not exactly one of her attendants and neither is my dad, but we come, too. The Captain doesn't tell us not to. All of us get into the executive lift and he takes us up to Level One. The whole way up, M and Rigel hold hands. Guess they figure there's no point hiding the truth now. I want to wrench them apart but I don't. I don't do anything at all.

Once we're inside the Captain's quarters, the same room where we had dinner last night, he turns to M. He doesn't look happy. None of us do.

"Excellency, I find myself in a very difficult position. I already have someone investigating how that recording was accessed and diverted to the Commons viewscreen. For that security breach, I apologize. However, I cannot ignore what I—what everyone—saw."

"I understand." M's voice is almost a whisper, like she's scared. "We never meant—" The door chime sounds, cutting her off.

One of the women we met yesterday on the bridge comes in, escorting Gordon Nolan. "Captain, I was able to trace the source of the breach to this man's cabin on Level Two. I thought you would want to question him at once."

The Captain turns to Gordon with a frown. "Explain yourself."

The guy doesn't say anything for a second, then he shrugs. "After hearing rumors about the Princess and her Bodyguard, I thought it important to find out if they were true—for the good of Nuath. It's the sort of thing our people should know about, given the new policy of openness after all of Faxon's lies. Don't you agree?"

The Captain just gives Gordon a long, cold look. "Exactly how were you able to pull off this bit of sabotage, sir?"

The guy positively smirks and I remember M never liked him. "Your security leaves a bit to be desired, Captain. Finding and copying that feed wasn't nearly as hard as I expected. Patching that copy into the feed downstairs was even easier."

"It appears to have been a sophisticated hacking job, Captain," the female officer says, "but not sophisticated enough to keep me from tracing it. I've already taken steps to ensure nothing like this can ever happen again."

"Thank you, Jana." Captain Liam turns back to M. "I do apologize for the intrusion into your privacy, Excellency. While I thoroughly condemn what this man did to prove his suspicions—" he glances angrily at Gordon— "I can't ignore what has been revealed. I'm afraid I am forced to take action."

Rigel speaks up before M can answer. "What sort of action, sir? Nothing that will compromise the Sovereign's safety, I hope?"

I snort, but Gordon actually has the nerve to laugh. "You're a fine one to talk about her safety after posing as her Bodyguard under false pretenses. I can't imagine how you managed to worm your way into such a responsible position without having your true intentions suspected, but now that you've been exposed—"

"He didn't worm his way into anything," M interrupts him, color coming back to her cheeks. "I myself convinced the *Echtran* Council to appoint him Bodyguard and the Council has known about our relationship all along. They only asked that we hide it in public. Rigel was completely trained for his Bodyguard duties, you can check with the Council. He passed their test and everything."

"The Council *knew*?" Gordon sounds scandalized. I wonder if he's faking it. "How could they allow such a thing? Just how long has this…relationship been going on?"

"They allowed it because I refused to become Sovereign if they didn't. And Rigel and I have been together since before I learned about Mars, or who I was, or…or anything."

"Together?" the Captain repeats. "Do you mean—?"

M huffs out a breath. "No! We're not sleeping together and we never have, no matter what people think." Her cheeks are bright red now. I wish I had my mum's ability to tell if someone's lying. "I wouldn't be alive right now if it weren't for Rigel. I thought everyone knew that story, how he saved me from Faxon's minions back on Earth? More than once?"

The Captain reluctantly nods, but Gordon just smirks and slants a look my way. "I'm betting your Consort didn't know about this."

"This does seem unfair to him in the extreme." Captain Liam looks at me, too, his expression sympathetic. Now I feel my own face getting hot.

"Sean knows," M tells them before I can figure out what to say. "He's always known, from the moment I met him. He doesn't like it, but he definitely knows."

The Captain frowns at me thoughtfully. "Now I understand your reaction to discovering that the Princess's Bodyguard would share her quarters. Still—" He turns back to M— "as Captain of the *Quintessence*, I can't in conscience allow a situation to continue aboard my ship that could jeopardize the future of Nuath. Your Bodyguard is hereby relieved and is not to approach you for any reason during the remainder of the voyage. Jana here will serve as his replacement until we reach Mars, where it will be up to others to decide how to proceed."

Though she looks stricken, M manages a tiny nod. "I can't blame *you*, Captain. But I won't allow you or anyone to punish Rigel for something that wasn't his fault—or, at least, no more his fault than mine."

"He won't be punished," the Captain says. "Not by me. A bed will be found for him in Steerage and he is to stay there except for meals."

Then, to Rigel, "Jana will escort you down immediately. Your belongings will be brought to you shortly."

Rigel looks at M questioningly and she looks back, almost like they're exchanging thoughts with their eyes, then he nods. "You're sure my replacement is capable?"

"Quite capable. Though Jana's primary duties aboard the *Quintessence* have been to monitor the sensors, she is also my chief security officer and has both the training and experience necessary to keep the Sovereign safe."

With another jerky nod, Rigel allows Jana to escort him out of the room.

As soon as they're gone, the Captain turns to Gordon. "Unfortunately, I don't have the authority to discipline someone of your rank, but I strongly suggest you remain in your quarters until we land. Then someone who *does* have that authority can deal with you. Now, get out of my sight."

Though he looks stunned someone would dare talk to him like that, Gordon doesn't argue. With a final, angry glance at M, he leaves without another word.

My dad frowns after him until the door closes. "I'm sorry you were put in such an untenable position, Captain. If you have no objection, we'll leave as well. I'd like to speak with the Sovereign and my children privately."

"Of course." Captain Liam looks stressed and tired and like he's more than ready for all this to be over. "Good night." He gives M sort of a sketchy version of the proper bow and we all head across the hall to her quarters.

M palms the door open—she still hasn't looked at me, except that once in the Commons—and we go in. When the door shuts, Dad looks at M, then Molly, then me. Then back at M.

"Do you have an explanation for what we saw?" he asks, but not accusingly, like I would have. He just asks it.

I can tell M is almost on the verge of tears, but she takes a deep breath and gives a little shrug. "That first night, after we boarded the ship, well, it had been so long… None of us had noticed the cameras yet, so the minute Molly was out of the room, I just couldn't resist kissing Rigel. I know it was dumb, but we're both so much stronger when we can…touch each other. Because of our bond. We…I needed that. I'm sorry."

"Molly?" Dad says. "Part of your duties—"

"I know." Molly looks embarrassed. "I told them that. I didn't see—"

"It wasn't Molly's fault at all, Mr. O'Gara," M breaks in quickly. "I promise."

Dad looks at her for a long moment but I can't tell what he's thinking. "Suppose you tell me about that second bit we saw. When was that?"

M swallows visibly. "Last night, after dinner. I know it looked bad, but we just really, really needed to talk, and not in front of the cameras or Molly or anybody."

"Talk. About what?" Dad looks almost as skeptical as I feel.

"I—" M darts a glance at me, then at Molly. "I'd rather not say."

He raises an eyebrow. "*All* you did was talk? How long was Rigel in your room?"

Now she goes pink again and I feel my gut clench. "We, um, might have kissed some, too. But it was *mostly* talking, I swear! He wasn't in there long, maybe half an hour."

My dad heaves a tired-sounding sigh. "There will be no way to keep this quiet once we reach Mars, as everyone on the ship witnessed that video. Word will likely spread within hours of our arrival, which means we need to focus on damage control now, before we land, if we are still to get you Acclaimed."

"Can't we just tell everybody the truth?" M looks up at him pleadingly. "It would be so much easier."

Oh, sure, and make me a colony-wide laughingstock!

But Dad's already shaking his head. "No. The traditionalists, your greatest supporters, could turn against you, and we can't afford that. Better to— Never mind. These decisions can wait for morning. We're all rather stressed right now and I need time to think things through."

He says good night to M and Molly and motions me to leave with him. I hesitate, wanting to talk to M myself, ask her again if all she and Rigel really did in her bedroom was talk and kiss, but I guess there's no point. If she lied to my dad, she'll lie to me. It's not like I can shake the truth out of her—or like I would, even if I could, no matter how she hurt and betrayed me.

I look at her, trying to communicate all that with my eyes the way Rigel seems to be able to do, but she barely glances at me before turning away. Again.

Dad insists his breakfast meeting with M be private, so even though I barely slept all night, I head down to the Commons as soon as he leaves. Before I even reach the recombinators, Brenna comes over, looking smug.

"Didn't I tell you it was more than a rumor, about the Princess and her Bodyguard? Didn't I?" A few people nearby look interested in our conversation and I remember again how much Brenna likes to gossip.

I shrug. "I really can't talk about it. Sorry."

"Rigel won't, either. He went straight to bed when that scary security woman escorted him down to Steerage last night. Rowena tried to talk to him this morning, but he's in a pretty foul mood." She glances over her shoulder. I look too, and see Rigel at a table alone, his back to the room.

"Excuse me." I get the default breakfast of scrambled eggs and toast, then take my tray over to Rigel's table, where he's pushing food around on his plate.

"Go away," he snarls, not even looking up.

I ignore him and plunk my tray and my self down across from him. "Want to tell me *your* version of what happened in M's bedroom?"

He glares at me. "No. I don't."

"So it's every bit as bad as people are saying, huh?"

Rigel makes a convulsive little jerk like he wants to stab me with his fork. "You mean what your *girlfriend* is saying? You do know she's the one who tipped off Gordon about the vid feed after eavesdropping on us yesterday, right?"

I didn't, but all I say is, "She's not my girlfriend."

"Right." Rigel snorts. "Maybe if you'd tried harder to convince *her* of that, she wouldn't have been so eager to spread stories about M."

"Which you two conveniently proved were true." Whether Brenna was involved isn't the point. "You know no one will believe nothing happened behind that closed door." Even I don't believe it, much as I wish I could. Ever since Trina's nasty trick with her phone, I've had nightmares about what M and Rigel might have done, might still be doing, in secret.

"We kissed. And talked. That's all. But it's enough for them to use as ammunition against M."

"Against M? Sounds like *you're* the one they—"

"You don't get it, do you?" He plants both fists on the table, his eyes narrowing to slits. "There are people, Royals, who want power for themselves and M is in the way. It was probably one of them who sent those guys after her back in Ireland, to keep her from going to Mars at all. Maybe they want me out of the way so they can get to her more easily, or maybe they just want some scandal to keep her from getting Acclaimed, but either way it's about politics, you can bet your life on it. I'm just a detail. One that screwed up, so now I can't even protect her."

I frown at him as that sinks in. "But she still has a Bodyguard, that woman from ship's security."

"For two days. Once we get to Mars, they'll probably put one of their own people in, somebody who won't even care about keeping M safe, who might even want to—"

"No!" That draws even more attention than we already had. I lower my voice. "I won't let that happen. No way. I may not be her official Bodyguard, but I sure as hell won't let anybody hurt her."

He looks at me for like ten seconds, then surprises me by relaxing a little. "Thanks. That helps a little. She thinks she can fix things, make them put me back in as Bodyguard, but..." His face twists with what looks like pain. "If my screwup gets her hurt, I'll...I don't know what I'll do."

Much as I'm enjoying watching Rigel beat himself up, I say, "The important thing is to keep her safe, right? Even if you don't much like me being the one doing it. Believe me, I know how that feels."

His mouth spasms into something he might think is a smile, but it's definitely not. "Yeah. I guess you do. Anyway...thanks."

He leaves and I start eating my cold eggs. I'm nearly done before it occurs to me to wonder when M had a chance to tell him about her plan to "fix" things.

23

Cosc damaste

COSC DAMASTE (KOSK DAHM-UH-STAY): *damage control*

Molly was super apologetic when she woke me the next morning to say her dad was on his way up to meet with me. I stifled my groan so I wouldn't make her feel worse, but I couldn't hide my swollen nose and crusty eyes. She didn't comment, just started laying out clothes for me.

I'd cried myself to sleep after wallowing in every possible worst-case scenario and a horrible black pit of self-loathing. Why, why, *why* hadn't I listened to the Council's warnings? Of *course* my every move was being watched, just like they predicted. Those cameras shouldn't have been a surprise at all. But instead of being extra careful, I'd flouted tradition the first chance I got, at that dinner, alienating my few Royal allies.

My detractors were right and my supporters were deluded. How could I possibly be fit to lead Nuath if I was making such stupid mistakes before I even got there? I'd never be Acclaimed now, which meant I'd ruined everything, and the Grentl would probably nuke Mars *and* Earth and it would all be my fault.

Another cry in a long, hot shower might have made me feel better, but I had to settle for a twenty-second ionic one instead. It got me just as clean, making my skin tingle and my hair lift around my head, but it definitely wasn't conducive to wallowing. The sink had water, so I splashed some on my face. Then, staring at my slightly-less-puffy face in the mirror, I took a cold, hard look at my options.

Giving up wasn't one of them, not with the stakes this high. No matter how badly I'd screwed up, I was still the only person who could respond to the Grentl, which meant I somehow had to get to the Royal Palace.

To do that, I'd have to act as responsibly, as regally, as possible from now on, which meant exerting a lot more self-control than I had so far. No snarky digs at Royals, no whining about rules. Maybe I shouldn't even try to get Rigel reinstated as my Bodyguard…except I'd promised him last night that I would.

No matter what, I had to keep moving forward, at least until I could answer the Grentl and avert whatever threat they posed. Only then could I afford to worry about what the future would hold for Rigel and me. Because if I failed, there might not be any future at all.

Mr. O and breakfast were both waiting when I emerged into the living room. He waited for Jana to taste my food and Molly to serve it to me, then asked them to leave. "I have private business to discuss with the Princess. You can both eat in the Commons while we talk, or take some of this—" he gestured at the table— "across the hall to the officers' quarters."

Once they were gone he turned to me, looking almost as tired and stressed as he had last night. "I've been working out a strategy to mitigate the damage done last night, since it's still imperative to get you Acclaimed as quickly as possible."

Before he could continue, I leaned forward, using all the "push" I could. "Are you *sure* the best thing wouldn't be to announce the truth about Rigel and me? About the *graell*? If everyone on Mars is going to find out about that video anyway—"

"I told you last night why we can't do that. Perhaps someday, after you're Acclaimed, after the people have a degree of confidence in you as a leader. But now, when your opponents' main weapons are your youth and inexperience? It would play right into their hands, give them enough ammunition to derail your Acclamation entirely. However, if we can convince people that Rigel was at fault, that you were misled by gratitude—"

"What?" I rocked back in my chair, horrified. "No! No way are you making Rigel a scapegoat when it was more my fault than his."

"I knew you wouldn't like the idea, but consider how much is at stake. I learned during my Resistance days that sometimes sacrifices have to be made for the greater good. As a leader, you—"

"Forget it," I snapped. "No leader worth her salt would let someone else take the blame for her own screwups. You sound like Allister. Remember what he tried to do to Rigel? And how Rigel almost died?"

He didn't look convinced. "Perhaps I should speak to Rigel. If he—"

"Don't you dare! It would be just like Rigel to...to fall on his sword, if he thought it was for my sake. Please, there *has* to be a better way."

After a long, frowning moment, he sighed. "Perhaps if we move quickly enough we can have you Acclaimed before word of that video spreads throughout Nuath. Unlikely, but I suppose it's worth a try. Can you tell me now what it was you needed to discuss with Rigel so privately that night?"

Caught off guard by the direct question, and positive the truth was a bad idea, I stumbled a bit over my answer. "Just...stuff about our bond, and...other things we haven't been able to talk about for a while. Like...Sean."

After regarding me narrowly for a long moment, he nodded. "Yes, the current situation has been difficult for all three of you. Unfortunately, this incident will likely make things worse."

No kidding. "Since we're definitely *not* making Rigel a scapegoat, what do you suggest I do?"

"Rise above the gossip. *Demonstrate* your worthiness in any way you can. Allow nothing else of a negative nature to attach to you." In other words, what I'd just told myself, in the bathroom. "Your best weapon is your likability, as we've seen in Bailerealta and aboard this ship. Therefore, I suggest you be yourself...your best self." He smiled, making me feel a *little* better.

While we ate, he gave me a quick rundown of what to expect when we reached Mars: crowds that might be welcoming or hostile or both, an official reception committee, and an escort to the lodgings had been prepared for me in Tullymayne.

"Why not the Palace? If we stay there, maybe I could...do what I need to do without getting Acclaimed."

"Unfortunately, that's not an option. Traditionally, it is a major event when a newly Acclaimed Sovereign enters the Palace for the first time, even if he or she lived there previously. Even your first visit to Thiaraway likely won't happen until after Acclamation, as there is more ceremony—and a parade—associated with that."

More stupid traditions and ceremonies! But I didn't say that out loud.

He went on to explain that to declare for Acclamation, I should have an approval rating of at least 80%, or at least one significantly higher than any would-be rival. If I couldn't manage that, and quickly, the contest for leadership would likely be long, contentious and destructive for Nuath and its people.

"Our people have never faced a situation like this," he reminded me, "so there are no laws or even traditions in place to smooth the process. While I would like to believe the majority are too averse to violence for things to degenerate to that point, there are no guarantees. Particularly if more factions, Royal or otherwise, enter the fray."

"On other ships coming from Earth, you mean?"

"As well as those who have come out of hiding since Faxon's overthrow, like Nels Murdoch, the Interim Governor. There are also the Royals who were released from Faxon's prisons who are now being treated for memory erasure and other mental trauma. Assuming they recover."

"Can they really cure memory erasure?"

"We don't know yet, though some therapies apparently show promise." He paused and I remembered this was personal for him, because of his daughter Elana. "In any event—"

He continued with his analysis of the current political climate of various Nuathan towns and villages, and which factions I most needed to be concerned with. It was a lot, and it kept me from working out a solid argument for Rigel's reassignment as Bodyguard. I didn't want to bring it up until I could be super convincing, which meant Rigel and I should probably brainstorm it—silently—over lunch or dinner in the Commons.

Finally, Mr. O stood to leave."Oh, I nearly forgot. I think it would be best if you remain here in your suite for the rest of the trip, certainly for the rest of the day. Let the worst of the gossip run its course. Otherwise you're likely to be subjected to unpleasant comments that might tempt you to say something that could damage your image further."

"But—" I broke off, reluctantly realizing he was right. If someone made a snarky crack about Rigel, I probably *wouldn't* be able to resist defending him, and that would set things back even further. "Okay. Fine."

For now.

I made the best of my virtual imprisonment, reminding myself repeatedly that this was the nicest place I'd ever stayed. I studied my book scroll, then practiced Taekwondo forms in the big living room when I started getting stir-crazy. Jana watched me with interest, then offered to teach me a few non-Taekwondo self-defense moves, which helped pass more time.

By dinnertime, I could swear I was already feeling twinges of Rigel-deprivation. So instead of watching the mindless comedy Molly suggested after we finished eating, I went to my room to fine-tune my arguments for getting him back.

When Mr. O'Gara arrived for breakfast the next day, I was ready. I bided my time at first, picking at my food while he updated me on the mood aboard the ship. The general outrage over the contents of that unauthorized video seemed to be fading, he said. Some were even making excuses for me, since it was common knowledge that Rigel had saved my life back in October.

I immediately seized that opening. "So, about Rigel." Mr. O frowned, but I continued anyway. "Since you won't let us tell the truth, shouldn't he be reinstated as my Bodyguard when we land? Jana has duties on the *Quintessence,* so I won't have one at all then."

"I'm sure a new Bodyguard can be assigned fairly quickly. In fact, one may already have been appointed, based on what the Council said before we left Jewel. We need to do everything possible to squelch speculation, so the less you and Rigel are seen together and, forgive me, the more you are seen with Sean, the better."

I'd expected this, so I moved to my next point. "But if it's already known in Nuath that Rigel is my Bodyguard, won't it cause even more gossip for him to suddenly *not* be? Maybe if we pretend nothing happened—nothing important enough to have him replaced, anyway —people will pay less attention to rumors."

When he began to look thoughtful, I pressed forward eagerly. "Also, don't you remember how sick we both got when we were apart for ten days last Thanksgiving? I'm already not feeling that great after just a day and a half away from him. I won't look much like a leader if I'm too weak to go out in public."

"As I recall, you were both given an antidote. I'm sure you'll be fine," he said drily.

"You can't know that. It's never been tested, since Rigel and I have never been apart longer than a day or so since getting it. Is it worth the risk?"

"I have perfect faith in our Scientists." But I sensed a thread of uncertainty.

"Even *they* said it should be tested, remember? That's the whole reason Rigel and I ran away, to keep them from separating us again. Besides, it's not like Rigel has any place to go once we reach Mars."

Mr. O regarded me for a long moment, clearly trying to decide whether those concerns were valid or if I just wanted to keep my boyfriend close by. Finally, he gave a small shrug.

"It's true that we should downplay things as much as possible, and that Rigel can't be left on his own, especially as he has never been to Nuath before. I'll consider the options."

"Thank you." It was the most I'd really expected. "And I promise neither of us will breach protocol again. At all."

Before he left, I suggested I should have my last dinner in the Commons that night, since it would be my only opportunity to demonstrate to everyone aboard that I was rising above the gossip. To my relief, he agreed.

I entered the Commons that evening, head held high, and was massively relieved to immediately sense Rigel's *brath*. I didn't even have to move my head to zero in on him, sitting alone at a table in the corner.

While Molly went to get my food, I headed straight for the table where Sean sat with a couple of other teens, careful not to so much as look Rigel's way. Desmond saw me coming and quickly vacated the chair on Sean's right, which made Sean look up.

"Dad said you might come down, but I thought maybe you'd changed your mind. You doing okay?"

I shrugged. "I've been better."

"Me too." I was surprised to sense irritation from him. "People are acting sorry for me and it's getting pretty old."

Oh. "Sorry." At his scowl, I realized that was exactly the wrong thing to say. "It's got to be better than what they think about *me* right now. So, what time do we land tomorrow? And what should I expect?"

Clearly relieved by the change of subject, he started talking about Arregaith, the town where the spaceport and most supporting industries were located, and nearby Tullymayne, where our temporary lodgings would be. Mr. O had already told me all this, so I just nodded and smiled while reaching out mentally for Rigel.

I've missed you so much! How are you holding up? He didn't answer right away, so I asked again, focusing harder.

Sorry, I heard you before. But 'fine' would be a lie and the truth would make you feel worse, so I didn't know what to say. Even from twenty yards away I could feel how upset he was, a combination of frustration, anger and guilt. Especially guilt.

Please *stop blaming yourself, Rigel! It was way more my fault than yours. Anyway, I have some good news.*

Molly interrupted me with my dinner then, which was probably just as well, since Sean's expression implied he'd noticed my distraction. I wasn't hungry, but pretending to eat would make it easier to disguise what I was really doing. I picked up my fork.

So, my news. I'm pretty sure I've talked Mr. O into letting you be my Bodyguard again once we land, so we just have to hang tight till tomorrow.

Yeah? That would be great. I hate not being able to protect you.

His response reassured me that Mr. O had kept his word and not tried to talk Rigel into martyring himself for my sake—or, rather, for the sake of "the greater good."

We'll figure out a plan. We always do. I projected all the confidence I could with the thought, but didn't get much enthusiasm back. Of course, he probably wasn't feeling great—physically—either.

Not so much, he sent in response to that thought. *Sorry you're not feeling well, either. Anyway, I should go. I'm done eating and that Jana woman is watching me.*

His mental tone bothered me. *Are you mad at me?*

No, just at myself. Love you, M. He was already walking out of the Commons on his last thought.

I'll see you here tomorrow, for the landing, I thought to him a little frantically as he left. *I love you, Rigel. Always!*

"Do you want to stay and watch the movie?" Sean asked as I continued to pick at my food.

I shook my head. "I'm a little soured on movies in the Commons, sorry. Besides, I should go to bed early, since tomorrow will probably be a long day."

Not wanting to look cowardly, I hung around until the movie started and eventually a few people came up to me. Some even made a point of telling me they still supported me, "no matter what." I tried to find that comforting, but a lot of the emotions I sensed around me were less than friendly.

Still, I thanked each person warmly, no matter what I felt off them, figuring it couldn't hurt. After half an hour of interaction, I was too drained to do more than drag myself back upstairs to my suite.

Molly woke me early the next morning so we could finish packing before heading down to the Commons for the landing.

The big room was again set up theater-style, people grabbing food and drinks from the recombinators before buckling themselves in to watch the screen. I sat next to Sean in the front row with Jana sitting where Rigel had before. He didn't seem to be here yet.

"What did you decide?" I whispered across to Mr. O when Molly went to get my breakfast.

He gave me a tight smile. "That we'll give it another try. For now."

Relief washed through me, though I belatedly realized that Sean's sour expression—and emotions—should have answered my question before I even asked. With a smile I couldn't suppress, I looked up at the viewscreen.

By now the Red Planet filled nearly the whole thing, looking every bit as dusty and lifeless as it had in every picture I'd ever seen from NASA's orbiters and rovers. Even though we'd been decelerating for hours, our approach still seemed awfully fast to me. A few minutes later, nibbling on a pastry with my eyes glued to the screen, I wondered how soon I'd be able to recognize our landing port. It was probably well hidden, like the one in Bailerealta. Maybe that flat spot off to the left—?

But even as I thought it, the *Quintessence* banked off to the right.

We were close enough now that the planet blocked out the horizon. For a moment I could make out hills and valleys and crevices, but soon we were so close and moving so fast that everything below us turned into a reddish blur.

We must have gone nearly a third of the way around the planet before we slowed enough that I could make out features of the landscape again, closer now, and clearer. The land darkened as we moved away from the sunlit side, but whether it was just before sunrise or just after sunset, I wasn't sure. I saw another likely flat spot in the twilight but we passed that, too, then descended into what looked like an impossibly small depression between three rocky peaks.

Just like in Bailerealta, a bright X appeared on the ground, then four triangular panels receded to reveal an opening that barely looked big enough to accommodate the *Quintessence.* I wondered if they used some kind of tractor beam, or if the pilot had to be that good. Either way, we descended smoothly through the portal, then down a long, long shaft.

A complicated-looking landing area below us grew larger and larger but before I could quite pick out details, the viewscreen suddenly went blank. A few seconds later there was an almost imperceptible jolt which I assumed meant we'd landed.

"Whoa," was all I could find to say.

Yeah. Pretty awesome, came Rigel's voice in my head. I turned slightly and saw him a couple of rows back, near one of the exits.

When did you come in? I was amazed I hadn't noticed, though I realized now that I did feel better than when I'd arrived.

That was *a pretty big distraction,* he pointed out. *Especially the part when we—*

He was cut off by the Captain's voice, coming from the speakers overhead. "Disembarkation will commence momentarily. Your belongings are already being transferred to the arrivals lounge, where they can be retrieved once you in-process. You will leave the ship by level and section, so please listen for your group to be called. Thank you for traveling aboard the *Quintessence.*"

So, did Mr. O tell you? I thought quickly to Rigel as everyone undid their harnesses.

Late last night. You must have been pretty convincing to get him to agree. Thanks!

I had a lot of incentive.

"What did you think of that?" Sean asked with a grin.

"Pretty awesome." I resisted the urge to look back at Rigel. "What was your landing on Earth like?"

"A lot bluer, but also awesome." He chuckled. The landing seemed to have improved his mood. "You nervous?"

"A little. I wish I could just blend in with the crowd and avoid all the craziness."

"I wish you could, too, but it'll be okay. If they don't love you right off, you'll win them over." He sounded a lot more certain than I was.

The first announcement came a moment later, clearing Level One—me—to disembark. I stopped to say goodbye to Jana, since she wouldn't be leaving the ship. She surprised me by smiling—the first real smile of hers I'd seen.

"It has been my great honor to serve you, Excellency, though I regret the circumstances that made it necessary. From what I now know of you, I have no doubt this will prove only a temporary setback. *Faoda byo Thiarna Emileia.*" Fist over heart, she bowed, and I could have sworn I saw the glimmer of a tear in her eye as she turned away.

Drawing some much-needed confidence from her reaction, I turned to the others with a determined smile. "Okay, let's do this."

24

Arregaith

ARREGAITH (AH-REE-GAYTH) (POP. 1,413): *town in southeastern Nuath containing spaceport and supporting industries*

Rigel fell into step behind me as we left the Commons. The four of us headed down the short corridor to the outer hull, where Captain Liam waited to bow his farewell. I thanked him warmly, then stepped through the portal, shoulders back and head high, determined to appear every inch a Sovereign.

My first impression of Nuath was a brightly-lit expanse the size of a football field and a wall of noise—the roar of a huge crowd standing behind a shiny barrier twenty yards from the ship. I paused at the top of the ramp, taking in the scene and gauging the mood of the crowd. To my relief, most seemed to be cheering, though a few shouted things that sounded vaguely hostile and there were two signs reading "*Na ga Rioga*" near the back—anti-Royals.

Vehicles of various sizes and shapes crisscrossed the area between us and the crowd, silently piloted toward different sections of the ship by official-looking people in red bodysuits. None of the cars, trucks or flatbeds seemed to quite be touching the ground. The underground landing area consisted of an enormous cavern with towering walls of pinkish-gray, punctuated by tall windows and occasional gaps in the wall wide enough for vehicles to pass through.

I was about to continue down the ramp when four men I hadn't immediately noticed in the confusion stepped forward to greet us. All wore silvery body suits under dark gray short pants with shoulder straps and holsters, very similar to Rigel's Bodyguard uniform. They also wore extremely serious expressions. At the foot of the ramp they stopped and bowed.

"Greetings, Excellency," said the tallest of the four, whose uniform had a star-shaped emblem on the right shoulder. "I am Kernan, acting Minister of Security, and these are three of my most trusted officers. As you can see, emotions are running high due to your arrival, so I thought it best to secure the landing area in order to guarantee your safety. We will escort you to the Arrivals Lounge."

"What about us?" came Gordon's panicked voice. I glanced back and saw that all the other Royals had come up behind us while I'd hesitated. "We were assured we'd be safe before booking passage. No one mentioned organized protests against Royals. I demand a security escort!" A few others nodded worriedly.

Suddenly realizing this could be my first chance to demonstrate leadership on Mars, I stiffened my backbone and my resolve and turned to the Royals behind me. "Please, everyone, calm down," I said, using a bit of "push." "You don't want to upset the other passengers, do you?"

Then, to my small welcoming committee, "Perhaps we should go someplace a bit more private so that you can tell us exactly what the current situation is."

Kernan was visibly relieved. "I completely concur, Excellency. Thank you. If you—all of you—will follow me?" He and his men led us across the broad floor of the cavern at an oblique angle to the crowd, which continued to shout and cheer. I smiled and waved as we approached. The cheers increased in volume and the shouts grew noticeably less hostile. Maybe I could win these people over after all.

As we continued walking, now away from the corralled throng, what I'd taken for walls resolved into individual buildings packed closely together, with occasional narrow streets between them. I looked around eagerly, taking in the crystalline look of some of the buildings, the thin strips of metal criss-crossing the darker pinkish-gray pavement beneath our feet.

With a start, I realized that we weren't in a cavern at all—we were outdoors! Something in the quality of the light, subtly different from real sunlight, had made me assume otherwise. Well, that and the knowledge that we were a mile or more underground. I looked up and instead of the dark shaft I'd half-expected, I saw an amazingly real-looking sky—blue, with thin wisps of cloud. There was no visible sun, so I glanced down at my shadow to figure out where the "sunlight" was coming from. I didn't have one. At all. Huh.

Yeah, definitely weird, Rigel agreed from behind me. *So, can we trust these guys?*

Oops. Feeling both foolish and guilty for not checking sooner, I focused my new ability on Kernan and his companions. What I sensed reassured me: concern, determination, and a fair bit of awe, presumably over meeting me. The only "bad guy" vibe I picked up from our whole group came from Gordon, and him I already knew about.

They seem okay,

We approached a building and the doors automatically whispered open to reveal a large, high-ceilinged room with a counter running along one wall. Two red-uniformed people stood behind the counter, presumably to in-process the arrivals, while a few others unloaded suitcases from a cart floating just off the floor.

Our group bypassed the counter to go through another door at the opposite side of the lounge, this one palmed open by Kernan. This was a sort of conference room, with a long oval table surrounded by more than a dozen chairs. We all sat, Sean on my left, his father on my right and Molly on her father's other side, still looking a little scared. Rigel stood behind me.

Kernan also remained standing, at the head of the table. "First, let me assure you all, and particularly you, Excellency, that we don't foresee the slightest danger to any of you. Cordoning off the crowd was merely a precaution, until we can gauge the strength and size of this new anti-Royalist movement, or 'Populists,' as they've begun calling themselves. Until today, we've considered them too small and disorganized to worry about. The Princess's arrival appears to have unified them somewhat, but I expect they will disband in short order, once they realize how little support they have from the general population—as all polls indicate is the case."

"What alerted you in time to set up the barriers?" Mr. O'Gara asked.

Kernan looked grave again. "Three hours ago the power across all of Nuath failed for a few seconds. Emergency backups kicked in for all critical systems, so the populace was never at risk. Still, this failure lasted twice as long as the one last month—long enough to be generally noticed, unlike the first one. These anti-Royalists immediately claimed responsibility, though we have not yet been able to ascertain how or if they could have done this."

"Such a thing shouldn't be possible." Devyn sounded almost angry. "Our Engineers have put in so many safeguards, so much redundancy, that the backups should never even be necessary." Several others nodded, some looking frightened.

Mr. O frowned. "Do you think it really was the anti-Royalists?"

"Personally, I think it unlikely. Not until after today's outage did they begin taking credit, saying it was a warning, an illustration of how the Princess's return bodes ill for Nuath. Whether they were responsible or not, they used it to bring more attention to their agenda."

Kernan glanced at me. "Having grown up on Earth as you have, Excellency, you may not fully appreciate how very frightening the prospect of a power loss is to our people. Ah, *your* people," he amended. Gordon shifted in his seat. "Indeed, I imagine they are far more worried about the possibility of future outages than about any political conflict."

That made perfect sense to me. "What worries *me* most is how many more of these anti-Royals are scattered throughout Nuath and how they'll react to my being here."

"Their numbers cannot be large, Excellency. Certainly not when compared to those eager for your Acclamation. In any case, I can assure you that my Ministry is fully prepared to ensure your safety for the duration of your stay. Can you give me an idea of how long that will be?"

"Not yet." Since no one had told *me* yet! "It will depend on how things, um, progress." I looked to Mr. O'Gara for confirmation and he nodded.

"The original plan was for the Princess to spend most of the current launch window on Mars. Of course, should her safety be in question, that plan would have to change."

Gordon apparently couldn't contain himself any longer. "And what about *our* safety? It's possible that every Royal on Mars is at risk! I demand a security detail. For every one of us." Though that last bit was obviously added as an afterthought, most of the other Royals muttered their agreement.

"That shouldn't be necessary," Kernan assured them. "None of the Royals already on Mars have been directly threatened in any way. Those who survived Faxon's depredations unharmed have stepped up in recent weeks to help with our recovery under the direction of Interim Governor Nels Murdoch. If anyone were going to be targeted, it would be him."

"And the Princess," Mr. O'Gara added. "Given this development, I assume you will assign extra security for the duration of her stay?"

Kernan nodded. "Cormac, here, has volunteered to act as her personal Bodyguard." He gestured toward the burly man on his left, then glanced at Rigel. "Of course, if she already has—"

"No, that will be fine," Mr. O broke in decisively. "Under the circumstances, someone more experienced seems wise. Rigel here can still be a part of her security detail, as he has proven himself both motivated and well trained to protect the Sovereign."

"Surely you can't—" Gordon broke in indignantly, but I interrupted before he could say any more.

"*You* have no say in the matter." I was startled by how authoritative I sounded. And though Gordon glared, he did shut up...for the moment.

Kernan's omni lit up in his hand and after a quick, low-spoken exchange, he smiled. "How very timely. The protesters have been segregated from the crowd for questioning and our investigators have determined that there is no immediate threat to *anyone's* safety, to include the Princess's. If you'll come this way, Excellency, we will shortly have you and your party settled in Tullymayne."

⁘

We all followed Kernan back to the big check-in area, where passengers from the *Quintessence* were claiming their luggage and waiting to be processed. I was expedited through, along with the O'Garas and Rigel, and Kernan led us all out a side door while the other Royals were still in line.

A long, brightly-lit hallway ended in an area nearly as large as the courtyard around the ship, only this one enclosed half a dozen sleek, futuristic-looking trains, all lined up across the middle. When I looked closely, I saw that, like the vehicles and luggage carts, they were suspended about six inches off the ground. I remembered then what Sean had told me about the trains here.

"The *tapacarrs*, ah, zippers, were temporarily deactivated as a security precaution. They'll resume running shortly, but this one will take us to Tullymayne before it's put back into general service." Kernan led us to the first train as he spoke.

A door that had been invisible a moment before slid open with a soft hiss. I followed Kernan inside, Cormac and Rigel immediately behind me. The other two security guys loaded our bags onto the train, then did a quick sweep of the car with little hand-held gadgets. One nodded to Kernan, who turned to me.

"The coach is secure, Excellency. This trip will be very brief, but please make yourself comfortable."

I took a window seat and Sean, of course, sat beside me. As the zipper started to move, I looked fixedly out the window while "talking" to Rigel, who was seated with Cormac behind me.

You okay with playing backup to that guy?

I guess, as long as you trust him. It's a heck of a lot better than either of us expected this time yesterday, he replied practically. *Shoot, I'd take a job as your janitor, if it meant staying close to you. This way I can still protect you. Officially.*

A not-quite-Earthly city scene flashed past outside, too quickly for me to notice much except that it seemed much cleaner than any Earth city and most of the buildings were of that same pinkish-gray stone, which I assumed must be the primary construction material here. The buildings thinned slightly, then grew denser again, and a minute later we slowed to a stop in another depot even bigger than the one we'd just left.

"Wait. Are we there already?" I asked, startled.

"Yep." Sean smiled for the first time since leaving the ship. "Tullymayne is the main transport hub, so it's only a mile or so from Arregaith. Here in the south, the towns and villages sort of flow into each other except for where the mines are."

I knew from studying Nuathan geography that the south was mostly industrial and was more densely populated than the northern, more agricultural region. I hadn't realized things were *this* close together, though.

"Doesn't look much like Ireland," I commented, remembering

what the O'Garas had originally told me about Nuath last fall. "I haven't seen so much as a blade of grass yet."

"Wait'll we get to Glenamuir. The north is totally different. You'll love it."

Before I could reply, Kernan ushered us off the train and toward a silver, bullet-shaped vehicle with a fancy logo on the side. Like the zippers, it hovered just off the ground. A few people were hurrying to various trains, probably trying to make up for lost time now that they were running again.

"No tracks?" I glanced back at all the trains, then ahead to our bus or van or whatever it was.

"Magnetic ones, but they're buried," Sean said. "They crisscross pretty much all of Nuath so the zippers and other transports can use them. I told you about that."

"Oh, right, sorry. It's all kind of—"

"Overwhelming?" He chuckled. "Don't worry, I'll explain everything as we go."

I sensed Rigel's irritation from behind me and stifled a sigh, wishing the tension between him and Sean could have been left back on the ship. Cormac climbed into the driver's seat of the floating transport while the other security guys transferred our bags, then bowed to me and left us. I got in, followed by the others.

"When will I be able to see Thiaraway?" I asked Kernan as Cormac maneuvered the hover-thingy out of the huge transportation depot. "Do I have to be formally Acclaimed first?"

"That's the tradition, but I'll be very surprised if that doesn't happen within the next day or two. That power interruption this morning will make people even more eager to have a proper Sovereign in charge again."

"That would be…excellent," Mr. O'Gara said from behind me, his hesitation echoing my own doubts. It *would* be great if I could get Acclaimed before the news about that video broke big time, but it seemed awfully unlikely.

Though shorter, distance-wise, this trip took longer than the first, since we had to go slower to navigate the confusing maze of buildings. Along the way, people stared at our van, then gathered into small, excited clumps. That logo must have told them who was inside. Of course, I did my share of staring, too, especially at the clothing they wore, subtly different from anything I'd seen on Earth.

The women mostly seemed dressed in colorful tunics over flowing, wide-legged pants, while the men wore bodysuits in shades of gray, brown and blue under knee-length pants and tunics shorter than the women's. A few wore ornate hats that glinted with metal or crystal embellishments.

Finally we stopped in front of a tall building that looked like a fancy hotel. A crowd immediately started to gather, some holding up omnis, probably taking pictures or videos. I was starting to worry I'd be mobbed when I got out when two large panels separated at the base of the hotel and Cormac drove us right into a tunnel. Glancing back, I saw the doors slide shut behind us, leaving the crowd outside.

"Cool," I muttered. "Like the entrance to the Bat Cave."

Beside me, Sean chuckled again. "There's stuff way cooler than that. I can't wait to show you."

I expected an underground parking garage but the tunnel ended in a lot only big enough for a couple of vans the size of ours. Sean handed me out and the others followed, while Kernan and Cormac unloaded our bags onto a waiting cart. Kernan then applied his palm to the hotel door and punched a code into the little holo-screen that popped up. The door opened to reveal a smallish, plushly-carpeted room that I belatedly realized was an elevator.

"Excellency?" Kernan bowed to indicate I was to precede him while Cormac took up the position behind me that should have been Rigel's.

The elevator only went up what felt like one floor, though at this point I wasn't willing to assume much of anything. The doors opened into a huge, gorgeous room with several sofas and scattered plush chairs, as well as numerous glass tables of various sizes, to include one at the far end that was big enough to seat two dozen people. Hotel lobby, I guessed, though I didn't see anything like a reception desk.

Kernan's next words proved I was making assumptions again. "This is the main living level. Your quarters are on the top floor, Excellency. There are twelve others on the two floors below, each with private bath. Kitchen is through there, recombinator fully stocked. Unless you'd prefer a human cook?"

"Sir?" Cormac frowned.

"Yes, I know you consider that a security risk, but it should be the Princess's choice." Kernan turned to me questioningly.

"Um, the recombinator is fine."

Molly was gazing around, her eyes wide. "Wow, and I thought your quarters on the ship were posh," she murmured. I felt the same way, but thought it might sound un-regal to say so.

"Before I go, Excellency, I need to give you this." Kernan held out a metallic red omni. "If you'll place your thumb here?" I did so and he gave the omni a complicated series of taps, after which a green light flashed from the end.

"There. It is now coded to your touch. No one else can access it, to include me. You will want to create a code—it can be spoken or keyed in—that you'll only share with a few trusted people, such as Mr. O'Gara. Anyone not using the code will be diverted to Mr. O'Gara's omni or to *techtract*, ah, voicemail, which I recommend you also have forwarded to Mr. O'Gara or an aide, for sorting. For non-private calls you can bypass the security settings, which I don't recommend, or use any vidscreen."

I nodded, staring at the device in my hand. My very own omni! This was *way* cooler than any cell phone. "Thank you," I said composedly, though I felt more like squealing.

Kernan proceeded to show me the omni's basic controls, then said, "As you now have both Cormac and your former Bodyguard here for security, may I have your permission to return to Thiaraway? There are still a few details to sift through in our investigation of the anti-Royalists."

"Oh! Of course. I'm sorry to have kept you from your job for so long already."

He smiled. "*Your* safety is my primary job, Excellency, and the main focus of my Ministry. But as this other matter may impact that, it is also important. I look forward to your speedy Acclamation and hope to see you in Thiaraway within a day or two." He nodded to the others, bowed to me, fist over heart, and departed, leaving Cormac the only stranger in our midst.

The moment he was gone, Mr. O pulled out his omni. "Let's see what the *grechain*, er, networks are saying, shall we?" He touched the omni to a faint blue circle on the oval glass coffee table and a rectangular screen several feet across materialized on the opposite wall.

I'd heard Nuathan communications had been disrupted and spotty since Faxon's overthrow. Would that maybe delay the scandal from the ship hitting the news? I braced myself as the screen lighted.

"—to us from the streets of Thiaraway itself," came a woman's voice, the screen showing a milling crowd of people. "Gaynor?"

"Yes, Moya, the mood here is extremely upbeat." A handsome man, obviously the reporter, now smiled from the screen. "To a person, the people of Thiaraway seem more than ready to welcome our new Sovereign home. Ma'am, what is your opinion about the return of our long-lost Princess? Are you ready to vote for Acclamation?"

The camera shifted to a dark-haired woman who was nearly bouncing with excitement. "I think we all are, Gaynor! Princess Emileia couldn't have come at a better time, with people spooked by that outage and all. Her return is just what everyone needs. What we've all prayed for ever since learning she's still alive!"

"Thank you. Sir?"

A middle-aged man appeared, smiling broadly. "You bet! My family is planning a celebration tonight, and we're counting the minutes until the call for Acclamation goes out, keeping our fingers on the 'aye' button."

"And that's been the story since I arrived here, Moya. What are your panelists saying?"

I was relieved when Mr. O'Gara switched to a different channel. All those strangers acting like I was some kind of savior weirded me out.

It's only going to get worse, Rigel remarked silently.

This channel seemed to be a series of text screens showing recent poll results—polls about everything from changes in the zipper schedule to willingness to restrict water usage. I remembered reading that the networks had become increasingly poll-driven before Faxon co-opted them all. Apparently they'd already reverted to that prior fixation on polls.

Mr. O flipped through the various poll screens until he found the one he was looking for: "Vote to Acclaim Princess Emileia as Sovereign?" Latest results stood at a whopping 91.3% in favor.

"That's it! We need to move quickly." Mr. O'Gara whipped out his omni. "I'll instruct the acting Elections Minister to arrange for an immediate vote. We may pull this off after all."

25

Tullymayne

TULLYMAYNE (TULL-EE-MAYN) (POP. 1,993): *town in southeastern Nuath containing main transportation hub and supporting industries*

While his dad spoke rapidly into his omni, Sean jumped up. "I don't know about anyone else, but I'm starving. Let's try out the recombinator in this place."

The rest of us followed him into the kitchen, which was super futuristic, with gizmos I hadn't even seen in Bailerealta. But still less bizarre than me being the top news story.

Sean started scrolling through the holo-menu of the recombinator. "Wow, I thought the selection on the ship was good, but this is amazing!"

Molly touched her brother's arm. "Excuse me. M, um, Princess, what would you like for lunch?" she asked pointedly, making Sean blush. "You can pretty much name it."

I tried not to grin since Sean was already embarrassed. "How about a cheeseburger and a side salad? Ooh, do they have Diet Coke?" They did. I usually drank tea, but right now I craved good old American cuisine.

Molly punched in my order and about ten seconds later my lunch slid out through the slot. I'd been told how it worked, but it still seemed more like magic than science. But then, so did microwave ovens.

I dutifully waited for Cormac to taste all my food before digging in, by which time the others had joined me. *Hey, silver lining,* I thought to Rigel. *I can eat broccoli again without you having to taste it first.*

Sucky tradeoff, but I'll take it. He felt more cheerful than he had in a long time. Those amazing poll numbers had boosted all our spirits.

"Cormac, you can sit." I figured I might as well be consistent. "Please," I added when he hesitated.

Though clearly uncomfortable, he complied, taking the chair to my right, while Molly moved down one. Sean, as always, sat on my left, with enough on his plate to feed a small village. Rigel sat across from me, his plate just as full. Where did boys *put* so much food?

A smiling Mr. O'Gara joined us a moment later to say that arrangements were being made for me to declare for Acclamation within the next two hours. "Once the announcement goes out, the vote can be held within twenty-four hours. You're as good as Acclaimed, Excellency!"

While they ate, he and Cormac talked about recent political developments, like the appointment of acting ministers and an interim legislature cobbled together from respected members of the Science *fines* and the few unimpaired Royals remaining on Mars when Faxon was ousted. I tried to listen, but my attention kept drifting to things like how close together my bedroom and Rigel's would be and the boggling idea that I might be heading to the Royal Palace—and the Grentl device—as soon as tomorrow.

"I'll turn the news back on, if you don't mind, Excellency?" Mr. O said as we finished.

I tried not to cringe visibly. "Sure, but…I'd rather you not call me that in private. Any of you."

He smiled back and nodded understandingly. Cormac raised an eyebrow but didn't say anything as Mr. O'Gara brought up the vidscreen again.

Sean plunked himself down on the big couch and looked up at me hopefully, but I elected to remain standing. Rigel silently assured me he was fine with me sitting there, but I could tell he really wasn't.

We caught the tag end of a press conference with the acting Minister of Energy assuring everyone that this morning's power outage had been an isolated glitch and that no one need worry about a repeat of it. Remembering what Kernan had said, I doubted both statements. After that, they launched into yet another report on my arrival, this one focusing on what I'd been wearing, of all things.

The frivolous story had barely begun, however, when the vidscreen abruptly switched to the same reporter we'd seen earlier, Gaynor, looking extremely serious and concerned.

"We interrupt this story with some disturbing news. Almost as soon as the first passengers from Earth in over two years disembarked, certain rumors began to spread, but we at Nuathan News Network pride ourselves on reporting fact, not rumor. Now, however, two different passengers have come forward with video evidence that substantiates those rumors. While we are not yet authorized to release those videos, it is feared that our much-heralded Princess may have flouted tradition by engaging in a romantic relationship with her Bodyguard, Rigel Stuart. Moya, what do you think this will do to her chances for a quick Acclamation?"

A blonde woman appeared on-screen, her expression even more worried than Gaynor's. "I'm afraid this revelation will come as a serious shock to many, Gaynor. You heard how upbeat everyone was earlier. This could trigger a dramatic shift in opinion. Earliest polls indicate that most want proof before condemning Princess Emileia out of hand, but unfortunately it appears that proof may be forthcoming very shortly."

"That's right, Moya." The camera switched back to Gaynor. "Informatics Engineers are working now to verify the authenticity of those videos, though the odds of two separate hoaxes matching so closely seem extremely small. Assuming those omni-made videos are validated, their publication should quickly be approved by the Interim Governor's office, in keeping with the new policy of transparency."

I turned to Mr. O in dismay. "Will they really show that video on the *news?*"

"They'll have no choice," he said grimly. "I knew word would filter out, but didn't realize the vid itself had been captured on private omnis. Because of Faxon's secrecy and abuse of the media, there is now strong public sentiment in favor of sharing everything openly, especially anything pertaining to the government. The networks obviously take their role in that process seriously."

Great. "So much for me declaring for Acclamation tonight. How long before reporters start demanding answers and interviews?"

As if in answer, Mr. O's omni beeped. He put it to his ear, then snapped, "No, I'm sorry. The Princess has no comment at this time." He broke the connection. "I won't be able to hold them off long. We'll need to decide—" His omni beeped again. "The Princess is resting from her voyage," he informed whoever was on the other end. "She'll release a statement soon."

Between the calls that now came in every few seconds, he reminded me that every town, village and *fine* had its own news feed. The "official" one we'd been watching was the most widely viewed, but the smaller outlets all liked to gather their own news and put their own spin on it.

"That could work to our advantage if we can sway enough smaller channels to throw their support behind you despite this issue. The Nuathan Network relies heavily on the polls, so if the overall numbers start shifting in your favor, they're likely to adjust their stance to match." His omni beeped again before I could point out that the reverse would also be true.

Might as well hope for the best until we know otherwise, Rigel thought, but he felt as tense as I did.

I was about to suggest we go upstairs and unpack, hoping for a lengthier private "conversation" with Rigel, when Mr. O suddenly replied to a caller with something other than his pat response.

"You are? I see. Yes, she'll meet with you. How soon can you be here? Very well, we'll see you in a moment." He hung up and turned to me. "This is someone you do need to talk to, but not about this matter on the news. For that, you'll need some preparation."

"Who—?"

"A Communications Engineer from Thiaraway." The significant look he gave me cleared up my confusion. "Eric Eagan."

∴

A chime sounded and Cormac went to the the fancy front door—the one we hadn't used—and returned escorting the oldest-looking Martian I'd ever seen. His snow-white, wispy hair and deeply lined face, made him appear far older than Shim, though his short stature and general air of frailty made him much less imposing.

As soon as he saw me he bowed deeply. "Excellency. Thank you for receiving me. I am greatly honored." His voice also held a quaver I'd never heard in Shim's.

"Thank you for coming, Mr. Eagan. Where can we talk privately?" I asked Mr. O.

Sean and Molly both looked confused and Cormac took a step forward. "Excellency, I must protest. Your security—"

"Is not at risk right now, Cormac, but thanks for your concern. Mr. Eagan and I need to discuss matters that are, um, classified. The *Echtran* Council on Earth was clear that I wasn't to talk about them in front of *anyone* except him." I almost added that Eric didn't look like much of a physical threat, but thought that might sound insulting.

"There is a small conference room on the floor above this one," Mr. O'Gara suggested. "I'd better remain here to field calls." He sounded regretful—and felt avidly curious. "Cormac can wait at the foot of the stairs in case you need him."

Though Cormac didn't look happy with that arrangement, he didn't argue. Indicating that Eric should follow me, I headed up the curving staircase with a silent promise to Rigel that I'd fill him in later. Eric and I entered the conference room, right off the landing, and I closed the door. "Sorry. Cormac is a little overprotective."

"Quite properly so, given that all our hopes rest upon you, more than anyone yet realizes. Is this room secure?"

"As far as I know. Do you mean it might be...bugged or something?"

Eric pulled a tiny black box out of his pocket and handed it to me. "Let us be certain. You will be able to sweep the room much more quickly than I can, Excellency, if you don't mind? This will emit a warning if any listening devices are present."

I took the box from him and walked around the room, waving it in front of me. I felt a little silly. Finally he motioned me to the table.

"That will do. Thank you." I handed the detector back to him and he pocketed it again. "After three centuries of secrecy, it wouldn't do to slip up now, when it might do the most harm. Shall we sit?"

I took the chair farthest from the door, just in case Cormac decided to stand guard in the hallway after all and Eric moved more slowly to take the seat next to me.

"How much were you told before leaving Earth? I take it you know about the Grentl, the device?"

Remembering what I'd been told so far, a little thrill of fear went through me. "Yes, but not many details. Just that the device is at the Royal Palace in Thiaraway and supposedly only I can use it. And that if I don't somehow respond to the Grentl soon they might do something awful, though nobody said exactly what."

"I'm afraid I didn't dare send much information to your Earth Council, even encrypted. But now you are here, I can tell you everything I know."

"Did…you know my grandfather, Sovereign Leontine?" I couldn't resist asking.

"Of course. And his mother, Sovereign Aerleas. In fact, I was in the room with her when she first imprinted on the device and have kept the secret of the Grentl ever since. No one else alive knows as much about the workings of the device, which, unfortunately has made me irreplaceable."

That meant Eric had to be well over three hundred years old—*definitely* older than Shim. Wow.

"Unfortunately?" I echoed.

He inclined his head. "I'd have followed my dear wife to the long home ninety years ago had the Sovereigns not had need of me. It is my hope that once the present crisis is averted, another Engineer can be trained to take my place, and I can go to my long-delayed reward."

I couldn't wrap my mind around the idea of living so long that dying would feel like a reward—but then, I was only sixteen. "So what exactly *is* the current crisis? Did that power glitch this morning somehow make things worse?"

"It would be more accurate to say that the 'glitch,' as people are calling it, brought to light just how dire our situation is."

"So you think these anti-Royalists are more of a threat than everyone thought?"

Eric fluttered a wrinkled hand in the air. "Those foolish protesters had no hand in the power interruption, though it is not surprising they were quick to take credit. We should probably let them. No, it was caused by the Grentl. And it was a warning."

⁘

I stared at Eric in horror. "The *Grentl* did it? How do you know? And *how*? Aren't they, like, hundreds of light years away?"

"The same way they communicate with us, using their quantum

entanglement technology. They made it clear many years ago, back during Sovereign Aerleas's reign, in fact, that the communication device is not the only link they still have with this colony. They also have direct access to our power grid, which they, after all, created. We have never been able to determine how that access works...or how to disable it."

This was feeling less real—but scarier—by the second. "Wait, you mean they screwed around with our power way back then, nearly three hundred years ago? We've *known* they could do that all this time and nobody told me?"

"We have, though by *we* I mean only the Sovereigns, myself, and two other Engineers, both now dead."

"So the *Echtran* Council doesn't know?"

He shook his head and my sudden fury at them died. "It has always been assumed our people would panic were they to learn that an advanced alien race is in direct contact with us. For them to learn that race also has the power to destroy us on a whim would guarantee that panic. Sovereigns Aerleas and Leontine both agreed that secret must be guarded at any cost."

Since it was taking every ounce of control not to panic myself, I got that. Shim would never panic, but remembering Alistair Adair, I had to admit it was just as well the Council hadn't been told.

"Shim Stuart of your Earth Council may guess," Eric continued, as though he'd heard my thoughts. "I remember him from his youth, an extremely bright young man who served a portion of his apprentice-ship under me and therefore knew of the device and the Grentl's exis-tence. Had he remained on Mars, he would have been my top choice for a successor—though I suppose he is getting on in years now, as well."

Though the idea of Shim as a young man was strange, it only distracted me for a moment. "But what's the point of causing power glitches? *Why* would the Grentl want to destroy us?"

I didn't question that they *could*. Without power, Nuath probably wouldn't last a day. A lot less, if the anti-grav supports were all that kept the roof from collapsing.

"I can only tell you that this is how they have expressed their displeasure before. The first occasion was shortly after the device was linked to Sovereign Aerleas, when a Linguist attempted to talk to them despite their prior insistence on speaking only with the

Sovereign. Then, more recently, when they attempted to communicate late in Faxon's reign and received no answer."

"But I thought Faxon did answer them?" I was sure the Council had said so.

"Eventually, but only after two brief power interruptions—which he attributed to the Resistance, which was growing stronger as news of your survival spread."

Nobody had told me about that part—because Eric hadn't told the Council, I reminded myself. "So how did he figure out what was really going on, if hardly anyone knew about the Grentl?"

Eric hesitated, looking troubled. "The room containing the device had long been sealed so that only the Sovereign could access it, though an Engineer was sometimes allowed in to take calibrations and ensure the device was not deteriorating in any way. On learning of the room's existence, Faxon forced entry, then compelled a fellow Engineer to help him access the device."

"How? Couldn't he just have claimed he didn't know anything about it?"

"My colleague did try," Eric said sadly. "He was loyal to the throne, but Faxon's methods were brutal. When he threatened the man's family as well, he capitulated—though Faxon still had him executed for his earlier resistance."

I'd known Faxon was a monster—he'd murdered my grandparents and parents, after all—but this seemed almost worse, since he'd had nothing to gain by the Engineer's death.

"So Faxon got to the device and did...what? I thought only a Sovereign could make it work?"

"Not precisely. Records show that within a decade or two of the device's first activation, our Linguists and Exobiologists were able to establish a very rudimentary means of communicating with the Grentl. But after a few years the Grentl made it clear they wished only to exchange thoughts with Sovereign Aerleas who, in addition to being the spokesperson for our race, also showed an aptitude for the peculiar sort of communication they favor. When Linguists later persuaded her to allow them to again attempt the more direct communication method, the result was very nearly disastrous, both for the Linguist involved and all of Nuath."

"So did they cut power again when Faxon tried to answer them?"

"They did not. I can only speculate as to the reason. Perhaps it was simple curiosity. It had been more than forty years since their last communication, so it's possible they at first assumed he was Sovereign Leontine's successor, though the genetic differences should have quickly told them otherwise. They did not, however, allow Faxon to access the embedded records of prior communications, as he'd hoped to do after learning such existed. Those, it seems, are available only to yourself—the only direct descendant of Aerleas and Leontine."

Now I was more confused than before. "Embedded records? Like…a computer file with some kind of genetic password?"

"A crude way to put it, but yes. You'll understand better after your first communication with the Grentl."

He sounded more confident than I was that I'd get the chance, but I saw no point in saying so. "The Council said that the Grentl somehow took Faxon out. Is that right?"

"Indeed. They allowed Faxon two fairly lengthy sessions with the device, but when he attempted a third, they used the device itself to render him unconscious—much as they did to that Linguist, back in Sovereign Aerleas's time. Fortunately, I was at hand and managed to drag him from the chamber and reseal it before calling upon the assistance of the few other loyalists who remained in the Palace. Together, we imprisoned Faxon and spread word of his overthrow before his own forces had time to react. Without his guidance—or threats—they quickly acceded to the will of the people." He gave me a thin smile.

It was hard to imagine frail Eric dragging anyone larger than a child, but maybe he'd been stronger a few months ago—or was simply stronger than he looked, like most Martians. "So why did they mess with the power this morning? Kernan, the head security guy, said it happened once before, too?"

"More than once, though the earlier ones required sensitive equipment to detect. As before, they appear to be warnings, sent when no one responded to the Grentl's most recent attempt at communication."

"The Council said the device activated again a couple of weeks ago. Did it?"

He shook his head. "I told them that in hopes of hurrying your arrival here, but that proved impossible by then. Not until last month's power interruption did I finally have enough data to predict how long we might have before the next. This morning's outage precisely confirmed my calculations. Now that you are here, we can decide how best to proceed before the Grentl take stronger action."

I swallowed. "How much stronger?"

He regarded me for a long moment with those watery blue eyes, as though gauging how close I was to panicking. "Each power interruption, dating from the very first, in Sovereign Aerleas's time, has been longer than the one before, occurring at ever shorter intervals after an unanswered message. This morning's lasted two point four seconds, long enough to be noticed by the population at large. According to my algorithm, the next will occur within ten days and last more than seven seconds. That will have the potential to cause at least minor damage and will likely cause panic among the populace. The one after that would follow less than three days later and last long enough to compromise the very integrity of the colony's physical structure. It is *imperative* that you be Acclaimed so that you can respond to the Grentl before that happens."

"Ten days?" My voice squeaked and I had a sudden flashback to my birthday party, when I was told how soon I'd be leaving for Mars. "I'll, um, do everything I can," I promised.

His expression softened slightly. "We must hope it is enough. This news about your dalliance with Rigel Stuart couldn't have come at a worse time, unfortunately."

Because so many secrets were being shared in this room, I decided to share another.

"It wasn't…isn't…a dalliance. Rigel and I are *graell* bonded. We have been since shortly after we met, seven months ago."

I waited for the usual disbelief, but it didn't come. Instead, Eric nodded his white head. "Yes, I remember a flurry of rumors when the news first came that you were alive. Most discounted that one, of course, but I've lived a long time and seen many things most people would not believe. I trust you would not make such a claim if it were not true."

"Thank you." I felt a rush of relief. "Everyone else who knows—the O'Garas, the whole *Echtran* Council—wants to pretend it never happened."

A thin hand grabbed my wrist with surprising strength and Eric's pale blue eyes burned into mine. "And so must you, Princess! At least until after you are Installed as Sovereign. You *must* gain access to the Royal wing of the Palace and appease the Grentl."

I started to protest, but he only tightened his grip. "You are young. If all goes well, you will have many, many years, more than you can now grasp, to live out whatever dreams you have. But if it does not—" he paused, commanding my absolute attention— "*no one* will have that opportunity."

26

Grechain

GRECHAIN (GREE-SHAYN): *Nuathan information network, both personal and mass-media; news channels within the greater* grechain

Eric asked for my secure code before leaving, forcing me to make one up on the spot. In a rush of nostalgia for those earliest days with Rigel, before everything got so scary and complicated, I blurted out, "Cornfield." Eric nodded, then synched my omni with his so I could easily reach him.

"Only contact me when you cannot be overheard," he cautioned, "and leave no unencrypted messages. None should be necessary, as I will have this on me at all times. Should the Grentl device activate again, I will of course contact you immediately."

"Thank you." I stood, holding out my hand—something I knew held particular significance from a Sovereign, an extreme level of trust.

Even though he had grabbed my wrist before to make his point, he hesitated before taking my hand. "My honor, Excellency. I know you will do great credit to your noble forebears. I feel it in my old bones." Stepping back, he bowed deeply.

We went back downstairs to find Cormac standing rigidly on the bottom step and the others standing around, looking nearly as tense.

"What?" I asked. "Did—?"

"Yes, they aired the videos," Mr. O said heavily, muting the vidscreen. "And your approval numbers are dropping even more quickly than I'd feared."

I glanced at Eric, since only he knew exactly how bad that news was, but to my surprise he just smiled. "It sounds as though you have your work cut out for you, sir. As do you, Excellency." He directed a final bow and a last, significant glance my way, then allowed Cormac to show him out.

You okay? Rigel thought to me as they went. I wasn't, and he could tell. I promised again to fill him in later, then turned to Mr. O.

"How far have my numbers dropped?"

He looked grim. "Your approval rating is already below fifty percent and still falling."

That rocked me back on my heels. "That much? That fast? Seriously? How did they even *do* another poll so quickly?"

"The same way they do all of them." Sean shrugged. "Same way they do elections and the way you'll get Acclaimed, eventually. Instant input into the network—everyone has access and a unique ID."

Mr. O'Gara nodded. "I fear our people have always been rather too easily swayed. It's a big reason Faxon was able to do what he did. Instant feedback tends to encourage a bandwagon effect."

I had to remind myself that even with a quarter-million people, Nuath was only the size of a large-ish town on Earth, so what might be impractical or even impossible for the whole U.S. would be much easier here, especially with their advanced technology.

"Well then, we'll just have to reverse that trend. Any suggestions?" I tried to sound matter-of-fact, to keep panic at bay even as my worst fears materialized. How would I ever get to the Palace, to the Grentl device, in time?

"Rise above the rumors, as I said before. It's all you can do. When you're questioned—as you will be—keep everything you say focused on the good of Nuath, on what you hope to accomplish as Sovereign. Don't deny anything that can be proven true, but the less you say about this matter, and the less defensive you sound, the less they'll have to spin against you."

Cormac, returning, nodded his agreement, though I could sense both concern and curiosity from him.

"How long before reporters actually come pounding on our door?"

Even as I asked, the door chime sounded loudly through the room.

"Not long." Mr. O's expression was wry. "Why don't you go

upstairs and unpack while I handle the first onslaught. Sean, Rigel, it's probably best if you go up to your rooms, as well."

Sean looked like he wanted to argue but just said, "Which rooms? Which floor?"

Remembering my earlier hope, knowing it was probably futile, I said, "Can't we all be on one floor? Wouldn't that be safest?"

Mr. O'Gara shook his head as the chime sounded again. "Your suite, which Molly and Cormac will share, is the entire top floor. Sean, Rigel and I can all take rooms on the floor below, if you'd prefer it."

"I would. Thanks."

Since the doorbell was getting more insistent, all of us except Mr. O piled into the elevator with our suitcases and headed upstairs.

⁘

I'd thought my suite on the ship was overkill, but this one was bigger than my aunt and uncle's whole house in Jewel. There were three large bedrooms off the huge, luxuriously furnished main area, while my own bedroom constituted a palatial apartment of its own. The over-the-top opulence was both impressive and slightly appalling.

"Sheesh! All six of us could stay here and still have room for more. Is this somebody's actual house?"

"Not precisely." Cormac set down my big new trunk before returning to the elevator for Molly's bags and his own small satchel. "It's a residence set aside for traveling dignitaries—members of the legislature, primarily. Prior Sovereigns have stayed here on occasion as well."

I regarded Cormac with sudden interest. It was hard to gauge Martian ages, but he wasn't a particularly young man. A tiny bit of gray showed at the temples of his dark hair.

"Prior Sovereigns? Did you know my parents? Or grandparents?"

He nodded. "I was on your grandfather Leontine's security detail and served briefly as your father's personal Bodyguard before he left for Earth." Though his face revealed nothing, I felt a wash of sadness from him.

An answering surge of emotion swelled my own throat. I had to swallow once or twice before finding my voice again. "Can you tell me about them? Not the stuff in books, but what they were really like? I was too young..." I trailed off.

"I remember," he said gently. "You were a…charming baby, Excellency. All of Nuath doted upon you. The news of your supposed death affected the people nearly as profoundly as your grandfather's assassination. It's a pity you never really knew your parents. Your father, Mikal, was extremely intelligent as well as a dynamic speaker, with all the makings of an excellent leader. Sovereign Leontine predicted that his son would outshine him one day, perhaps become the best leader Nuath had ever seen."

"And my mother?" I prodded, overwhelmed at discovering such an unexpected source of information.

Cormac smiled for the first time since I'd met him this morning. "Consort Galena was an amazing woman. Beautiful, of course, but also kind and compassionate. Before Faxon—" he nearly spat the name— "she already had built a reputation as a tireless humanitarian, spending a great deal of her time improving the lot of our less fortunate. How anyone could have—" He broke off, the subject clearly painful to him despite his stoic demeanor.

I totally understood, but I had to ask one more question. "Did… did they love each other?"

He gave a terse nod. "They were both such completely admirable people, how could they not? Even though their joining was a matter of tradition and political necessity, over time they developed great affection for each other."

Turning slightly away to hide the tears I felt threatening, I let out a long, shaky breath. "Thank you, Cormac. I hope you don't mind if I ask more about them later?"

"Of course not, Excellency. It will be my honor to share whatever I can." His voice was gruffer than usual.

Molly awkwardly cleared her throat, clearly affected by the exchange, as well. "I'll, um, go unpack for you."

I followed her into my absurdly huge bedroom, still trying to get my emotions under control. I'd thought learning a little about my parents would make me happy, but it only brought home more forcefully what I'd lost. Maybe, if I'd grown up knowing them—

M? Rigel's thought came faintly, distracting me from my melancholy. Can you hear me?

I can! Are you in the room right under mine?

I think all of our rooms are under yours, since you have the whole fifth floor. I was worried it would be like on the ship—

But it's not! I sent excitedly. *This is great! I can tell you all about—* I broke off when I noticed Molly looking at me strangely. And no wonder, since I'd stopped dead in the middle of the room to stare into space. I gave my head a little shake and smiled at her, then went to help her unpack my clothes.

It turns out this Grentl thing is even scarier than I thought, I continued, putting underthings into a drawer. *After we all go to bed tonight, I'll tell you everything. We can finally talk as long as we want!*

Okay, tonight. Try not to worry till then. I love you, M.

I sent all the love I could back to him. Tonight couldn't come soon enough—especially since the intervening hours would probably suck, what with reporters and political opposition and all. I was glad I had Rigel to look forward to.

Molly unpacked her own stuff while I freshened up in my bathroom, by which time Mr. O had messaged Cormac that we could come back downstairs.

Sean and Rigel joined us in the lift—Rigel and I managed to brush hands for a delicious half-second—and a moment later we were back in the living room. "Did you get rid of the reporters already?" I asked.

"Only for the moment." Mr. O grimaced. "And only because I promised them a press conference first thing in the morning. I told them you were resting from your journey now and could not be disturbed."

"A press conference? I'll have to talk to all of them at once?"

"It's your best chance to start spinning things back our way before your opponents can organize. We'll go over appropriate answers to the questions you're most likely to be asked. I've already made a few notes based on what they were throwing at me outside just now."

Though I cringed at the prospect of facing planet-wide scrutiny so soon, I nodded. "And I should fill you in on what Eric Eagan told me." He might as well know how high the stakes really were.

"Ah, yes. Let's use that same conference room, shall we?"

Sending a silent suggestion to Rigel that he listen in, I gave Mr. O the gist of what the Grentl had done and would likely do if I didn't reply within two weeks. When I finished he was silent for a long moment. I could feel him trying to subdue his horror at this new knowledge.

Finally, he drew a long breath and nodded. "Failure is clearly not an option. Let's get you Acclaimed as quickly as possible, shall we?"

When we rejoined the others downstairs, he was again all business. "The important thing is to prepare you with a few solid talking points that you can go back to anytime things start to get awkward—but without seeming as though you're evading. We can spend the rest of today practicing."

Sean was radiating curiosity, but only said, "Molly and I will hit the recombinator for afternoon tea while you get started."

Though we'd only had lunch a couple of hours ago, I didn't protest. Hot tea might help dispel my chill from the spectre of what failure would mean.

I'll help any way I can, you know that, Rigel promised silently, also sobered by what he'd just learned.

I remembered the awful suggestion Mr. O had made on the ship and quickly shoved that thought away before Rigel could pick it up. *Thanks. Just having you here is a huge help.*

For the next couple of hours, Mr. O threw increasingly difficult—and more insulting—questions at me while I fumbled for answers that wouldn't make me sound guilty or, worse, incompetent. A few, like the most personal ones about Rigel and me, he asked me over and over until I could reply without stammering or blushing.

Sean and Molly kept us supplied with tea and snacks, while Rigel sat at the other end of the table fighting down the anger some of the questions produced. I couldn't blame him. Even hearing Mr. O ask those questions shocked and irritated me. The thought of complete strangers demanding such private information was much worse.

My brain was starting to feel fried when Mr. O stood up and stretched. "Let's take a break, shall we? We should check the latest news stories and polls, in case there's anything else out there you'll have to address tomorrow."

We headed back to the living room and he powered up the vidscreen. I was bringing up the rear, hoping for another chance to brush hands with Rigel, when a familiar voice caught my attention.

"Now, don't misunderstand me," Devyn Kane was saying. Hurrying forward, I saw him sitting at his ease in a comfy-looking chair, being interviewed by Moya. "I found Princess Emileia to be a sweet-natured girl who relates well to people, and certainly not unintelligent. Unfortunately, the incident aboard the *Quintessence* would seem to confirm what so many had already feared: that she simply isn't yet mature enough for the role that has been thrust upon her young shoulders."

Someone behind me, either Mr. O or Sean, hissed with irritation while Rigel growled silently.

Moya nodded gravely. "This news was a shock to all of us, Devyn. Still, the Princess *is* the last—the only—heir to the Nuathan throne. Especially if she chooses a strong Regent, don't you believe that in time she can become what our people need?"

Devyn smiled at the camera, a sad, understanding smile that looked amazingly genuine. "I very much want to believe that, though after Faxon's near-genocide of the Royal *fine*, I fear there are very few qualified candidates for Regent. Given enough time, the Princess *might* possibly find someone she trusts who is both strong enough and experienced enough to guide her through what will undoubtedly be a rocky few years. But, Moya, can Nuath afford to wait? The people have already been without a proper leader for fifteen years. Now, during this difficult time of rebuilding our government, our infrastructure, and our very society, they will surely need a steady hand at the helm from the outset."

Though I'd expected this, a sick knot formed in my stomach. The interview continued for several more minutes, Moya asking questions that almost seemed designed to let Devyn press home the point that the people needed a strong, mature leader *now*. Without ever actually saying anything directly critical of me, he also made it clear that I was not that leader.

Mr. O shook his head in frustration and switched over to the latest polls, which were worse than ever. "We already knew Devyn and others would use your youth and inexperience against you," he reminded me when I cringed at my 33% approval rating. "It's a shame they have this new ammunition, but it also gives us an angle we can use."

We continued watching the news during dinner, Mr. O using his omni to convert one of the big windows in the dining room into a vidscreen. He kept clicking between the various *fine* and local networks, which helped me understand how they differed in style and viewpoint.

The Informatics network was the slickest—not surprising, since those were the computer geeks—and also one of the most sympathetic. Their reporters insisted that outdated traditions were less important than my ability and willingness to lead, though they also seemed open to the idea of a free election for Sovereign. Ballytadhg, a village heavy on the arts, also seemed willing to give me the benefit of the doubt.

At the other end of the spectrum was the People's Network, which Mr. O said was popular with the "lower" *fines* like Mining and Maintenance. They broadcast an interview with Crevan Erc, the main spokesman for the anti-Royal or "Populist" faction. He was now disavowing knowledge of how the power outage had happened, but claimed it still underscored why mere blood was no way to choose a leader.

"When our antiquated hereditary system serves up an untried girl with no knowledge of what it means to be Nuathan," he said, "it is clearly time to change that system. Our very survival may depend on it."

Some of the traditionalists were nearly as bad. One went so far as to hint that both Rigel and I should be charged with treason against Nuath.

The others fell somewhere between those extremes, but momentum was growing for the idea that Nuath's next leader should be chosen from among a handful of "strong, experienced" Royals. Devyn's name was frequently mentioned in that context, as was that of the Interim Governor, Nels Murdoch.

Rigel was almost universally vilified, even by those most strongly in favor of my eventual Acclamation. Sean, by contrast, elicited sympathy everywhere, much to his disgust.

Mr. O pushed his plate away, switched off the feeds and pulled up the notes on his omni. "Looks like we have a lot more work to do." He then resumed his nonstop barrage of questions, punctuated by drill sergeant-like demands to try again every time I stumbled.

Three long hours later, Mr. O'Gara declared that I was as ready as I'd ever be. "Try to get a good night's sleep." He spoke more gently than he had all evening. "Molly, I'll trust you to choose her an appropriate outfit for this. Breakfast at eight."

I was completely wrung out as we all headed up to bed, taking the beautiful, winding staircase this time since we'd been sitting for hours. "I hadn't even thought about what I'll wear. I hope you have some ideas?"

Molly grinned, reminding me she had no idea what was really at stake. "Don't worry. There's lots of great stuff in your new wardrobe."

Nodding absently, I shifted my focus to Rigel, half a landing back. *I hope I can stay awake long enough to talk with you for a while. I've been looking forward to it all day!*

We'll get more chances, he assured me. *Just falling asleep in each others' thoughts will be awesome.*

Once in bed, we did manage to communicate briefly, but I soon felt myself drifting off. Still, it was inexpressibly sweet when the last thing I heard before sleep claimed me was Rigel wishing me sweet dreams.

27

Probalreith

PROBALREITH (PRO-BAHL-RETH): *opinion poll; public opinion*

When Molly tapped on my door the next morning I jerked instantly awake, a delicious, gentle dream about Rigel fleeing beyond recall as dread of my coming ordeal flooded back.

Molly dressed me in a dark gray tailored skirt and silvery blouse that looked a little, but not *too* much like a uniform, and fixed my hair in a conservative, pulled-back style. Rigel sent soothing thoughts up to me the whole time, but I didn't manage more than a *Thanks* in response, I was so nervous by now. The moment Molly declared me ready I headed downstairs.

Mr. O'Gara greeted me with an approving nod. "Good choice, Molly. Very businesslike. A little on the severe side, but that's no bad thing. Do you remember all your talking points, M?"

He ran over a few of the tougher questions again over breakfast, which I was too keyed up to eat anyway. When Sean and Rigel both commented on my abstinence, I promised to make up for it after the press conference.

Then, suddenly, it was time.

"All right, M, come over to this window." Mr. O'Gara's nervousness nearly matched my own, which didn't help at all. "In a moment

I'll switch it to two-way. You'll answer their questions from here. Would you rather stand or sit?"

"Stand. I'll fidget if I sit."

I looked out at the street, only six feet below us. A small, expectant group—the reporters—waited there, with a much larger crowd ranged behind them. It was obvious none of them could see me…yet.

"How does this window work?" I asked, stalling.

"Similar to what I did for the vidscreen last night, just a shifting of electrons in the reactive glass. Sean can give you the details later, if you'd like. Ready?"

I straightened my shoulders, clasped my hands firmly in front of me so no shaking would be visible, and nodded.

Mr. O did something with his omni and immediately I could hear everything from outside as clearly as though the glass had simply disappeared. At the same moment, every head outside swiveled my way.

"Hello, everyone, and thank you for coming." I willed my suddenly magnified voice to stay steady. "I can't tell you how much I've looked forward to finally seeing Nuath and its people with my own eyes. This is a very exciting moment for me."

A murmur swept through the crowd of onlookers, but whether of surprise, excitement or condemnation, I couldn't tell. Some of them bowed, fists over hearts, but not all. Not nearly all. The little group of reporters took a step closer, their expressions so avid I almost took an instinctive step back. Almost. Holding my ground, I spoke again before they could start flinging questions or accusations at me.

"I'm sure you're all aware that my life was as disrupted by Faxon's tyranny as any of yours, and my losses as great. I hope, however, not to dwell on the past, but instead to press forward into a hopeful future. To rebuild Nuath into the land of peace, plenty and dignity that it was before his regime, with an eye to making it even better, a place where every single citizen will have his or her voice heard and needs met.

"To do this, I will need the support of each and every one of you. I realize that you don't really know me yet, but I plan to change that. My goal is to earn your trust, as well as the support I will need to lead Nuath into its best possible future."

That concluded my prepared opening. The final line seemed well received, if not so enthusiastically as in Bailrealta.

"I understand that many of you have questions for me, and I'm glad, as it will help us get to know each other. Yes?"

I nodded to a man up front, who I recognized as Gaynor, the reporter from the main Nuathan News Network. I recognized a few of the others as well, from the various *fine* and local news feeds we'd watched last night.

"Thank you, Princess," Gaynor began respectfully enough. "All of Nuath has been just as eager for your arrival as you have been, and hopeful that you might eventually be able to pick up where Sovereign Leontine so tragically left off."

I smiled slightly and inclined my head, but didn't relax. Just as well, given his next words.

"That is why those videos from the *Quintessence* we've all seen by now are so distressing. I hope very much that you will be able to reassure us by explaining exactly what sort of relationship exists between you and Rigel Stuart, your former Bodyguard."

This was the question Mr. O'Gara had drilled me on most, so I had my answer ready.

"Rigel was the very first person of Martian descent I met on Earth. He and his parents were the ones who discovered my true identity and informed me about Nuath and its people, as well as my own ties and responsibilities to it. When Faxon's followers attempted to kill me, Rigel Stuart saved my life—more than once. I have always considered him a close and trusted friend."

Not the whole truth, but certainly no lie.

"Are the two of you *romantically* involved?" a female reporter near the back called out.

"We dated for a couple of months when I was fifteen." I forced myself to shut up before I could elaborate about the happiest two months of my life. Mr. O'Gara had been adamant that I not volunteer any more than strictly necessary.

"And what about now?" the same reporter persisted. "Those videos of you kissing—"

"As I said, I still consider him a close and trusted friend."

A storm of questions broke out then, along with some derisive laughter from the crowd in the back. I was losing them.

"How does Sean O'Gara feel about this *friendship*?" shouted a blond man I recognized from the Agricultural network. "Was *he* in favor of Rigel Stuart being appointed your Bodyguard?"

"I can't speak for Sean," I replied, grasping at another one of my talking points, "but he has been aware of my relationship with Rigel since meeting me and did not attempt to block his appointment as Bodyguard." Not formally, anyway.

"Will this rekindling of your relationship with Rigel Stuart prevent you taking Sean O'Gara as your Royal Consort, or him from accepting?" a different reporter, a woman, asked.

"I would prefer not to speculate about the future, especially as I have not yet been formally Acclaimed Sovereign."

"But what about that kiss?" the interviewer from the People's Network called out. "You two looked like a lot more than friends in that video."

Palms sweating, I arranged my expression into the solemn, slightly apologetic one I'd practiced last night. "It's true that we were both guilty of a momentary lapse in judgment during the stress of our very first space voyage. It *was* only momentary, however. After being informed last year of the reasons a personal relationship between us would be unwise, we have done our very best to set our early romantic attachment aside for the good of Nuath."

That seemed to go over fairly well. I saw people in the crowd nodding to each other, as though in understanding. But then came the question I'd dreaded most.

"Exactly what happened behind that closed door, Princess? The people have a right to know."

Personally, I thought that was crap. Princess, Sovereign, whatever, I was entitled to *some* privacy! But I couldn't say that. Instead, I repeated the words I'd rehearsed earlier with Mr. O'Gara. "Rigel is not only my good friend, he is my trusted advisor. I needed to speak with him about matters I couldn't discuss openly in front of my *Chomseireach* so that we would be better able to conduct ourselves as was fitting for both of our stations. I regret that I chose to do so in a way that was open to misinterpretation."

Laughter and another storm of questions broke out, some of them downright rude. Among others, I heard, "How physical was your relationship?" "Did Stuart force you?" and "Are you still a virgin?"

To my relief, Gaynor spoke again before my reluctance to answer turned them actively hostile. "I apologize, Princess, for the personal and speculative nature of some of my colleagues' questions, but accusations have been leveled at the media in the past for our failure to dig deeply enough. Given our experiences of the past fifteen years, we can no longer afford to take everything we are told at face value."

"I understand. In fact, I think that's admirable." I projected all the warmth I could, given that my insides churned with ice. "I grew up in a society where the freedom—and persistence—of the press is both guaranteed and expected."

Realizing that I was perilously close to crying or shouting, either of which would be distinctly un-Sovereign like, I abruptly launched into my prepared closing statement before they could ask any more questions.

"Again, thank you all for coming. I understand that my youth is a concern for many of you. I cannot, of course, pretend to be anything other than a sixteen-year-old who only learned of her heritage six months ago, nor will I pretend that coming to terms with my true identity has been easy. What I *can* assure you is that I have now accepted my heritage and have striven to the very best of my ability to prepare myself for the role I was born to assume. I fully intend to continue learning how to best benefit Nuath and its people, not only until I reach adulthood, but for the rest of my life.

"Despite my extremely full schedule, I very much look forward to more opportunities to speak with you, so that we can all get to know each other better."

Another chorus of questions broke out, but I gave the tiny bow I'd been taught for leave-taking and stepped back, ending the press conference. Mr. O'Gara quickly flipped the window to privacy mode.

The second the sound outside was muted, I flopped limply into a chair and looked over at Mr. O and the others, who'd been standing just out of sight the whole time. "Well. That was pretty much a disaster."

"Not a disaster," Mr. O'Gara assured me, though I sensed his disquiet. "You did cut it a little short—certainly much shorter than they'd have liked—and didn't get a chance to use any of your policy talking points, but overall I thought you handled yourself extremely well. That bit about freedom of the press was a particularly nice touch."

Molly, Sean and Cormac also seemed to approve, but it was Rigel I was mainly concerned about and he didn't seem as happy.

You didn't like it? You knew I had to say—

No, it's fine. I know you did. I just don't much like hearing it. You were great, really. It's bound to help your poll numbers.

I doubted that, but turned back to Mr. O. "How soon till we know if it did any good…or made things even worse?"

"Within the hour, I'd say." He switched the window to a vidscreen, like he had last night. "If your numbers go up, we'll try to use the bandwagon effect to your advantage to turn things around quickly. Meanwhile, let's see what the networks are saying."

"And get some breakfast into you," Sean declared. Molly immediately jumped up and headed to the recombinator.

He's right. Eat, Rigel agreed when I started to protest. *Last thing you need is to get weak or cranky, right?*

Once food was in front of me, I discovered I was hungry after all. I ate while we watched the initial reactions to my press conference.

"—well received," a male reporter was saying. "But many are still concerned that this romantic attachment, confirmed by the Princess, will undermine her relationship with her future Consort, Sean O'Gara. Until we receive a statement from him, however, we have no way of knowing how valid those concerns might be."

We all glanced at Sean, who looked startled.

"Now, with more from Tullymayne, we go to Gaynor, who is still interviewing those who were on the spot for the Princess's first-ever press conference."

The picture switched to Gaynor, this house in the background.

"Thank you, Peter. The mood here is slightly more upbeat after the Princess's surprisingly competent performance. Some feel that for a girl of sixteen to display such maturity and poise bodes well for her future—and ours."

Told you you did great, Rigel thought to me with a smile.

"Others, of course, still have strong reservations." Gaynor turned to a bystander, who parroted back some of the insinuating stuff I'd heard shouted just now.

Mr. O'Gara clicked around to some other feeds. The reports were generally more favorable than I'd expected, though there were notable exceptions. When Mr. O's omni started buzzing, he glanced at it, then switched off the vidscreen.

"Interview request. You'll be getting a lot of these today." He wandered into the living room to deal with them while I finished my breakfast, Sean and Rigel both keeping me company with "snacks" that put my breakfast to shame.

Mr. O turned the vidscreen back on when the rest of us returned to the living room and the first story stopped me in my tracks.

"Did Bodyguard Take Advantage of Princess's Innocence?" splashed across the top of the screen in bold letters, followed by what appeared to be a live interview with Rory Glenn.

"Innocence, gratitude, call it what you will," he said angrily to the camera, "but I'll never believe Rigel Stuart didn't know what he was doing, playing on our Princess's vulnerability at a time when her entire world view had been turned upside down. For all we know, he was acting on Faxon's orders to undermine her chances of eventually supplanting that tyrant. How else do you explain two teenagers almost single-handedly fighting off two dozen trained soldiers?"

Before I could even wrap my head around such mind-boggling logic, they switched to someone else, a woman. "Of course Princess Emileia is grateful to Rigel. It's why she's not willing to publicly put the blame on him, where it belongs. I just think it's a shame she met him before Sean, her real destiny. My heart just breaks to think what he must be going through."

My stomach started to roil, making me wish I hadn't eaten so much. Rigel was being made into a scapegoat after all!

"What I want to know," a man was saying, "is whether that Stuart kid compromised our Princess. What if the whole succession has been polluted?"

I gasped. "Turn it off, please. I can't stand to listen to any more of—"

"Wait! Look!" Sean exclaimed, pointing to the lower corner of the screen where an inset showed the latest poll results. My approval rating had climbed to 48%, fifteen points higher than it had been last night—though still a long way from the 80% I needed.

"I know you're not happy with the direction the spin has taken." Mr. O gave me a look I interpreted as *I told you so.* "But it's clearly moving your numbers in the right direction, and quickly. Though your first instinct might be to defend Rigel—"

"You can't," Rigel finished for him in an emotionless voice that belied his anger and humiliation. "He's right. If putting the blame on me will get you Acclaimed, we have to let them do it."

I stared at him helplessly, frustration and panic making it hard to think. The very thing I'd feared if Mr. O suggested his plan to Rigel was happening anyway. I shouldn't, *couldn't* allow it, but if I insisted on telling the truth now, I'd never get Acclaimed and the Grentl would kill us all.

"I'll *only* go along with this if I can reveal the truth—the *whole* truth—the moment I'm Installed as Sovereign." I pinned first Rigel, then Mr. O with the most determined glare I could muster. Out of the corner of my eye, I saw Sean make a gesture of protest, but he didn't say anything.

Good by me, Rigel thought, but Mr. O'Gara was frowning.

"Let's just focus on getting you Acclaimed before we worry about what will follow, shall we?"

I kept my glare in place. "I *won't* let anything happen to Rigel because of this. Not even if it means—" I broke off, but Mr. O grudgingly nodded.

"Very well. We'll do whatever is necessary to keep that from happening. But for the moment it's clearly to our advantage to let the misconception stand. With luck, it won't be for long."

The next two hours proved Mr. O'Gara's assessment true, much as I hated to admit it. My approval numbers continued to rise as public sentiment turned increasingly against Rigel. Almost as disturbing as the calls for Rigel's arrest or punishment were those demanding proof of my "purity."

"What is this, the middle ages?" I huffed after the third mention of that. "There's nothing in Nuathan law about virginity tests for Sovereigns. I mean, I could pass but...ew. Where are they getting this?"

Mr. O shrugged. "No, it's not law, but one reason heirs to the throne have always been encouraged to become acquainted with their intended Consorts at an early age was to prevent any other attachments from forming. I suspect your opponents are behind this new idea, in hopes it will convince the traditionalists to withhold their support."

We kept the news on while Mr. O'Gara sorted through more interview requests on his omni. "You'll need to grant some of these but we'll be selective, start with the interviewers most likely to show you in a positive light." He kept reading, occasionally typing a response—declining the ones I shouldn't accept, I assumed.

After lunch, we caught the end of an interview with Gordon Nolan that confirmed Mr. O's theory on where the "purity" nonsense had come from.

"—also noticed how evasive she was," he was saying to the interviewer. "All Nuathans should be greatly concerned to know whether the Princess has been compromised, physically or emotionally. Our people, and especially our Sovereigns, have always tended to faithful monogamy and it has been repeatedly demonstrated that a strong bond between Sovereign and Consort creates a more effective leader. There is also the succession to consider. I, for one, would very much like to know *exactly* what happened behind that closed door we all saw in the video."

"Nothing happened!" I shouted at the screen, making everyone jump. "Sorry. But I'm not sure I can take much more of this."

Hey, try to focus on how your numbers are improving instead of all this talk show crap, okay? Rigel thought to me comfortingly.

How come this horrible stuff isn't bothering you as much as it is me? I sent back. *Especially since they're insulting you way more than me?*

That's why. Trust me, if it was you they were attacking, I'd be even more upset than you are. Try to chill a little, okay?

Mr. O turned off the vidscreen. "I know it's upsetting, M, but we do need to stay abreast of what's being said so you can more effectively counter it. But perhaps a break is in order. In a few minutes I expect—" He broke off as the door chime sounded.

"More reporters? Already?" I just might throw something at them, the way I was feeling.

"Er, I don't think so. Just a moment."

Mr. O went to the door himself and we could hear him speaking quietly to someone outside. A minute later he returned, accompanied by an imposingly handsome woman who somehow struck me as vaguely familiar, even though I was sure I'd never seen her before. Maybe it was her expression, which reminded me disconcertingly of Aunt Theresa's, whenever she disapproved of something I'd said or done. The woman's auburn hair was threaded with gray, which probably meant she was on the elderly side for a Martian.

"Excellency, everyone," Mr. O said formally, "this is Morag Teague."

The woman bowed to me, fist over heart. "I am most honored, Excellency." She didn't sound honored, though, she sounded pissed.

But that barely registered because at mention of her name Rigel stiffened visibly and I was hit by a blast of shock from him—shock tinged with both eager excitement and fear. Even as I tried to decipher what that could mean, the woman turned her head to look squarely at Rigel.

"I assume you know why I'm here?" she asked him, confusing me further.

He gave her a fleeting, uncertain smile. "It's...it's good to finally meet you...Grandmother."

———————————————————————————————

28

Scar a cheila

———————————————————————————————

SCAR A CHEILA (SCAR AH KAY-LAH): *separated; torn asunder; ripped apart*

Stunned, I looked back and forth between Morag Teague and Rigel. Was this Shim's wife? Hadn't I been told she'd died? Then, with a start, I realized why Morag seemed familiar. She looked like an older —and much more severe—version of Dr. Stuart, Rigel's mother.

I kept expecting Morag and Rigel to hug or at least smile at each other. Instead, after several seconds of uncomfortable silence, Morag spoke again.

"You look even more like your father now than in the picture your mother sent a few years ago. Still, you are my grandson, and therefore my responsibility while you are in Nuath."

She turned to me then with a slightly more pleasant expression, though when I focused I mainly sensed anger and resentment from her. "I must apologize for the role he played in potentially delaying your Acclamation, Excellency. Rest assured I won't allow him to interfere further in matters of state."

"As I tried to tell you, it's not completely—" Mr. O'Gara began, but she waved him to silence with an imperious hand.

"I don't blame you, Quinn. I'm sure you've done your best with him, but recklessness is in his blood, from both sides. Neither of his parents respected propriety or tradition, either."

216

"Excuse me?" Indignation overcame my surprise. "You will please, Madam, not insult Rigel's parents or Rigel himself in my presence. They have all been of great service to me many times over, including saving my life. I owe them a huge debt of gratitude."

Morag inclined her head to me deferentially, though there was no lessening of her anger. "Your defense of them speaks very highly of you, Excellency. No doubt it is that gratitude that prompted you to shield my grandson from the consequences of his poor judgment. But as his natural guardian it falls upon me to ensure nothing of the sort will be necessary again."

"How?" I tried not to let Rigel's growing anger and worry distract me.

She primmed her lips, again reminding me of Aunt Theresa. "I intend to take him home with me to Pryderi before he can do any more harm to your reputation, or to my family's."

"Thanks for your *concern*, Grandmother," Rigel practically snarled, "but I have a job to do here. I'm part of the Princess's security detail."

Morag sniffed audibly. "I'm certain they can find someone far more suitable for that position, Rigel. It has taken seventy years for your mother's flouting of tradition to be forgotten and I will not have it dredged up again because of her son's improper association with someone so completely above his station. As you are underage, you will do as I say. Get your things and let's be gone with no more nonsense."

Rigel started to refuse, but Mr. O touched his shoulder. "Go ahead, Rigel. We don't want more rumors that could damage the Princess further."

Though he looked—and felt—furious, Rigel gave an abrupt nod and headed up the stairs without a backward look.

I'll stop her somehow, I thought after him. Angry as he was, I doubted he could hear me.

"You can't just take him," I told his grandmother the moment he was out of sight. "You don't have the authority—"

"Actually, she does," Mr. O informed me gently.

"How? She can't be his guardian. Both of his parents are alive, even if they're not here on Mars."

"As the eldest member of Rigel's immediate family, Morag is indeed his guardian according to Nuathan law. That would be true even if his parents were here." He paused to let that sink in. "And I believe it *would* be best for Rigel to go with her, given what's being said in the media."

"Not to worry, Princess." Morag gave me a thin smile. "This has in no way altered my intention of voting in favor of your Acclamation. I, at least, hold your lineage in the highest respect."

Implying that Rigel didn't.

"None of this is Rigel's fault," I insisted. "When he and I started dating, no one knew whether I'd ever get to Mars or become Sovereign. And even if I did, Dr. and Mr. Stuart didn't know my supposed traditional Consort was still alive, so they never told Rigel it might be a problem."

"Again, your defense of the Stuart family is commendable, Excellency. I have no doubt you will be a most effective Sovereign in time. However, all question of blame aside, Quinn and I both feel it is best—for Rigel, for you, and, most importantly, for Nuath—that my grandson stay with me from this point on. That will minimize the risk of any further scandal that could imperil your Acclamation."

I turned to stare at Mr. O'Gara. "Wait. You *knew* about this?"

He at least had the grace to look uncomfortable. "Until Morag messaged me a short while ago, I didn't realize Rigel still had relatives living on Mars. I was about to tell you when she arrived. Please, Excellency, remember what is at stake. I'm sure Rigel will agree with our reasoning, once he's calmed down."

A cold fist seized my heart as I realized he was probably right. Feeling blindsided and betrayed, I tried another tack. "Won't you hustling him away only start more rumors? Make everyone assume we really do have something to be ashamed of?"

Morag dismissed that argument with a flick of her fingers. "If anyone asks, I will simply tell them that I desired to become acquainted with my long-lost grandson and that you were gracious enough to allow it. I would suggest you say the same."

"But—" I sensed Rigel approaching and broke off.

"Rigel, your grandmother and I both agree that the best way for you to support the Princess is to go with her now," Mr. O said the moment he appeared. "It will help to defuse speculation and improve her chances of Acclamation."

He stopped on the bottom step, frowning from the two of them to me. *He…he has a point, M. If this can help you get Acclaimed faster—*

"Are you ready, Rigel?" Morag asked briskly before I could respond. "Let's go, shall we?"

He nodded, thinking to me as he joined her, *Will you be safe? Do you trust Cormac?*

Yes. He knew my father and grandfather. But you can't go, Rigel! Maybe if we tell her about our bond? If I get sick, it'll be even harder for me to get Acclaimed or do anything about the Grentl.

It would only make her more determined, Rigel assured me. *Just get yourself Acclaimed before you can get sick, okay? Then maybe I can come back to help with the Grentl. Be safe, M. I love you.*

I looked directly into Rigel's eyes, which reflected the anguish I was feeling no matter how much he pretended it was for the best. *Call me as soon as you can—my secret code is cornfield.*

His grandmother put her hand on his arm to lead him away.

Cornfield, Rigel. Did you hear me?

I felt him struggling to control his emotions enough to communicate and after a few anxious heartbeats he sent back, *Cornfield. Got it.*

I love you, Rigel! Always. We'll be together again soon, I promise! Then I made myself say aloud, "Thank you for everything, Rigel. I hope to see you again very soon." It sounded formal, even cold, after my impassioned silent vow. I saw him wince slightly.

Mr. O, Sean and Molly all said their goodbyes, then Morag Teague and Rigel left while I just stood there, numbly staring after them.

✦

"I, ah, have a list of interview requests to go over with you," Mr. O'Gara said after a moment, breaking the awkward silence.

I rounded on him. "How could you agree to this? Don't you remember what happened when we were apart over Thanksgiving? How am I supposed to convince people I'm a leader if I get that sick again?"

"I agreed because it will help you get Acclaimed. Nothing else is as important right now, you know that. *If* you get sick, we'll deal with it. Right now, we need to line up interviews and appearances so that you can undo the damage that's been done as quickly as possible." There was no compromise whatsoever in his tone—or in his emotions.

"Fine," I snapped, still furious. "Where do I need to be when?"

No one else said a word as he led me back to the table, pulling up his omni screen as he went. "The main Nuathan Network should be first as it has the widest viewership. Regan Ryan has a morning show and a reputation for informal, chatty interviews, so it shouldn't be too adversarial. She has a studio right here in Tullymayne. Ten a.m.?"

"Fine," I said again. I tried to tamp down my anger, telling myself that the quicker I could get Acclaimed, the quicker I'd get Rigel back. And if I *was* going to start feeling yucky, it made sense to do my most important interviews first.

"Excellent. I'll confirm that one." He touched the holo display. "Then I suggest a couple of village square appearances, with moderated questions. Ballytadhg and Glenamuir are the most sympathetic. An Informatics interview would be good as well. They're open-minded and likely to show you in a good light. After that, things could get trickier unless we turn perceptions around quickly."

He proceeded to line up six or seven appearances for me over the next couple of days, a ridiculously tight schedule. I agreed to all of them, doubting I'd stay healthy much longer than that. I hoped I was wrong, for Rigel's sake as well as my own. And Nuath's, of course.

"That will do for now." He closed the display. "Let's see how these go before considering other requests."

We joined the others, who were still watching the interminable news, switching back and forth between live reporting and more in-depth text updates. Nothing much had changed. Some people were making excuses for me while others seemed to think I was unfit to do more than sweep floors. Nearly everyone talked about Rigel like he was some kind of vile seducer. They only disagreed about whether I'd been a willing participant or a hapless victim, either through understandable gratitude or arrant stupidity.

I tried to keep track of which groups held which views so I could do a better job winning over the unsympathetic ones and solidifying support from those already on my side, but my attention kept wandering back to Rigel. Would he even be allowed to contact me? I didn't dare check my omni in front of everyone else, so when Sean announced he was hungry I jumped up.

"I'm going to run upstairs and change before dinner. No, that's okay, Molly, I don't need help. You can stay here too, Cormac. I'll only be a few minutes. Feel free to start without me."

The moment I reached my bedroom, I pulled out my new omni.

Unfortunately, the only message was from Eric, sent half an hour ago. *Heard RS is with grandmother. Wise decision. Stay focused.*

Irritated, I threw the omni on the bed. Was every single person on Mars against us? I yanked off the conservative outfit I was still wearing from my press conference, fuming at the injustice of my whole stupid life. Vowing to get Rigel back whether I got Acclaimed or not, I stalked into the bathroom to splash water on my face and brush my hair into a less severe style.

As I discontentedly pulled on a more comfortable outfit, I suddenly remembered something. Morag Teague *wasn't* Rigel's only relative on Mars. His father had a brother here! Could he help me? Before I even finished that thought, I snatched up my omni from the bed.

"Stuart," I said to it, dredging Rigel's uncle's first name from my memory. "Um, Tor Stuart?"

It was my first time using an omni, so I was a little surprised when it worked. A little holo-screen popped up, showing a man's face. "Excellency?" He looked shocked. "I, ah, wasn't anticipating—"

"No, I know. And I apologize, especially since we've never even met. But you're Rigel Stuart's uncle, aren't you?"

He inclined his head. He was as handsome as Rigel's father—in other words, extremely—but noticeably older. "I am. How can I be of service?"

I quickly explained about Morag taking Rigel away. "Mr. O'Gara says she has that authority, but is there anything you can do to get her to bring him back?"

"I doubt it, Excellency." He looked genuinely regretful. "Her family and mine have not been on speaking terms for over a century, and as Rigel's guardian she has precedence, as the elder. The only person with the authority to overrule her would be Shim, my father, but as he is on Earth—"

Though I'd known it was a long shot, disappointment settled heavily in my stomach. "I understand. Thank you anyway. Um, have a nice evening."

He bowed and I cut the connection, fuming again. If only Shim were here— But all I could do at the moment was go down to dinner.

The others were still in the living room watching the feeds and Sean waved me over to join him on the couch. "Come look! Your numbers are still inching up, though not as fast as before."

I glanced at the vidscreen. Sure enough, my approval rating was now over 50%.

When I didn't sit, Sean stood. "I'm doing my bit to help, too. Dad had me record a statement while you were upstairs and I'm doing a couple of interviews tomorrow. That looks better on you, by the way."

I glanced down at my pants, the closest thing to jeans I'd found, and simple blue blouse. "Uh, thanks. So, dinner?" I wasn't hungry, but Sean's compliment—and the admiration I sensed from him—made me uncomfortable. Better to turn his attention to food, which never seemed far from his thoughts anyway.

While I picked at my meal, Mr. O gave me a rundown on the sorts of questions I could expect during my three appearances tomorrow.

"Be prepared for personal questions, since that's what the media is focusing on right now. Let's practice again how you'll deflect those back to policy issues, shall we?"

After dinner, Sean again urged me to sit next to him on the couch. This time I did. "You didn't eat much," he commented. "You okay?"

"I'm fine." Actually, I could swear I was already feeling the first hints of Rigel withdrawal, but that *had* to be purely psychological. "Just a little tired."

"We'll make sure you get an early night." He reached over to give my hand a light squeeze. "Busy day tomorrow and all."

His hand felt surprisingly warm and comforting around my cold one, but after a moment I eased my hand out of his grasp with an apologetic smile. "Good idea." I turned my attention back to the screen.

My approval rating had inched up another fraction, but there were also opinion polls on every aspect of the "scandal." Mr. O pointed out a new one showing 27% willing to break with tradition to elect someone other than me as leader, followed by a short list of names, each with a favorability rating. The top name was Interim Governor Nels Murdoch, with Devyn Kane in second place. "That's the important one to turn around."

Then I saw a different poll, one that almost made me lose what little dinner I'd eaten. *What penalty should Rigel Stuart face for breaching his oath and defiling the Princess?*

"Penalty? Defile? What the—? How long has that one been up?" I demanded.

"First time I've seen it." Sean frowned in apparent concern, but when I "read" him, I picked up as much satisfaction as worry. "Seems a little harsh."

I stared at him. "A *little?* When Rigel didn't do *anything* wrong?"

"Okay, sorry. It's way harsh."

But I could tell he didn't mean it. Irritated, I scooted a few inches away from him on the couch.

"I doubt Rigel will be charged with anything," Mr. O reassured me. "Some of the news outlets lean toward the sensational. This is one of them." He quickly switched to a feed where the top story was water management instead of the latest spin on my personal life.

A few minutes later, I was hit by an intense wave of exhaustion. "I think I'm going to turn in. You guys can fill me in on any developments in the morning."

Mr. O'Gara nodded understandingly. "Probably a good idea. It's been a stressful day for all of us, but especially for you. We'll talk more about how to handle tomorrow's interviews over breakfast. Sleep well, Emileia."

Yawning, I headed to the elevator, too tired for the stairs. Molly went up with me, claiming she was sleepy, too. On the ship I'd felt weird when Molly helped me get ready for bed, but tonight I was grateful. I wondered why I was so wiped, then reminded myself that over the past two days I'd arrived on *Mars*, learned all that scary stuff about the Grentl, conducted my very first press conference, and had Rigel snatched away from me without warning.

Anybody would be exhausted after a couple of days like that.

29

Ballytadhg

BALLYTADHG (BAH-LEE-TEEG) (POP. 1,106): *east-central Nuathan village known for Arts* fine *and industry*

Sean

M seems a little out of it when she comes down—late—to breakfast. I can tell Dad's worried, though he pretends not to be. He just reminds her what to expect at each of today's appearances.

"Regan Ryan generally tries to put her guests at ease and engage them in conversation. She'll focus on the personal but will likely keep things upbeat. I don't foresee any problems there. Ballytadhg is likely to be more policy oriented, though if the forum moderator takes direct questions from the audience, we can't know for sure. In Glenamuir all questions will be screened by the moderator, which should keep things under control. Still, you'll need to stay on your toes for all three."

She nods, but I can't tell if she's taking in his words or not. She's definitely not taking in much breakfast.

"You okay?" I whisper, looking at her plate.

She immediately sits up a little straighter and nods. "Fine. Just too nervous to eat much. You can finish this if you want."

"No time." Dad throws down his napkin and stands, his own

breakfast only half eaten. "We need to be going."

During the few minutes it takes to reach our destination, Dad quizzes M again with likely questions. She answers, but slowly. I'm worried about her.

Regan Ryan's Tullymayne studio is in a high-rise, so we're escorted up to the ninth floor, then into a little waiting room.

"Regan will be introducing you in just a moment, Princess," the woman tells M. "Your companions can remain here during your interview."

Molly goes to sit down. "Isn't Regan interviewing you today, too, Sean?"

"Right after M, I think, unless she calls me in sooner. That'll probably be up to you," I say to M.

"Oh. Um, okay." She still looks like she's not totally awake.

The door opens again and the same young woman motions to M, whispering that the broadcast is already live. She frowns when Cormac follows but doesn't try to stop him. I wish I could go with M, too. She looks like she could use the support. I settle for watching her on a vidscreen in the corner.

The studio is set up like a living room, with a couch and chairs, probably to help the guests relax. I hope it works for M. Regan Ryan, a tall brunette, bows to her. "Welcome to Nuath Newsworthy, Princess Emileia. I'm honored to have you here today. Please, won't you make yourself comfortable?"

M sits in one chair and the hostess sits in the other, both half-facing the camera.

"Thank you, Regan, and thank you for having me here." M's voice is steady, to my relief. "As I said yesterday, I'm looking forward to letting the people learn more about me."

"That's exactly what this interview is for, Princess." Regan gives her a big, fake-looking smile. "So, tell me, how did it feel to learn the truth about who you are, who your father and grandfather were?"

For the next half hour they talk about everything that happened last fall. Just like Dad coached her, M hardly mentions Rigel at all. Regan acts more interested in M's feelings than the events everybody already knows about. She keeps trying to get M to elaborate on how shocked she was to learn about Nuath and her real identity and all.

"Yes, it was pretty heady stuff for an unpopular nobody who'd never left Indiana, or even owned a cell phone, to find out I was a

Princess," M says with a little laugh. But it sounds forced, and she looks paler than when she went in.

Regan, still with that fake smile, acts all surprised. "Unpopular? You? That's hard to believe, I must say." No kidding. But according to M and everybody else at Jewel High, it was true.

"Well, my adopted aunt and uncle aren't particularly well off," M explains. "And until I started spending time with other *Echtrans*, I was nearsighted, so I wore glasses. One thing that helped convince me the Stuarts were telling me the truth was the way I changed once I was around them."

"And then, of course, the O'Garas came to Jewel, which must have made even more of a difference?" Regan says, her smile getting even bigger and faker.

"Um, yes. Of course." I can tell M wants to say more—probably stuff Dad told her not to.

"So, how did you feel when you learned that Sean O'Gara was your destined Consort? It must have seemed like meeting your very own Prince Charming, to borrow a term from your Earth fairy tales."

I hold my breath, since that's not a question Dad coached her on. It obviously flusters M a little, because she waits just a hair too long before saying, "Oh, yes, Sean and his family have been great." Not exactly an agreement, but not a contradiction, either. I let my breath back out.

Now Regan turns her plastic smile to the camera. "As it happens, we also have Sean O'Gara here in the studio today. I know our viewers are dying to meet him, so if you have no objection, Princess, I'd like to invite him to join us."

Dad warned me this might happen, but I'm still caught off guard. It helps a little when M smiles and says, "No objection at all, Regan."

The woman that took M into the studio is already motioning urgently to me, so I follow her, then sit in the chair on M's other side while Regan introduces me.

"Thank you for joining us, Sean. I've looked forward to meeting you as much as our viewers have, after hearing so much about you. Let's start with a little bit about your background. You grew up here in Nuath, didn't you?"

I shoot a quick glance at M. She looks even sicker up close. "Um, yes. I was born in Thiaraway, but my family moved to Glenamuir when I was two, after Faxon...you know."

Regan fires more questions at me about my early life and my parents' involvement in the Resistance. I try to answer without letting my distraction show, but I can tell M is close to losing it. There are beads of sweat on her upper lip and her face is almost white now. Regan doesn't seem to notice, totally focused on me, but I'm afraid M is about to either pass out or throw up, neither of which will do her any good at all in the polls.

I rattle off a canned response to Regan's next question while frantically trying to think of some way I can help M hold it together until we're off camera. She swallows like she's about to hurl and suddenly I remember Thanksgiving dinner at her house, when she looked almost exactly the same. And I remember what helped.

"You were in Bailerealta, Ireland, when you first learned that Princess Emileia was alive, weren't you?" Regan is asking me. "Tell me, how did you feel when you heard the news?"

I smile down at M, desperately hoping my idea will work. "Like I'd been struck by lightning. Like the universe had suddenly expanded with bright possibility." True, even if I rehearsed it earlier.

"So you were excited?"

"Excited is a massive understatement. I couldn't get to the United States, to Jewel, Indiana, quickly enough. And obviously I wasn't disappointed when I got there." I reach over and put my hand on top of M's, where it's resting on the arm of her chair.

I feel the wonderful tingle I always get from her even though she flinches slightly, like she does before pulling away. But she doesn't pull away. She glances at me, her green eyes wide and startled. Then, as I watch, color creeps back into her cheeks and she sits up a little straighter, paying attention again.

Elation and relief lance through me that I really can heal her like this—but then those feelings evaporate as I realize what that means: that the reason she was sick in the first place is because of Rigel. Again.

✦

M doesn't look at me again as the interview continues, but she also doesn't move her hand away from mine. She must know as well as I do that she can't afford to while we're on camera, both because of how it might look, and because she'll start feeling sick again.

"And what about you, Princess?" Regan asks. "Sean O'Gara must have seemed quite something after only knowing Earth boys all your life."

"Yes, definitely," she replies after a slight hesitation. I know she's thinking about Rigel. "Of course, I had no idea who he was at first. That he was supposed to be my Consort one day, I mean."

"It must have been very exciting to learn that," Regan prompts. I tense, worried she'll finally goad M into saying something about Rigel on the air—maybe something about how upset they both were when Uncle Allister blurted out the truth about me at Rigel's birthday party.

"Exciting is an understatement." M is echoing my words from a minute ago but I know her meaning is totally different.

I can't help it, I take my hand off hers. But I try to do it casually, so it won't look like it has anything to do with what she just said. Her hand gives a little twitch, like she wants to grab my hand back—or maybe that's my own wishful thinking.

"It did take me a little while to get used to the idea." This time her little laugh almost sounds natural. "After all, I was raised in the United States, where arranged marriages are pretty much unheard of."

Regan's laugh sounds more forced than M's did. "And now?"

M sends a fond-looking smile my way, though I notice it doesn't reach her eyes. "What do you think?" Then, before Regan can ask anything else, "It's been lovely of you to have us here today, Regan. I hope I get a chance to talk with you again. As you can imagine, though, my schedule is extremely tight right now."

"Oh, of course!" Regan never loses a single watt of her high-powered fake smile. "I can't tell you how much I appreciate you giving me, giving our viewers, so much of your time today, Princess, especially so soon after your arrival. I very much hope we can schedule another interview soon. Needless to say, that goes for both of you. *Such* an adorable couple!"

M doesn't react to that, just stands up, nods to Regan and the camera and walks out of the studio with me, Cormac right behind us.

By the time we return to the car, the color is already starting to drain back out of M's face. I'm tempted to touch her hand again but figure I'd better not press my luck—not yet. Dad and Molly both chatter about how great the interview was, how well M and I both did. Dad's already predicting a bump in the polls. Neither of them seem to notice how quiet M is.

We don't need to be in Ballytadhg for two hours, so we head back to our mansion of a guest house for lunch. When we step out of the elevator I'm already thinking about what I'll order from that awesome recombinator but then M excuses herself and makes a bee-line for the downstairs bathroom. Even from here, we can hear her retching.

Dad, Molly, Cormac and I stand around awkwardly, the rest of them finally worried about her. But by the time she comes back out, all white and shaky, I'm getting pissed. Because I can only think of one possible explanation for her feeling *this* sick *this* soon after Rigel's departure.

"M? Are you okay?" Molly rushes forward to help her to the couch.

"No. I'm not. It's the whole *graell* separation thing. I'm feeling pretty crappy—and I'm guessing Rigel is, too."

"But...you can't be getting sick already? You haven't even been apart twenty-four hours!"

M just shrugs. "I know it makes no sense, but I'm definitely not faking."

I plop down next to her and grab her hand before she can stop me. "You're not faking this, either." I force my voice to be more gentle than I'm feeling. Sure enough, she starts to look better again almost instantly. "You think I didn't notice before?"

She stares at me. "You mean—you did that on purpose? During the interview?"

"I could tell you were about to lose it."

"Thanks. But—" She regards me uncertainly. "Why are you so angry?"

Guess I'm not hiding my feelings very well after all. "Because you getting this sick this fast, especially after that antidote the Council gave you, proves you and Rigel must have done a lot more than talk that night on the ship. When he was in your bedroom."

M snatches her hand away from mine. "I already admitted we kissed. But that was *all*. Besides, it was just that parlor room with the chairs, not the bedroom." Like that makes a difference.

"Yeah? So why would just kissing change anything? It's not like you hadn't done *that* before."

"Sean," Dad says warningly, but I keep watching M, waiting for her answer.

"I don't know." She looks away from me. "I got sick on the ship, too, when they sent him down to Steerage—faster than in November, though not as quickly—or as badly—as this time. It's like every time we're apart and then get together again, our bond gets stronger and being apart gets worse."

Her eyes snap back to mine, and now she looks pissed, too. "And you *know* we haven't had a chance to do anything since landing on Mars, not even kiss. So don't go talking about *proof* when you don't have any!"

I'm so relieved there might be a different explanation than the one I assumed, I immediately back down. "Sorry. You're right. I shouldn't jump to conclusions." I reach for her hand again, but she leans away from me, still mad.

"No. You shouldn't. And don't feel like you have to help, either. I mean, if you think I'm such a liar, why would you even *want* me to get Acclaimed?" She's already turning paler again and I feel like a monster. A jealous monster.

"Look, I said I was sorry, okay? And of course I want to help if I can. Any way I can. Please let me, M."

She looks away again with a sigh. "I'm sorry, too." I can almost feel the anger draining out of her. "I'm just...stressed, I guess. I really did appreciate what you did during the interview. I...wouldn't have made it through otherwise."

"I'm here whenever you need me," I promise her. She still doesn't look at me, but gives a little nod. I'll take it.

My dad clears his throat. "We only have an hour to eat before we need to leave for Ballytadgh."

⁙

"—so yes, I think we should go back to a truly representative legisla-ture," M is saying to the moderator in Ballytadhg's town square. "If you read the documents that originally outlined our government, you'll see that's what the first Sovereign and his Cabinet had in mind, giving every *fine* a voice. We have a chance now to go back to that ideal."

I can't believe how good she is at this, even with all that prepara-tion. She's handling this Q&A like a seasoned politician...with my help. Even if it's just some bizarre DNA thing, I'm happy I can make her better. Happy that she *needs* me.

"So, are you saying Faxon decimating our government and killing half of our Royals was a *good* thing?" comes an indignant question from the audience.

I glare in the questioner's direction and see it's that prime *twilly*, Gordon Nolan. Crap! Why wasn't that guy arrested or something? This was supposed to be one of the *easy* crowds. I guess her opponents saw her rising numbers and figured they'd better do something.

M tenses slightly at the question, but I doubt anybody but me notices. I slide my hand an inch or two over until it grazes her wrist and she sits up straighter, looking her heckler in the eye. "Of course I'm not saying that, Gordon. Those murdered Royals included my entire extended family, in case you've forgotten."

The jerk flinches and the people sitting around him frown in his direction. Good.

"I'm saying," M continues, "that out of all the evil Faxon perpetrated on our people, this could be *one* good thing we get out of it, something to give more of our people a chance to be heard as we rebuild Nuath and move forward into a better, brighter future."

Spontaneous applause erupts, and I remember M telling me on the way here that the Arts—what Ballytadhg is mostly known for—were one of the *fines* that got marginalized in the legislature over the centuries.

After that, most of the "questions" are excited suggestions about other ways Nuath could be better off. M doesn't have any trouble responding, since they play right into the talking points she and my dad have rehearsed. Still, when the session ends—with more applause—she slumps a little, like somebody let some air out of her.

Not caring if she objects or not, I take her hand firmly in mine. "Great job, M," I whisper.

"Thanks." She squeezes my hand slightly. Then releases it. She waves at the still-applauding crowd as we walk back to the car to head to her next appearance, in Glenamuir—our old village.

As soon as the car pulls away, she leans back against the seat and closes her eyes. I start to reach for her hand again, just a few inches from mine, but stop myself. Maybe if I wait, she'll touch me instead.

Molly, meanwhile, is bouncing with excitement to see Glenamuir again. Even before we reach the outskirts, she's pointing stuff out to M. "See? I told you there are sheep on Mars. Some goats, too, but not as many, and they're mainly around Bailecuinn, to the east."

"You guys were right." M sits up and looks out the window. "This part does look a little like Ireland. I didn't quite believe it from what I've seen so far."

"Yeah, until we got to Ireland, I figured stone walls were just a Nuathan thing." Molly points as we pass one. "Of course, they're reddish here instead of gray, but otherwise they're *exactly* the same."

"I guess that makes sense, if the original colonists were brought here from Ireland." M perks up a little as she looks around. I'm glad to see her interested in something other than politics. Or Rigel.

The car stops at the edge of the Glenamuir village square, where a crowd's already waiting. Cormac steps out to check security and Dad and Molly follow. M hangs back for a minute, then suddenly reaches over and grabs my hand. I try to hide my happy shock as she clings to me, soaking up as much healing as I can give her before she faces the crowd.

After a few seconds, she gives me an apologetic little smile. "Sorry. I just needed a little—"

"Hey, it's *totally* okay. You can grab my hand or—whatever—anytime you need to, I told you that."

"I know. But…it doesn't seem fair, using you like, I don't know, a recharging station or something."

"Seriously, don't worry about it. I'm happy to help. Patriotic duty and all that." I grin to lighten her mood but she still looks serious.

"Even though—"

I don't want to hear what she's about to say, so I interrupt her by saying it myself. "Yeah, even though I know you'd rather it was Rigel here instead of me. And that you're worried about him seeing us together on the news and stuff. I get it." I don't like it, but I get it.

She looks at me for a few seconds, then nods. "Okay, then. Thanks, Sean." She lets go of my hand.

I pretend she did it reluctantly.

———————————

30

Glenamuir

———————————

GLENAMUIR (GLEN-uh-mer) (POP. 898): *largely Agricultural village in northwest Nuath; longtime home of O'Gara family during Faxon's reign*

In spite of Sean's words, I still felt guilty as I stepped out of the hovercar and looked around at the little village of Glenamuir. It was similar to Bailerealta, but bigger, with red stone buildings and gray metal roofs.

"It hasn't changed at all. Oh, look, it's the Corcannons!" Molly waved enthusiastically and a family near the front of the crowd waved back. "They were our next-door neighbors when we lived here."

Sean extended his arm to lead me to the platform and I took it, since it would look odd if I didn't.

This forum started out exactly like the one in Ballytadhg, with the mayor of Glenamuir giving a little speech about how honored they were to have me here, me responding with my prepared opening statement—which was well received—and then the first questions, which were read by the stunning older woman acting as moderator.

"Yes, I hope to have a properly elected legislature up and running as quickly as possible," I was saying several minutes later, when a disturbance broke out near the back of the crowd.

Mairi, the moderator, frowned in that direction, then repeated what she'd said at the beginning. "Anyone with questions or comments, please message them to my omni. I'll relay them in the order received."

In response, a man shouted, "You're only asking the easy ones! I want to know why anyone would want a girl who can't even keep her Bodyguard in line to lead our whole country? Because her grandfather did? She's no Leontine, just look at her!"

A few people standing near the man nodded their agreement, but most of the crowd started shouting him down.

"Give her a chance!" one woman cried.

"Leontine was young once, too!" another yelled.

"Please," I said, taking advantage of my microphone. "Everyone is entitled to an opinion. I don't claim to be my grandfather, but in time I hope to lead effectively in my own way."

The moderator quickly jumped in with the next submitted question, one about allocation of resources. But as I answered, I noticed a few reporters converging on the dissenters in the back to collect statements. There seemed to be at least a dozen of them, more than I'd thought.

I was flagging again by the time Mr. O signaled the moderator for the final question. I managed to answer in a reasonably steady voice, then gave a shortened version of my closing statement. Sean was waiting as I stepped from the platform, ready to give me the boost I needed. Grateful, I clung to his hand for a second, but when I noticed news cameras and omnis turned our way, I let go and waved.

Sean didn't protest but I could feel his disappointment, just as I'd felt his elation when I'd grabbed his hand in the car earlier. None of this was fair to him, but it was even less fair to Rigel. Not only did he have no way to mitigate his symptoms, he had to watch me cozy up to Sean on national TV.

"Want a tour of the village before we head back?" Sean asked, his spirits reviving.

I didn't have the heart to say no, he and Molly were so eager to show me around. Several of their old friends came up to greet them, some with hugs, then a few shyly asked to be introduced to me. Others kept their distance, though. When I focused, I picked up definite hostility from a few of the girls near Sean's age.

As we moved on, I heard one girl loudly whisper, "Of course he has to pretend he doesn't mind. What else can he do?"

"She so doesn't deserve him," another girl said, not bothering to whisper at all. "Little cheat. Good thing for her I'm not old enough to vote."

Sean's ears turned bright red. "Ignore them," he murmured. "They've been watching too much garbage on the feeds, that's all."

Molly didn't say anything but I could tell she was bothered as well. I hated that I was indirectly spoiling their excitement at being back in their old village, but what could I do? Confronting those girls would only make the gossip worse.

He and Molly determinedly showed me their old school, house and favorite haunts, but I could tell the visit had become bittersweet for them. Not only weren't they coming back to stay, I was sure being here reminded them of their sister Elana, who apparently still hadn't recovered much memory.

The Corcannons invited us to stay for dinner, but Mr. O and I were both eager to get back to Tullymayne. He wanted to analyze the latest news updates to prepare me for tomorrow and I was desperately hoping to talk to Rigel. I hadn't had so much as a one word message from him yet and I was starting to worry.

As soon as we got back, I headed for the bathroom again, but not to throw up this time, since Sean's frequent touches were keeping my symptoms to a manageable level. Locking the door, I pulled out my omni. *Still* no message from Rigel. Stifling my disappointment, I waited a moment, flushed the toilet, then rejoined the others.

"—buzzing about our Princess's visit to Sean O'Gara's home village of Glenamuir today," a reporter was saying. "Many say it speaks well of the Princess that she would include one of the smaller villages in her tour of Nuath. Perhaps more importantly, the videos we've seen should help quiet fears that the relationship between the Princess and her future Consort might have been irreparably damaged by the events on the *Quintessence*."

The screen showed Cormac, Molly and Mr. O getting out of the car on our arrival at Glenamuir, then zoomed in on Sean and me, still inside. I'd assumed the tinted windows gave us privacy, but I was wrong. In the close-up, I grabbed Sean's hand and hung on to it while we had a conversation that looked deceptively intimate without any sound. Then they showed me holding Sean's hand again right after my closing remarks but cut away before I let go to wave.

I cringed, imagining how this must look to Rigel if he was

watching—which he probably was, unless he was already too sick to stay awake. Meanwhile, Sean was regarding me both sympathetically and a little warily.

"Should have guessed they'd do that," he said as the reporter moved on to a dissection of today's interviews. "But it'll probably help your numbers, even if it's not what you—"

"I know. And I'm not mad at you, Sean. It's not your fault at all. It's just…I'm worried about Rigel."

He held my eyes for a long moment, then his gaze fell away and he nodded. "Yeah. Yeah, I get that. Dad, can we call Rigel's grandmother and see how he's doing?"

Though clearly as startled as I was, Mr. O pulled out his omni. "I'll try." I could feel his reluctance.

A moment later, Morag Teague's face appeared on the vidscreen in place of the news. "Yes? I'm rather busy at the moment, Quinn."

"Thank you for taking my call, Morag," he replied pleasantly, though with a slight edge. "The Princess would like to speak with your grandson, if that's possible."

I leaned forward eagerly, but she pursed her lips, again reminding me forcefully of Aunt Theresa. "I'm afraid it isn't, at the moment. I'm still at the research center and he's at my home."

"Can we reach him there?" Mr. O persisted.

"No," she said bluntly. "I haven't had time to get Rigel an omni of his own. In any event, he wasn't feeling well when I left earlier, so I recommended he stay in bed."

I quickly scooted sideways on the couch to get in front of the screen. "Ma'am, I know what's wrong with Rigel, and staying in bed isn't going to make him better. If I could just visit—"

She raised an eyebrow but gave me a *fairly* respectful bow. "Yes, he told me this morning what he thought the issue might be, but what you suggest is out of the question. Even assuming it's true that you and he have developed some semblance of that mythical *graell* bond—"

"Of course it's true! Didn't Dr. Stuart—your daughter—tell you?"

Her face became shuttered, expressionless. "My daughter and I have not been in close communication in recent years. But in the unlikely event such a bond could exist, it makes far more sense to develop a cure than to indulge it, given the difference in your stations. Don't you agree?"

I swallowed, aware not only of her judgmental regard but Mr. O's, as well. "Ah, no. I'm afraid I don't. Without our bond, I doubt I can become the kind of leader Nuath needs. Rigel and I are both stronger, healthier and…*better* when we're together."

That skeptical eyebrow went up again. "I suppose it is understandable you would believe that under the circumstances, Excellency. If he is not feeling better tomorrow, I will bring him in for testing and confer with my colleagues on the best course for him. For both of you."

"But scientists on Earth—Martian Healers—already tried a cure. They did a bunch of tests and came up with something they called an antidote, but it obviously didn't take, since Rigel and I are both getting sick again now."

She actually smiled, though not a very nice smile. "With all due respect for those *Echtran* Healers—" she used the word *Echtran* like a slur— "and while I'm sure they did their best with whatever equipment they have, I can't say I'm surprised they were less than successful. In Pryderi we have the most advanced Healer research facility in existence, with resources that go far beyond anything available on Earth."

I drew myself up, doing my best to look and sound regal, though I was feeling less so by the moment. "Madam, I must insist—"

"Once you are Acclaimed, Princess, we can discuss this further. At present Rigel is my responsibility, and I must do what I feel is best for my grandson. When our researchers develop a cure, it will of course be shared with you immediately."

"But—"

"And now, if you will excuse me, I must return to my work." With a final, perfunctory bow, she broke the connection.

I sat back, suddenly limp as a dead fish. "I can't *believe* her!" I practically wailed. "Even his own grandmother won't believe we're bonded? Why didn't Dr. Stuart tell her?"

"You heard what she said." Mr. O switched back to the news with a shrug. "Now that you've met Morag, can you blame Ariel? It's clear her mother still hasn't forgiven her for marrying outside her *fine*. No doubt she was abusive enough toward Van that it caused a permanent breach. Sad, of course, but these things happen."

Sean took my hand and squeezed it, which felt better than I

wanted to admit, even to myself. "We just need to hurry and get you Acclaimed, M. Then she won't dare go against your wishes."

I glanced up at him in surprise and saw the shadow of pain behind his smile. He wasn't happy at the prospect of me getting Rigel back, but he'd help me do it. Because he really did care about me.

It hit me again, strongly, how unfair this was to him, since I could never care for him the same way. Still, I'd accept whatever help he was willing to give.

What choice did I have?

.⁺.

My approval numbers did get a slight bump from the day's efforts, though less than Mr. O had hoped. Probably because, while I was answering questions and wandering around Glenamuir, my opponents were busy undercutting my support. Like the press conference Devyn Kane gave late that afternoon.

"Clearly this recent stress is taking a toll on our Princess," the feeds showed him saying. "She looked so ill during her conversation with Regan Ryan this morning that I was extremely concerned for her, as I'm sure many of you are, as well." He nodded to a large screen behind him that showed my face, pale and sweating, magnified to several times normal size. "She seemed to rally somewhat afterward, but it seems obvious she is on the verge of some sort of breakdown. And who can blame her? She's little more than a child, one who has had multiple shocks in recent months."

Then there was the footage with those men who'd disrupted my forum in Glenamuir. "You implied earlier that Princess Emileia is unfit to lead Nuath. Can you tell us why?" a reporter asked one of them.

"Are you serious? Look at her—she's just a kid! Think about the state of Nuath these days: legislature barely functioning, cobbled together from the few Royals healthy enough to serve and some random Scientists. We've got disruptions in half our supply chains, not to mention that power outage the day she got here. You really think she can handle all that? When she couldn't even keep her Bodyguard's hands off her?"

Worst was a panel discussion on the *Comeadach* Network, which pandered to Nuath's staunchest traditionalists—the ones Mr. O had originally claimed I could count on.

"We can't only look to the next decade or two, but must consider future Nuathan generations," Gordon Nolan said. Others on the panel, including Rory Glenn, nodded in agreement. "That is why it is essential, before Acclamation can occur, to know for *certain* that the Royal bloodline has not been polluted. We owe it to our children and grandchildren—and their grandchildren."

Though fewer than 10% were in favor of Gordon as Nuath's next leader, more than twice that many agreed with his stance about my "purity." That bothered me more than Devyn's approval rating, which was now 42% and rising, nearly even with the Interim Governor's 47%. Mine was currently at 58% but that would be hard to maintain now that my "easy" interviews were over.

Over the next few days, as my opponents got better organized, my appearances became more confrontational, just as Mr. O had predicted. Though I tried hard to keep my focus on the issues, people kept demanding to know exactly how "serious" my relationship with Rigel had been. Two different interviewers baldly asked whether I was still a virgin. (I said yes.)

My schedule became more and more grueling, with Mr. O constantly prepping me as we traveled from one appearance to the next, all over Nuath. Sometimes I even had to change outfits in transit to better relate to whatever audience I needed to reach.

I never could have survived any of it without Sean. Not only his physical touch, which was the only thing keeping me healthy enough, alert enough, to function at such a level, but also his unwaveringly supportive presence. Not once did he let slip a single snarky word about Rigel or our bond, or even try to take advantage of our forced closeness by getting too cuddly.

Still, I was continually, uncomfortably aware of his feelings for me. Touching as often as we had to for my health, his emotions were coming through more and more clearly, sometimes even when I didn't focus. That bothered me almost as much as the emotions themselves, since it reminded me way too much of the earliest days of my bond with Rigel, when emotions were the only things we could pick up from each other, and only when touching.

Despite all our efforts, my numbers slowly began to erode. Devyn and I were now neck and neck on the question of who Nuath's next leader should be, with Nels Murdoch a not-too-distant third. Bringing up the rear were Gordon Nolan and Crevan Erc, spokesman for the "Populist" movement.

According to Mr. O'Gara, when Nels had been pressed to assume temporary leadership, he'd only accepted because no other qualified Royal was healthy enough to serve. But apparently two months in power had given him a taste for it. Both he and Devyn constantly hammered home my lack of experience. The traditionalists, goaded by Gordon, continued to shout for Rigel's head, while Crevan Erc spun my own comments about a representative legislature against me.

It looked less and less likely I'd be able to deal with the Grentl in time to stop the next power glitch Eric had predicted. Finally, I suggested to Mr. O that we just go public about the aliens, since colony-wide panic was obviously preferable to its destruction, but he shook his head.

"Only if all else fails. That news could do nearly as much harm to Nuath as Faxon did."

"How about just telling Nels Murdoch?"

Mr. O sighed. "I've already suggested he put in extra safety precautions against the chance of another outage. He brushed me off, claiming everything possible is already being done. I rather doubt he'd believe the truth now, but that may have to be our next step."

Crazy as my schedule was, I tried several more times to talk to Rigel but his grandmother never answered, forcing me to leave message after message—which I doubted she even relayed to him. In desperation, I even sent a message to Shim, on Earth, begging him to do something. Finally, after more than a week, I received a text from Morag, but it only read, "Rigel comfortable, stronger daily, research ongoing."

I was glad he wasn't getting sicker, but I still wanted to talk to him more than anything—especially after a news story that ran that same evening.

As he always did, Mr. O turned to the main Nuathan Network after dinner to check the day's numbers and we saw the blonde reporter, Moya, chatting with her colleague, Gaynor.

"Not a bad day for our Princess, all told. Many thought those technical questions from the acting Minister of Planetary Resources would point up some chinks in her armor, but I didn't notice any. Did you?"

"She did hesitate once or twice, but overall her performance would have done credit to a woman twice or three times her age. Even so, most predict that Devyn Kane will pull ahead of her in the polls any day now."

Moya nodded. "Yes, I'm afraid the only thing keeping Princess Emileia alive in the polls is how charmed people are by the real-life romance unfolding right in front of our eyes between our Princess and her prince-to-be, Sean O'Gara. Let's look at some responses to this afternoon's vid-poll."

I cringed, then cringed again, as they showed brief clips of Nuathans from all over the colony sharing their opinions on that topic.

"It's like a fairy tale, only it's really happening," said a young woman from Monaru, the big manufacturing city where my most recent interview had been held.

"I didn't think I had a romantic bone in my body, especially at my age," said an older man from the mining village of Einion, "but watching those two together puts me in mind of when my wife and I first fell in love."

The network cut back to one of yesterday's interviews, where I was answering a question about Nuath's power supplies while clinging tightly to Sean's hand. He was gazing at me with complete absorption and I looked totally okay with it, even glancing over to smile at him once or twice while I talked. Then they cut back to the videos from today's poll.

"Aren't they just the most adorable couple?" gushed a middle-aged woman from Thiaraway, the capital city.

A dozen more flashed up, interspersed with other clips of Sean and me together, like that first one in Glenamuir. Not all the comments were positive—some referenced the "scandal" with Rigel—but most focused on Sean and me as a couple. Over and over, I heard words like "charming," "adorable" and "sweet."

Sean must have noticed my appalled expression. "Hey, silver lining, it's keeping your numbers up."

"He's right," Mr. O agreed. "We need something more substantial, though. Tomorrow will be your first chance to face all of your opponents at once. All of Nuath will be watching this one, so it's *imperative* you be impeccably prepared."

He launched into the questions I needed to be able to answer, keeping the fear I could sense from him out of his voice and expression. Though I was equally aware of how short our time was, my answers were rote, automatic.

Because all I could really think about was Rigel, wherever he was, watching that same news report. Watching Sean and me, looking for all the world like two people falling in love.

31

Nimhic

NIMHIC (NIV-ɪк): *antidote; cure*

I went up to bed that night both depressed and frightened.

If Eric's prediction was correct, the next power glitch would happen the day after tomorrow. If tomorrow's debate didn't turn the tide in my favor, Mr. O and I had agreed our next step would be to sit down with Nels Murdoch and perhaps Devyn Kane to inform them of the Grentl threat—and hope they believed us. In fact, Mr. O had already tried to arrange an appointment with Nels, but the Interim Governor's office hadn't confirmed it.

Squashing down my panic—I had *lots* of practice by now—I let Molly help me undress, then finished getting ready for bed. Just before lying down, I glanced one last time at my omni…and saw the message indicator blinking. I picked it up off my nightstand, expecting another totally unnecessary reminder from Eric that time was getting short, since it had been more than two days since his last one.

Instead, to my delighted astonishment, it was a message from Rigel!

Testing if this works. Quick chat tonight after MT asleep?

I quickly touched the reply button, which opened a holo-keyboard. *Works!* I typed. *What time? Love you!* I was about to hit send when it occurred to me that he might be using his grandmother's omni, which meant she'd see anything I wrote. Reluctantly, I deleted the last two words, then sent my message.

Quivering with eagerness, I slid between the sheets, the omni on the pillow next to me, and waited. And waited…

A soft pinging in my ear woke me more than an hour later. I blinked, disoriented, thinking for a moment that I was in my old bedroom in Jewel. Then memory flooded back and I sat up. Rigel! I quickly smoothed my hair with my fingers, unsure if we'd be able to see each other or just talk.

"Rigel?"

"M! I can't talk long—or loud—but it's great to hear your voice."

"Ditto! How are you? Can you do that holo-video thing?"

"Not sure. I'm using the the vid in my room. I had to reprogram it to send that text and I spent the last hour getting voice to work. Just a sec, let me try something."

While he did more tinkering, I made sure my own ultra-security setting was in place. According to Kernan, that encrypted my conversations and made them unhackable—by anyone.

"Okay," Rigel said, "try your holo button."

I did, and after a long second or two, a fuzzy image of Rigel appeared in midair in front of me.

"You did it! Can you see me, too?"

He nodded. "Probably better than you can see me. Best this ancient thing's camera can do."

"You said you have to be quiet. Does that mean your grandmother will get mad if she knows you're talking to me?"

"She didn't *specifically* forbid me to contact you, just made a point of telling me my vid's comm settings didn't work."

"So you're not *exactly* disobeying her, since she didn't make it a rule." I couldn't help grinning, since I'd similarly skirted the line with Aunt Theresa on plenty of occasions. "Has she been awful to you?"

His blurry image shrugged. "She's gone on and on about me and my parents and how we've all let her down and disgraced the family and stuff, but she hasn't put me on bread and water or anything. The worst is all the tests and treatments she's putting me through."

"But are they working? Are you feeling better yet?"

"Finally, as of yesterday. But I hate what Grandmother has the Mind Healers doing. It's like they're trying to brainwash me, make me forget we ever had a bond. Which I won't. Unless...unless it would help if I did?"

"What? No! Why? Because of all that junk on the news, about Sean and me? That's just media spin. The only reason he's staying so close is to keep me from getting sicker."

He gave a single nod. "With the side benefit of helping you in the polls."

"Yes, but please don't think—"

"I'm sorry, I shouldn't have said that. I can't even imagine the pressure you're under right now. How are you holding up?"

"Talking to you helps," I told him truthfully, "but I wish you were *really* here. I...I'm afraid I can't do this on my own, Rigel."

Suddenly, I was pouring out all the fears I'd had to keep bottled up over the past week. It was an incredible relief to finally share everything I was feeling with the one person in the universe who completely, totally understood.

"So if I can't turn things around tomorrow and Nels won't meet with us, we'll have to go public with the truth to get me Acclaimed," I concluded. "In which case it'll be up to me to keep the whole colony from going into a panic meltdown. Then I *still* have to be some kind of...intergalactic diplomat, to somehow convince the Grentl not to destroy us. Oh, and I *hate* all the awful stuff they keep saying about you on the news, Rigel. I'm scared a mob will show up at your grandmother's with torches and pitchforks!"

"I'll be fine." Of course he'd say that. "Grandmother won't let anyone actually hurt me. Please don't worry about me, M, on top of everything else. If casting me as the villain gets you Acclaimed without spilling the beans, it's good news for everybody, right? We can worry about my reputation once you take care of...everything. Meanwhile, I'll just lie low."

I stared at him helplessly, wishing I could sense his real feelings and thoughts, know for sure if he *really* believed he was safe. "Oh, Rigel, I need you so much!" I whispered.

He gave a convulsive little twitch. "I'm sorry, M. I wish we could— But there are bigger things at stake right now. Don't let me—missing me—screw that up, okay? I don't need that on my conscience, too."

"Your conscience? Rigel, none of this was *ever*—"

"Yeah, yeah, I know. Look, I'd better go. I'll make sure Grandmother sends you this new serum first thing tomorrow, okay?"

"You don't think it'll screw up our bond?" I asked fearfully.

"We won't let it. And hey, once it works, you won't need Sean to keep you healthy. Bonus." He tried to grin but even pixelated it looked fake. "Now get some sleep so you'll look your best on camera tomorrow."

"I'd rather talk to you."

This time his smile looked real. "We'll manage it again soon—as long as I don't get caught."

"Can you erase the record of this on your end, in case your grandmother checks?"

"Yeah, I made sure of that before I texted. Don't want to give her an excuse to make rules I'd have to break. Sleep tight, M."

"I'll try. I love you, Rigel. I'll do my best to get Acclaimed really, really soon, so we can be together again."

"Among other reasons. I love you too, M. G'night."

The second he broke the connection I fell back against the pillows, only realizing then how hard I'd been working to appear alert and healthy so Rigel wouldn't worry even more. As I drifted off to sleep I wondered if he'd been doing the same, or if that new serum worked as well as he claimed.

And whether I really wanted it to.

✦

After that cathartic but frustrating talk with Rigel, I slept like the dead for nearly ten hours. Even so, it was all I could do to drag myself down to breakfast the next morning. Sean greeted me at the elevator and gripped my hand, like he'd been doing every morning. It helped, but I was still achy and yawning when Mr. O startled me with a big smile.

"We had a courier from Morag Teague half an hour ago with this." He held up a vial and a device that looked like a syringe without a needle. "She says it has been effective for Rigel and hopes you can benefit from it, too."

"Oh!" I don't know why I was surprised, when Rigel had promised. "That's, um, great. How does it work?"

"The message said to administer it as a standard hypospray. I'm no Healer, but I think I can manage it—unless you'd rather call in someone more trained?" Mr. O'Gara hesitated with the vial halfway to the syringe.

I glanced at the others. Sean, still holding my hand, was frowning slightly, while Molly looked hopeful and Cormac was as impassive as always. "I'm fine with you doing it," I said.

"Shall we, then?" He clicked the vial to the syringe, then, when I nodded my permission, he pressed it against my upper arm. The little hiss startled me but didn't hurt at all.

"Did she say how long before we'll know if it works?"

Mr. O glanced at his omni, where I guess he'd saved her message. "Within a few hours. Let's hope it makes a difference before that round table debate."

Even as he spoke, I felt—or imagined I felt—a lessening of my headache beyond what Sean's touch had accomplished. Since the outcome of today's debate would decide whether or not we had to break the news of the Grentl colony-wide, I really, really hoped what I felt was real and not just wishful thinking.

"Sean, maybe you should keep your distance for the next hour or two, to avoid clouding the results," his father suggested.

"Oh. Um, yeah. I guess that makes sense." He reluctantly loosed my hand, worry and a silent plea creasing his brow. "Unless you'd rather I—?"

"No, your dad is right. It's the only way to know for sure."

He gave a curt nod and went to sit across the breakfast table instead of beside me like he usually did. Now that he was no longer touching me, I couldn't feel his conflict as strongly as before, but it was obviously still there. And understandable, I supposed. He really did want me healthy, but if this worked, he'd lose his ironclad excuse to stay close to me—touch me—constantly.

By the time we finished breakfast, it was obvious to everyone that the serum was helping. I'd eaten twice what I had at any one meal since Rigel left, and both Molly and Mr. O remarked on my improved color. My energy and mental clarity were creeping back, too, an even bigger relief. Rigel hadn't been faking last night after all.

Mr. O had cleared my schedule so we'd have time for some last-minute grilling before this afternoon's all-important debate. When we finally left for the studio, on the outskirts of Thiaraway, I felt sharper and better prepared than I had all week. But would it be enough to make the difference we needed?

An hour later, I was seated at a long, curved table with my primary opponents: Devyn Kane, Nels Murdoch and Gordon Nolan. Crevan Erc's petition to be included had been denied on the basis of his *fine*, so he was already organizing more protests.

The moderator explained to the cameras that he would take questions from a small, hand-picked audience consisting of acting ministers and various other high-ranking Royals who had arrived on Mars over the past week. The one questioned would have ninety seconds to respond, after which each of the others would have one minute to comment.

At first everything proceeded smoothly, the questions touching on the various policy issues Mr. O had prepared me for. I felt like I was acquitting myself well, even with Sean sitting all the way at the back of the room.

"Tell me, Princess," the acting Minister of Terran Obfuscation asked early on, "how you can possibly oversee the emigration of our people to Earth over the next century without compromising the secrecy my Ministry has worked so hard to maintain, given your background?"

"If anything, Minister, I believe my background will be an advantage. Having been raised as an Earthling, a *Duchas*, if you will, I know better than most how they think and how much we can risk them discovering without endangering our people's future there. Believe me, growing up in Jewel, Indiana, gave me firsthand experience of just how bigoted and fearful people can be when they don't understand something. Small, rural towns are hardly known for being broad-minded."

A few questioners chuckled, reminding me that while most Nuathans were familiar with American television programs, for many that was the extent of what they knew about us. Maybe I could use that to my advantage.

"Even in ignorant backwaters like Jewel, or, say, Mayberry, people can be educated, if it is done gradually and without condescension. Such education will be essential if our people do not want to live out their lives in hiding or deception. With strictly controlled, *gradual* release of information, I am confident that our children, or at least our grandchildren, will one day be able to take the prominent place in Earth society that will benefit both them and the *Duchas*."

"She makes it sound easy," Gordon responded the moment I indicated I was done. "But who decides what information gets released, and when? A teenaged girl who grew up, as she says herself, in an ignorant backwater?"

Devyn's response was less patronizing but essentially the same. "While I have no doubt the Princess's intentions are good, a leader with a broader, more adult experience of the various facets of Earth culture might be better able to carry her stated goals to fruition."

Nels, who had never visited Earth, made a different argument. "There is also much to be said for extensive, firsthand knowledge of our own people and what they've endured in recent years. Without that, it would be difficult to orchestrate the sort of orderly emigration and education the Princess hopes to achieve."

So it went, for the next hour and more. The moderator repeatedly reminded the audience that questions could be directed to any of the four of us, but most seemed to be for me. And, as Mr. O had predicted, once the important policy issues had been addressed, the questions became more and more personal—as did the comments from my fellow panelists.

"Yes, yes, you've stated repeatedly, Princess, that nothing beyond a kiss occurred between you and your Bodyguard while on the ship." Gordon's expression was frankly disbelieving. "Yet we've still heard no specifics whatsoever on what *did* happen behind that closed door. After suffering Faxon's abuses and lies, Nuathans will no longer tolerate secret dealings by their leaders."

I looked him straight in the eye. "I'd say hacking into a ship's security system to violate the privacy of someone's personal cabin involves 'secret dealings' as well, Gordon. Nuathan law does not require a Sovereign, or anyone else in government, to relinquish *all* claims to privacy in the name of openness. I have admitted that kissing Rigel was an error of judgement—*my* judgement. I've also stated that nothing else of a physical nature occurred between us, either aboard the *Quintessence* or elsewhere. I still maintain that position."

"Well said, Princess," came Devyn's response. "I have a daughter only a few years older than yourself, and I would not dream of prying into the details of her romantic activities—though in her case, of course, the Sovereign bloodline is not at stake."

Gordon immediately leaped on that. "In this case, however, that bloodline is of *supreme* concern. I have spoken with countless Nuathans in recent days and many are reluctant to vote for Acclamation without *proof* that their would-be Sovereign has not been compromised, perhaps even now carrying a mixed-*fine* child. Are you willing to have your story independently verified, Princess?"

Mutters swept through the audience, some nodding in agreement while others shook their heads and frowned at Gordon. I glanced at Mr. O'Gara, sitting in the back next to Sean. He lifted a shoulder and gave a small nod, as if to say there was only one way to settle this.

Beyond tired of tiptoeing around the issue myself, I lifted my chin and spoke to the whole room. "Yes. Fine. I'll submit to whatever tests are necessary to *prove* that I haven't been 'compromised.' Bring in Healers, Geneticists, whoever you trust, and let's settle this, once and for all."

After several seconds of stunned silence, Rory Glenn protested from the audience. "Surely no one is suggesting that the Princess *herself* be subjected to any sort of distasteful or degrading procedure? I, for one, won't stand for it."

Nearly everyone in the room seemed to agree, much to my surprise—and secret relief, since a virginity test *did* sound pretty degrading. Maybe they had some kind of infallible lie detector they could use on me instead? That wouldn't be nearly as icky. I was about to suggest that when Gordon spoke again.

"Certainly not." He managed to sound nearly as shocked as Rory had. "The Princess need not be involved at all. With her permission, our Mind Healers can perform a simple memory extraction on the Stuart boy and discover *exactly* what occurred that fateful night. Then our people will be able to choose a proper course with all facts in hand. Thank you, Princess, for agreeing to set everyone's minds at rest."

32

Pryderi

PRYDERI (PREE-dairy) (pop. 1,127): *Nuathan town southwest of Thiaraway, home to most major Healing facilities*

"What?" I stared at Gordon, aghast. "That's not what I—" But Mr. O'Gara shook his head urgently from the back of the room, so I broke off. "I mean, we should make sure that's okay with Rigel and…and his grandmother first, shouldn't we?"

Gordon just smirked, clearly believing my backpedaling was an admission of guilt. I thought Devyn and Nels both looked a bit smug, as well. Finally, belatedly, the moderator took control again.

"Any details can be worked out later," he said. Then, to the audience, "Are there any final questions for any of our participants? We have time for one or two more."

Now that I'd defused the personal issue—at least temporarily—the questioners seemed willing to return to matters of policy. It was good I'd been drilled so thoroughly or I never would have managed coherent responses, I was working so hard not to panic in front of everybody.

Thankfully, after another ten minutes, the debate was over. We each gave our prepared closing statements—again, I was grateful for all that rehearsal—and then the audience members came forward to shake our hands and chat. I excused myself as quickly as I reasonably could, trying to signal to Mr. O that I needed to talk to him *now.*

He must have caught my frantic silent plea, because he announced loudly, "Anyone with further questions or communications for the Princess, please message me. I need to get her to her next appointment."

I made my way to his side and he and Sean shepherded me back to the car, Molly and Cormac just a step behind.

Not until we started back to Tullymayne did Mr. O'Gara turn to me, worry creasing his brow. "What is it? I hope you're not having second thoughts, now that you've so effectively undercut one of the main arguments against your Acclamation. I would have suggested this course sooner if I'd thought you'd agree."

"But I don't! I thought I was volunteering to have *myself* tested. I figured it would be embarrassing, but worth it to shut up all the gossip. I *never* would have suggested it if I'd known they'd go after Rigel!"

Mr. O shrugged. "The traditionalists hold you—your bloodline, at least—in too much respect to allow any tests on you. This is a far better solution and should be just as effective."

"No, it's not," I assured him. "Believe me, we do *not* want them extracting that particular memory and making it public."

He frowned—though not as ferociously as Sean did. "But you've claimed all along that nothing of significance happened that night. Are you saying now that's not true?"

"Nothing to 'compromise the Royal bloodline.'" I used air quotes. "But we did talk about stuff that shouldn't be made public—unless it's time for our last-resort backup plan?"

Mr. O's eyes widened as my meaning penetrated. "But you promised the *Echtran* Council—"

"Only because that was the only way they'd agree to let Rigel come along. So I…waited till we were already on the ship."

Sean and Molly looked back and forth between us in growing confusion until Sean broke in angrily. "So you're saying that you and Stuart really did—?"

"No." I glared at him just as angrily. "We didn't. We haven't. Why does *everyone* find that so hard to believe?"

"Then what—?"

"Not now, Sean," his father snapped, still frowning at me. "You're telling me Rigel *knows?*"

I nodded. "He was my Bodyguard. It only made sense." Out of the corner of my eye, I saw Cormac, who was driving, twitch slightly.

"So if they extract his memory of that evening and make it public…"

"Then *everyone* will know. Yes."

"Know what?" Sean and Molly demanded together.

Mr. O'Gara huffed out a frustrated sigh. "Matters of state that neither of you are cleared for at this time."

"Except Stuart knows?" Sean was glowering at me again. "If he knows, why—?"

"I said, not now, Sean," his father repeated sharply. "While a panic might achieve our ultimate goal, it would be at far too steep a price. No." He thought hard for a moment. "We'll simply have to limit who witnesses the extraction and then trust to the common sense and patriotism of those present to prevent word spreading further."

"Word about *what?*"

"Not *now,* Sean. Ah, good, we're back. I need to make some calls."

So did I.

The moment we were inside, I excused myself to my room so I could securely text Rigel—though by now he'd probably seen my goof himself, on the news. I also called Eric Eagan, on the off chance he'd missed it. When he didn't pick up, I left an encrypted message about what Rigel's memory would reveal.

Mr. O was just setting down his omni when I got back downstairs, looking somewhat relieved. "The memory extraction is set for tomorrow morning and they've accepted our conditions. Other than the necessary Healers and Rigel's grandmother, only Devyn, Gordon and Nels will be present, as will you and I, Princess. The networks will of course petition to have reporters there, but none will be granted admittance. We'll have to trust your opponents will see the wisdom of keeping what they learn to themselves. I've also sent a message to the *Echtran* Council, apprising them of the situation."

"Dad…" Sean began. Molly also looked pleadingly from me to her father. Cormac looked as stoic as ever, but I could sense his curiosity, too.

"We might as well tell them," I said. "I trust Molly and Sean—and Cormac—way more than I trust Gordon Nolan to keep it quiet."

After a long, tense pause, Mr. O exhaled noisily. "I suppose you're right. No sense leaving them to speculate." He turned to the others. "It happens that there is a lot more riding on Emileia's Acclamation than almost anyone realizes."

He went on to briefly explain about the Grentl and the threat they posed, to include the power glitches. I watched—and felt—the others' growing horror, though all three of them did their best to hide it. Interestingly, even though Cormac looked the calmest on the outside, I felt more fear and confusion from him than I did from Sean or even Molly. Maybe because he'd never lived anywhere but Mars?

"So, if Eric Eagan's prediction is correct," Mr. O concluded, "the next power failure will happen late tomorrow. Assuming he believes what he learns, Nels Murdoch *should* have time to put extra safeguards in place to minimize the potential damage."

There was a long silence. Molly was biting her lips, but wasn't falling to pieces like I'd worried she might. "What…what if M *can't* convince the Grentl?" There was only the slightest hint of panic in her voice. "Once she gets Acclaimed, I mean."

"I'll just have to make sure I do." I pretended a lot more confidence than I really felt and was rewarded when her fear started to ebb.

"Dinnertime," Sean announced before anyone else could voice their worries.

More questions were asked and answered over dinner—I noticed that not even Sean ate quite as much as usual. By the time we'd watched the day's news recap (I'd edged ahead of Devyn again in the polls) everyone was ready to call it an early night.

Before turning off my light I checked my omni one last time, but unlike last night, no happy surprise awaited me. Neither Rigel nor Eric had responded to my messages. Devoutly hoping tomorrow's procedure wouldn't blow up in all our faces, I eventually fell into an uneasy sleep.

⁙

Breakfast the next morning was subdued. Sean and Molly were still clearly a bit freaked by last night's revelations, Mr. O'Gara was deep in thought and I was worried because I still hadn't heard back from Rigel *or* Eric. I mentioned the latter worry to Mr. O, who frowned, then shrugged.

"Time enough for that later. There's little he can do to help until you're Acclaimed."

Since they weren't among the agreed-upon witnesses, Sean and Molly remained behind when Cormac drove Mr. O and me to the Pryderi facility where the memory extraction would take place.

"How will this work, exactly?" I asked on the way there. "Do they, like, download a particular memory into a hard drive or something? How do they know which memory is which?"

"I don't know all the technical details, but memory engrams have specific characteristics that vary by age, allowing them to pinpoint a time range for a memory. It's how they erased Allister's knowledge of the Grentl after he was ejected from the Council in December. As for what they'll do with it...you'll see. It's really rather impressive technology."

From someone who'd spent his life on Mars surrounded by technology way beyond anything we had on Earth, that was saying something. Worried as I was about what was going to happen, I was also increasingly curious.

The Mind Healing Facility was one of dozens of large, angular, crystalline structures lining the main thoroughfare of Pryderi. We were ushered through a sky-blue lobby and down several corridors of the same, soothing color. A few people did double-takes, then bowed, as they realized who I was.

When we reached a sealed silver door, our guide touched a panel in the wall next to it and the door slid silently into the ceiling. The man then bowed and hurried back the way we'd come. Cormac took up a position in the hallway and Mr. O and I entered a large, sky-blue room. The entire opposite wall was transparent, with a dozen or so chairs lined up in front of it.

At our entrance, Nels Murdoch, Devyn Kane and Morag Teague turned, then bowed, as did an auburn-haired woman I hadn't met. I noticed she bowed more deeply than the others.

"Welcome, Excellency. I am Adara Walsh, head Mind Healer, and I will be overseeing today's procedure."

I nodded, then peered through the window into the next room. Rigel, attended by two other Healers, reclined in a sleek gray chair with several bizarre-looking instruments attached to it. It reminded me slightly of a dentist's office.

"This won't hurt him, will it?" I asked anxiously. Rigel appeared conscious, but unnaturally relaxed.

Are you okay? I thought at him through the glass, as Adara assured me the procedure was painless.

The only thing that indicated he might have heard me was a slight movement of his eyes toward the window. There was no change in his expression, and no response.

"Is he all right? What have you done to him already?"

"Just a mild sedative," Adara said soothingly. "The procedure works best when the subject is in a dreamlike state."

"So he doesn't know we're here?"

"It's doubtful."

I stared through the window, aching with all my being to tell him how sorry I was, how much I missed him. To touch him. *Rigel? Rigel, can you hear me?*

Still no response. I tried, hard, to tap into his thoughts but all I sensed from him was calm tainted by a tiny bit of confusion. Had they even told him what they were doing? I was about to demand more information when Gordon Nolan entered the room.

"Sorry if I've kept you waiting." He made a perfunctory bow in my direction. "There were a few things I had to take care of before, well, let's get started, shall we?"

"A moment." Mr. O pulled out a tiny black box like the one Eric Eagan had used to make sure the conference room back in Tullymayne was secure. Standing in the middle of the room, he turned in a slow circle, the box held in front of him. Suddenly the box chirped—and Gordon flinched. The box was pointed right at him.

"Did you perhaps forget to turn off your omni?" Mr. O asked with exaggerated politeness.

Gordon didn't meet his eye as he fumbled in his pocket to pull out his omni. "Um, I must have. Sorry." He touched a control and the black box stopped beeping.

"Now we can proceed," Mr. O'Gara told the Healer. "You'll all know soon enough why we insisted on this level of security."

Adara, along with everyone else, was looking askance at Gordon, but now she turned to the window and touched a spot near the edge. "You may begin."

We all sat down and watched as the two Healers in the room with Rigel pulled up holographic control screens from each of the instruments in turn, making adjustments to a few of them. One of them touched a similar screen on the wall and the window in front of us instantly became opaque.

"What—?" I began, but then an image appeared on the window-turned-vidscreen—an image of my quarters aboard the *Quintessence.*

It was like watching a movie, with Rigel as the camera. He crossed the big living room, stared at my parlor door for a second or two, then knocked softly. Unlike the vid feed on the *Quintessence,* this one had sound. I opened my door and pulled Rigel inside, then threw myself at him. Gordon snickered audibly, making me cringe. At least they weren't getting Rigel's actual *thoughts,* just his memories.

After several long, embarrassing seconds, Rigel pulled back—it was so weird seeing myself through his eyes!—and we sat down. The others in the room flicked glances my way when they heard me admit I really didn't want to be Sovereign, that Devyn would be a better leader. But then I started telling Rigel about the Grentl and everyone's attention was immediately riveted on the screen in front of us.

When I got to the part about the communication device and Faxon, the fear and tension in the room was so palpable it made me squirm. I heard audible gasps from Morag Teague, Adara and at least one Healer on the other side of the window.

After I finished, Rigel asked a few questions, like why I hadn't told him sooner, and I answered. Then we cuddled and kissed for like half an hour. Everyone kept watching, but I could feel them getting restless, fear now warring with raging curiosity.

Finally Rigel left me, saying, "If I stay, you know as well as I do we'll do something we shouldn't. I need to go while I still can. I love you, M."

It was all I could do not to cry. Would we *ever* have a chance to be together like that again?

As soon as Rigel left my parlor, the image faded and the window became transparent again. Swallowing back emotions I couldn't afford to indulge right now, I turned to face the others. Morag's face was white as a sheet, and the rest looked nearly as shaken. Devyn hid his fear best, but I could still sense plenty from him. He was the first to find his voice.

"Surely it can't be true?" He looked from me to Mr. O'Gara and back. "Everything you told him? How—?"

"Not only is it true, there's more." I was careful to keep my voice calm and reasonable. "Things I didn't learn until after I arrived in Nuath." I repeated everything Eric Eagan told me, including his prediction that there would be another power outage that very evening. "If you don't believe me now, you will after tonight."

All three of my opponents exploded with questions, their voices getting louder and louder as they talked over each other until Mr. O raised a hand. To my surprise, they shut up.

"I can attest to everything you have just learned, as can the Palace Engineer Eric Eagan and the *Echtran* Council on Earth. The real question is, what are you prepared to do about it? At the very least, I hope you, Nels, will put additional safeguards in place before tonight's outage."

"But...it *can't* be true! Can it?" Nels Murdoch was almost pleading, more frightened than ever. "Why would these aliens—especially if they're the ones who brought us here in the first place—want to destroy us? You said this Engineer is old. It's possible his mind isn't completely sound, that these outages have nothing to do with this outlandish story. The anti-Royalists already claimed responsibility, after all."

"Which Crevan Erc later recanted. Those people would say anything to bring attention to their cause, you know that. You've found no proof they were involved have you?" Mr. O challenged him.

"No, but—"

Devyn Kane broke in. "Nels, I recommend you take those precautions. If no outage occurs this evening, as I devoutly hope it won't, we'll know the risk is not as great as the Princess and Quinn wish us to believe. I'm sorry," he said to me, "but you must admit this all seems rather self-serving, an elaborate ploy to convince us to withdraw from consideration for leadership."

I blinked. "What? You think we somehow implanted a false memory into Rigel? Would that even be possible?" I asked Adara.

"Not by anyone outside of this facility." Her terror receded with something else to focus on. "The procedure would be extremely complex, requiring equipment existing nowhere else. Only a handful of people—myself and three others—know how to do such a thing. And I assure you—" this to the others— "none of us have done so. What we just witnessed is what the boy actually remembers."

"All right, so she actually told him all that. But how do we know it's *true?*" Gordon demanded. "It could all be a setup to convince everyone she *has* to be Acclaimed whether she's the best person for the job or not."

Mr. O gave a disgusted snort. "Until that video on the ship was leaked, her Acclamation was never in any doubt. You all know what her approval ratings were when we first landed. Besides, if it were a ploy, we could have broadcast this news to all of Nuath from the start. I leave it to each of you to imagine what the reaction would have been."

"Mass panic," Devyn said heavily. "If this *is* true, then you—and the *Echtran* Council back on Earth—had good reason to keep it quiet. I suppose we'll know for certain this evening. Meanwhile, Nels, you should probably err on the side of safety. You can say it's a mere precaution, because of the outages we've already experienced."

Though clearly still distressed, Nels nodded. "Our Engineers have already reinforced the existing backups, but some systems should probably be taken completely offline before…beforehand." He pulled out his omni. "If I may?"

Mr. O'Gara nodded, but Gordon rounded on him. "Well, I for one refuse to believe it until this supposed outage actually occurs. And I'm not sure I will even then. Maybe you've somehow rigged it—"

"Listen to yourself, Gordon," Devyn snapped. "How could they possibly have done such a thing? The last outage occurred before the Princess even arrived. I, for one, will be convinced *if* this next outage takes place as predicted. At that point…we'll discuss our options."

"I believe some should be discussed now," Mr. O said. "Princess, why don't you have Cormac take you back while I hash out a few details on how we might move forward?"

Eager as I was to get away from Gordon and the others, I hung back. "Can't I at least talk to Rigel before I go?"

Morag Teague spoke for the very first time since our arrival. "Certainly not! With respect, Princess, seeing you now could seriously set back my grandson's recovery. Apart from that, it would be most improper after what we all just witnessed. I gave permission for this procedure hoping that it might squelch the gossip tainting our family, but now—"

"I can't imagine anyone here will wish to make public what we've just seen," Devyn assured her, flicking a steely glance at Gordon. "But I agree, Excellency, that it would be unwise for you to interact with Rigel Stuart at this time."

"As do I," Mr. O'Gara concurred. "You should go now, Princess. I'll join you in Tullymayne shortly."

I opened my mouth to protest further, but Mr. O gave me a look that stopped me. Realizing he probably wanted to negotiate some kind of compromise to get me Acclaimed quickly, I reluctantly left the room, though every cell in my body was straining to return, to get back to Rigel, to touch him.

After one last, longing look through the window, I turned away. If the next power glitch happened on schedule, odds were good I'd be Acclaimed. Mr. O would see to that. And once I was, *nobody* could stop me from getting Rigel back. Meanwhile, I had to hold it together, be ready for what would come next.

Be ready to save us all.

33

Reghnuchan

REGHNUCHAN (REN-NEW-HAHN): *Acclamation, as of Sovereign*

"Well?" Sean demanded the the second Cormac and I stepped out of the elevator. "Did it work? Were they convinced? Will they support you? Where's Dad?" He and Molly both radiated fear and tension.

I shoved away my lingering frustration about Rigel so I could calm them. "Your dad stayed to talk with them—to negotiate, I think. Gordon's in total denial but I think Devyn and Nels Murdoch will come around, especially once the next power glitch happens."

Molly managed a tiny smile. "I'm really glad you're back. I thought Sean would wear a rut in the floor, pacing." He shot her an irritated look but she didn't notice. "What happened, exactly? What was it like?"

"It was weird, watching Rigel's memory replaying on a big screen for everyone to see. Seeing myself from Rigel's perspective. Seeing—" I broke off. There was no point sharing the parts that would hurt Sean. "Anyway, now they know the whole truth. Once they get over being freaked out, I'm sure they'll realize the important thing is to stop the Grentl from pulling the plug. All the political and personal stuff can get hashed out later, as long as we *get* a later."

Sean shuddered visibly. "Yeah. They're smart guys, even if a couple of them are jerks." I wasn't sure if he was trying to reassure himself or Molly. Probably both. "How long till tonight's power failure, exactly?"

I glanced at my omni. "Almost six hours."

Those six hours felt like at least a week. We tried to eat, but not even Sean had much appetite. When Mr. O joined us about two hours into our wait, his report was reassuring.

"Everyone was shaken by what they learned, of course, but Devyn and Nels are reasonable men. Assuming the power outage occurs on schedule, they are both willing to do whatever is necessary to safeguard Nuath—which includes helping you get Acclaimed as quickly as possible."

We watched the news feeds, which mostly consisted of speculation about what that secret memory extraction had revealed. At least until Nels Murdoch released a statement cautioning people to remain indoors between five and seven o'clock that evening while maintenance was done on the power grid.

"Ah, good." Mr. O was clearly relieved. "That should dramatically decrease the chance of injuries."

I kept sneaking peeks at my omni as we waited, desperate for *some* word from Rigel or even from Eric, but there was nothing.

Finally, it was time.

We all held our breath, caught between hope and fear that the blackout would really happen. My heart beat once, twice…then everything went black. Terror erupted in waves from Molly, Sean and Cormac, even though they'd known it was coming. Mr. O's fear was less pronounced, but definitely present. I tried hard to keep my own panic in check, counting seconds.

"How long?" Molly whispered into the dark.

"Not long." Mr. O's voice was surprisingly steady. "Three. Two. One."

And the light returned as abruptly as it had disappeared. As one, Sean and Molly ran to the window, apparently needing to see for themselves that their world had survived. Mr. O and I followed more slowly. Everything looked just as it had, the street still deserted. Even craning my neck, I couldn't see anything out of the ordinary. Yet.

"Let's check the feeds," Mr. O suggested after a relieved few minutes. "If there was damage, they'll be reporting it soon."

A visibly distraught Moya filled the vidscreen. "—despite Nels Murdoch's earlier assurances. People are understandably frightened and angry that this so-called maintenance resulted in the longest power outage in Nuathan history." Over her shoulder was a live image of people venturing into a street somewhere, a few sobbing, others shouting.

"Earliest reports reveal only minor damage so far, thank goodness. The suggested precautions no doubt saved countless lives. Had zippers and private vehicles been running, casualties could have been extensive."

She glanced off to the side, gave a small gasp and turned back to the camera. "This just in, from near Keary, in the far northeast corner. Several large pieces of rock apparently fell from overhead, damaging one home and injuring livestock, sparking new concerns about Nuath's structural integrity. Keary is low-tech, so some there may not have heard the directive in time to protect their animals. We'll have someone on the spot shortly. Now we go to Gaynor, in Thiaraway. Gaynor, you've been there since before the blackout. What can you tell us?"

"People here are scared, Moya," said Gaynor, the Royal Palace behind him. "This blackout has reminded us all that our colony's very existence depends upon uninterrupted power. Already, some are calling for accelerated emigration to Earth, a topic barely discussed since Faxon's ouster. We're hoping for a statement from the Interim Governor soon."

Over the next half hour, reports continued to come in from all over Nuath, everything from escaped sheep and chickens in the North, when force fences shut off, to the failure of two improperly secured anti-grav construction cranes in the South, resulting in significant property damage. Then the first fatality report came in—a woman in Strahancill whose roof collapsed because she'd illegally replaced physical supports with anti-grav ones to save space when remodeling. I swallowed hard. Could I have somehow prevented that death? I really, really hoped it would turn out to be the only one.

Sean and Molly were both still paler than usual and I realized how much harder this had to be for them. Nuath was their home in a way it could never, ever be mine. And they were only two of the nearly quarter million people it was my job to protect. If only Rigel—

At the sound of Nels Murdoch's voice, my attention snapped back to the vidscreen. "I deeply regret that our upgrades were not sufficient to prevent this latest power failure, though they should keep such a thing from ever occurring again. Still, given the current mood of our populace and the need for a stabilizing influence in these uncertain times, I have decided to step down as Interim Governor and to withdraw my name from consideration for more permanent leadership. It is my hope that our born Sovereign, Princess Emileia, will step forward to lead Nuath into the future and I ask all of you to join me in Acclaiming her our natural leader."

My breath whooshed out of my lungs. "Wow, just like that? Do you think Devyn—"

Before I could finish, Devyn Kane stepped onto the dais where Nels was giving his statement, standing shoulder to shoulder with the man who just this morning had been his political opponent.

"I must agree with our esteemed Interim Governor. While he has done an admirable job during the difficult weeks immediately following Faxon's fall from power, it is now time for Nuath to unify. I hope, under the leadership of Sovereign Emileia, we can all pull together to complete the work Nels began. Princess, if you are listening, please accept my sincere apology for any criticisms I previously voiced."

"My apologies, as well, Princess," Nels echoed. If I hadn't seen it this morning, I might not have noticed the fear still lingering in his eyes. "We hope to hear from you or your representative soon so that all necessary arrangements can be made for your Acclamation."

⁂

"Do they mean it? Can it really be that easy?" I exclaimed, not quite daring to believe.

"It's what they agreed to this morning," Mr. O assured me, "though once the Grentl threat is averted they'll want favors in return. Devyn implied he'd like to be considered for Regent. But the important thing now is to get you Acclaimed and into the Palace." He pulled up the screen of his omni and a moment later, Nels Murdoch's face appeared in midair between us.

"I presume you heard?" The fear he'd mostly hidden while on camera was more evident now. "You've made your point, so let's move quickly, shall we? I recommend you contact the Elections Minister as soon as possible to make the necessary arrangements. Good luck, Princess." He cut the connection before I could thank him.

I glanced at Mr. O, confused. "Doesn't my approval rating still need to be above eighty percent?"

"Traditionally, yes, though I'd be surprised if…ah, look, they're already putting up the latest numbers."

In a dramatic turnaround, my rating had jumped from barely over 50% to 83%. Neither Nels's nor Devyn's names appeared at all now and, while Gordon's was still there, he had a mere 12% rating, even worse than Crevan Erc's 19%.

"Excellent." Mr. O'Gara placed another call and a youngish woman appeared on the screen. "Princess Emileia!" she exclaimed, her face reflecting none of Nels's fear. "I'm Deirdra Scully, recently appointed acting Minister of Elections. The Interim Governor told me to expect your call. Are you ready to declare for Acclamation?"

Her enthusiasm made me smile in spite of myself. "Yes, I am. How soon can the vote be held?"

"According to the protocols, your official declaration must first be announced throughout Nuath, after which twelve hours must elapse before the vote. Probably a holdover from when communication was less instantaneous, but it's still in the rules."

"Can the official declaration go out tonight, then? To start the, um, clock ticking?" The important one already *was* ticking, but she didn't know that.

"Certainly. I'm sending the text to you now. All you have to do is read it back to me. I'll capture it, then make the broadcast through the government channel that everyone is required to carry. It will display instantly, then again at two hour intervals until the vote is held."

The text of the official declaration—in Martian—popped up on my screen. I had a sudden, vain temptation to check my hair and makeup before reading it, but that would waste more precious time. Taking a deep breath, I pinned a smile on my face and immediately started reading aloud.

"Me Banfriansa Emileia go hofiguill is run dom teacht i chorioin eri Thiarna ar barr Nuath." (Which, roughly translated, meant "I, Princess

Emileia, do formally declare my intention to ascend to the position of Sovereign of Nuath.")

Deirdra did something on her end I couldn't see, then I heard my declaration repeated back to me. I winced a little—I always hated how my recorded voice sounded—but Deirdra smiled brightly.

"Perfect! I can see you've worked hard to master Nuathan, Excellency, even though English is almost universally spoken now, as I'm sure you've noticed."

"I have, yes. And thank you. So what happens next?"

She glanced down, then back up at me. "I'm feeding your declaration into the government channel now. It's nearly seven-thirty, so the vote can be held any time after seven-thirty tomorrow morning."

"And it stays open for three hours, correct? Let's have it start right at seven-thirty, then."

For a second she looked startled, but then nodded. "Very well, seven-thirty it is. People can vote before leaving for work. They'll have just breakfasted, which should help to assure a favorable vote, not that I imagine it would be otherwise, now the others have withdrawn their opposition." She was smiling again.

"Thank you so much for your assistance, Deirdra. Please let me know if anything else is required of me."

"It has been my very great honor, Excellency! You'll hear from the Interim Governor to arrange for your Accession and Installation after the vote has taken place."

Within minutes of my declaration airing on the official channel, it was the main story on all the networks, interrupted by occasional reports of additional, mercifully minor, damage around the colony. We kept watching while we ate dinner, all of us with better appetites now.

Both Nels and Devyn made more statements about what a good thing this was for Nuath. To my dismay, they also both claimed that after this morning's procedure they were convinced that Rigel was out of the picture for good, and that Sean and I were forming the "necessary bonds" to lead as Sovereign and Royal Consort.

The networks responded by re-showing—again!—every cozy-looking moment Sean and I had shared on camera over the past week and gushing about what a perfect couple we made. I hoped Rigel wasn't watching.

"And now, back to the studio for another look at the polls. Early indications are that better than eighty-seven percent will vote in favor of Acclamation tomorrow morning."

We all turned in early since Mr. O assured us we'd have a very long, busy day tomorrow. Before getting into bed, I sent another encrypted message to Rigel, apologizing again for the stupid stuff on the news and promising that the moment I was officially Sovereign I'd make his grandmother send him to the Palace. I hoped it would reach him, since he still hadn't responded to my last message.

The only thing that finally calmed me enough for sleep was vowing to get Rigel back by my side within the next day or two. No matter how much his grandmother or anyone else disapproved.

When my alarm woke me at six-thirty the next morning, I was deep in a disturbing dream in which Rigel was trapped in a cage, insisting that his grandmother had made him swallow the only key. Relieved to find *that* problem, at least, wasn't real, I jumped out of bed. Ignoring the nice outfit Molly had laid out for me the night before, I threw on my old Earth jeans and t-shirt and hurried down to breakfast so I wouldn't miss any of the voting reports.

And got sent right back upstairs by Mr. O'Gara.

"You'll be expected to do a few quick interviews they can show while the voting is going on and you may have to respond to your remaining detractors. You need to look the part, especially until the last votes are in. It will also be good practice for…afterward."

Even though he was right, I grumbled as I followed Molly back to my room to be properly decked out in a silvery green tunic and flowing pants of deeper green. Then she fussed with my hair until I insisted it was fine.

"I won't look very regal if I'm still stuffing my face for the first interview. Let me go down and eat something, okay?"

She stepped back, looking hurt. I immediately apologized, but she just smiled and shook her head.

"No, it's fine. You have to be way more nervous than I am. C'mon."

Sure enough, when I finally got back to the breakfast table, my stomach was too jumpy for me to eat much of anything. I told myself this wasn't nearly as bad as when I'd waited for the *Echtran* Council to vote on Rigel's fate, back in December. This was practically a sure thing, in comparison.

I couldn't relax, though, until the first returns came in at a quarter to eight, overwhelmingly in favor of Acclamation. Everyone in the big living room—the three O'Garas and even Cormac—let out a cheer. I just let out the breath I hadn't realized I was holding.

"Things are getting lively here in the Governmental Center," the reporter Moya said from in front of the Royal Palace. Behind her, a few anti-Royal protestors waved signs, but most of the crowd seemed to be in a celebratory mood. "Let's see if we can get the Princess's take on how the vote is going, shall we?"

Mr. O's omni buzzed a second later. "Ready?" he asked, his hand hovering over it. Taking a fortifying breath, I nodded.

"Thank you so much for speaking with us on this momentous morning, Princess," Moya said directly to me—and all of Nuath. "You must be pleased with these early returns, but what do you think of the continuing claims some are making that you are too young and inexperienced to lead?"

"Good morning, Moya." I was momentarily distracted—and a little freaked—to see my face in an inset over her shoulder. "I, um, yes, I'm delighted that the Nuathan people seem ready to have a Sovereign in place again. As for my age and lack of experience, I fully intend to surround myself with advisors who are both older and wiser than I am, as we begin the task of rebuilding the government that Faxon so foolishly dismantled."

"Well said, Excellency." Moya smiled into the camera. "I hope we can speak with you again as this morning's vote progresses."

"It will be my pleasure." Not exactly true, but I'd do whatever I had to.

They went back to counting votes, tallying up the returns by *fine* as well as by region, city, town and village. It reminded me of CNN back home during the last Presidential election night, right down to the maps and graphs.

As the voting went on, the numbers continued to trend in my favor. In fact, by nine o'clock, with the time allotted for the vote only half over, nearly 90% of the vote was already in, with 86% in favor of Acclamation.

I'd given two more quick statements by then in response to Moya's questions—though it seemed more like she just wanted to fill air time than get any real info from me—and Nels Murdoch had been on as well. Now his face popped up again, looking genuinely pleased.

"Yes, it's clear now that our Princess will be Acclaimed Sovereign. Given that, I very much hope that all of our people will unite in their unwavering support for her, and that no prior considerations will cause any person or group to attempt to undermine our new leader. I, at least, will treat this historic event as a cause for celebration."

At ten-thirty the vote closed with over 97% accounted for, the remaining 3% apparently comprised of those still in the hospital and a few technophobes who abstained on principle. 86.2% had voted for Acclamation. At one minute past eleven, I read the traditional acceptance speech (in Martian), then added a brief bit (in English) that Mr. O had helped me to write between interviews.

"Truly, I am both honored and humbled by your faith in me and will do everything in my power to justify it. I absolutely agree with everything I just read to you about honoring the vision and sacrifice of my ancestors and putting the good of Nuath ahead of my own personal interests. And I plan to get started right away on the first steps toward bringing our people into their best possible future. Thank you."

I disconnected from the direct link into the colony-wide news feed, then sat back and looked around at the others, still feeling more than a little bit stunned.

I was now really, truly, officially, Sovereign and supreme leader of Mars! I was finally going to get Rigel back!

And I had just over forty-eight hours to stop the Grentl from killing us all.

34

Thiaraway

THIARAWAY (THEE-AH-RAH-WAY) (POP. 81,155): *capital city and center of Nuath; seat of Nuathan government; traditional home of Royal family*

Mr. O pulled out his omni and stood. "I'll have Nels Murdoch let the Palace staff know we're on our way. Normally they'd take days to prepare everything for your arrival and Accession, but we obviously can't wait. I suggest you all go pack."

Half an hour later, the five of us said goodbye to our sumptuous temporary quarters and headed for the Royal Palace, a place I'd only seen in pictures...and in my dreams. My heart beat faster as we approached Thiaraway. It wasn't as large as Monaru, the big industrial city to the south, but it was more imposing, its crystalline skyscrapers visible from more than a mile away.

When we reached the outskirts, people were already lining the main thoroughfare into town, waving flags and what must have been very hastily-prepared banners of welcome. I was reminded of Bailere-alta when I heard chants of *"Faoda byo Thiarna Emileia!"* along with the English version, "Long live Sovereign Emileia!" There were also scattered shouts of "Allegiance to the Sovereign," and even, "We love you!"

Despite my anxiety over what lay ahead, my heart swelled and my eyes prickled with unshed tears of gratitude that I could inspire such a display of emotion from these people. *My* people. People only I could protect.

Touching the control that switched my window from tinted to transparent, I smiled and waved at the crowds as we slowly made our way toward the Palace. The people responded, waving back frantically and chattering excitedly to each other. For the first time ever, I felt like maybe I could get used to this kind of rock-star treatment.

Assuming, of course, that I could keep every last one of us from being buried under a gazillion tons of rubble the day after tomorrow.

Don't lose sight of the goal, I told myself firmly before the adulation could go to my head. Then we turned the last corner and I gasped in wonder. All thoughts of rock-star-ness and even my goal vanished. Up close, the Royal Palace was even more splendiferous, more breathtaking, than I'd imagined, its pink crystal facade and fantastical spires sparkling like diamonds in the faux sunlight. No wonder this image had stuck in my infant brain when nothing else had, spawning the dreams and fantasies of my childhood.

"Isn't it beautiful?" Molly murmured. "I'd forgotten…I haven't seen it since I was little."

"Spectacular." I stared like I'd never drink it in deeply enough as it filled my whole field of vision, more and more exquisite details becoming visible. To think I'd actually lived here when I was a baby…that I might live here again! Suddenly the idea of staying on Mars didn't seem *completely* terrible—as long as I could have Rigel with me.

Just like at the guest house, a previously invisible door appeared at the bottom of the castle and we drove down a long, winding tunnel that opened into an underground parking lot many times larger than our one in Tullymayne. A man and a woman in matching uniforms greeted the car with synchronized bows, fists over hearts. The man opened the car doors and, at some silent signal, two other men appeared to whisk our bags into a lift. The woman bowed again, this time specifically to me.

"It is the honor of a lifetime to welcome you back to the Royal Palace, Excellency! I am Sheila, head housekeeper, and this is Powell, head butler. If you will come this way, I will show you to the Royal chambers." She led us to a separate elevator, this one with crystal and gold detailing.

"The Interim Governor sent word that your official Accession might occur as early as this afternoon, but surely you would prefer to settle in for a few days before taking on official duties?"

What I might prefer was irrelevant. "Thank you, Sheila, but no, any time after lunch will be fine."

If she was startled, she hid it well. Leading us through an enormous, glittering reception hall, then down an opulently paneled and carpeted passage, Sheila indicated a hallway on the right. "Your Consort and his father can lodge in the Royal family quarters. The Sovereign's apartments are this way."

Motioning for Molly and Cormac to follow her, I hung back for a moment, putting a hand on Sean's arm. "You haven't said a word since we reached Thiaraway," I murmured, so softly even his dad couldn't hear. "What's wrong?"

He shrugged. "Just…wondering how long before you make them bring Rigel here."

Conscious of Mr. O watching us curiously from a few paces away, I managed not to frown. "You get why I have to, don't you, Sean? If having him here can help me—"

"Yeah. I guess. Just…don't forget what really matters, okay?"

Sean's mention of Rigel made me long for him so fiercely, it was a physical pain in my chest. Unable to answer, I just nodded to Sean, then hurried after the others, already waiting in front of a set of ornate double doors.

"Sorry! You could have gone on in."

"Only you can open these doors, Excellency," Sheila corrected me. "They are keyed to the Royal Sovereign bloodline. If you'll place your palm here?" She indicated a smooth spot in the center of the right-hand door.

At my touch, the doors silently parted in the middle, sliding back into the walls to reveal a big room furnished in muted shades of purple and gold with deeply upholstered chairs and sofas, highly polished tables and crystalline sculptures everywhere. It was gorgeous, the very height of decadence.

"If only I can open the door, does that mean no one's been in here since…since my grandfather died?" I asked. "Faxon didn't use these quarters?"

"There is a service entrance, used by trusted staff for cleaning and maintenance, which your Handmaid and Bodyguard will also be able to use. Faxon—" Sheila primmed her lips as she said his name— "did insist on using these apartments at first, via that entrance, but soon moved to other quarters, claiming they were more comfortable. Certain amenities, such as the hot-water shower, bedroom and office vidscreens, and various storage vaults are only usable by those of the ruling bloodline," she clarified in response to my puzzled expression.

"Ah." The poetic justice made me smile.

As Sheila proceeded to give me a tour of my new digs, I felt increasingly overwhelmed. Every place I'd stayed since leaving Jewel had been bigger and more luxurious than the last, but this put all the others to shame. The Royal Apartments consisted of *twelve* rooms, including private bedrooms for Molly, Cormac and at least three other attendants, a nursery, two offices, one for me and one for my eventual Consort, a "private" dining chamber for twelve, two parlors and of course my own absurdly opulent bedroom. Not to mention half a dozen cupboards and safes that only I could open and enough closet space for a good-sized village.

Every room had its own color scheme, but none of them clashed. Some of the walls, like in my big office/parlor, were covered in what I first took to be patterned silk, but which turned out to be non-reflective metal sheets studded with decorative crystals.

"You can make and receive calls on any vidscreen." Sheila indicated the largest one, back in the first room we'd entered. "Various security settings are available on each, though you will likely want an aide to screen most incoming calls."

I nodded, remembering what Kernan had said when he gave me my omni—which was what I'd still use for *really* private communication, like with Rigel or Eric. If only they'd communicate!

"Shall I leave you now?" Sheila broke into my thoughts. "I trust your Handmaid is familiar enough with the standard amenities to assist with anything you might need."

"Oh! Of course. I'm sure you have lots to do. Thank you, Sheila. We'll have lunch with the others in half an hour, if that's okay?"

"Certainly. You can call up a map of the Palace on a vidscreen or simply follow the blue line to the main dining room." With another bow, she left us.

Puzzled, I glanced at Molly. "Blue line?"

"Yeah, most of the big government buildings have a guidance system like that. Makes it super easy to find the office or exhibit or whatever it is you're looking for."

"Oh. Cool." I looked forward to trying it. But first, I had calls to make, one official, one not. "I'll, um, be out in a few minutes." I headed into my ridiculously fabulous bedroom and closed the door.

I'd never operated a vidscreen myself, but I'd seen the others do it enough times that it only took me a moment to figure out how to synch my omni with the one in my room, then bring up the little holographic pad to control it. I tapped the "vidphone" option and the vidscreen lit up, showing an attractive garden screen saver.

"Morag Teague, please."

Almost immediately, the garden scene was replaced by the face of Rigel's grandmother, her background surroundings blurred out— something I'd learned most people did by default when answering calls. Her expression was more pleasant than I'd ever seen it, but as soon as she spoke, I realized it was a recording.

"This is Morag Teague, Director of Sub-cellular Research. I am unavailable at the moment, but if you will leave a message, I will return your call at my earliest convenience. Thank you."

I found the holo-button to record a message and touched it. "Morag, I would like Rigel to call me or, better, come to the Royal Palace as soon as possible." I hesitated, wondering if I should make it a Royal order or something, but just concluded with, "Thank you."

She had to know I'd been Acclaimed, so I was pretty sure she'd have no choice but to do what I asked. With any luck, she'd have Rigel here by the end of the day. My spirits lifting at the prospect, I next used my omni to call Eric.

Unfortunately it went to voice mail yet again, which effectively re-dampened my spirits. Without Eric's help, I had no clue how to operate or even *find* the Grentl device.

After freshening up in a bathroom bigger than my whole room back home, I rejoined Molly and Cormac, trying to smooth my expression so they wouldn't pick up on my anxiety. "Let's go get some lunch," I suggested as brightly as I could.

"Dining room," Molly said clearly as we stepped into the hallway. Sure enough, a faintly glowing blue line appeared on the floor ahead of us.

"Cool!" I breathed, momentarily distracted from my worries about Rigel and Eric. Once, as we followed the line, I stepped right on it to see what would happen. Nothing. Glancing back, I saw it had disappeared behind us. How did it *know?* Some kind of sophisticated sensors, I guessed. The line itself was either embedded in the floor or holographic—I couldn't tell which.

We followed the blue line around a dizzying number of turns and through half a dozen doorways, then suddenly emerged into a long, high-ceilinged room hung with six crystal chandeliers along the length of the polished black stone table that ran down the center of the room.

"Whoa. Overkill much?" I muttered, staring at the long, long table and three dozen or more chairs set along the sides. At the near end, I saw three places set for a meal, but no food yet. "This *can't* be the only dining room?"

"There are several," Cormac responded. "But as you didn't specify, we were directed to the main state dining room, the default for visiting guests. The housekeeper clearly anticipated this, as they seem prepared to serve you here."

I glanced at the table again. "We need two more place settings, though. No, Cormac, you two are still going to sit, since it's just us. I promise to let you do the stand-behind thing for state functions, okay?"

"Very well." He had stopped protesting my insistence on this while in Tullymayne, but he still looked uncomfortable with it. Tough.

Mr. O and Sean joined us then, followed immediately by two women in staff uniforms carrying covered dishes. The older one bowed to me.

"Excellency. I am Mada, head cook. I've taken the liberty of preparing a selection of the more popular luncheon dishes rather than delay your meal by having you specify."

"Hello, Mada, and thank you. But I need places set for my Bodyguard and Handmaid. Yes," I said quickly when she frowned and opened her mouth, "I know it's not customary, but it is my preference when dining with close friends."

She bowed again and flicked a glance at the younger woman, who instantly whisked dishes and silverware out of the long sideboard by the door and set places for Cormac and Molly. We all sat, Sean on my left, as always.

After asking me how I liked my apartments, Mr. O'Gara proceeded to carry most of the conversation, going over the details of my impending Accession and Installation, along with everything else lined up for this afternoon and evening.

I had a hard time paying attention, my mind flitting back and forth between eagerness to see Rigel and worry about Eric's continued silence. I really needed to talk to Mr. O about what we'd do if I couldn't contact Eric, but couldn't think how, with Palace staff within earshot.

I'd meant to let Mada know which of the gazillion "samples" were my favorites, hating the thought of so much wasted food. But when lunch was over, I realized I'd mechanically eaten everything that appeared on my plate without even noticing what it was. As soon as we rose from the table, I turned to Mr. O'Gara.

"So when can we talk about the, um, important stuff? I still haven't—"

His eyes flicked to the still-hovering staff. "Soon. First, the forms must be observed, beginning with your formal Accession and the Passing of the Scepter." He glanced at Molly, who nodded. "We should have time to talk after the Royal Reception."

"But—"

"I know. But now is not the time. Try to relax for a few minutes before your Accession. If you can."

.⁺.
⁺

Back in my quarters, I retreated to my bedroom with the excuse that I needed a shower. Which I did, but first I tried yet again to contact Eric. When he still didn't answer, I left an encrypted message, something he'd *claimed* I wouldn't need to do, because he'd supposedly have his omni on him at all times. The fact that he didn't was starting to scare me.

"Eric, I don't know where you are or what's going on, but in case you somehow missed it, I was Acclaimed this morning. I'm finally here at the Royal Palace, where you said I need to be, but there's still a lot I don't know about that, um, thing I need to do. So if you can *please* call me or, even better, come to the Palace, I would really, *really* appreciate it. Thanks."

I glanced at my vidscreen then and saw the little message light flashing. Rigel? I fumbled with the controls, I was so eager to bring up the message screen. *Seven* messages were showing. I recognized the names of two reporters and a government official...and Morag Teague. Adding "find an aide to screen calls" to my growing mental to-do list, I tapped her name.

Her image appeared, then bowed to me, though I thought her expression looked wary. "Allow me to congratulate you on your Acclamation, Excellency. Unfortunately, Rigel is undergoing necessary therapy today but I will pass along your message as soon as I speak with him again." She bowed again and my screen reverted to the garden scene.

I remembered what Rigel had said about those "therapy" sessions, how they seemed to be trying to undermine our bond with them. I was determined that this would be his very last one. I quickly called Morag back—and again got her canned message.

I squared my shoulders, trying not to let my frustration show. "While I appreciate your concern for Rigel, Morag, I insist you bring him to the Royal Palace as soon as possible, no matter what sort of therapy you've scheduled for him. It's *extremely* important."

I sent that, then left yet another message for Rigel, though by now I doubted he'd ever see it. Maybe she'd found out he'd hacked his vidscreen and disabled or confiscated it. Still, after my last message to Morag, *surely* she'd have him here at the Palace by tonight. Tomorrow at the latest. Maybe together, Rigel and I could find and figure out how to use the Grentl device even if I didn't hear from Eric?

With that hopeful thought to fortify me, I headed into my bathroom. Though it boasted the first real, hot-water shower I'd seen since leaving Earth, I took an ionic one anyway, to save time.

After that, I let Molly array me for my Accession and Installation, trusting she knew what she was doing when she fitted me into an outrageously sumptuous gown and matching jewelry. I couldn't seem to stop staring at myself in the mirror, finding it hard to believe that vision in deep purple silk was really me. The dress was studded with about ten pounds of diamonds, which also sparkled at my ears and throat, and in the tiara securing my upswept hair.

"You're *sure?*" I asked for the third time.

"It's the traditional Accession gown, so yes, I'm sure," she said with a grin, also for the third time. "We should go. Unless you want to make a grand entrance after everyone else is already there?"

"Uh, no. Let's go."

When we reached the Royal Audience Hall, the two elaborately uniformed Palace staff members on either side of the double doors bowed deeply, then flung the doors wide. Suppressing a gasp, I paused on the threshold.

I'd seen pictures of this room, the equivalent of the Sovereigns' throne room, but pictures hadn't come close to doing it justice. For one thing, it was beyond enormous, at least twice the size of Jewel's Town Hall. And the opulence was off the charts, the walls covered with artwork and silk hangings and the ceiling painted with a huge mural of planets and stars, with what looked like real gold highlights.

At the far end, on a dais, was the *cathoir*—a beautifully ornate golden chair with purple velvet cushions. Actually sitting on that thing suddenly seemed ludicrously impossible…just like everything else in my life lately.

Mr. O'Gara and Sean arrived just then and I turned to them in relief, hoping I didn't look as nervous as I felt. "Oh, good! What am I supposed to do? I know you told me, but I've totally spaced it."

Mr. O's smile was understanding. "You'll greet the dignitaries and reporters who will arrive in just a few minutes, then Nels Murdoch will present you with the Royal Scepter. Here is the text of the ceremony. It's very brief."

He punched it up on his omni screen for me and now I recognized it from my earlier reading. After saying my part under my breath twice, I was pretty sure I had it memorized.

"Thanks. And I really have to sit there?" I pointed to the *cathoir*.

"You do. In fact—" He glanced at the time on his omni— "I suggest you do so now."

35

Insealbau

---

*I**NSEALBAU** (in-SALL-baw): Installation, as of Nuathan Sovereign*

I moved to the dais as quickly as my elaborate gown would allow and sat in the intimidating throne-thing just as the doors flew open again, this time to admit a whole crowd of people.

I recognized Nels Murdoch, Devyn Kane, Gordon Nolan and a few others, and Mr. O quietly identified the rest. "The entire acting legislature—both Houses—as well as at least one reporter from every network."

The hundred-plus people arranged themselves in a semi-circle facing me, then Nels stepped forward, thumping his right fist smartly against his chest before bowing.

Everyone else in the room followed suit, then chanted, *Emileia, Thiarna ar barr Nuath, failte a Thiaraway agus cumacht,* the traditional greeting welcoming me to Thiaraway and to the throne.

Then Nels recited, first in Martian, then in English. "Sovereign. It is my honor to welcome you to Thiaraway and to cede leadership of the Nuathan people into your august hands. I hereby present the Royal Scepter, which I deliver into your hands as a token of your authority to rule. May you do so with wisdom and mercy."

He bowed again, the action as stilted as his speech, and the man Mr. O had identified as acting High Chancellor came forward to hand the glittering staff to Nels, who presented it to me with another bow. I hesitated for a second, then reached out and took the Scepter in both hands. It was lighter—and warmer—than I expected. It also felt surprisingly...*mine.*

"*Go raibhe mile maith agat. Me aidh bhunach go deo.* Many thanks," I said. "That will ever be my goal."

Now the whole room chanted along with Nels, "*Thiarna Emileia ar barr Nuath, failte a agus cumacht go deo,*" roughly, "Sovereign Emileia, we look forward to your long reign." Then they all bowed again.

I did the proper inclination of my head in response, which freed everyone to start moving around, some toward the door, others coming forward to offer their personal greetings and congratulations. That took a while, but once the reporters were gone and most of the crowd had dispersed, Nels came up to me again.

"May you rule long and well, Sovereign. I wish you much success in *everything* you do." He felt sincere, which wasn't really surprising, considering what my first task needed to be.

"Thank you, Nels. You served well as Interim Governor during a very difficult time for the Nuathan people. You were chosen because they trusted you to do what was best for them, and clearly that trust was well placed. I hope you will accept a post on my Advisory Council. Your experience would be very valuable to me."

His eyes widened in surprise, but then he smiled—the first real smile he'd directed at me. "It would be my great honor, Excellency. My allegiance, of course, is yours. Always." He bowed deeply.

Relieved to have him as an ally instead of an opponent, I smiled back. "I appreciate that more than I can say. If you have suggestions for other members of my Advisory Council, I would very much like to go over them with you."

"Absolutely, Excellency."

I glanced down at the scepter I still held. "Did Faxon carry this while he was in power?" Nothing in my reading had mentioned it either way.

Nels blinked, then shook his head. "He did have it brought to him at the very beginning, but then ordered it locked in the Royal Treasury, where it has remained for the past fifteen years. Why?"

"Just...curious." I suspected the Scepter might be one of those things specially attuned to the Sovereign bloodline. When I got a chance, I'd have to study up on it.

But first I had to get through this afternoon's stupid Royal Reception, so I could get on with the two things that *really* mattered—stopping the Grentl and getting Rigel back.

"That was well done, inviting Nels onto your Advisory Council," Mr. O'Gara commented as we left the Royal Audience Hall twenty minutes later. "I must say, I'm impressed, Excellency."

His use of my title still made me blink. "Thanks. It seemed like the right thing to do, somehow."

"Indeed."

"How long until that reception? Is there time now to talk about… you know?" There were still Palace staffers nearby.

He shook his head. "It's scheduled to begin in the main function room in about forty-five minutes and you'll need to change first. As will Sean and I. Molly will know how to dress you."

I glanced at her and she nodded eagerly, clearly distracted from her earlier fears by the prospect of again treating me like a living Barbie doll.

"But we'll talk after, right?" I pressed, before Mr. O and Sean left us to go to their quarters. "I *still* haven't heard back from Eric and we need a plan for…everything." No one was close enough to hear, but I had no idea what kind of surveillance system the Palace might have. No point taking chances.

"Of course. I haven't lost sight of what's important, Excellency, not to worry." With that, he bowed, which felt weird, too, and turned away.

Sean hung back. "I thought you did great just now, too." His blue eyes were warm and, at the moment, unshadowed by fear or jealousy. "Try not to worry too much, okay? It'll all work out somehow."

I hoped he was right.

⁘

Half an hour later, arrayed in a *different* purple-with-diamonds dress that was nearly as gorgeous as the Accession one but easier to walk in, we left for the Royal Reception. This time Mr. O and Sean were waiting in the hallway to accompany us to the main function room. Sean's eyes lit up with frank admiration when he saw me.

"Wow. That last outfit was great but this one suits you better. You look awesome."

I felt myself blushing, stupid as that was under the circumstances. "Um, thanks. You guys look great, too."

They did. Their costumes for the Accession had been nearly as ridiculous as mine, but now Sean and his father wore discreetly embroidered navy tunics over dark gray body suits that made them both look very distinguished. Maybe not as impressive as Rigel in his Bodyguard uniform, but...

"Shall we?" Mr. O said, turning toward the corridor on the left.

After a five minute walk, we reached our destination and I gasped yet again. "Main function room" was an absurdly dry description for the most sumptuous ballroom I'd ever seen or even imagined. Chandeliers of pink crystal illuminated gem-encrusted frescoes of flowers and foliage on the walls and intricate gold-inlaid mosaics on the floor. Tables laden with all kinds of delicacies and drinks were scattered around, adorned with fantastical ice—crystal?—sculptures in every color of the rainbow.

People were already entering through another door, decked out nearly as lavishly as the room. Molly and Sean stared around, as stunned as I was, but Mr. O appeared unfazed. Of course, he'd probably been here before, when my grandfather Leontine was alive.

"There will be a receiving line," Mr. O informed me before I could ask. "You, Sean and the senior acting ministers and their spouses." He nodded toward the other early arrivals. "This way."

Soon every healthy Royal in Nuath was there, well over a hundred of them by now, along with the heads of every *fine* and the few non-Royal town or village mayors. Each formally greeted me with bows and congratulations before moving on down the line to the ministers.

Some of these Royals, Mr. O whispered during a brief break, had only recently been released from treatment for memory or other impairments inflicted by Faxon. Another two dozen or so had arrived from Earth three days ago, on a ship from Montana.

"I'll *never* remember all these names and titles," I murmured at one point, as the introductions went on and on. Didn't Mr. O get how distracted I was right now? Wasn't *he*?

"Not to worry. I'm recording everything so you can go over it after, ah, afterward." He tapped his breast pocket, which I assumed contained his omni. "We'll have time to talk later, I promise. For now, just keep smiling."

He and Sean stayed by my side after the interminable receiving line ended, Mr. O'Gara deftly steering conversations away from undesirable topics, but there was no chance for private conversation. Slowly, we made our way around the enormous room, Cormac and Molly trailing behind me. I smiled and nodded as one government official after another outlined what they hoped I'd be able to do for their particular Ministry, and at least a dozen Regent hopefuls politely tried to convince me they'd be my best choice.

Several of the Royal guests still had obvious memory issues, like Jeremy, the former Minister of Elections, who told me at least four times that he'd once visited the Midwest during the six years he'd spent on Earth in his twenties. And Thora, once a Legislator from Monaru, who kept calling me by my mother's name, Galena, then blushing and apologizing profusely, swearing I looked just like her.

Some unimpaired Royals made me uncomfortable, too. There was one in particular, Cora, a recent arrival from Earth, whose bright blue eyes held an almost fanatically intense gleam whenever she looked at me, giving me the creeps. Gordon, at least, kept his distance, merely smiling with exaggerated politeness any time I looked his way.

As we went, Cormac and Molly tasted and served me whatever food or drink I showed an interest in, though Mr. O frowned me away from the prettiest glasses. Sean informed me in a whisper that those contained an alcoholic beverage called *spakriga*, the Nuathan version of champagne.

If it weren't for the terrible threat looming over everyone, I might possibly have enjoyed myself, at least at first. But as the evening wore on and people kept talking at me, I had an increasingly strong urge to yell at everybody to shut up—that they had no idea what was *really* important, that their whole complicated colony might be *gone* in two days.

Instead, I smiled my thanks to Molly as she handed me another adorable little canapé, then whispered to Sean, on my left. "How soon till we can politely get out of here? I can't believe your dad's making us do this when we need to be working on…you know."

"Yeah, I know. But he thinks following the traditions will keep people from panicking."

Before I could argue the point, the acting Minister of Transportation came up to ask me a question about getting the trains onto their old schedule, forcing me back into Sovereign mode.

Though I'd been dying for the reception to end, when it finally did, the fear I'd managed to push to the back of my mind resurfaced. The ornate clock above the door showed it was nearly eleven, which meant I now had less than thirty-seven hours to save Nuath…or not.

Late as it was, when I suggested we all go back to my quarters to talk, Mr. O immediately agreed.

"You were a very good sport tonight," he said the moment we were safely behind closed doors. "All of you were. I know pretending everything is fine wasn't easy, but I do believe it will go a long way toward undermining any rumors certain people might start."

Gordon, in other words.

"Let's quickly check the feeds, shall we?" he continued. "Then we can discuss what our next step needs to be."

As he moved to the main vidscreen, he noticed the message light flashing. "I hope you haven't been bombarded. I meant to have your messages routed through me for sorting before you receive them, at least until a permanent aide can be found. We'll check what's there in a moment."

There was nothing particularly surprising in the news. A few stories, still, about last night's power glitch, but mostly it was all about the happenings at the Palace today. The entire colony of Nuath had apparently been throwing an incredible, all-day party. Some of the shots of people celebrating in the streets—celebrating *me*—were both embarrassing and heartwarming. And made me hope all the more I could somehow keep them all safe.

After ten minutes, Mr. O turned off the feed and pulled up my list of waiting messages. To both my relief and disappointment, none were from Rigel or Eric, but one was from his grandmother.

"Interesting," Mr. O'Gara commented after shunting half a dozen messages into his own in-box for evaluation. "I wonder what Morag Teague can want?" He clicked it.

This time Morag's bow looked forced and mechanical. "I cannot, of course, refuse your direct order, Excellency," she said without any introductory niceties. "Though Rigel's Healers have strongly advised against it, I will inform them he is to be at the Palace by noon tomorrow. Your good health." With another perfunctory bow, she signed off.

Mr. O turned to me with a frown. "What was that about? Did you contact her?"

"Of course." I lifted my chin, refusing to feel guilty. "I sent her a message almost as soon as I got here. She's refused to let me talk to Rigel ever since she took him away." He didn't need to know about the one conversation we'd managed. "But the vote is over now and I'm Installed and everything, so what difference does it make if we're together? Especially if having him here can help me stop the Grentl?"

"I thought Eric Eagan was going to help you with that? Rigel Stuart only knows what you've told him." His voice was heavy with disapproval.

"That was the plan, but as I've been *trying* to tell you all day, Eric isn't returning my calls and I'm getting really worried. I think he's the only one who knows where the Grentl communication device is or how it works."

"Eric never shared that knowledge with anyone else, as a safeguard?"

"A couple of other Scientists knew at one time, but they're both dead now."

"Then he should have given you more information at the outset, against the chance of something happening to him." He swallowed, his alarm now matching mine—finally. "We need to track him down immediately. We're running out of time."

"I hope Eric is okay. But especially if he's not, I need Rigel here." I sent Sean an apologetic glance, which he ignored. "I knew you wouldn't approve, but I'm going to need every advantage possible and my bond with Rigel is an advantage."

"That serum you were given—"

"Keeps me from getting sick, yes. In fact it makes me feel mostly normal. But when Rigel's with me—" *when he's touching me, kissing me,* I thought but didn't say— "I'm *better* than normal. I'm stronger, faster, smarter, more confident—all the things I'm going to need to be, to deal with the Grentl and save Nuath."

Mr. O'Gara continued to glare at me for a long moment, apparently deep in thought, then sighed and shook his head. "It's far more important to find Eric Eagan. We can deal with this…other matter later, after the main threat has been averted. You're sure Eric told you *nothing* about where the device is located?"

"Just that it's in a sealed room somewhere in the Palace. I think—I hope—if I find the room I'll be able to open it. From what he said, it's probably one of those Sovereign-bloodline-only things, like the door to this apartment. But first we have to find it."

He nodded, then stood. "Yes. Well. It's late and we're all tired. Let's tackle that problem in the morning, shall we? A discreet inquiry into Eric's whereabouts will likely turn him up, then we'll go from there."

Sean stood, too, but hesitated when his father moved to the door. "So...you're okay with Rigel Stuart coming here and starting those rumors back up?"

"I didn't say that, Sean," Mr. O'Gara snapped, "but now is not the time to discuss it. Come along."

I could feel Sean's anger, jealousy and resentment—partly at his father—as he reluctantly followed him out of the room. When the door closed, I let out a sigh of my own, which Molly echoed.

"Poor Sean," she said. "I'm pretty sure he was starting to think, well—"

"I know. But you get why I need Rigel here, don't you?" I looked at her pleadingly, hoping for *one* ally.

She lifted a shoulder. "I guess. I just...hate to see Sean hurt."

"Me, too, and I'm really sorry about that. He's a great guy. He's just not...Rigel."

⁺_₊

Once I was ready for bed and alone again, I turned on my bedroom vidscreen and replayed Morag Teague's last message—quietly.

"Though Rigel's Healers have strongly advised against it, I will inform them he is to be at the Palace by noon tomorrow."

No, I didn't see how she could wriggle out of that promise, or how those Healers could refuse to do as she asked. She was his guardian, after all, the only one in Nuath with full authority over him—except me. I should definitely have Rigel back by noon tomorrow!

Sean had been right earlier: everything *was* going to work out okay. Mr. O would track down Eric and, with Rigel's help, I'd be able to do whatever I needed to do to keep Nuath safe. Right at this moment, I was absolutely sure of it.

For the first time in nearly two weeks, I fell asleep with a smile on my lips.

I was still cheerful at breakfast, which made Sean glower and Mr. O avoid my eye. We were all eating in my apartment today, so we could talk. "Any luck finding Eric?" I asked brightly as we sat down, earning a quick frown from Mr. O.

"Not yet. He's not at his home, so I'm making inquiries elsewhere, to include all of the Healing facilities."

That sobered me a little. "Do you think he's sick? Or hurt?"

"Perhaps. He's extremely elderly. He might even have died."

I'd tried hard not to think about that possibility. "Well, um, let me know as soon as you hear anything."

Finally subdued, I finished my breakfast in silence while Mr. O ran down the list of people who'd applied for audiences and what excuses he'd used to put them off. For the next twenty-four hours, *all* our attention needed to be on averting the Grentl threat.

As soon as Sean and Mr. O left, I checked for messages—first on my omni, which only Rigel and Eric could access. Nothing. Then I went into my bedroom to check the vidscreen, where almost three dozen waited, though most had already been copied to Mr. O to deal with. I scrolled quickly down the list, then suddenly sucked in my breath. There, third from the bottom, was one from Rigel! It had come just ten minutes ago.

Hoping against hope he wouldn't say he'd be delayed getting here, I touched "play"—and there he was, my Rigel, big as life and so gorgeous my heart turned over.

"Hey, M," he said. "You might want to sit down to listen to this."

What? Why? I wanted to shout at his image, my bubble of happiness punctured by his wooden tone, his sad smile. Backing up, I dropped onto an ottoman, my eyes glued to the screen.

"I've had time to do a lot of thinking," he continued in that same awful, expressionless voice, "and I've come to a decision. You're not going to like it, but I think it's the right thing to do. What we had together was wonderful, but I think we both knew it couldn't be forever. You hold a position now that requires you to make sacrifices and I need to be one of those sacrifices."

No no no no no, I started chanting silently as the terrible words kept coming.

"I've decided to go back to Earth immediately. You need to be with Sean now, for the good of Nuath. But because it will hurt too much to see you two together from now on, I've asked to have the last year of my memory erased before I go."

"NO!" This time I said it out loud, leaping to my feet. But he continued talking, while I kept shaking my head like I could make it all not true, make him not really be saying these horrible things.

"I know I'm taking the coward's way out, and I'm sorry for that, M, and sorry I can't tell you a proper goodbye. I hope in time you'll be able to get over me and be happy with Sean. He's not a bad guy, you know, even if I haven't always been his biggest fan.

"By the time you get this message, the procedure will already be done, and I'll already be on board the *Luminosity*. I'm bringing along a letter for my parents explaining what I've done and suggesting we move away from Jewel, so please don't try to come after me. Your focus right now needs to be on keeping Nuath safe, both from this immediate threat and into the future. Please do your best to stay safe and to be happy. Goodbye, M."

The screen went blank.

I was left staring at the spot that had been Rigel, too stunned to cry.

36

Iobirt inghlactha

IOBIRT INGHLACTHA (EE-BURT EN-HWAHK-THUH): *acceptable sacrifice*

Sean

"I see," my dad is saying to someone on his omni when I come out of the bathroom and join him in the living room of the huge two bedroom apartment we're sharing. "Thank you."

He clicks off and turns to me with a sort of grimace. "Good news and bad news. I've located Eric Eagan at one of the smaller Healing facilities in Pryderi. He's alive, but that's all they would tell me, as I'm not a family member."

"But they'll have to tell M, won't they, since she's Sovereign? If she insists?"

"That's my hope. I was just about to call her with this development."

"I'll go tell her myself," I offer, heading for the door. "If that's okay?"

Dad's expression tells me he knows why I want to do this, but he nods anyway. "Tell her the more quickly she can get Eric here to the Palace the better—though she knows that already."

"Right." I hurry toward M's apartment, rehearsing how to give her this news. I was kind of a jerk at breakfast just now, too jealous to think about the kind of pressure she's under. Hopefully this news will make her happy—happier than she already is, what with Rigel arriving any minute now.

I shove that thought away, telling myself—again—that if having him here will help her do what she needs to do, I should be all in favor of it. I guess I'm still having trouble wrapping my head around this Grentl thing. A few days ago I thought Nuath's problems were mostly over, with Faxon gone. All we had to do was get M up far enough in the polls to be Acclaimed. And I was totally on board to help with that.

But now there's a threat way worse than Faxon hanging over the only place I've ever thought of as home, and I can't do *anything* to help. But maybe this news will.

I tap the door chime on M's apartment and Molly opens the door, her face white and scared, which makes me forget for a second why I'm here.

"What? What's wrong? Are you okay? Or is M—?"

Molly flaps a hand toward M's bedroom and my gut clenches. "No, M's not okay, but I can't get her to tell me what's wrong. She's just sitting on the floor in there muttering to herself. Sean, I think she's finally cracked under the pressure! What are we going to do?"

Pushing past Molly, I shrug, like it's no big deal. "We'll snap her out of it, that's all." It might not be that easy, but I want to erase that scared look from Molly's face—even though I'm scared now, too.

M is sitting on the floor of her bedroom, in between a white leather ottoman and the vidscreen, which is blank. She doesn't even look up when I come in, just keeps rocking forward and backward, chanting, "No, no, no," over and over and over.

I squat down on my heels in front of her. "M? M, it's Sean. Can you hear me?"

She doesn't respond, just keeps rocking and chanting, so I put a hand on her shoulder to stop the rocking, at least. For a second she pushes against me, but then a kind of shudder goes through her and she looks up at me.

"Sean?"

Relief explodes through me. I nearly hug her to my chest, but stop myself in time. "Yeah, M, it's me. What's going on?"

First horror fills her eyes, then tears. She waves a hand at the blank vidscreen in front of her. "It's Rigel. He— Oh, no, no, no, no." She tries to start rocking again, but I don't let her.

"What? What about Rigel? He's not coming here after all? Did Morag do something to him?"

"Not...not Morag. He—" She breaks off with a wail, then suddenly starts sobbing so hard I'm afraid she'll hurt herself, her breath coming in gasps that sound almost like screams.

My fear floods back, almost choking me. I'm careful not to look at Molly. I don't want her to know how scared I am. If Rigel's dead or something, will we be able to pull M out of this crash in time?

We have to, that's all. With Nuath's survival on the line, we have no choice. M has no choice. Stiffening my backbone, I grab M by both shoulders and make her look at me.

"M! M, snap out of it and tell me what happened! Please!"

It's several long moments before she can stop herself from sobbing and gasping, but slowly, slowly, she does. Still sniffling a little, she wipes her nose with the back of her hand, then finally starts talking.

"I got...I got a message. From Rigel. He said...he said..."

"Did you erase the message?"

She shakes her head.

"Then can I watch it? So you don't have to tell me?"

"Oh. Oh, I guess so. But I don't think I can—"

I loosen my grip on her shoulders, instead stroking them lightly. "Hey, it's okay. Everything is going to be okay, M. Somehow. You'll see." It's a stupid promise, one I have no power to make come true, but I don't want her to fall apart again. "I'm going to watch the message now, okay? You don't have to if you don't want, though. You can go in the other room with Molly."

At my glance, Molly holds out her hand to M. "C'mon, M. Let's get you a cup of tea, okay?" M lets Molly pull her up, lets her lead her out of the room. Molly sends a helpless glance over her shoulder at me as they go. I want to reassure her, too, but that will have to wait.

As soon as the bedroom door closes behind them, I power up the vid and play Rigel's message. My mouth falls open as I listen. Because even if I happen to agree his leaving is the right thing for Nuath, I can't *believe* he'd really do something like this to M. *Especially* not right now. As soon as the message ends, I hit "play" again.

As I watch the video for a second time, a suspicion starts to niggle at the back of my brain. But it would be beyond cruel to say anything to M unless I can verify it. Besides, it would be guaranteed to distract her from what she needs to do over the next twenty-four hours and *nothing* is worth risking that.

After a third watching that unfortunately makes my suspicion even stronger, I turn it off and join M and Molly in the living room.

They're sitting at the table, both with cups of tea, and I'm relieved to see M actually sipping hers. Molly isn't. She looks questioningly at me but I shake my head slightly. I'll tell her later.

"I'm sorry, M." I sit down next to her but don't touch her. "I don't blame you being upset. But can we worry about that problem after we keep Nuath from being destroyed?" I'm careful not to say Rigel's name, afraid it might set her off again.

She sets down her teacup and gives a huge, shuddering sigh. "I don't— No. You're right. I have to at least try." She lifts her chin an inch and looks at me, misery still clouding her green eyes. "Thanks, Sean."

"Hey, what kind of friend would I be if I didn't help you save the world?" I say it lightly, though it's taking all my willpower not to touch her, to hold her. She seems to need comfort so badly. Later, I promise myself. "I came to tell you Dad found Eric."

"Alive?" She looks afraid to hope, like she's bracing herself for another disaster.

"Yes, alive. But he's in the hospital and we need you to get him out. They won't even tell Dad anything about his condition."

M takes another sip of tea, then stands up, squaring her shoulders. "Okay. Just tell me who to call."

I'm incredibly proud of her but don't say that, either. "Let me ask Dad." I message him and two minutes later he joins us in M's apartment.

He shoots a curious glance at M, who still looks pretty fragile even though she's holding herself together at the moment. Before he can ask her what's wrong, I touch his arm and give him a quick shake of my head. He frowns, then nods before turning to M again.

"Sean told you we found Eric Eagan? He's in the Whelan Healing facility in Pryderi, condition unknown. I couldn't get any information from the person who answered my call, but you should be able to."

M doesn't say anything, just goes to the big vidscreen and pulls up the controls like she's done it a million times. "Whelan Healing facility," she says firmly.

A second later a blonde woman appears. She looks shocked when she realizes who's calling, then bows to the screen. "Apprentice Healer Gilda at your service, Excellency! May…may I help you?"

"Yes," M says. "I need to have Eric Eagan sent to the Royal Palace as soon as possible."

"Eric Eagan?" The woman taps something in front of her and frowns. "According to his records, he's not in a condition to leave the facility. In fact, well…"

"Well what?"

"I'm sorry, this is the sort of thing that's normally only shared with next-of-kin, but—"

"But I *am* the Sovereign," M reminds her.

The blonde pales slightly. "Of course. Also, he doesn't seem to have any next-of-kin listed. I'm ah, afraid Eric Eagan isn't expected to leave the Healing facility at all, Excellency. His condition is both fragile and terminal."

Oh, crap! Dad and I exchange worried glances and I hear a little sound somewhere between a gasp and a sob from M. "Terminal? But—"

"His birthdate does show him to be well over three hundred years old. I've never heard of anyone choosing to stay alive for so long. Unfortunately, there are still *some* limits to what we can do to slow the aging process."

"Can…can I at least talk to him?" M asks after a second.

"I don't know whether he's lucid at the moment, but I can try. Just a moment."

The screen saver pops up, then a quavery voice says, "Yes? Hello?"

"Eric?" M says. "Eric, it's M. Um, Sovereign Emileia."

"Excellency. Thank God." He breaks off and we hear coughing. Then, his voice a little stronger, he says, "They took my omni when I was admitted."

I see M swallow. "I'm so sorry, Eric. I just found out—"

"No time," he interrupts. "You need to have me brought to the Palace immediately. Make it a Royal order, so they can't refuse."

"Can't you just…tell me what to do?" M looks like she's about to cry, but not about Rigel this time.

"No. Everything here is monitored. Not secure." He starts coughing again, for longer this time. Finally, he just says, "Hurry. Please," and breaks the connection.

M turns to look at us. "What if he's too sick to move?"

"Eric is dying anyway," Dad says gently. "I imagine he'd rather save Nuath first, if he possibly can. Call again and ask for Eric's Healer."

She does, and Gilda transfers her call.

"Healer Alban, Sovereign. Honored, of course." The guy gives her a sketchy bow, not looking honored at all. "I'm afraid I was in the middle of— What can I do for you?"

"Healer, I require the presence of Eric Eagan at the Royal Palace. Immediately." M's voice is so authoritative it startles me. Good for her!

But the Healer frowns. "I'm sorry, Excellency, but that is not possible. His condition—"

"Yes, I've been informed, and I'm sorry to hear it, but I'm afraid it's irrelevant. This is a matter of vital importance and no one but Eric will do. He is in full agreement that he must come. He can be brought on a stretcher, if necessary. Please make the necessary arrangements."

His frown becomes a scowl. "I really cannot sanction—"

"Noted. Should his condition worsen as a result of my request, I will take full responsibility."

"I'll see what I can do," the guy snaps. "It may take a few minutes to—"

M cuts him off again. "Thank you. I'll wait."

The next five minutes seem to last forever. Again I want to tell M how proud I am of her, but again I don't. Finally the blonde Apprentice Healer appears on the screen again.

"I apologize for the delay, Excellency, but Eric's Healer— Anyway, he has authorized Eric's visit to the Royal Palace, once all possible precautions have been taken. I was told we can have him there tomorrow morning, if that will be acceptable?"

"If they can possibly get him here today, please tell them to do so. I appreciate your assistance Gilda." M ends the call and lets out a long breath, her shoulders slumping a little now.

Dad shakes his head. "That's going to be cutting it too close. Now that they've authorized his release, I'll go there in person to see if I can hurry the process—with your permission, of course."

"If you think it will help. The sooner we can get him here, the better."

"Do you want me to come, too?" I need to tell Dad what Rigel did to M, but I'm kind of afraid to leave her right now, in case she falls apart again. So I'm mostly relieved when Dad shakes his head.

"No need. Do what you can here to help prepare for Eric's arrival." He shoots a concerned look at M. For a second he looks like he's about to say something else, but then just leaves.

As soon as he's gone, M sort of collapses in on herself. I help her to a chair before she can fall down.

"Hey, easy. Just relax for a minute. You did great just now, by the way. Every inch the Sovereign."

M looks up and gives me a sad little laugh that makes my gut twist. "Guess I'm a better actress than I thought." Then her face crumples and she starts crying again. Not sobbing this time, just tears flowing silently down her cheeks.

"M, don't! Please. Try to hold it together for the next twenty-four hours and then we'll figure something out, okay? Maybe you can order somebody to restore his memory like they've done with the people Faxon messed with."

"What—?" Molly starts to say, but stops at my look. She needs to know, though.

"M, can Molly watch that message, too?"

M nods, tears still running down her face. I motion to Molly to go into M's bedroom and do that. No way I want M to see it again, not now.

While Molly's gone, I bring M more tea and sit next to her, talking the whole time but not really saying much. Trying to comfort her with my voice, mostly.

"Dad'll do what he can to get Eric here faster and you'll want to be ready for that, right? So drink up and I'll ask Molly to pick you out something to wear. What kind of outfit would be appropriate for saving the world, huh?"

She doesn't laugh but she does take a sip of tea. Then another. Good enough for now.

Molly rejoins us after a couple of minutes, looking shell-shocked and almost like she might cry herself. I send her another warning look so she won't start telling M how sorry she is. We need to keep her mind off that message as much as possible.

And that's what we spend the rest of the day doing.

Molly putters around the apartment asking M's opinion on stupid stuff like where a vase of flowers should go or which shoes she'd rather wear with a certain outfit. I turn on the news feeds and scan for stories I think might distract M, then try to get her talking about them. Half the time she doesn't respond to either one of us, like she's too deep in her own tortured thoughts to hear. But other times she does, so we keep it up, keep trying to draw her out of herself.

Dad comes back late that afternoon, but he doesn't look happy.

"That Healer Alban is a piece of work," he says. "Even though I said I was acting on behalf of the Sovereign, he put me off for hours, then finally agreed to have Eric brought here this evening. But that won't help us much, because he insists Eric be sedated for the move and can't be awakened before morning. Still, better this than having Eric arrive sedated in the morning—which would have kept him from helping in time."

M doesn't react but Molly looks scared again.

"Good thing you went, Dad," I say quickly. "Now we'll have a few hours to spare. It'll be fine." That's for Molly. And M. For all of us, really.

Dad and I go back to our apartment to change for dinner—in M's private dining room again—and I finally have a chance to tell him about Rigel.

"Hm. She seems to be coping fairly well, at least."

I look at him like he's nuts. "Coping well? She was a basket case when I first got to her. Ask Molly. Why would Stuart do this, especially now? He had to know what it would do to her."

"Youth doesn't always think ahead, but in this case it's probably for the best. Perhaps his grandmother suggested this course, as it will go a long way toward clearing their family name."

"Yeah, but—" I start to mention my suspicion about that message, but something in Dad's expression stops me. It's almost like he expected this, only…how could he? Either way, there's nothing we can do right now—not until after M stops the Grentl.

"I'm sure M will get over this, in time." Dad still sounds way too calm, almost dismissive. "Meanwhile, we'll help her to do what she needs to do tomorrow. As Nels Murdoch has called to remind me half a dozen times today, that's the important thing. Let's not lose sight of that."

"Don't worry. I won't." But M is important, too, and I wonder if Dad hasn't maybe lost sight of *that*.

37

Gaiscigh

GAISCIGH (GAH-SHEEG): *heroism; act of extreme bravery*

I lay on my bed, staring at the ceiling as the fake Nuathan daylight gradually turned it from dark gray to pale blue. Yesterday's events were still a blur and I was trying to keep them that way.

My soul-deep shock that Rigel wouldn't be here for me, that he'd actually made the *choice* to leave me, had left me almost incapable of thought. If Sean—and Molly, and their Dad—hadn't been here, making me almost literally put one foot in front of the other, I might have fallen so deeply into my black hole of misery I'd be stuck there forever. I still wasn't sure they'd done me a favor by dragging me out.

Last night, when Molly finally left me alone, the enormity of what had happened crashed over me all over again. Sure, I'd been upset when Rigel was sent down to steerage on the ship and I'd been forbidden to talk to him. And even more upset when his grandmother took him away with barely a goodbye. But this…this might just destroy me completely.

Those other times, I'd at least been secure in his love and knew the separation was as painful for him as it was for me. And I'd had *some* reason to believe it wouldn't be permanent. Not only was this separation permanent, but I was in pain all by myself. By now, Rigel didn't even know who I was. Didn't remember…anything that mattered.

I'd cried until no more tears would come, leaving me with a dull numbness that lasted all night. I welcomed it, clung to it even now. Numb was better. Easier. Maybe if I stayed numb long enough—

"M?" Molly's voice filtered through the locked bedroom door. "Dad's here. He says Eric Eagan is finally awake."

At her words, my sluggish brain started working again in spite of me. I resisted at first, fighting to hang onto the numb, because renewed capacity for thought meant renewed capacity for pain. But it was no use.

With a groan, I heaved myself to my feet and went to the bathroom to splash a bit of precious cold water on my face. It didn't help—my eyes were still red-rimmed and puffy. I shrugged at myself in the mirror. Appearances didn't matter any more. Nothing did. Not to me.

But I still had to put one foot in front of the other, at least for the next few hours. "Game on," I said to my reflection, forcing myself to muster all the strength I had left for the challenge I'd come to Mars to face. Even with my heart ripped out, I had to do what I could to save Nuath from the Grentl.

After that, I could go back to numb. Maybe for good.

The others were waiting in the living room to urge breakfast on me before going to see Eric, but I refused everything but a few sips of tea.

"Let's get on with it." In a detached sort of way, I noticed how dead my voice sounded. If the others noticed, they didn't comment on it.

Mr. O led the way to the guest wing, where Eric had spent the night. I followed docilely, Sean close by my side, Molly and Cormac two steps behind.

"How long do we have?" I heard Molly whisper fearfully to Sean as we walked.

"Nearly two hours," he responded. "Plenty of time. Don't worry, Mol."

Two hours didn't sound like plenty of time, but I couldn't seem to summon any worry. Some remote corner of my mind knew I should be nervous, even afraid, but I wasn't. Probably just as well.

Mr. O stopped in front of a door, pressed the chime, and it slid open. Inside, a woman in a metallic green uniform was helping Eric into a complicated-looking silver chair that hovered a few inches from the floor. At our entrance, both of them bowed to me, Eric from his chair.

"Thank you for coming, Eric," I said mechanically. "I'm sorry it was necessary."

"Quite all right, Excellency." His voice was barely above a whisper. "It was my wish to come. You may leave me now," he told the attendant. "This chair has everything I need, and it will notify the facility should my condition change. Whether I want it to or not."

The woman frowned disapprovingly, but nodded and left. Forcing myself to really focus on Eric, I was momentarily shocked out of my numbness by the change two weeks had wrought. Old as he'd appeared before, now he looked like an animated, emaciated corpse, his skin sunken against his bones and his hands impossibly frail. Only his eyes showed that he was alive and conscious.

"I'm sorry," I repeated, this time meaning it. "I had no idea—"

"My choice," he interrupted wheezily. "Only reason I'm still around. Had I known I might deteriorate so quickly, I would have given you more information when we last met. Now..." He paused to catch his breath before continuing. "Now we have little time to waste. If my calculations are correct—"

I nodded. "Right. We have to do this in the next two hours. I know. Can you tell us where we need to go and exactly what I have to do when I get there? Then I can handle things myself and you can...rest." He really did look and sound awful.

But he shook his head with surprising fierceness. "No! I—" He coughed, then cleared his throat. "I must take you. Show you. The room...intentionally difficult to find. Come."

Eric led the way into the hall, guiding his chair around one corner, then another, taking us back the way we'd just come.

"It's in my own apartment?" I asked, startled, as we approached the door.

"Not in. Through." He paused by the door while I palmed it open. "Special access created for Sovereigns to avoid notice."

Which made perfect sense, now I thought about it.

We followed Eric across the huge main room to the Sovereign's office, a room I'd only glanced into during my initial tour of the apartment. He led the way past several plush chairs and the big desk with its vidscreen to the far wall, which was of that crystal-studded non-reflective metal I'd noticed earlier. There, he finally stopped.

"Is there a...a secret door or something? How—?"

Eric pointed at one of the crystals, a blue, star-shaped one. "Blue.

Your signal, when device activates. Otherwise, colorless. All these know?" He gestured weakly toward the others.

"Yes, I tried to message you. Quite a few people know now. It wasn't my intention but it's what got me Acclaimed in time."

His eyes wandered from face to face. "You and you, accompany us," he said to Mr. O and Sean. "You others wait here. Not enough space for all."

Before either Cormac or Molly could protest, Mr. O said, "He's right. No point all of us going. If we're all still here two hours and—" He glanced at his omni— "seven minutes from now, you'll know we were successful."

They both bowed and left, Molly still obviously scared despite Sean's whispered reassurance.

"Your hand," Eric said to me. "There." I touched the spot he indicated, just next to the blue crystal, and sure enough, a door that had been invisible a moment before slid down into the floor, revealing a tiny, softly-lit room. It was empty.

Eric motioned me inside, then followed, as did Mr. O and Sean, looking as confused as I was. Eric was right—there definitely wasn't room for two more people in here. The door slid shut and I felt the floor descend beneath us.

A few seconds later the door opened again to reveal a long, dimly lit hallway. When we stepped out, the elevator door closed—and disappeared. A barely-discernible oval, marginally shinier than the surrounding wall, was the only indication of its location.

Now Eric led us down the hallway, past a series of huge doors spaced at regular intervals—storage rooms, maybe?—then stopped in front of one near the end of the passage. "Through here," he whispered.

Mr. O touched the door's access panel and the big door slid up into the ceiling. Behind it was a huge room filled with plastic and metal crates. Eric propelled his chair through the towering maze of stacked containers, turning corner after corner until we arrived at what appeared to be a blank wall.

"Again. Your palm." He motioned me toward the wall.

I pressed my hand against it and the wall simply...disappeared. Behind it was a room maybe twice the size of the secret elevator.

"Come." Eric moved ahead of me to an alcove on the far side that held what I assumed must be the Grentl communication device.

It was much smaller than I'd expected, a cube maybe ten inches on a side that appeared to be composed mostly of some kind of crystal, with copper projections at the near left and far right upper corners. Looking closer, I saw more coppery bits woven all through the semi-transparent crystal, from which emanated a faint glow.

"What…what do I have to do?" I whispered. My numbness gone for the moment, fingers of dread crawled up my spine.

"I'll show you. But first, this." Eric pointed to a tiny panel in the wall next to the Grentl device's alcove.

The panel was so small I could cover the whole thing with my palm—which I tentatively did. I felt it slide open and jerked my hand away to see a small recess that held nothing but a smooth, flat, circular something.

"Take it," Eric whispered.

Tensing for I'm not sure what, I reached in and pulled out the object, a purplish crystal two inches in diameter and not quite an inch thick. I turned the thing over in my hand. "What is it?" There were no identifying markings, nothing to give a hint of its purpose.

"Archive." I had to stoop to hear him, his whisper was so faint now. "Can access after imprint on device. May help. Now." He faced the square device again. "Left hand here. Right hand there. Simultaneous. Don't…let go."

Nodding, I set the archive stone back in its little cubby and positioned myself directly in front of the communication device, my heart pounding. My earlier numbness would have helped now, because I was as scared as I could ever remember being in my life. I could hear my own breath coming in shallow, frightened gasps.

Sean place a comforting hand on my shoulder. "Go on, you'll be fine," he whispered, but Eric waved him back.

"Mustn't…touch her. Not for this."

Taking one more fortifying breath, I extended my right hand until it was directly over the back projection and put my left over the nearer one. Then, counting silently to three, I grabbed both projections at the same instant.

A searing current arced through my body, from one hand to the other and back, making me gasp and *almost* forcing me to let go. I gritted my teeth and held on. The current continued to race across me —not quite electrical in nature, more like alternating hot and cold sensations that bordered on painful. I tightened my hands to a death grip, determined not to let go until Eric said I could, and the current slowly diminished to a gentle warmth that was almost pleasant. I was suddenly reminded of how the Royal Scepter had felt when I'd first touched it. This had the same *mine*-ness.

I turned my head to ask Eric if I could let go, but before I could form the question I was suddenly assaulted by a series of images—no, more than images. *Experiences.*

I was a child being led by the hand into the Royal Audience Hall, then handed onto the knee of the man on the throne—my father. I was older, about my own real age, being introduced to a handsome young man by my mother. He and I were studying together. Now I was a few years older, being handed the Royal Scepter, feeling it warm in my hands. Older still, I faced this same Grentl device, felt the current running across my body. Years later, I held my first child in my arms, a son. I named him Leontine.

The flashes came faster and faster, each one later in Aerleas's life. I was elderly now…then abruptly I was a child again, a boy this time.

Leontine-me listened while my mother, Aerleas, handed out an edict from the throne. I visited the People's House and asked questions of some of the legislators there. I met a beautiful girl but she left and I was sad, but then I met a different girl—no, a woman—and we took vows together. I held our firstborn, also a son. Now I was handed the Scepter, felt it become *mine.* The Grentl device again, and I approached it fearfully, nearly letting go during the imprinting process. Much older now, I stood in front of an angry mob, trying to calm them.

And then I was younger again, in my late teens, and angry, fighting with two other boys on a dirty city street beside a dumpster. Still angry, I sat by the bedside of a woman, my mother, as she died. I walked down the ramp from a space ship, scared and excited, taking in my very first glimpse of Nuath. Now I was giving an impassioned speech to a large group of people, shaking my fist. And again, to an even larger group. They're cheering. An old man is lying at my feet, dead. Finally, the Grentl device again. It hurts terribly, searing my hands, but I can't let go.

That last image faded from my mind, leaving me shaking and confused. Then, before I could release the device, I felt something totally different—something even scarier. Images again, but this time they were mine—experiences from my own life, beginning earlier than

I'd ever consciously remembered, as an infant here in this very Palace, and continuing on through every year of my childhood right up to the present. It was like my thoughts, my very brain, was being sucked out of my skull, faster and faster, through the device to some unknown end.

Finally, finally, it stopped. While I was still gasping from the ordeal, the copper projections I held abruptly cooled, which I assumed meant they'd hung up. Carefully, gingerly, I let go. My palms were still tingling and my temples throbbed, but I didn't seem to be injured in any way.

I took a step back, away from the terrifying device, and slowly turned to find Sean and Mr. O'Gara staring at me, clearly alarmed.

"M," Sean said, reaching a hand toward me. "Are you okay? For a while there, we were afraid you might— That you—"

"What happened?" his father interrupted. "Were you communicating with them? Did it work? Will they stop manipulating the power supply?"

"I…I don't know," I stammered, still shell-shocked from my experience. "They didn't…didn't *say* anything to me. It was…it was…"

Mr. O held up his omni so that we could all see it. "We'll know in a moment. The next outage was to occur in…seventeen seconds."

Had I really been communing with the device for two whole hours? It had felt like seconds…and days.

We all tensed, barely breathing, as we watched the seconds count down on Mr. O's omni. Two seconds. One. And…nothing. No change.

Mr. O went to the door of the room and looked out. "The lights are still on. I think…I think we may be all right."

"You did it!" There was awe in Sean's voice, and disbelief. Then, loud and exultant, "You did it!" Without warning, he hugged me to him and I was too stunned—by everything—to protest, or even to comprehend.

Slowly, by stages, it sank in. I *had* done it. We were still here. Nuath hadn't been destroyed. Relief bubbled up in me, bittersweet because I couldn't share it with Rigel, but relief all the same. I turned excitedly to Eric.

"Eric, we did it! Thank you so much! I could never have done this without you."

He didn't respond or move, slumped down in his chair, his head tilted at an awkward angle. I reached over and shook his shoulder gently, reluctant to wake him. "Eric?"

Slowly he opened his eyes, but didn't sit up any straighter. "Contact established?" he whispered.

"Yes, I think so. They didn't disrupt the power, anyway."

"Done, then. You…Emileia…saved Nuath." Those last two words were a mere breath, but accompanied by a smile so happy, so peaceful, that I felt like I'd been given a medal. Then Eric's eyes closed again and he sank even deeper into his chair, his head lolling back, his breathing stilled.

"Eric?" I repeated, tears starting to my eyes, but I knew even before I touched him again that he was gone, his life's work finished.

The three of us gazed down at Eric's lifeless body for a long, somber moment.

Mr. O was the first to find his voice. "He held on for decades longer than anyone should have to, just so he could accomplish this last task. All of Nuath would honor him as a hero, if they knew."

I swallowed. "I wish we could tell them. There should be a…a holiday in his honor or something."

"A nice thought," Mr. O agreed. "But now, we need to get him back upstairs before someone from the Healing facility arrives. They'll know already that he's dead."

He motioned to Sean to help him maneuver the chair around so they could guide it out of the room. Sean nodded, but then paused to look closely into my face.

"Will you be all right?"

I shrugged. I didn't see how I ever could be, with Rigel gone. The Grentl threat was all that had kept me moving forward, and now it was over. My sense of purpose was gone. I looked up at Sean helplessly, not sure how to put any of that into words. Knowing that even if I could, it would pain him.

"I just—" I began, when a hum interrupted me.

We all turned to see a faint bluish glow emanating from the Grentl device along with the hum, which was intensifying. I glanced questioningly at Mr. O'Gara, since Eric could no longer advise me.

"Do you think I should—?"

He nodded urgently. "Yes. You must. We can't risk ignoring them again."

Terrified at the prospect of another session like the last one, I moved slowly to the device. Exactly as Eric had instructed me before, I grasped the two projections simultaneously. The current was milder this time, the sense of *mine*-ness even stronger.

"Hello?" I said it aloud, but also tried to project it with my mind, not at all sure how this communication actually worked.

There was a pause, during which I could feel my heart beating. Then, without warning, a thought intruded itself into my brain, unmistakably from without.

From the device.

From the Grentl.

"WE ARE COMING."

.˙.

*Read **Starfall**, the electrifying conclusion to the original Starstruck series!*

About the Author

Brenda Hiatt is the New York Times bestselling author of twenty-three novels (so far), including traditional Regency romance, time travel romance, historical romance, and humorous mystery. She is as excited about her STARSTRUCK series as she's ever been about any of her books. In addition to writing, Brenda is passionate about embracing life to the fullest, to include scuba diving (she has over 60 dives to her credit), Taekwondo (where she is currently pursuing her 4th degree black belt), hiking, traveling, and pursuing new experiences and skills.

For a free Starstruck short story and the earliest news about Brenda Hiatt's books, subscribe to her newsletter at:
brendahiatt.com/subscribe

Connect with Brenda:
brendahiatt.com

www.ingramcontent.com/pod-product-compliance
Lightning Source LLC
Chambersburg PA
CBHW051248210726
48287CB00002B/406